Red for Rachel

Everything in the room was bathed in a reddish glow from the curtains. It was neat, almost up to my own standards. The furniture didn't match, but it was all solid stuff: pricey-looking for a student. At the side of the table there was an alcove which opened onto a kitchen. A room divider ran up to the window frame making a separate bedroom. I strode across and knocked gently on the closed door and then opened it slowly.

I was more than half expecting to find Rachel stoned out of her mind and curled up with lover boy. What I actually saw next hit me like a kick in the guts.

This room was also bathed in red filtering through the curtains. The light revealed a young man, lying on the bed. I thought he was asleep but looking I realised his eyes were open and that the redness was darker than the red from the window. He was lying there covered in blood. His throat had been cut from ear to ear.

The author was born in the Lever district of Bolton but has worked for most of his career in South Manchester. He has worked with adults and children in a variety of educational roles.

Frank Lean

Red for Rachel

Mandarin

A Mandarin Paperback
RED FOR RACHEL

First published in Great Britain 1994
by Mandarin Paperbacks
an imprint of Reed Consumer Books Ltd
Michelin House, 81 Fulham Road, London SW3 6RB
and Auckland, Melbourne, Singapore and Toronto

Reprinted 1994

A CIP catalogue record for this title
is available from the British Library
ISBN 0 7493 1669 1

Phototypeset by Intype, London
Printed and bound in Great Britain
by Cox & Wyman Ltd, Reading, Berks

To my wife and sister
for their help
and encouragement

Acknowledgements

Many thanks to Terri D and Joan M
for their extra-mural assistance

1

Manchester June 1993

If I'd known the trail of bloodshed and violence resulting from my journey I think I'd have stayed away.

My secretary and part-time lover Delise had reached me on the car phone at 7 a.m. I'd been up all night staking out the home of a junior manager of the Happyways Hypermarket in Rochdale. The case cracked at 6 a.m. when I saw an unmarked van driving away with a load of Happyways' cigarettes.

As a result of my labours I had done myself out of a job and was on my way to sort out Delise. After my wife's death I drifted into a relationship with Delise. The problem was she wanted more from me than I could offer. Seeing me only on Sundays while I used most of the daylight hours to track down light-fingered retailers had been a problem for her.

Hell, it's a living! What did she expect? A nice safe nine-to-five job with a pension and widow's benefits? Yes, that was what she expected . . . and fringe benefits like seeing her lover by daylight occasionally as well.

There was no way I was going to get a job like that. Even if that was what it took to keep Delise happy, too bad. I'll never hold a regular job down for long. I'm too full of bile and bad temper to work for anyone but myself.

I owe Delise plenty, she pulled me back when I was seeking oblivion at the bottom of a booze bottle; and it isn't that I'm not attracted to her. She's an exceptionally beautiful woman. A rare blending of Irish and Caribbean features: a snub nose and firm chin, full lips and a lovely warm, dark-honey coloured complexion. But it's her eyes which give her face such striking beauty. Large, melting, liquid, brown: they change with her mood.

I was ready to do practically anything for her except change my job.

I'm a renegade from a police family, and it shows. I just have *a* job but my father and both grandfathers have been in the job. At six foot two, and built like the proverbial brick outhouse, I've inherited the physique but not the temperament to become a copper myself.

From earliest childhood I've continually disagreed with my father and rubbed him up the wrong way. I'm one of those hopeless cases who has a built-in sympathy for the underdog. I suppose having a son who sometimes regards criminals in a kindly light was a hard thing for my father to bear when I was a child, but it's not got any easier for him.

When I left college I ignored all entreaties to go and sign on at the cop shop and drifted into manual labour. A year on a building site toughened me up but when I got a job working on the Channel Tunnel Mum pleaded with me to give it up.

As a compromise Dad was able to use his contacts to get me some training and work as a bodyguard. Shepherding Arab sheiks and jumpy Japanese businessmen about had been interesting for a while, but nursemaiding mean old rich men gets boring. Using a small legacy from my paternal grandfather for finance I set myself up as a private enquiry agent, thus avoiding what my father saw as my predestined role in the next generation of Cunane coppers.

That didn't go down too well, but it really soured the cream when I married an African student. The prospect of future generations of brown-skinned Cunanes was even less pleasing to them than my refusal to become a policeman. They didn't come to the wedding or speak to me for eighteen months afterwards. The ice was only just beginning to thaw when my wife, Elenki Alloway Cunane, solved their problem for them by dying.

If it hadn't been for Delise I might have sunk into despair and spent the rest of my life wrapped round a bottle. She'd kept me turning out for work through the worst period and things began to improve. Making the best of what they saw as a bad job, Mum and Dad were coming round to Delise as a prospective daughter-in-law. At least they could relate to her only living close relative: her Irish mum, Molly Delaney.

Even more to their surprise, the business Delise and I were building up was doing well.

I'm good at the job. People take one look at my honest open mush and decide I'm too thick and too straightforward to get to the bottom of their devious little schemes. Quite a few have made that mistake.

I'm in the process of carving out a niche for myself as a specialist in catching supermarket rip-off artists. The security department at Happyways think the world of me. I'm not a threat to anyone's career. I'm a 'quick fix' for a plague of plundering employees, a plug-in crimefighter without a cape. The police say they haven't the time or funds to check out the bent employees of private companies. They want the companies to bear the expense of being self-policing. My corner-cutting methods save time and cash.

I pride myself that I can spot the sleek, self-satisfied air of the successful in-house larcenist at quite a distance. Supermarkets often complain about shoplifting by the public but they like to keep the problem of theft by employees under wraps. Hence my usefulness. Even if I make a mistake and the firm sacks the wrong man it still makes commercial sense. Tough but true: stock leakage falls sharply after an investigation.

From my point of view, intuition is a mixed blessing because it means that my employment is usually successful but brief. Then I'm hanging round the office getting under Delise's feet. That doesn't please her either. She really wants her bread buttered on both sides.

This latest job in Rochdale is a case in point. The guys involved had been very cheeky. They had a local computer genius hacking into the inventory and providing them with false invoices and delivery notes. The branch was so huge that it was months before anyone at head office began to twig that high value items were going astray: a little bit here, a little bit there. There were only half a dozen men who could have been involved. Catching them meant spending my evenings cuddled up with a telephoto lens. Delise had to spend her evenings on her own.

Then when I finally gleaned a few choice photos my reward was a pat on the head from the boss and now a kick up the backside from Delise. Talk about swings and roundabouts . . . rewards and favour from Happyways, sour phone calls from my girlfriend. The trouble was, Happyways' cheques were often late, but I would be seeing Delise that afternoon.

Formalities in Rochdale didn't take long. Once the local

managers are convinced, they don't waste time in organising prosecutions. As the police aren't interested in company crime, they deal with matters themselves using sacking, blacklisting, even blackmail to try to get some money back. So now, with all my business completed, I was on my way to Manchester in the middle of the afternoon. It was thirty-six hours since I'd clocked up any zeds but I was willing to try to salvage the only halfway decent relationship I'd had since my wife died.

From her Irish mother and Jamaican father Delise has inherited a mixture of Celtic melancholy and Caribbean warmth; or is it the other way round? I'm never entirely sure where I'm up to with Delise. I think that's what I like about her. I tried to phone her.

The M62 approaching Manchester isn't the best place in the world to use a car phone. Solid ranks of heavy lorries driven by certified road-hogs, along with massive road-works, make driving a tricky business requiring every ounce of concentration.

Still, my mind kept going over the events of the last few days. The experience of catching the Happyways perpetrators had brought me intense satisfaction. If I hadn't had that early morning call from Delise I might have spun things out in Rochdale for a bit longer. There was always some extra item of proof: another incriminating photo; a peek at a bank statement . . . But never mind! It was all for the best; there was no need to gild the lily. I had them bang to rights and supermarkets were getting boring. There was a sameness about them and their parasites that was becoming tedious.

I had to keep my mind on the traffic as I turned off the A627 onto the M62. Instead of threading my Nissan Bluebird into the central lane for a fast run into Manchester I stayed in the inner lane and turned off at Birch Services.

I parked the car and phoned. I phoned the office, I phoned her flat, I phoned my flat, I phoned her mother. No Delise. Great! She demands to see me and then does a vanishing act.

When I got back on the motorway I didn't dare let my attention stray. The sun was shining directly into my face. I was dazzled and in addition to the eye strain was the massive pollution from dust and fumes coming at me from all sides. I was glad to get off the motorway at Stretford and turn down Chester Road heading for central Manchester.

The ring of hills to the east had trapped a blanket of humid air over the city. Manchester is built on reclaimed swamp land and the warmth of June combined with the motionless atmosphere created almost tropical conditions of sticky heat. Even driving along the Mancunian Way with the windows open didn't bring much relief from that clammy air which had once attracted textile manufacturers to the city.

On my left I passed the stumpy towers of the Institute of Science and Technology. No dreaming spires for down-to-earth Manchester. Behind them, the bleak and dirty red bricks of the warehouses which provide the city with the sites for its newest industry were ranked. Here ecstasy pills and acid house music had replaced King Cotton as the source of economic growth. The heat wasn't preventing a steady stream of traffic heading for the densely built-up area.

At the end of the Mancunian Way, crossing newly laid tracks for the Metro-Link trams, I took the London Road and then a left turn down Whitworth Street towards my office in the Atwood Building. I took a right into Navigation Street and stopped the car. I turned on the car alarm for all the good it might do me and got out. Crossing the road and going left, I entered the narrow street where the headquarters of Pimpernel Investigations lay.

The Atwood building, with its curious chisel-shaped top, has seen better days. It had been the headquarters of a textile wholesaler and the upper floors consisted of a massive angled skylight extending down several floors so that buyers from the big stores could examine fabrics in natural light. Now the original purpose has gone but no one wants to pull the place down. It's a Grade two listed building. The entrance hall with its tiles and plasterwork give an impression of grandeur which rapidly fades as one reaches the first floor. Large rooms are partitioned off into cubicles and the treads on the stone stairs are well worn.

The old building does have a lift or 'hoist' as Fred Lumsden, the caretaker, insists on calling it but, as usual, there was an 'Out of Order' sign on the lift door. With less than bounding energy, I made my way up the stairs to the top floor where the rabbit hutch which I call my office is situated. Still, the rent's low.

My plywood cubicle's at the end of the long corridor which runs alongside the former sample buyers' viewing room. It's not much better than a converted store room but I always console myself that 'great oaks from little acorns grow'.

The initials on the glass door, '**P.I. Ltd**', are a private joke, but I'm proud to have an office of my own. It's the symbol of my independence. I rarely spend much time there, Delise sees to the routine mail and helps me to work out my expenses. Money is tight, but as long as it keeps coming in I've enough to pay Delise, keep up the rent, and live, but not enough to afford any luxuries like fitted carpets or designer furniture.

Although the furnishings are spartan, it's neat and tidy and gives an impression of seriousness which I couldn't project if I worked from home, or, like some of my rivals, from the lounge bar of a pub. All the furniture is well used, there's an outer section with desk and armchairs where Delise presides when she's so minded, and an inner office which is my domain.

My desk has a big piece of veneer missing along one side. There's a large captain's chair upholstered in black leather right next to it and two small armchairs in green imitation leather standing against the wall to the right of the desk. These provide what comfort there is for visitors and customers. An air of business efficiency is demonstrated by the three large filing cabinets ranked along the wall opposite the desk. These also do duty as a bookshelf for my few reference works. An overgrown Swiss cheese plant and a photograph of Elenki, taken two years before she died, are the only personal touches.

Today there was another personal touch. Propped against the phone to distinguish it from the neat pile of bills there was a letter labelled 'Bastard' in red lipstick. From Delise I supposed.

I opened it.

Dear Bastard

I've had enough of hanging round here waiting for you to decide whether you want to play at cops and robbers for the rest of your life or settle down to a normal existence. I can't stand it any more, I've moved all my things from your flat and your things from my flat.

I've met some one else and I don't want to see you again, ever. Bastard. (underlined in red)

Delise

P.S. Don't try to get in touch, I'm moving to London today and my mum won't give you the address

P.P.S. A man came to see you. He seems a cut above your usual clients. He wants your 'personal services in a private matter' and he will meet you at 4 p.m. in the Pullman restaurant at Voyagers. He didn't want to give any details, but his name is Ellington or Elsworth. I told him to look out for an oversized Chippendale reject with a broken nose and black curly hair.

I sat there breathing heavily for a few moments. Then a feeling of relief came over me. I wasn't going to get a bollocking about my absences; I wasn't going to have to continue with my awkward efforts to back out of the relationship. Delise had solved her own problems and mine.

Call me a cold-hearted bastard if you like, but that part of me that was supposed to have feelings just wasn't there: it had been surgically removed. Elenki's death had lobotomized the area of my personality that felt normal emotions like sadness or regret.

Still, it was a wrench. Before she got too bossy Delise had always been able to take me out of myself and lift my mood when things weren't going well . . . that had been quite a lot of the time. I wondered if she really had someone else or if that was just a ploy to make me feel jealous. God knows, she'd had time enough and opportunity enough to latch onto any number of blokes while I was neglecting her. I hoped she did have someone and part of me even hoped he treated her better than I'd done.

Besides removing herself from the scene Delise had done me another favour. She'd fixed an appointment with this Ellington character. The name was unfamiliar to me, so perhaps he was attached to another retail chain. If so, it was good news. I needed something to tide me over until Happyways' cheque came through. I looked at my watch. It was two forty-five.

It struck me that I should replace Delise with an answering service so I phoned and engaged one for a week's trial. I'd some time to kill before meeting Ellington. I hoped he'd recognise me despite Delise's unflattering and inaccurate description. I decided to sort through the mail. She'd left quite a pile of it.

Most of it was junk mail: insurance ads or bills. Delise had neatly arranged the bills in order so I binned the junk mail and the insurance ads and started working through the bills. I wondered what insurance I should get in my line of work.

Delise had set out the bills in order of priority with those demanding immediate payment first. I decided to pay the poll tax but to leave the National Trust card for another month – a cowardly decision, but the NT wouldn't put my name on a list of the uncreditworthy if I didn't pay. I'd part pay my phone and electricity bills. It only took three minutes to do this. I never read bills, only look at the colour.

The room was getting warm so I opened the window. Pimpernel Investigations doesn't run to air conditioning. Nor does it run to windows that work. The sash cord's broken and the window slowly shuts itself. I propped it open with a forensic medicine text book that I once brought in a fit of enthusiasm for the minutiae of detection. So far, propping open the window is the best use I've found for it.

I started working out my invoice for Happyways, being careful to include as many incidental expenses as possible. I usually had a brain-storming session with Delise when doing this, so it took me a while to get through it on my own. When I finished I needed to photocopy it.

Old Fred Lumsden's allowed to use the photocopier belonging to the firm that occupies the ground floor of the Atwood Building. He's supposed to do a copy of his time sheet on it, but in exchange for a pleasant smile from Delise and the occasional bit of gossip he shares his code number with us and lets us into the copier room when there's no one about. When I got there I found the door locked. This wasn't usually a problem, the lock was easy to turn with a picklock, but somebody had fitted a hasp and a brand new padlock. It didn't look like Fred's handiwork, the firm must be economising on photocopying. Cursing, I started back up to the top floor.

There was a small wardrobe in Delise's room where I kept a change of clothes. I opened the door and looked at myself in the mirror. I was wearing grey trousers and an old bomber jacket, serviceable for all night stake-outs but not for business meetings. I had a bag of clothes in the boot of the car, but I always keep a change of clothes in the wardrobe.

I quickly changed into a navy-blue business suit and white shirt, then checked my appearance. Apart from my complexion, which was grey from eating too many chips in the Happyways Hypermarket canteen and from lack of exercise, I thought I would pass as a businessman. Delise hadn't thought to tell me how I would recognise Ellington but there wouldn't be too many businessmen in the Pullman on a Wednesday afternoon. It was an unusual choice of rendezvous really: a very anonymous place. Maybe he only had a very limited expense allowance.

The departure of Delise was affecting me less than I thought it would. My overactive conscience was trying to make me feel guilty about being so relieved but I was still feeling relieved. There was a spring in my step as I walked through Piccadilly Gardens past the huge statues of Queen Victoria and other nineteenth-century anachronisms. They looked out of place standing there on their pedestals amid the litter and pigeons.

As usual, a stroll down Market Street was like entering a time warp to Lowry-land. Even on a Wednesday afternoon there were poorly dressed and ill-looking people hurrying up and down. Manchester's as bad as Johannesburg for the way people segregate themselves. The poor on Market Street, the rich on King Street and St. Ann's Square . . . with Marks and Spencers and Deansgate as neutral ground in between.

Voyagers is a recent addition to the Arndale Centre which developers had inflicted on the end of Market Street. It's the best thing in the Centre – a complex of restaurants and sandwich bars that's actually large enough to meet demand without giving a sensation either of being a barn or of being overcrowded.

I mounted the massive escalator which gave access to the restaurant from the street and turned towards the bar – a restaurant decorated as a railway carriage. There were several men sitting on their own. I discounted a number for not being well enough turned-out to fit Delise's 'cut above my usual clients' description and approached a swarthy looking gent in a well cut grey-suit. He seemed to be on the look-out for some one.

'Excuse me, but are you Mr Ellington?' I asked.

He gave me an appraising stare.

'That's a new approach, chuck; I'm not Duke Ellington but you can have a blow on my trumpet any time you like. Have a seat . . .' He spoke in a nasal northern drawl and extended his hand to me.

I recoiled from his invitation as if I'd put my hand on a hot-plate.

Then I saw another man waving a rolled-up copy of *The Times* at me. I hadn't noticed him before because he was seated behind a wide pillar. I headed in his direction. A tall slim figure, there was a suggestion of nervous energy and tension in his movements. When I got closer I could see that although he was elegantly dressed there was something indefinably care-worn about his appearance. A man with problems, I surmised, in his early fifties, who had worn well until recently when his troubles had come on him.

'Are you the private detective?' he asked. His tone was firm and brisk, he spoke with a posh northern accent that had more Yorkshire than Manchester in it. I glanced over my shoulder; the character in the grey suit was rolling his eyes at me.

'That's me, David Cunane,' I said, offering my hand. He didn't seem inclined to shake it and impatiently gestured at me to sit down. He looked me over with a dubious expression on his face. I thought it was my turn to ask him a question.

'You're the gentleman who spoke to my secretary this morning?' I asked politely. 'Er . . . Mr Ellin . . .?'

'Elsworth, man! Elsworth!' he barked back.

For a second I thought he was swearing at me. I must have looked at him oddly. 'Nice one, Delise,' I thought, 'you've made me blow it before I get to round one.'

'Elsworth is a proud and honourable Yorkshire name, I'll have you know!' I noticed the veins standing out under the pale skin of his high domed forehead.

Fortunately he calmed down and resumed speaking, but still under the grip of some powerful emotion. 'Yes, I made an appointment with you but I must say I'm reconsidering my course of action,' he said. He wouldn't look me in the eye, he focused his gaze about six feet above my head and fluttered his eyelids in a curious way. Apparently this was the external sign of the reconsideration process.

'I'm sorry about getting your name muddled up, but *you* made the appointment. I've been on a case all night. I could be on my way home by now. I could be soaking in my bath or fixing myself a meal,' I replied, in as humble a tone as I could manage.

He seemed to finish the internal debate and come to a decision. The muscles in his face kept clenching and unclenching. Whatever the problem was it was affecting him strongly. He had a sensitive and emotional face. There were lots of deep lines round his mouth and eyes. His sandy hair was receding from a prominent forehead. The eyes were a washed out blue colour, deep set in well-developed cheek bones.

Still not looking me in the eye, he shifted in his seat so that he was perched on the edge. His right hand went up to his clean-shaven face while his left busied itself smoothing down his beautifully cut, blue chalk-striped suit. Then he pulled out a handkerchief and gave his fingers work by knotting and unknotting the corners. He was in a mess.

'The reason I asked to meet you here and not in your office is that my problem is of a delicate personal nature . . . and I prefer not to divulge it where there is risk of er . . . er . . . contact with other er . . . persons besides yourself.' I took this to mean that he didn't want Delise overhearing him.

'Yes, Mr Elsworth, my secretary did say that you were reluctant to tell her what the problem was. I can assure you that anything you say will be treated in strict confidence. I can supply you with references if you like,' I said, slipping into my sales patter.

This seemed to soothe him because he continued with his slow revelations. 'My wife and I just have the one child, Rachel, we'd both have liked more but she's our only child.' Disclosing this much seemed to drain Elsworth, his head slumped to his chest and he sighed heavily. There was a world of regret in that sigh. I couldn't help but feel sorry for him.

Sensing that I was about to speak he put up his hand to silence me. Then looking at me directly, he asked 'What's the expression they use these days? "Natural parent"?' After sighing again he continued, 'Well, I'm not Rachel's "natural father" but I'm the only father she's ever known . . .' His pale eyes were blinking and he seemed to be on the point of tears, always a bad sign in a Yorkshireman. There was something very heavy going down.

Whatever it was, he had me biting my knuckles in suspense. This wasn't one of my usual bread and butter, plain as a pikestaff 'Trouble at t'mill' sort of cases which ended with the bad boys getting their knuckles rapped and handing back the stolen goodies. Kidnapping, rape, blackmail and child molestation were flashing up at the forefront of my tired brain like the winning row coming up on a fruit machine.

'She's disappeared . . . been missing for more than a week. My wife's at her wits' end. Neither of us can take much more of this . . . My wife and I want her found and returned to us.'

'The police —' I said, but that was as far as I got because he again cut me off. I was there to listen, not to advise.

'We can't go to the police,' he said brusquely. 'She's over eighteen and she's not really a missing person. She's got the cause of all her problems with her.'

I was puzzled; it sounded as if he needed a priest more than a private investigator, but he was definitely starting to annoy me. Speaking with elaborate care, doling out his words like a nineteenth-century workhouse master ladling soup out to orphans, he was radiating the message that the whole business was distasteful; particularly having to arrange secret meetings with shady characters like me. I felt that I needed to respond to him with exquisite politeness and perhaps needle him into saying more than he might otherwise.

'Look,' I said, 'why don't you tell me more about what's happened? Then I can tell you if I'll be able to help you.' As I spoke the waitress came and took my order. Glancing at the table I ordered the same as Elsworth: a cheese sandwich and a slim-line tonic.

He went into his facial contortions once more and then finally looked me straight in the eye again. I was making progress.

'I am the Chief Executive of the Northern Pioneers' Bank.' He announced it in a magisterial way, as well he might.

I sat up and began to get very interested. The Northern Pioneers is the biggest independent bank in the North-west and has its headquarters here in Manchester. Delise was right, he was a cut above my usual clients.

In a very polite voice I asked, 'Can I have some details about your stepdaughter? Nothing you tell me will be passed on, I can assure you.' As I spoke the waitress returned with my order and there was a pause until she'd gone away again.

'You were recommended to me by Ian Watson of the Beacon Insurance Company. He said you were very discreet.'

I'd sorted out some phony fire damage claims for Beacon a couple of years ago. Watson is their chief executive. I'd barely met the man.

'Oh good old Ian, great golfer. Yes, discretion's part of the service. I can give you references if you'd care to make certain before trusting me. I may only be a one-man band but at least you'll know who to blame if anything goes wrong.'

This was more on his wavelength. I was enjoying continuous eyeball to eyeball contact with him now.

'Well, as I said, Rachel's my stepdaughter but she's really like flesh and blood to me,' he seemed on the point of relapsing back into his highly emotional, word-a-minute, way of talking when he said this but he kept going, and information started to flow. 'Rachel's been so alone all her childhood, that's why we wanted more children. She's always related more to Dee, that's her mother, and myself, than to her own age group. Old head on young shoulders . . .' he paused for a moment, then went on.

'We call her Rachel Elsworth but she's originally Rachel Rankine, my wife's daughter by her first marriage. She's been missing for a week now. I'm sure the reason she's disappeared is that she's been er . . . rusticated from her hall of residence at the Poly, or whatever they call it, and is too scared to get in touch with us.'

'Rusticated eh, sounds painful,' I said trying to interject a lighter note. 'What happened, Mr Elsworth.'

'Her boyfriend,' he replied, pronouncing the words with distaste, 'a youth by the name of Andrew Thwaite, asked her to look after some plants for him. It turns out that they were cannabis plants and a cleaner with above-average botanical knowledge found them.'

I raised my eyebrows in mock surprise. 'Oh dear, oh dear. So what happened next?'

'Rachel telephoned us at once, of course. But we were out. She left a message on the answering machine but failed to stress the urgency of the matter. She said she was in trouble with the warden of her hall because of some plants but she thought she could handle the matter herself. Her mother thought nothing of it, she certainly didn't connect it with drugs.'

Elsworth's tone was more relaxed than it had been, looking at my honest face must have been having a calming effect, but there was something irritatingly pedantic about the way he spoke. He was like Queen Victoria on her pedestal.

'We were horrified when her mother returned the call to find that she couldn't get in touch with Rachel. I spoke to the warden of the hall and he said he'd been forced to tell Rachel to seek other accommodation as from the next day. She hasn't been home.'

'Surely she left an address before she moved out of the hall?' I said.

'No, she didn't. I had to go to great lengths to impress on this warden individual, Kinvig by name, that his own position might be in jeopardy, before he cared to inform me that Rachel had moved in with her young man. He lives in a street which I believe to be notorious for drug dealers and other low life. There can be no question of me seeking her out in person.'

Elsworth's implication wasn't flattering to me.

'So you want me to delve into this street of shame and recover Rachel for you?' I responded in a mildly sarcastic tone of voice. 'Why don't you wait a little while? She's bound to get in touch when she wants some money.'

'Are you trying to argue yourself out of the job?' Elsworth replied sharply. 'Her mother is dreadfully worried. It's easy to see you've no children of your own.' Once again, his tone was that of someone explaining something to a moron. My simple, honest face was having its usual effect. I looked at him blankly.

He tried again. 'If you were a parent you might understand that one of the hardest things in life is to see a child you love and care for more than anything in the world ignoring your advice and doing things that are certainly going to lead her to disaster. I told you Rachel grew up among adults: well we're frightened that she's not street-wise . . . she's . . .' he caught his breath for a moment as if about to reveal something, but then changed tack and went on.

'You hear of such dreadful things. Her mother's frightened . . . Well, Rachel's a very good-looking girl . . . and she thinks the best of people . . . Her mother thinks . . .'

It seemed to be getting harder and harder for him to say what he wanted.

'It's difficult for me to say it as her father, you'll think I'm biased, but Rachel really is extraordinarily beautiful, I've never seen anyone in her age group who could hold a candle to her. Her mother . . . Dee thinks . . . She thinks someone might . . . er . . . see an advantage in trying to exploit Rachel's really striking appearance. You see someone tried to do something similar to Dee when she was starting out in life.'

He didn't need to say more. I was getting his drift. He thought Rachel might end up on the streets earning a crust for this Thwaite character. It seemed a bit extreme to me but he knew his own daughter better than I did. She wouldn't be the first naive girl to go that way. The drug connection was worrying too . . . still, it was a bit of a jump from a cannabis plant in a student's bedroom to a pimp enslaving his tart by getting her hooked on heroin.

'You're quite right to be worried,' I said. 'I'm sorry, I didn't mean to sound unsympathetic but have you any concrete evidence that this so-called boyfriend is up to something like you suggest? There could be serious criminal charges against him, and for you own sake you might do better to involve the police right away.'

'Do you think I'd have waited a week before acting if there was?' he snapped. 'There's nothing tangible apart from Thwaite getting her ejected from her hall of residence. There's nothing to go to the police with but our fears! I suppose I was a fool to see a private detective but Dee is so worried, I must do something.'

Elsworth was reading his words from the invisible Teleprompt six feet above my head again, eyelids fluttering away like a pair of moths trapped in a spider's web.

There was definitely something odd about the guy quite

apart from his problem with his daughter. He needed help but wanted to fend off any human contact or warmth from a person who could help him. How had he lived for fifty-odd years without ever needing help that he couldn't just demand as of right from someone? His tone was despairing and angry, as if I was accusing him of neglect.

Fine! If he found it more comfortable to keep things to a cash-only basis, that was just fine by me. This must be how the rich always get things sorted. Dealing with supermarket managers hadn't prepared me for this kind of thing.

'Calm down Mr Elsworth, I was just making sure that you know what the alternatives are. My services don't come cheap. You've no idea how much trouble I can get into by taking something on and then having to turn it over to the police. I'll want a down payment of £400 and then £150 a day plus expenses.' I knew I was chancing my arm, I've worked for a lot less than that.

To my surprise, Elsworth was already opening his wallet. He put £550 in cash down on the table.

'I'd have taken a cheque you know,' I said.

'That's all right, I prefer it this way. My wife and I definitely don't want police involvement. We're not going to wash our dirty linen in public at any stage in this business. You can be quite sure of that.' He spoke in a supercilious, almost sneering tone, as if the cash transaction gave him the right to treat me with contempt. He thought he could order me about now that he'd got me where he wanted me. I didn't like it one little bit.

'Have you got a picture of Rachel?' I asked.

With an air of having thought of all these details, Elsworth placed a postcard sized photo of Rachel next to the cash. I picked it up and studied it. The intense conversation with Elsworth had given me tunnel vision; concentrating on him in a crowded restaurant meant I'd had to exclude all other stimuli. Looking at Rachel more than made up for my visual starvation.

The photo had been taken at a wedding, and by a good pro who'd got everything just right.

Keen intelligence in the eyes gave her looks a sophistication which didn't go with her years. Her raven black hair was parted in the middle and shaped into the nape of her neck in a bun which kept it off her bare shoulders. She was wearing an elaborate head band of white silk flowers which matched the tie straps of her white broderie anglais bodice. From the slightly wistful smile I could surmise that she'd missed catching the bride's bouquet. The brightly coloured vegetation in the background suggested a tropical location.

Elsworth was right to be worried. This was a face that could tempt the wrong man into any kind of indiscretion. She looked like a beautiful virgin who'd been prepared for sacrifice to appease the anger of some savage god.

I don't know how long I gazed at the photograph. Elsworth didn't interrupt while I worshipped at the shrine of his daughter's icon, but I became conscious of time passing and of the job I was taking on.

'I'll need that address, the name of the hall and a phone number where I can reach you,' I said, in as down-to-earth a tone as I could manage.

Elsworth dictated the address – Clydesdale Road, Didsbury – and the name of the hall – Abbotsford – to me but he seemed reluctant to part with his phone number. I was surprised at the Didsbury address, I must have missed the latest news about the local drugs scene because I'd never heard about any pushers' paradise in Didsbury. Delicatessens yes, crack-cocaine, no. Still the drugs scene was changing all the time. In the end Elsworth gave me his home phone number and told me he could be reached there after 7 p.m. most evenings.

'Don't speak to my wife. If she answers just ask for me and ring off if she says I'm not there.' He gave me his orders in the tone of one who is not used to being challenged by his underlings. I could imagine a teenage girl would find a lot to dislike about him but, as the man said, I'd no children of my own, so how would I know? He was paying the bill but his suggested method of speaking to his wife seemed calculated to increase anxiety. Still, mine not to reason why.

'Another thing Mr Elsworth. I can find out where Rachel is but I can't make her come to you if she doesn't want to.'

He shook his head irritably. 'I understand that. We just want you to make sure that she's not come to any harm. How soon could you commence? You could go down to Abbotsford Hall tonight.'

'Why would I do that Mr Elsworth?'

'Well, you check the address this Kinvig person gave me and find out the exact number. You could see if Rachel has been back to the hall.'

'That sounds reasonable but I'll have to charge you for a full day if I start now.' I was hoping he wouldn't agree, I was aching for a good meal and a night's sleep.

'That's immaterial, just send in your bill. Money isn't a problem,' he said with the air of one who'd never had to worry about paying his poll tax.

'It's just that I've been working all night and I'll be better for a night's sleep before I start looking for Rachel. You've waited a week, a few more hours won't make any difference,' I said.

I still hadn't picked up his money and he must have calculated that it was getting late in the day to find someone else so in the end he reluctantly agreed to me getting an early start tomorrow. I took his cash and gave him a standard service contract as a receipt.

He was now showing signs of wanting to leave. He kept making little bounds out of his chair as if something was pinching his behind. Presumably back at the bank his minions scurried to bring their business to a close when they saw that the great man was getting impatient.

I decided to wind him up a bit.

'Just a moment Mr Elsworth. I can't do the job unless you tell me a great deal more about Rachel than you have so far.' Elsworth seemed taken aback. He wasn't used to having underlings prevent him from drawing meetings to a close. 'Think about it Mr Elsworth. If you went to the police you'd spend two hours talking to one set of detectives and then they'd pass you on to someone else and you'd have to repeat it all over again.

'Even if you were to pull rank, as I'm sure you could, you'd find yourself having to tell every relevant detail about Rachel to at least two people before you got to the Chief Constable or some high-up at the Home Office.'

Elsworth stared at me for a long time; he was trying to decipher something in my face. He was having a hard time deciding whether or not to trust me. I pushed his cash back towards him to help him make up his mind.

He gave me a forced smile. 'I can tell you that if I wanted to speak to the Home Secretary I wouldn't have to go through all the rigmarole you mentioned. God knows, we give the party enough money. But what do you want to know? Where shall I begin?' he asked in a more pleasant tone than any he had used so far.

'Just tell me anything about Rachel that might help me to find her. Remember I'm a total stranger. It would be helpful if I could see her room, her belongings, anything that would help me to form a picture.'

'No, no! That's quite out of the question. My wife mustn't be disturbed.'

'Look, I don't have the resources that the police do but it can take even them weeks to find someone who wants to stay missing. You've got to give me more to go on.'

Elsworth sighed. 'Rachel's always had the best of everything, the best education money could buy. Her mother didn't want to send her to boarding school as she's an only child. I wanted her to go to a Swiss finishing school this year, but no, of all possible places she insisted on going to Manchester Polytechnic or the Metropolitan University, as I suppose we must call it now.'

Such behaviour was obviously quite inexplicable to Elsworth.

'She wouldn't even do Business Studies or anything in which I could help her. She's doing a BA in Fashion. She's got a lot of her mother in her . . . headstrong, won't be told anything. She gets enthusiasms, she was into sport and horse riding. Very good she was too, she won lots of trophies.

'Rachel can be very competitive, she's got to come first in whatever she's doing. She can get very upset if things don't go the way she wants them to. She's not short of guts either, she used to go right up to the judges at gymkhanas and tackle them if she thought she'd been unfairly faulted.

'Then all the interest in horses stopped and she wanted to be an actress and singer. She went for singing lessons and was doing well but since this Thwaite appeared on the scene all she's shown any interest in is in being a sound engineer or glorified electrician. She even wants to change her course to sound engineering.'

'What does Thwaite do with himself? Is he a student?' I asked.

'He's some kind of DJ, works in several of these sleazy clubs that are springing up everywhere. I believe he also claims to be a student. Wherever that unwholesome young man is, that's where you'll find Rachel. Wherever he is, that's where danger lies for Rachel.' He stood up abruptly. The interview was definitely terminated this time.

As he got up to go he snubbed my offer of a handshake for the second time. He'd no desire to be matey. He just strode off into the Arndale Centre as quickly as his long legs could carry him and disappeared from view.

I picked up the menu and ordered a well-grilled sirloin steak, onion rings, chips and a pint of bitter. On the whole the day had ended rather better than I'd had any right to expect. I'd nabbed the villains at Rochdale, Delise had withdrawn her affections in the most pain-free possible way and I was having money thrown at me to do a trawl round the clubs for a missing girl. All I needed now was a decent night's sleep.

2

I woke up bright and early without benefit of an alarm clock. My first feeling was one of relief: I didn't have to go to Rochdale. It was no good trying to go back to sleep, I'd only wake up with a headache. I got up and put on my cycling kit. Exercise helps me to think and being on the wrong side of thirty-five, I need to keep in condition.

I cycled through Stretford and crossed the Mersey at Flixton Bridge. It was going to be a warm day but the air was still fresh and crisp, the humidity would rise later. Bumping along on the south bank of the river I came to Sale Water Park and took the footbridge at Jackson's Boat back into Chorlton. It was fifteen miles of firm going and I was sweating freely when I got back to the flat.

I stripped, tossed my things into the laundry basket, and took a long luxurious shower. I hadn't had any great thoughts about Elsworth except that there must be more involved than he'd told me. The man was so eager to pay, there must be a snag. Maybe the boyfriend was even more obnoxious than Elsworth had implied and he was paying me danger money in advance.

I poured silver top milk over my muesli and tucked in. I used to get through a lot of bacon and fried bread but concern about cholesterol had changed my breakfast to cereal and gold top Channel Islands milk. Females always shrieked in horror at the sight of gold top, so now I am down to silver. I expect to be on skimmed if I ever reach pensionable age.

I made a cup of instant decaff and looked around the flat. Everything was in order. Tidying up is another of my peculiarities. I love scouring grease off remote crevices in the kitchen. It concentrates the mind even more than cycling. Elenki couldn't stand it; she liked to live in a comfortable confusion of scattered possessions.

Delise hadn't made much of a mess, but then she'd never spent much time here. I noticed that she'd removed all her things from the bathroom. I must remember to ask her mother for my key back. Or perhaps not. It might be better to wait for events to take their natural course. I didn't want to seem callous.

I was feeling cheerful and confident. Cash in hand and the money coming from Happyways were responsible, not the absence of Delise. I'd be able to renew my N.T. membership this month after all. Feeling as cultural as a government Heritage minister, I whistled Mozart's 39th Symphony as I went into the bedroom. Before facing my wardrobe, I shook the duvet and made the bed.

I chose a pair of multi-coloured argyll socks from the neat ranks, then teal boxer shorts and an open weave long-sleeved cotton shirt. I decided not to wear a tie. A pair of beige trousers and a tan nubuck jacket completed my outfit. I checked my appearance in the mirror and changed the black belt for a brown one. I looked great. I'm thirty-eight years old and nothing's begun to sag.

Delise's description of me as a misshapen lump of male cheesecake was unfair. She must have been feeling very bitter towards me. OK, I'm quite broad across the shoulders, but at six foot two I don't look out of proportion and my nose isn't broken; well, not any more. It's been reset and is straight enough. My physique has been developed by honest labour, not by pumping iron, and it's not out of a steroid bottle.

The cycling preserves my fresh complexion which gives me such a guileless appearance in the mirror. I looked as if I'd just stepped out of a health food commercial.

My old man claims I look like him. I've certainly inherited the black curly hair and blue eyes of the Cunanes but he's slightly taller than me with an erect posture given him by his years in the police that I could never hope to match. He often orders me to stop slouching about. I don't think I do and I tell him I'm much better looking than he is with his fierce hawk-like face and permanent frown. Though we look alike my face is broader and more open and friendly. Anyway I've never had any trouble attracting the opposite sex. Maybe the very slight twist in my nose gives me a rugged charm which the regular features of a male model wouldn't.

One way I certainly am like my father is that we're both very particular about our appearance. When I was going to school he used to inspect me before I left the house and make all kinds of critical comments. 'If you want to get on in life, you've always got to be well turned out,' was his constant refrain.

He's done thirty-odd years in the police – a straight copper who never got the promotion he deserved. Not that it rankles with him; he loves the Force. He's always telling me it's not too late to join up. Eileen, my mother, is an ex-teacher who's determined that I'm going to do well. She was never satisfied with me at school. I worked hard and passed all my exams. I got a good degree but then, by her reckoning, I stumbled at the final stage. I refused to put my foot on the career ladder. Perhaps the pair of them had driven me too hard.

They can't accept that I'd rather work digging holes in the road than settle into the routine of a nine-to-five job. In fact, when commissions have been slow coming in, I've done quite a bit of navvying. I'd rather work with my hands than sit answering the phone all day or brown-nose to some inferior superior.

As I wouldn't be able to get into the office until later I put in a call to my answering service. It was working efficiently. There'd been a call from Charlie Sims, head of Happyways' security in Luton . . . 'Was I interested in an investigation in Middlesborough? Call him back before noon.'

I called him. The job sounded like a good chance to leave Manchester for a while. If Delise could clear off, so could I. It wasn't as if we needed to go through any formalities, her letter had said it all: she'd found someone else. I took the opportunity to pester Sims for prompt payment.

My bank is in Chorlton and the nearest I could park was three streets away. I paid in £300 and left in a moral glow. I lived to keep that bank balance healthy. Crossing the road, I strolled to the electricity shop and paid half my bill. Next came the Post Office to send my invoice to Happyways.

I hummed the catchy Happyways jingle to myself as I walked away from the Post Office.

'If you want to spend a nice day,
You can't do better than Happyway,
Hap, hap, happee, way . . .'

At least I'd be able to spend a few days without that rattling round inside my head.

Then on to Didsbury, weaving my way through traffic-clogged streets. The hall of residence was in the grounds of a Victorian nabob's residence. The mansion still stood, complete with outbuildings; pleasant gardens had been replaced by accommodation blocks. Concrete was in stark contrast to the nineteenth-century work.

There was no obvious entrance to the architectural mish-mash. I spotted a security man in a peaked cap behind one of the doors.

I tried the door. It had an electronic lock but the man didn't seem inclined to open it. He looked up from his paper and pointed around the side of the building. I located a tradesmen's entrance by the dustbins. When I opened it I found myself in a kitchen. A black lady took a break from slicing apples to direct me to the Warden's office in the old building.

I met another locked door, this time with a bell to ring. A middle-aged woman in rimless glasses opened the door. The glasses gave her a severe appearance, she didn't look likely to stand for any lip from the likes of me. I explained my business to her. She invited me into her office.

A no-nonsense sort of woman with the cares of the world on her shoulders, she introduced herself as the Warden's secretary, Janet Rushford. Her plain face and grey hair were enlivened by expressive eyes which she used to the full to communicate her feelings. She dealt with most of the problems concerning students. The warden wasn't around much.

That was her ploy to explain being harassed and having no time for idle questions. I told her I was enquiring into Rachel Elsworth's whereabouts on behalf of the family.

'A very demanding young lady, Miss Elsworth,' she said, rolling her eyes upward.

'What do you mean?' I asked.

'Oh, nothing,' she said, clamming up as if she realised that she couldn't afford to make personal remarks. 'Just that she seemed very hard to please. Seemed to think the place was a private hotel, but we've very little time to give anyone much individual attention.'

I was about to ask her to explain further when the phone rang. It was a student.

'You can see how it is,' Rushford said as she put the phone

down. 'We're snowed under with students wanting to get into Hall. So we can afford to be choosy. If they don't want to keep our rules, they're out.'

I took this to be a reference to Rachel. I told Rushford I already knew the story about the cannabis plants.

'Metropolitan University policy is strict about drugs. We've our reputation to think about. The warden will always ask students to find their own accommodation if there's any drug involvement. It doesn't matter who they think they are, even important people's children like your precious Rachel. That's explained to them when they take up residence here. They're adults and we don't inform their parents if they're asked to leave,' she spoke briskly in a local middle-class accent.

'That seems harsh,' I commented, oozing an insincere-sounding concern into my voice. 'Have you seen Rachel since she was barred?'

'You don't understand,' Rushford responded angrily. 'We're offering students supervised accommodation with full board, but we're not their moral guardian. I'm sorry she had to be put out. She hasn't been back to the Hall since her removal as far as I know.'

Rushford turned back to her typewriter and began determinedly inserting a fresh sheet of paper into it. It was obvious that the interview was at an end. I asked her what she knew about the boyfriend but, if she knew, she wouldn't tell me anything.

I coaxed her into checking if Thwaite was a student at the Poly. She phoned Administration for me. Thwaite was a current student living at 90 Clydesdale Road, Didsbury. That was the same street Elsworth had given me; and now I'd got the number.

Back in the car I hauled out my street directory. Clydesdale wasn't far. It was one of the few terraced streets in the area. Although many of the big houses round here have suffered the fate of Abbotsford there are still millionaires living in the leafy lanes of Didsbury.

A short drive through narrow streets shaded by over-grown trees brought me to Clydesdale Road. It must have been a while since the banker had been in this part of Manchester.

In the early sixties the street had been decrepit with the

big houses full of transients and the pavements heaving with pushers and the CID. Since then it had been transformed. The houses had nearly all been converted into expensive flats. There was no reason why the managing director of the Northern Pioneers' Bank shouldn't have lived in the street if he'd wanted to: it was perfectly respectable. Perhaps Elsworth was relying on memories from a misspent youth.

The question was how a student like Thwaite could afford to live here. Number 90 was right at the end of the street. The builder had solved the problem of building a corner house by putting two frontages on it. One with two large bay windows and a big front door faced Clydesdale; the other with identical bays, but minus the front door, faced the main through-road. It was a large house, but Edwardian not Victorian like the others, and had been built later during the development of the main road into Didsbury village.

I walked up to the main door which had a leaded light and five named door buttons. The lowest button had the name Thwaite over it. It looked as if I was going to earn Elsworth's money pretty easily.

I pushed the button. No reply but I could hear the bell ringing in the ground floor room to my right. The curtains were closed at ten-thirty in the morning. When Clydesdale Road had been the way Elsworth described it back in the sixties there would have been nothing unusual about this, nowadays I wasn't so sure.

The sky was heavily overcast and it felt warm and damp – a typical summer's day in Manchester. I debated whether to wait or come back. I went and sat in the car for ten minutes. There was no movement in the house nor in the street. I went back to the door and rang each of the bells in turn. Nothing happened. People were moving up and down the main road, some further down the street, but no one was taking a blind bit of notice of me. I felt along the top of the door ledge. No key. Nor was there one under the mat, nor behind the milk bottle holder.

I went through the yard to the back door. No key in any of the obvious places, but on the low retaining wall at the side of the doorstep I noticed a loose brick. I lifted it out and there it was. I carefully opened the back door. There was no sound of an alarm. I put the key back.

The new people who lived in Clydesdale Road were all at work earning the money for their expensive mortgages. There were no little old ladies to watch from behind lace curtains. I went inside. My years of poking and prying into other people's business have left me with few inhibitions about unauthorised entry.

The back door opened on to a wide, well-lit hall. What had once been a kitchen and scullery had been converted into the unit now occupied by Andrew Thwaite and, I hoped, Rachel. A wide staircase carpeted with cheap tiles led upstairs. The door to Thwaite's flat was an original Edwardian door tarted up with a layer of hardboard.

I knocked. Still no reply. There was no sound at all in the house apart from the noise of traffic. The lock looked fragile. I considered getting out my picklocks but there was no need for anything so dramatic. The door wasn't locked.

I stepped into the room.

This was what Elsworth was paying me to do: walk into a complete stranger's flat. I wasn't nervous. I'm used to bluffing my way out of awkward situations on 'private property', I could always claim I'd come to repossess the TV, or even leg it if things got rough. Being chased out of buildings is an occupational hazard. Fortunately most of the people I deal with aren't too fussy about their right to privacy anyway. They're only too used to people in big boots trampling all over their lives. If I always had to get court orders to gain admittance there wouldn't be much need for private investigators in the first place.

Everything in the room was bathed in a reddish glow from the curtains. It was neat, almost up to my own standards. The furniture didn't match but it was all solid stuff: pricey-looking for a student. At the side of the table there was an alcove which opened onto a kitchen. A room divider ran up to the window frame making a separate bedroom. I strode across and knocked gently on the closed door and then opened it slowly.

I was more than half expecting to find Rachel stoned out of her mind and curled up with lover boy. What I actually saw next hit me like a kick in the guts.

This room was also bathed in red filtering through the curtains. The light revealed a young man, lying on the bed. I thought he was asleep but looking I realised his eyes were open and that the redness was darker than the red from the window. He was lying there covered in blood. His throat had been cut from ear to ear.

My eyes bulged as I took in the scene. There was an unreality about it: it looked like a wax tableau in Madame Tussaud's Chamber of Horrors. I could feel my heart pounding. I took a step forward. My feet wouldn't move. They were sticking in the congealed blood which had soaked into the thin carpet. After a while I remembered to draw breath. I strained my ears expecting to hear a police siren.

Then it hit me. This was why Elsworth had been so anxious for me to find his daughter and make enquiries about Thwaite all over the Metropolitan University. No wonder he'd avoided looking me in the eye. The bastard had fitted me up as a murder suspect.

Paying me in cash was a clever touch, he'd have given me £2000 if I'd asked. Then when the police found me with my pockets crammed with untraceable cash there'd be no link to him. I hadn't even made him sign a contract. I'd been so impressed by his claim to be the boss of a bank that I'd forgotten the first rule in the detective manual: always check out your client. I deserved everything that was coming to me.

My story would sound feeble – a wealthy banker had employed me to round up his daughter, of whom there was, of course, no trace. The number he'd given me so unwillingly was probably as phony as he was. So no banker, no daughter, no phone number; but my prints would be all over the murder scene. The police would say I'd returned to finish cleaning up the job I'd been hired to do.

If I was going to clean up I'd better get started. The police would be in here with their portable lasers. If I left even one print it would show up as a fluorescent glow. I had to retrace my steps and wipe down everything I'd touched. It wasn't difficult, I'd only touched the doors. Before I left the bedroom I carefully scanned round. The victim was lying peacefully in his gory bed. It must have been quick: there were no signs of a struggle. Tearing my eyes away from the corpse I noticed a framed photograph on the bedside table. It showed the murdered man with Rachel. I leant forward and took it. The victim must be Thwaite, he wasn't likely to have someone else's photo by his bed.

At least it was proof that Rachel had a connection with the murdered man. The photo showed Thwaite with his arms twined round Rachel in a very proprietorial way. He was smiling like a cat that's just been granted an extra nine lives. She was looking up at him, her dark hair over her shoulders, that same faintly quizzical smile on her face that she'd had in her father's photograph.

As I moved to leave the room I could see the imprint of my feet in the congealed blood. I was bound to leave tracks. I slipped my shoes off and left them where they were. On the table in the living room there was an open newspaper. I grabbed it and hastily wrapped the shoes up.

My instinct was to get out of that room as quickly as possible. But if I could just find some connection between the victim and the man who claimed to be Rachel Elsworth's father I might still be able to put myself in the clear with the boys in blue.

I looked through the papers on Thwaite's table. They were arranged with meticulous neatness: essays, notes, folders, textbooks. The bookcase was the same – a few novels, a lot of textbooks – nothing to interest me. Then my eye was caught by a red bookmark in a black leather-bound book. It was a diary. I flicked through it. The name Elsworth appeared on several pages. I took it, picked up my shoes and tiptoed out into the hall.

I closed the door and gave the handle and general area a good wipe down and then did the same for the back door. I even remembered to take the key out again and wipe it. Walking as casually as I could manage in my socks, I got in the Nissan and drove away.

The traffic was much lighter than earlier but there were still plenty of vehicles about. The entrance to my building makes an awkward angle with the road and I had to wait for several minutes for the traffic to clear before turning in to the communal garage block.

Once behind my own door I started to breathe normally

again. I stripped off all my clothes and put them with the shoes into a black bin bag. Next, I took a shower and dressed in jeans and an old polo shirt.

It was time to take stock. Having left my flat this morning as happy as a pig in clover I'd returned to it in as much trouble as it was possible to be in. I had to think my way out of this mess.

Elsworth was the start and end of the problem. I needed to be able to prove that he'd commissioned me to go round to Clydesdale on a bona fide job before the police turned up looking for me.

All right, maybe I shouldn't have actually entered the flat but if people leave their keys lying around what do they expect? I hadn't broken in. I'd only been trying to find a mixed up teenager and persuade her to get in touch with Mummy. The trouble was, I couldn't be sure what Elsworth might say. He might deny ever having met me.

Delise had arranged the meeting and then done her vanishing act. Was there a connection? There couldn't be. Delise wasn't like the mysterious Rachel. Delise's mother would have been on my doorstep yelling blue murder last night if she'd thought her precious daughter was missing. I had to assume I wouldn't be able to get in touch with Delise until she decided to surface in my life again. If she ever did.

God! Was I missing her already? She'd only been gone a day. No. Who could miss someone as critical as Delise? She was like a nagging toothache. I ought to count my blessings and hope I'd seen the back of her. We'd had our bust ups in the past but she'd never done a runner on me. Still, it might do no harm to try to get her phone number from her mother: the fact that she'd arranged the meeting between me and Elsworth at all showed that she still had some feelings.

That left the man in Voyagers who'd witnessed my meeting with Elsworth and Elsworth himself. Both of them were problematical. And there were now all kinds of connections between me and the murder scene. Janet Rushford at Abbotsford Hall could link me with Thwaite. The police laser might pick up a fingerprint I'd missed. There were bound to be traces of fibre left in the room from my clothes. Most damning of all . . . those bloody footprints.

I wasn't a pathologist but the half congealed blood suggested that Thwaite had been murdered not long before I found him. It must have been murder . . . there had been no sign of any knife in the bedroom.

I'd heard of a bloke who'd killed himself by trying to poke wax out of his ear with a matchstick. He'd been drunk at the time and the match had punctured an artery. The police had treated that as murder until the postmortem found the match in his ear.

Thwaite's throat had been cut while he was lying on the bed. It must have happened there. There was no blood anywhere else. How could a dying man, life's blood spraying from his throat, find time to hide the knife? His fists were clenched with sudden pain, as if death had caught him in his sleep.

It had to be murder.

And if I didn't want it pinned on me I must get rid of anything which could connect me to the scene. All the clothes I'd been wearing would have to be destroyed. There was no point in just washing them, any trace of fibre that had brushed off the trousers or shirt could sink me.

I decided to take the stuff to a municipal tip. Burning or burying were both too visible. Scurrying round the flat I assembled more rubbish, old newspapers and magazines, and filled another black bin liner. Having two bags would look far more normal. As I checked that the clothes didn't have anything in the pockets I noticed that the newspaper I'd wrapped my shoes in at Clydesdale Road had a feature article about Mike Dyer and his Paloma club in it. Nothing special about that, the papers are always carrying stories boosting him: the great Manchester success story, the man who'd built up an entertainment empire out of nothing.

That paper was the last thing that Thwaite must have read before going to bed. Dyer was promising to improve the security at his clubs and stop the drugs gangs plying their trade on his premises.

I had my choice of three local tips. At two I'd have to get out of the car and walk some distance to the dump but at Northenden I'd be able to drive right in and sling my rubbish over the wall into the huge concrete basin to join thousands of identical bags. Northenden it would be.

As I put the bin bags in the car I looked at my watch. It was just noon, only a couple of hours since I'd set out on my day's work so cheerfully.

Everything was all right at the tip. I joined the queue of people disposing of their refuse and my clothes went to play their part in Britain's land-fill programme. That would teach me not to spend so much time in front of the mirror.

On my way back I took the long way round and drove through Brooklands and Sale onto Washway Road. I followed it onto Chester Road and turned into the new White City Retail Park opposite the Greater Manchester Police HQ.

As soon as factories and homes had been swept away in this part of Manchester vast shopping developments and blocks of offices shot up in their place. Most of them had been financed by the Northern Pioneers' Bank. At least five other new developments stood within a half mile radius. There was a noticeable lack of customers for the shiny new superstores, each housed in a metal and plastic unit. The massive car park was almost empty.

Should I pay GMP Headquarters a visit to 'assist the police with their enquiries'? It was the honest thing to do, but was it the best policy? The police have a record of disliking private detectives that goes back to the days of the Bow Street Runners. So why should they believe anything I said? They would more likely turn my perennial near-bankruptcy against me and claim I'd started doing contract killings on the side.

True, Manchester wasn't as bad as some places but the same relentless pressure to make a case out against anyone who was even marginally 'in the frame' operated here as well. Even if some ambitious detective didn't try to pin the job on me I'd be tied up for days answering the same questions over and over. The best thing I could do was to forget that I'd ever paid a visit to Clydesdale Road and hope that it was never discovered.

The new boss at the GMP, Bill Benson, was said to be hostile to private detectives, certainly more unsympathetic than his two predecessors who had managed to hold out against the general prejudice to some extent. They'd had special reasons for that – it was rumoured in the trade that the GMP had employed private detectives to find out what the Yorkshire police were up to during the Ripper case.

Benson was also said to be very tidy-minded, very keen on correct administration: a new broom come to sweep clean. He had certainly taken over at the GMP in inauspicious circumstances. His immediate predecessor, a man well-liked in the Force, had been drowned in a yachting accident soon after getting the job. The chief before him, a great bearded bear and a man after my father's own heart, had been nationally famous for his trenchantly stated religious and moral views. My father had loved him.

I've no quarrel with the GMP myself, my father and uncle pounded the beat for years. But some promotion-hungry coppers are only interested in making out a case against a suspect. It was up to the courts to sort out justice and there was more than enough evidence to make a case out against me.

I got out of the car and walked over to the Pizza Palace for a meal. All this serious thinking was making me hungry. I had a deep dish pepperoni with extra cheese topping. As I chewed my way through the tacky mozzarella I thought about Rachel Elsworth and her father.

I wondered where Rachel was now. Would she be shattered when she found out about Thwaite? According to Elsworth, being with Thwaite was danger enough for her, so she was still in danger now he was dead?

Judging from the strength of Elsworth's emotions yesterday he had very strong feelings towards his stepdaughter. Did my casual approach tip him over the edge? Had he overcome his reluctance to go round to Clydesdale Road?

There was still time to do what I should have done when he started pushing money into my hot little hands – check the bastard out. The best place to begin was at the bank he claimed to be running.

I got into the Bluebird, drove down Chester Road and sat in the traffic jam on Deansgate for half an hour. Then I parked at Long Millgate. As I walked towards the bank I noticed that the name of the street was 'Hanging Ditch'. I was glad I wasn't superstitious. Fending my way through the throng of homeless beggars on Corporation Street stopped me getting too morbid.

The Northern Pioneers have done themselves proud. No one was going to describe their head office as a carbuncle on the face of Manchester. Everything that money could do had been done. The high tech, neo-Brutalist building reeked of rampant capitalism.

As soon as I entered the foyer I realised that I'd made a mistake, I should have gone home and changed into a suit. I probably still had cheese on my face. I went to the reception desk and asked for Elsworth. The dainty blonde receptionist opened her mouth in surprise and said 'He isn't available. If you want an appointment you'll have to write stating your business. Then if he decides to see you it'll be at least two weeks before you hear anything.' She gave me a form to fill in in triplicate.

I decided to try the charm that had worked on Janet Rushford earlier in the day but this one wasn't having any of it. I smiled and said 'Mr Elsworth does work here then, does he? He is in the building?' in my most syrupy tones.

'I'm not at liberty to give out that information. His whereabouts are only of concern to his senior colleagues. Please fill in the form if you want an appointment,' she stonewalled back.

'That's just it. I need to see him urgently. I'm doing some work for him and I need to get in touch . . .'

'State your name, then,' she interrupted with the intonation of a speak-your-weight machine.

'Can't you just see if he's available? I could leave a message for him. I don't need to speak to him personally,' I wheedled.

'Senior executives can only be reached by appointment or through the proper channels. State your name and number and I'll check the computer to see if you're listed as an employee,' she said with the same mechanical intonation.

I was getting nowhere. I tried oozing the charm out. 'Look Miss, a man named Elsworth has hired me to do some work for him personally, not for the Bank. He says he's the chief executive of this bank. I need to make sure that's true before I go to a lot of trouble and expense. I can see you're not going to get in touch with him, but have you got some sort of brochure with pictures in of the top executives that I could just have a look at to see if he's there?'

An expression of triumph crossed her features. 'Do you have an account at this bank, sir?'

I shook my head.

'Do you intend to open one?'

I shook my head again.

'Brochures may only be given out to our customers,' she said with a smile, baring her sharp little teeth.

I began to get annoyed. A group of interested spectators had gathered behind me. I was game for the next round, but before I could get another word out of my mouth I spotted a massive Frankenstein-clone in commissionaire's uniform bearing down on me. She must have pressed the panic button. I considered sprinting up the stairs but if getting past the receptionist was this tough who knew what else the Northern Pioneers' Bank had in store for awkward customers.

I got clear of son-of-Frankenstein by walking quickly to the revolving doors and into the street.

I went directly to the Central Reference Library and looked up Elsworth in *Who's Who*. He was listed as the chief executive of the Northern Pioneers' Bank.

The discovery of the corpse had thrown me into a spin. I wasn't my usual charming self. I ought to get back to my little grey home in south Manchester and work out what to do. I walked back to the car and as I headed south tuned to local radio.

There was no mention on the news of any murder.

3

Safely back in my kitchen I turned the television on, tuned to the cricket on BBC2, and watched Merv and his XXXXers demolishing the Tetley Bittermen. The Bittermen were playing in such a lacklustre way that they didn't deserve to be known as the England team. It looked as if the Bittermen needed a few XXXXers playing for them. I had a green 'Scotchbrite' scouring pad in my hand and, having taken the white enamelled drip pans and hob cover off the cooker, I worked at the top of the oven and gas jets to remove any minute blemish which had appeared since my last session.

Two fingers of Bell's whisky were adding to the soothing effect of my labours. When I was satisfied that the underside of the hob was gleaming I went into the living room. The cricket on the television had been replaced by the antics of Huxley Pig with his catchy signature tune so I turned it off.

A mood of lethargy was creeping over me – reaction from the shock I'd had, but I couldn't afford to switch off. I had to find Rachel now, this was personal. I had to find her if only to give myself an excuse for not reporting the death of Thwaite to the police. This reminded me of the evidence I'd taken from the scene of the crime.

I picked up the black diary I'd removed from Thwaite's flat. It was quite substantial, with a full A5 page per day. Thwaite had neat, well-formed handwriting. The diary contained a full record of his movements over the past year from September. As well as studying for a master's degree in environmental management at the Metropolitan University Thwaite was DJing at half the nightclubs in town. He must have been good because he'd worked the best-known clubs as well as some I'd never heard of. A top DJ who could spiel his way through all the latest evolutions of the pop scene – hip-hop, garage, techno etc – could earn up to £600 an hour in one of the big clubs.

There were also references to Rachel. She went with Thwaite on most of his weekend gigs. No wonder Thwaite could afford to live in yuppified Clydesdale Road – judging by his earning power this guy was a suitable prospective son-in-law for any wealthy banker. Of course the punters would eventually get tired of his patter but by then he would have got his degree in environmental management and a healthy bank balance to fall back on.

One mystery about his flat was that there was no sign of expensive audio equipment there. Most DJs spend part of their earnings on the latest Technics turntables, records, mixers, amps and speakers not to mention fairy lights in tubes etc. As a successful DJ Thwaite had to have somewhere to keep all his equipment and some transport to shift it.

There was no address for his parents or next of kin in the 'In case of accident please notify . . .' slot in the diary.

He had a North of England sounding surname but that didn't tell me anything about where his parents lived. I'd need the Metropolitan University records for that . . . which might not be readily forthcoming at the moment.

It was coming up to half six so I turned the television back on for the Northern News. Thwaite was a minor local celebrity so his death was bound to feature. I sat through the whole half hour. There was no mention of a murder in Didsbury. Waiting for something to happen was making me jumpy. Not expecting a reply, I picked up the phone and dialled the number Elsworth had given me.

'Hello, Dee Elsworth' replied a lady sounding like the Queen in 1952. Obviously a suitable mate for Elsworth. No one could fake that tone of voice, she had to be his wife: so he was who he said he was.

'This is David Cunane here, Harold asked me to call,' I replied, slipping naturally into the servile tones developed by generations of working class conditioning.

'Yes, he said you'd be calling. He's had to go to Brussels for a meeting with the Commission about the new banking laws. He caught the 10.15 p.m. flight to Brussels last night. He's opened an account for you at our bank's branch in Deansgate. You'll be able to draw up to £150 a day and if you need more the manager, Mr Blomely, will let you have any reasonable sum.'

'That's very civil of Mr Elsworth,' I said, surprised. Instead of giving me the push he seemed to be handing me the keys to his piggy bank. There must be something wrong. Since when had bankers started chucking their own cash around like drunken sailors on the spree? Still, Elsworth could hardly be setting me up as a murder suspect if he was dishing out the cash with such a free hand. There must be some other motive for his open handedness.

'If you hear from him before I do please tell him that there has been a significant development, and I'll have some news for him shortly.' Mrs Elsworth didn't sound very distressed; there was a faint hint of strain in her voice, but nothing that would justify her husband's demands for reticence. According to him she was at her wits' end. Perhaps some of these upper-class types don't show their feelings like the rest of us, or maybe she knew more about Rachel's disappearance than her husband suspected.

If Delise had been missing for a week her Mum would have been on national TV by now. She was very close to her mother.

Come to think of it, Delise should have called by now. Typical of her to time her exit for the one period in my life when I really needed her. I wasn't missing her but her absence was like the sudden disappearance of a well-scratched itch: it created a void. Anyway Delise came in useful for phoning the likes of Mrs Elsworth. She always managed to extract more information from a phone call than I did, especially when she put on her 'posh' voice. Her Mum had spent a small fortune on elocution lessons for her. Delise could aspirate with the best of them. Her splendid vowel sounds had won me a lot of commissions over the last two years.

The moment I'd been avoiding all day had now arrived. It seemed I'd have to phone the police and tell them about the corpse in Clydesdale Road. I decided to phone the local police at Sydall Lane. I went out to a public call box. I might be paranoid but I felt safer at a pay phone. Using a Merseyside accent I reported the presence of a corpse at 90 Clydesdale Road. It would take some time before Sydall Lane got someone from Didsbury out to Clydesdale Road.

Back at the flat I fixed myself a tuna salad. I noticed that Delise had cleared all the yogurts out of the fridge. Perhaps she hadn't gone as far as London after all. Maybe she was lurking at her mother's waiting for me to go and beg her to return.

Well she could wait a while longer. It was nearly seven hours since my last meal. I had fresh strawberries and ice cream as a dessert. They filled a corner.

Thwaite's diary mentioned that his most recent gig had been at the Paloma club. He seemed in demand there. So perhaps that would be a good place to pick up Rachel's trail. I dressed with care for my visit to clubland, hoping that these clothes weren't going to end up in a land-fill as quickly as the last lot. I selected a dark linen suit with a terracotta silk shirt. I would wear the shirt open collared: anyone over thirty in a tie is automatically regarded as a snooper from the Drugs Squad in these places.

When I got down to the Paloma there was a queue, although it was still early, but I didn't have to wait long before having to pay my £3.50.

At the door were both male and female bouncers wearing black t-shirts with a white dove logo and the word 'Paloma' on their chests. Some were searching customers for drugs or concealed weapons.

'Step through the screen' said one of them, a short, muscular man who had the aggressively healthy appearance of a military P.E. instructor. He wore a police-style radio communicator clipped to a strap across his chest so he could call for quick assistance if needed. His manner discouraged any jollity from the punters, who were queuing for their night's fun with the enforced sobriety of a bunch of Welsh chapel elders sneaking round the back of an off-licence.

'Remove any metal objects and step through the screen,' he repeated firmly, ushering me through an airport-style detection screen. When I stepped in it began bleeping. I pointed to the buckle on my belt. Mr Health and Fitness looked dubious, gave me a quick frisk, but let me through.

The club consisted of a giant L-shaped room. Each section had a bar running along its full length. The shorter part had many alcoves and nooks for seating. There was space for dancing in the longer segment. A balcony running round the outer part of the L, where the rooms met, completed the internal arrangements. You could look down into both rooms from the balcony. There was another bar in a cellar under the shorter room. The decor was ultra-modern and expensive.

Ear-shattering house music blared out of every speaker. Or was it 'garage', the latest offspring? Most of the customers were teenagers dressed in baggy jeans and loose t-shirts. White trainers were much in evidence, I felt conspicuous in my brown suedes. I walked over to the bar.

Any chance of seeing Mr Dyer?' I asked the youth behind the bar.

'I only serve drinks round here, you should have come in before we opened,' he said in a surly manner, busily moving down the bar from me. Before he could break eye contact I gave him a hard stare and he turned away to look towards the bouncers. I didn't see what happened next in the crush, but he must have connected because a thick-set man with massive forearms parted the crowd and stood in front of me. At five foot six in height he was as broadly built as he was long. His nose had been broken many times and was spread all over his face. The barman now reappeared with a smirk on his face. It was a well-practised tactic.

'Look I'm a friend of Andrew Thwaite, I've come to talk to Mr Dyer about him,' I said quickly.

'Oh, why didn't you say that right away?' he said dismissing the muscle man with a wave. 'Ms Mather's been asking for him all day. If you knew how many people we get walking in here, expecting to see Mr Dyer, you wouldn't have asked.' He picked up a phone at the back of the bar and spoke into it, then showed me through to a door at the corner of the bar which he opened with a special key chained to his waist.

'First on your left, mate,' he said, indicating a narrow way almost blocked by stacked crates of mixer drinks. As I manoeuvred my way along trying not to rip my suit, the door at the end opened and 'Popeye', the body-builder with the overdeveloped arms who had made a recent appearance in the bar, popped out beckoning me forward.

I stepped into a wide, high ceilinged room furnished with couches round three of the walls and a small bar opposite me at the fourth. A morose collection of body-beautiful characters in t-shirts and jeans lounged on the couches. It looked like the casting session for an American wrestling film. My friend with the muscular forearms led me to a more normally shaped group standing in front of the bar.

'This is the guy that was asking after Andy, boss,' he said in a broad North Manchester accent. The man he introduced me to made a sharp contrast to the steroid-and-embrocation crowd. he definitely wasn't one of the health and strength brigade.

Short and fat, of indeterminate age, and wearing black trousers and matching black shirt, he was a high-grade weirdo. He looked like an unfrocked Catholic priest who'd converted to Satanism. Instead of a dog-collar he had a beaten silver neckpiece fastened at his throat by studs in his shirt. The piece was about four inches across. Black winkle-pickers completed the satanic rig. His heavily gelled hair was close shaven at the sides and long on top. His face, with piggy eyes and double chin, looked as if it had damaged a lot of meat pies in its time.

My instinct for spotting a villain was shrieking, watch out for this guy! Hardly a case for much professional pride on my part, he seemed to have gone out of his way to label himself a villain like one of the baddies in an old fashioned Western film.

If the impression he'd set out to create was evil, he'd succeeded. It was reinforced by the furrows on his brow and impatient expression as he peered at me short-sightedly. I stared back at him. The thought came to me that his appearance was meant to be some sort of clever, camp joke. A blonde stood at his side.

'Who the hell are you then?' he asked, scowling at me all the time. 'Do you know where the bugger is? He should have been set up hours ago.'

'You must be Mike Dyer, then?' I replied. I knew I was out-numbered and meant to be overawed in the presence of Manchester's leading club boss but something made me want to cheek him so I answered his question with a question.

To be fair, he took it well.

'That's right, cocker. You're not from the press are you? I don't give interviews after 10 p.m.' he said, running a comb through his oily locks.

'No, I'm not. I'm looking for a girl called Rachel,' I said hoping to provoke some reaction. He was too hard-boiled to give anything away but he didn't throw me out.

'If you're looking for a girl, you should have stayed round at the front. We don't encourage pick-ups in here, do we lads?'

There was a sycophantic titter from the tide of muscle men. 'Unless one of this lot's called Rachel. Thick-set sort of girl? Cross dresser? Is that it?' he asked again.

I stared back at him.

The woman standing next to him was far easier on the eye than he was. An attractive blond with curves in all the right places, she was ill-matched standing next to the pear-shaped Dyer. They looked like beauty and the beast. It must have been intentional on Dyer's part, an angel to put alongside his carefully crafted Satan. Although she joined in the laughter at his joke, everything else about her was a complete contrast with him.

She was in her late twenties, about five foot four in height. Her hair was thick, curly and blond: a real mop. Her eyes were cornflower blue and she had a lop-sided grin which made her expression not so much mocking as amused. A fresh complexion suggested that she had a life in the daylight hours, she wasn't a hot-house plant.

Her features were a little too firm; her nose, cheek bones and chin a shade too pronounced. Her beauty could be ranked as classic, rather than contemporary. The sculptural quality of the bone structure suited her rather long face. There was character there. I guessed that she was nobody's moll, not a tart or kept woman. She had an air of competence and ability out of keeping with Dyer's collection of hangers-on.

She was contemplating the world from a long way off, probably as far away as the orbit of Venus. Her air of detachment from this squalid little back room and its inhabitants made a pleasing impression on me, as if she was an ally before I'd even spoken to her. Her well-shaped figure didn't repel me either.

'Are you going to tell me who you are then?' demanded Dyer, his tone more hostile as he noticed my attention straying.

'My name's David Cunane and I'm a private detective.'

'God, we've got bloody Mike Hammer here lads, or is it Magnum?' Dyer's cronies were all paying attention now. Popeye gave an appreciative chuckle at his boss's sparkling wit. Dyer spoke in a heavy 'stage Northern' accent of the kind popularised by public school comedians.

'Oh, don't be so rude Mike,' said the blond, confirming my favourable impression of her. 'I'm Sylvia Mather, Mike's personal assistant, Mr Cunane. Can you tell us where Andy's got to? He should have been on here tonight. We don't get many people breaking their engagements at the Paloma.' Mather's voice pointed up the contrast with her boss even more than her appearance , it was a sweet, beautifully modulated voice that could have charmed the birds off the trees. The expressions 'honeyed tones' or 'dulcet tones' didn't really do justice to this rich rolling speech. I felt myself warming to her even more.

'He'll not be keeping too many engagements from now on,' I said.

'What the hell does that cryptic remark mean, Hammer?' said Dyer giving me an unfriendly poke in the shoulder. 'Is this like a crossword puzzle? Give us another clue.'

'It means that Andrew Thwaite won't be coming, he won't be doing any more gigs for anyone.' As I spoke I was looking right into Dyer's eyes. There was no change at all in his sneering expression as I gave him the news. 'I'm trying to get in touch with his girlfriend Rachel, I need to see her.'

'No you're not, Mister Private Bloody Detective. You're going to tell me exactly what's up with Andy and who the hell sent you here.' As Dyer spoke threateningly I was aware that several of the mini-Schwarzeneggers had stood up and were forming a circle around us. My options seemed to be narrowing.

'Do you want me to handle him for you boss?' butted in a very tall, gaunt-looking bruiser with a Glasgow accent and red spots all over his face.

The pimply Scotsman's intervention seemed to change Dyer's mind for him.

'Mind your own bloody business Jock! Get out round the front and see everything's all right. In fact, all of you bastards can get the fuck out. It's time you started earning the money I'm paying you,' ordered Dyer, glancing at his heavy gold Rolex.

'Come over here, you,' he said to me, leading me into the corner, Spotty Jock and Popeye and their crew of muscle-bound clowns obediently trooped out leaving me alone with Dyer and his personal assistant.

'Sorry about that. They're all so hyped up on steroids and aggression I sometimes forget who I'm dealing with. What would you like to drink, Mr Cunane? Sylvia, get him a drink.'

Dyer's manners were dramatically improved by the departure of his gallery as was his accent, now just standard North Manchester.

Dyer made a big play of lighting a huge cigar while his assistant attended to me. I wondered what he was thinking. He'd been pleasant enough when he thought I might be press, then aggressive when he learned I was a detective. Now he was puzzled about who I was and what I knew, he was fishing for information. He had me pegged as a brainless mug who'd soon spill the beans over a glass with his lady.

'What'll it be?' said the luscious Sylvia.

'Oh, I'll have a large malt whisky if you've got one,' I said.

''Course we have,' said Sylvia. 'Mike wouldn't dream of drinking anything else, would you pet?'

Dyer glared at me through thick blue smoke as Sylvia handed me a generous measure of his whisky. His show of hospitality hadn't extended as far as offering me a cigar. Then he made a conscious effort to turn the charm on again.

'Just what has happened to Andy? He's one of my best DJs.' Dyer showed me his pearly teeth as he spoke. He'd paid his orthodontist a mint.

'He's been found dead in his flat in Didsbury. The police are saying it looks like suicide,' I improvised. An outright lie would have been quickly detected and have thrown suspicion on me, but telling the truth might be just as dangerous.

I'd never intended things to get this far. The last thing I wanted was to be answering questions which might link me to the murder. I'd thought I'd have a quick look round to see if Rachel was on the premises and then clear off. Now here I was getting myself even more into the clag than I'd been before.

Sylvia sat down heavily, she turned pale. I'd have dearly liked to know what was going on behind that pretty face.

'I should have thought Andy would be the last person in the world to kill himself,' she said slowly. The news had obviously been a big shock for her.

'I don't know, some of these young people can't take a setback can they Mr Cunane?' said Dyer nastily. 'They've no staying power, all piss and wind . . . Maybe he was using something.'

'You'd know more about that than me,' I replied cheekily. The breezy way he was taking the news offended me.

His face flushed, the angry scowl came back and he stood up.

I must have struck an exposed nerve. I'd only meant that he knew Thwaite better than me. My mind flashed back to the paper which had been open on Thwaite's table. No wonder Dyer was sensitive about drugs. Still, his reaction to the news was peculiar. When you hear that someone you know's just killed himself you don't start sneering about him. His assistant's reaction was a more normal one.

'Sylvia, you see if you can get some sense out of this smart-arse will you? I'm going before I lose my patience with him.'

Turning to me he snarled, 'I've only got to say the word and my lads'll hammer you into the ground, Mr Private Eye Clever Dick Cunane. Yes, you cheeky bugger,' he added, jabbing the cigar at me, 'you'll wake up with men in green coats and face masks all round you.'

'I'm being paid to ask questions, not to sort out your DJs for you, Dyer. What do you know about Thwaite's girlfriend Rachel? She's missing.'

'So you said, and what makes you think I know or care anything about her? Just keep your nose out of my business, smartarse!' he rapped back.

Dyer left the room, but then put his head back round the door. 'And don't give him any more of my best whisky either . . .' came his parting shot to Sylvia.

So, it hadn't taken many minutes for him to revert to type and start flinging threats around again.

I didn't seem to be making much progress in finding anything out about Rachel. Swallowing Dyer's excellent malt far more quickly than it deserved I turned to Sylvia. She was still looking good, not smiling not but wearing a sympathetic expression on her face.

'Your boss is a charming guy. Is he always so sweet?' I said.

Sylvia laughed. She seemed completely untouched by Dyer's outburst. It hadn't taken her long to get over the news of Andrew Thwaite's demise.

'Do you fancy going out for a bite to eat?' I asked her in my smoothest style. I didn't feel any pangs of betrayal towards Delise, this was a purely business occasion.

'Well thank you, kind sir. I certainly would like to have something to eat and you heard what my dear boss said, didn't you? I've got to get some sense out of you.' There was no havering or coyness. I liked that. No sooner had I made the suggestion than we were on our way out.

There was a back exit to the club, and Sylvia led the way. I took her to the Trattoria Milano in Albert Square, just a short walk from the club. The Trattoria is in a cellar below some old-fashioned legal offices and serves a pretty good tagliatelle. It's an expensive little place, usually full of lawyers. I don't go there very often but the bill would go on Elsworth's expenses. We had Parma ham for starters, tagliatelle with ham and mushrooms followed by osso bucco with wine, onions, tomatoes and parsley. The 'torta della casa' turned out to be a rather sickly-sweet cake.

We took a table in the corner. The intimate cosy atmosphere and subdued lighting encouraged an exchange of confidences, which is why the place was so popular with lawyers.

Sylvia and I made small talk over the meal and we split a large bottle of sweet Orvieto Classico DOC. It was expensive but Elsworth was paying. Over the wine she began to open up about her boss. She'd worked for him for four years during which the club had gone from strength to strength.

'You mustn't be too hard on Mike, he's under a lot of pressure at the moment,' she explained.

'What sort of pressure would that be, Sylvia? His club's supposed to be the tops isn't it?'

'No, it's not that sort of pressure. The police are pushing to close us down because drug peddlers keep infiltrating the club to sell their stuff. It's very unfair, we search people, we've undercover men and hidden cameras but they still get in.'

'With all those young people there are bound to be pushers trying to sell to them,' I sympathised. 'But I'm really concerned about Rachel Rankine. You might have known her as Rachel Elsworth. She's missing.' As I said the name Elsworth there was a distinct change of atmosphere. I could sense that the name was some sort of trigger for Sylvia; she suddenly seemed to be a lot more interested in what I was saying.

'Can you tell me anything at all about her?' I asked.

'Well I never heard anyone call her by her surname. All these DJs have their girlfriends helping them you know. It can take some of them hours to set up. Rachel certainly stood out from the bunch, she's very pretty but my God doesn't she know it! A real little poser.'

Noticing the interested expression on my face as she made her revelation Sylvia blushed slightly under her tan.

'Sorry. Are my claws showing?' she said. 'Yes, Rachel's a beautiful girl but she doesn't half flaunt it. Most of her efforts were wasted at the Paloma, silly little fool! Mike's more or less the only normal man there . . .'

I laughed loudly.

'It's true, most of the men who work for Mike are more interested in how they look in the mirror than in girls. They're always flashing their muscles at each other. As for the DJs, they're worse. Most of them are too doped out of their minds to be interested in sex.'

'So the famous Paloma ban on drugs doesn't extend to the staff then?' I asked.

'Don't be naive. If we banned everyone who used drugs we wouldn't be able to employ many people from the pop scene. We're not running a church social. The ban is on selling drugs, we can't control what people do outside.' Sylvia spoke brusquely. Despite her charming appearance and sunny expression, she was all business now.

'I understand that, but what about Rachel and Thwaite? What were they on?' I countered.

'Well I don't know about Andy Thwaite, from what he's done he must have been on something, but it wasn't as obvious as with some. He always seemed to have his head screwed on the right way. Rachel now, she gave the impression of being so taken with herself and her wonderful personality that I don't think she needed any kind of stimulation, but there again you never know. She might have used snow. They were both in the scene.

'How did they get on with each other and with Dyer?' I asked.

'Andy was always the boss even though she is a masterful type. There were one or two sharp little confrontations but

Andy always got his way. She needed him more than he needed her, I suppose, but anyone could see she resented it. A dominatrix in the making that one!'

'You don't like her much do you? But how did they get on with Dyer?'

'Well Mike seemed to be very interested in Rachel at first but lately not so much. He definitely knows who she is though, take no notice of what he said in the club. Thwaite was quite close to the boss, he got a lot more than the usual number of bookings. 'Course he was good, but I never thought he was that good.'

'What do you mean, he'd some sort of hold over Dyer?' I said suspiciously.

'No, nothing like that, but now I think about it, Mike did spend more time with him than he usually did with a DJ and was more anxious to please him than you might have expected. He even invited him round to the Prohibition Club quite a bit, not that Andy went much.'

'What's the Prohibition Club, then?'

'You know when they changed the law on drinking hours? Mike opened this club where you can drink all afternoon. It's like the Paloma but without the dancing.'

'Did Rachel ever go there, Sylvia?'

'Oh yes, at least I saw Andy in there with her once or twice but it wasn't their sort of place. They were keen on performing, not sitting and boozing,' she replied.

'Look Sylvia, I'm being paid to find Rachel and I have to ask you this, but don't take me wrong. Is it possible that Andy and Rachel and Dyer might have got themselves mixed up in something heavy, something that's really bad news and that this is why Thwaite's dead and Rachel's disappeared?' I pressed.

'No of course not! What are you saying? Mike's had them bumped off? You've got a vivid imagination,' she said angrily.

'Calm down Sylvia,' I said, reaching across the table to pat her hand. 'You said yourself that they were in the scene, she might have used cocaine, and her father is convinced that she's mixed up in drugs, or at least that Thwaite was.' I told her about the cannabis plant at the hall of residence.

Slightly mollified by my explanation Sylvia continued to

defend her boss. I could see that I wouldn't get anything more out of her.

'I didn't know Andy Thwaite well enough to say what he might have been involved with,' she said. 'He was probably a user, but Mike Dyer would never have had anything to do with him if he'd been selling drugs. Mike would do anything to stop his club being closed down. He's got everything to lose from being involved with drugs.'

I remained sceptical, but what was the point of spoiling the start of a beautiful friendship by getting argumentative about an ugly customer like Dyer. I changed the subject, and we concentrated on the wine for a while. When I did return to the subject of Andy and Rachel it was to a less contentious area.

'Have you got any addresses for Andy apart from his pad in Didsbury? He must have somewhere he kept his stuff,' I asked.

'I did hear some mention of Southport, but that sounds a long way for a Manchester DJ to go to store his equipment. I could look it up for you tomorrow,' she replied pleasantly.

Sylvia had recovered from the moment of reaction she'd shown when I mentioned the Elsworth name and the tension caused by my suggestions about her boss, she was smiling at me again and I wasn't impervious to her charms. I was ready to sit listening to that beautiful voice all night. She kept flickering her eyelashes at me like someone having trouble with their contact lenses but after looking at her for a while I decided it was being done for my benefit. I tried to rein in my wayward libido, at least for the time being.

We finished our meal with brandy and coffee. Sylvia told me some more about herself. She was a career girl, not from Manchester originally. She'd trained as a chartered secretary and the first jobs she'd had were with boring insurance companies and banks; she'd been unhappily married to a solicitor for four years and when the chance came for a job at the glamorous Paloma club she'd jumped at it. She was like that, she liked doing exciting things like gambling and free fall parachuting, nothing dull. Mike had a rough side to his tongue but he made up for this in other ways, he could be very generous.

It was certain I wasn't going to get far with Sylvia by criticising her boss. She told me that Mike was married and had a big house in Handforth.

How interesting.

Sylvia lived out in the sticks at Heaton Mersey; she suggested getting a taxi home but I gave her a lift in the Bluebird. Her home was in a block of newly built flats. She invited me in for a drink. I declined but not before I'd got her home phone number and a promise that she would try to find Thwaite's Southport address.

As I drove back through Didsbury and Chorlton towards my flat I didn't feel too pleased with my day's work. I'd taken on what seemed like a simple job of tracing a missing girl but at the very first hurdle I'd almost come a cropper.

I'd panicked when I found the corpse in Clydesdale Road, I'd incriminated myself by removing evidence. I'd imagined all sorts of plots to fit me up as the chief suspect in a murder case with Harold Elsworth as the master criminal. He'd been in Brussels at the time the murder took place. At least I think he'd been there. How long does it take for all the blood to drain out of a human body? The murder must have been committed some time in the morning before I got there, not the afternoon or evening before.

So if it wasn't Elsworth, who else would have wanted to kill Thwaite?

Dyer had shown no emotion at the news of the death nor had he shown much interest in the details. He'd a lot to lose if his club was shut down for drug pushing but there was no hard evidence that Thwaite had been involved in drugs unless you counted the hysterical denunciations of Harold Elsworth. Thwaite might have been a casual user but that didn't make him a dealer.

My route took me past the end of Clydesdale Road. There was no sign of activity there. The lights were on in several of the rooms at number 90 but there were no police cars or incident vans around.

Instead of going home to South Manchester I drove back into town down the Princess Parkway and stopped the car along the street from the Paloma Club. Things were still humming, wailing music blaring out and throngs of young people crowding the pavements. I decided not to go back in. Popeye and Spotty Jock, Dyer's chief henchmen, might not be too friendly.

I wasn't quite sure where I was aiming but I felt I had to do something more to earn my fee.

At 2 a.m. the mobs began pouring out of the club right into the road, blocking the taxis and police cars. It was like a football crowd pouring out of Old Trafford on a Saturday afternoon. There were lots of police on view as well as Dyer's dove t-shirt brigade standing in the doorway of the club. Some kids banged on the car window thinking I was a taxi. In half an hour the crowds dispersed. The police climbed into their vans; the bouncers withdrew to the inner recesses of the club and calm returned to the street. By 3 a.m. I was beginning to think I was wasting my time when activity began again at the club.

A huge white Mercedes pulled up outside and Popeye, Spotty Jock and their mates rolled out of the club. They started scanning the street so I lay sideways on the seat peeping out of the back window. Then the fat man himself emerged clutching an outsized executive briefcase and accompanied by a young woman. They got in the Mercedes with the minions. I turned my engine on and as they drove away tucked myself in at a discreet distance behind them. I was careful to keep myself from view. Dyer wasn't the type to accept surveillance with a friendly wave and a nod.

They drove down Medlock Street and onto Princess Road and the Parkway. At the end of the Parkway they turned left onto the M56 for a couple of miles before making for the A34 and Handforth where they turned into the Esplanade, a sort of reservation for rich people in the middle of Handforth.

The Esplanade wasn't a through road and I couldn't follow them. I pulled in for a moment and then drove on slowly. Dyer and his henchmen were getting out at the sixth house down on the left. Popeye was on sentry duty. He didn't look alert.

From the distance I was it was impossible to tell if the girl with them was Rachel. I cursed myself for not having my night glasses or telephoto lens with me. She looked young and rather awkward in her movements, perhaps she'd had a skinful. It could be Rachel, she seemed to have dark hair. I wasn't too sure about identifying her anyway, the photo her stepfather had given me gave no idea of whether Rachel was tall or short and like a fool I'd failed to ask Sylvia Mather for a physical description. 'Good looking' and 'pretty' weren't really much help in identifying someone two hundred yards away in poor light.

This girl could be Rachel, could be anyone. She might be doped or merely drunk, but what could I do about it?

I parked and sat for a while. Several police cars drove slowly past and it was only a matter of time before one asked me what I was up to. Dyer hadn't emerged again so the chances were that they were settled for the night. I drove round Handforth and passed the end of the Esplanade several times; the Mercedes was still parked. There was no sign of activity.

I turned for home along the empty motorway. When I got in I poured myself a whisky and went to my lonely bed.

I woke at 9 a.m. The family of thrushes under the guttering outside my bedroom window were in full voice. I crept into the kitchen and poured a glass of orange juice. I felt sluggish, not hung-over but heavy-limbed, not the agile detective of yesterday morning. It was bright so I decided to begin my day with a token training ride.

I keep my mountain bike in the lock-up garage attached to my flat. I have it heavily chained, the local criminals do a roaring trade in stolen bikes. It's a Raleigh Mustang with 18 gears – not indexed. The frame's heavy but that doesn't matter as I use it only for training purposes. I've got a pannier on the back so I can carry a heavy load if I want to use it for shopping. My cycle shorts were in the laundry basket so I was wearing a pair of old jeans.

It was late in the day to be cycle riding in safety so I thought I'd better put my helmet on. I feel over-dressed wearing it but there are plenty of drivers in Manchester who think nothing about having stunt races down both sides of the highway. I put on my cycling gloves.

The biggest open space near my flat is the Mersey Valley. The river flows between steep artificial banks but from time to time spills over onto the plain. This is a wide area between 'edges' on either bank. The land between the edges is several miles wide in places. Danger of flooding has kept the builders at bay.

I rode down to Chorlton Ees nature reserve: an area which the Valley Authority is trying to return to its original state. There are tall stands of reeds and lots of low birch trees growing as they must have when the ice melted twelve thousand years ago. Bird life has been coaxed back to the river bank but the existence of a model aero-club on the opposite side doesn't do much to support the illusion of wilderness. Winding through this nature reserve are narrow paths, which it is my pleasure to cycle along.

Pedalling through the reeds I could hear the high-pitched

whine of a model aircraft engine coming closer. I didn't think anything of it, the aero-modellers fly their planes over the marshes onto this side of the river.

Then the noise began to get louder, louder than a model aircraft. Over my shoulder I caught a glimpse of a scramble bike ridden by an unhelmeted black man, with a passenger, coming up at speed, and as I was pulling sharply to one side felt a terrific blow across my back and shoulders. I went off the track and over the top of the bike as the wheel sank into the mud. As I cartwheeled the sight of the rider's head and shoulders and heavy chain, swinging in his pillion passenger's hand, fixed in my memory like a flash photo before they shot away. I had a soft landing but I blacked out from the pain in my back.

I must have lain in the mud for at least ten minutes before I came round. I pulled the bike upright: apart from being covered in mud it was fine, but I wasn't. My back felt as if it was on fire. I thought I'd been shot but there wasn't enough blood. I could hardly move my arms and shoulders. With difficulty I climbed aboard the bike and freewheeled down the slight slope back the way I'd come. There was no sign of the pair on the scramble bike.

While I was on the Meadows none of the passers-by even gave me a second glance. Figures on mountain bikes covered in mud from head to foot were a familiar sight. Even in my crippled condition it didn't take me long to get back home.

I left the bike in the garage, not bothering to chain it. Moving crabwise, I got myself to the front door of the building. Luck was on my side or I might have lain in the doorway for a while. One of my fellow residents, a good friend, gave me a cheery good morning as she walked past me on her way to the shops.

'Fiona,' I croaked, 'I've had an accident, can you find somebody to help me up the stairs?' Short of crawling, there was no way I could have got upstairs on my own.

Fiona Salway, a retired infant school teacher, looked me over. Her expression conveyed the unflappable calm that had dealt with a thousand emergencies in the classroom. She's got a friendly owlish gaze and rosy cheeks which make her look much younger than her sixty years. Fiona's a very kind person, much more than a neighbour to me in many ways. She's always happy to do those little favours which make living on your own in an anonymous block of flats more human and bearable. The only fault I can find with Fiona is that she's got an insatiable curiosity that can sometimes get oppressive.

'Finbar's in, I'll get him to come down,' she said, inspecting me very closely with her hazel eyes. Finbar's her twin brother, he's a retired regular soldier. Fiona's never been married, she lives with her brother off and on. They stay together until they have a difference of opinion about something, then Finbar goes away for a while. They re-unite when their need for company is stronger than their differences, a sensible arrangement. She pressed the button on her door bell and spoke into the microphone. Finbar came down at once. He was no more put out by an emergency than his twin. He supported me and I was able to make it to my front door.

'It's a good job you were wearing this, look the back's all stoved in.' Fiona was holding my helmet. 'What on earth happened to you? We'll phone for the police and an ambulance, you've been attacked haven't you?' She wanted to come in and sort me out but I insisted on being on my own. The last thing I wanted was the police snooping around.

Finbar looked at the helmet disbelievingly. 'How did you manage to do that to it? It's almost as if you've been bashed over the back of the head with a hammer,' he said, shaking his head in disbelief.

'No, it was an accident. I came off the back of the bike. I must have landed on a stone.'

He pushed the door open looking disbelieving. 'You'd better let me have a look at you.' I knew that if I submitted to the Salway's well-meant ministrations I'd end up in hospital. I gently pushed Finbar out into the corridor and shut the door.

I struggled into the bathroom, ran a bath and stripped. I poured half a box of Radox into the bath and climbed into the hot water. The pain in my back and shoulders was exquisite. The scramble biker's passenger must have lashed me with a heavy ball and chain. It hadn't been just an attempt to frighten me. If I hadn't been wearing a helmet he'd have crushed my skull. Gradually the heat and the paracetamol I took before getting into the bath began to ease some of the pain out of my back. I lay there soaking for half an hour.

My back was a mess. I could see the imprint of individual links of chain right across my shoulders. I wondered whether to call James McNeil. James is a doctor, he teaches at the University School of Life Sciences, the fancy new name for the Medical School. He and his wife Margaret are two of my oldest friends. A middle-aged couple, I'd met them with my wife at university do's for African students. Elenki had been studying medicine. Later, when she was dying from anaemia, they did everything they could to help. They live half a mile away from me with two enormous dogs for company.

In some ways I value their advice and friendship more than that of my parents.

I decided not to bother them. I got dressed and put on a business suit. I practised walking up and down my living room. I could move. I went round the flat gathering up laundry and loaded it into the washing machine.

The morning paper I get doesn't have much local news and there was nothing in it about Thwaite. I got the mid-morning local news on the television: nothing about any murder in Didsbury. I phoned Ted Blake, an acquaintance who works on the news desk at Alhambra Television, the local commercial TV station. I'd met Blake through my former interest in strong drink. He's a larger than life character in every sense of the phrase. A couple of years ago we spent many evenings together trying to drink each other under the table. There are no friends like the ones you've been chucked out of pubs with.

He said he'd ring me back with any news.

He came back on shortly. 'There *was* an item not included in the news. Here goes . . .

' "The body of a man believed to be that of student DJ Andrew Thwaite was found in his flat last night. Foul play is not suspected." Then this part's not for release . . . "He was found with his throat cut, the knife still clenched in his hand." '

I was so gobsmacked that I asked him to repeat it.

'A friend of yours, was he, Dave?'

I was biting my knuckles, not from the pain in my back but from sheer surprise. When I'd told Dyer that Thwaite's death was suicide I'd been improvising to keep myself in the clear.

I'd never dreamt the police would say it really was suicide. There hadn't been a knife clenched in his hand when *I* left him.

'He was a friend of someone I'm trying to help,' I said. It was never a good idea to give Ted information. He's a genius at making bricks without straw.

'Thanks very much Ted, I'll get back to you if there's any story on this.'

'Think nothing of it, just remember that it's me who's your friend not the *Evening Banner.* So pass any juicy items to me first,' he said genially.

The *Banner*'s the local evening paper: it's the sister of a heavy daily paper which doesn't report much crime. To make up for this the *Banner*'s full of local crime stories. It certainly brightens up many a dull evening. As well as working on the newsdesk at Alhambra TV Ted's a stringer for a national tabloid which is in competition with the group which owns the *Banner.* I thanked him again and rang off.

Trying to concentrate on the job in hand and not on the pain in my back I got the car out of the garage and drove into town. I parked in a multi-storey near my office and set off down to Deansgate. I should've been using a zimmer frame.

Eventually I made it to the Deansgate branch of the Northern Pioneers' Bank. I felt like a Klondyke miner struggling through snowdrifts to strike gold. I surprised myself at what I was prepared to go through for money.

I got to see the manager without any trouble when I mentioned Harold Elsworth's name. Whether it was the blow I'd suffered or just natural greediness I don't know, but I'd no trouble with my conscience in asking Mr Blomely for £400 expenses incurred yesterday for loss of clothing in addition to the £150 for today. Blomely raised his eyebrows ever so slightly when signing the cheque for his cashier. He said nothing: he must have been told to ask no questions. I was sorry I hadn't asked for more. For me he was the perfect bank manager: ready to hand out someone else's cash without a murmur.

I limped back to my office. For once the lift was working and I managed to get myself seated behind my battered desk. I eased my back by propping myself up with two cushions. I took the Remington portable typewriter out of the desk drawer and began typing a message to Rachel Elsworth. I kept it simple:

RACHEL
Contact David Cunane,
a friend of Andy Thwaite,
tel: 061 978 4567

I tried to get up out of the chair again but the pain across my shoulders was so sharp that I decided to stay where I was and make a few phone calls.

I phoned Charlie Sims at Happyways' Head Office in Luton. When I finally got through to him he asked if I'd made up my mind about Middlesbrough. The job he was offering was similar to Rochdale – undercover work by a one-man clean-up squad. Charlie said he believed in staying with a winner. When I hesitated again he offered me more money. Flattered, I asked him if it could wait a couple of weeks and he said he'd have to think about it and get back to me.

Then I called Janet Rushford at Abbotsford Hall and asked if she'd mind if I came in for another chat. She wasn't pleased to be interrupted at her endless labours but she'd heard about the death of Thwaite and would give me a few minutes if I came round.

Finally I gave Sylvia Mather a call at her home number. While the phone rang I glanced at my watch. It was still before noon. Sylvia picked the phone up.

'Hello, David Cunane here,' I said. 'How are you this morning? Meeting you last night really made my day worthwhile,' the words slipping from my tongue as smoothly as a politician's promises.

After a pause for breath Sylvia came on . . . 'I'm surprised to hear from you so early. I should've thought you'd have needed a long lie-in after all that wine and whisky last night,' she sniped away breezily. There was something thrilling about that rich voice of hers. I felt as if I couldn't hear enough of it.

'You're joking. Detectives all have cast-iron livers. I was up with the lark and back on the job.'

'Back on the job? Does that mean you're still looking for Rachel?' she said sweetly.

'Yes, can't let the grass grow under my feet . . . Last night you said you might have an address in Southport where Andy stored his DJ kit. I think that's where Rachel might be.' I felt I wanted to impress her.

'Oh yes, I've been thinking about that. I never actually heard there was an address in Southport. Andy was talking about picking some stuff up there and I just assumed . . .' Sylvia paused, '. . . Would you like to meet up for a drink? We could go to the Prohibition Club, Mike won't be there.' She had obviously got the message about my feelings toward her boss.

I hesitated before replying. I wasn't sure that I ought to be socialising with her until I'd found Rachel. After all, Thwaite had turned up with his throat cut, and someone was anxious to slow me down. Rachel might be next in line for the razor. Still, meeting Sylvia would be combining business with pleasure if she knew more than she'd already told me about Rachel. She was my only firm lead. As if she could read my mind she offered me the excuse I was looking for . . . 'I might have a look round in the office to see if there's any more information about Andy . . .'

'That's fine. What time would suit you?' I didn't like to sound too eager but I wasn't turning down an invitation from someone who wanted the pleasure of my company, even if I did feel as bruised as if I'd been trapped under a road roller. It could be that Sylvia's motives were as mixed as my own. We arranged to meet at 10 p.m. I would spend the time up till then tying up every loose end I could think of in tracking Rachel down.

I took a couple more paracetamol and struggled out of my chair, picked up the message to Rachel that I'd typed and headed for the basement and a loan of old Lumsden's photocopier. There was activity in the building at this time of day. One floor had been converted into a sales room for tents. They were erected with their pegs nailed into the wooden floor. There was a steady stream of the public making its way up the worn stone steps as I made my way down.

When I reached the basement Fred roused himself from his lair and came out to meet me.

'Morning Chief, seen the padlock I fixed,' he said, sneering all over his wrinkled face. Fred's grin was short of teeth; he was missing his front teeth and, although he had a set of false ones, rarely wore them. He made a bad situation worse by his habit of opening his mouth wide and showing off the remaining yellow canine fangs. The director of a cheap horror movie couldn't find a better natural than Fred. I wasn't in the mood for his humour.

'Look Lumsden, I always pay for any photocopies I take. You know I leave the money in your tin. So what's the idea of locking me out?' I said, giving him a hard stare.

' 'S not me Boss, honest. That copier belongs to 'Glo-Worm Enterprises', they said someone had been doing hundreds on it. I conned them into thinking they'd made a mistake but they still made me put a padlock on the door.'

'OK, but is there any chance of using it now?'

'You're in luck, they've all gone out to lunch and left the padlock off. Come on.' He gave me what he intended as a conspiratorial chuckle, it came out like the croak of a sick vulture.

'Hey, where's that secretary of yours? I've missed her the last couple of mornings. Always stops for a word does Delise, not like some,' he said, looking at me inquisitively.

'She had to go away for a few days, Fred. Don't look so worried, I've not done away with her. I'm in a hurry, can you get a move on?' I explained grudgingly.

Leading me to the room, he opened it with his ordinary pass key. I did two copies and then rearranged them on the copier so that the message came out three fold on each piece of paper. Then I did twenty copies of that. I gave the old scavenger £2 and went back to the office in the lift.

I cut out the messages, stuck them on postcards and put them in my pocket. It took some time. I hobbled down the stairs and across to the multi-storey, eased myself into the Bluebird and drove to Didsbury.

When I got to Abbotsford Hall I made for Rushford's office. As before, the warden was absent and Rushford was seated at her desk, beavering away. She was definitely one of the world's workers.

'Well that was a coincidence! . . . You asking about Thwaite and then him turning up dead like that,' she said, looking up from her desk at me. There was more than a question in her eyes: I detected a hint of pleasure there. Was she secretly pleased to see one of the students landing up on a mortuary slab, I wondered. Or was there something about Thwaite I ought to know about?

'If you put it like that, it was a coincidence. I'm looking for any information you can give me to help me find Rachel Elsworth. She's still missing and for all I might know there might be some connection with this lad's suicide.'

'I don't see why I should help you, there's a police force to do things like that,' Rushford replied unhelpfully. I could see I was going to have to persuade her again. Part of the secret of my success, such as it was, was my ability to get people to open up to me.

'If your warden hadn't been so quick to throw Rachel out for looking after a few plants for a friend she wouldn't be missing,' I said in the concerned, more in sorrow than in anger, tones that had got Rushford going on my last visit. 'Do you think the police are going to be worried because an eighteen-year-old hasn't phoned her parents in a few weeks? It was you who said the Metropolitan University doesn't bother telling parents when they throw students out, so why should the police be concerned?'

I was trying to box clever and get Janet Rushford angry so that she would open up. The trick might have backfired but she rose to the bait nicely.

'Just you hold on a minute!' Janet said angrily. 'That'll be quite enough of your nonsense. I'm only the warden's secretary. It's him you should be haranguing.' She paused, almost on the point of tears. 'I hate people coming in here ticking me off for his mistakes. Perhaps he was a bit hasty but he's got the rules on his side.'

'I'm sorry. I only want to ask you if there are any students here who might be able to tell me where Rachel is.' I changed my tone and spoke sympathetically. 'I can't see how that would breach anyone's rules.'

She nodded her head in agreement. She didn't want to seem hard-hearted and officious.

'I've had an enquiry from Rachel's department. She hasn't been in for lectures or tutorials for a week. They didn't know she was no longer resident here. She has a friend called Lisa

Goody who lives at the top of "B" block. We could go and see her.'

She led the way into the glass and concrete block and up the stairs to the top floor. We came to Goody's door. There was the sound of loud house music coming from the room. Rushford knocked. A rough male voice bawled 'Go away'. I could hear giggling. Rushford gave me a knowing look and knocked again much louder. 'It's Mrs Rushford here,' she said in the nicest possible way. 'I just want to ask you if you've seen anything of Rachel Elsworth.'

After a moment the door half opened and a large youth wearing Batman boxer shorts leaned round into the corridor. I got a quick peep at a naked girl pulling on a pair of black leggings before he closed the door.

'What you looking at? Got your eyeful then?' he whinged in a nasal Liverpool accent. His lank, greasy hair was parted in the middle and his full lips were also parted in an unpleasant sneer. My impulse was to give him a 'Moss Side kiss' – head-butt him – but with my sore back I decided it would be better to let Janet handle things by grovelling to the lout.

Speaking very politely, she asked him if she could have a word with Lisa about her friend Rachel.

'Just leave us alone will you? We don't know anything about that stuck-up bitch,' said the lank-haired lover from Liverpool as he slammed the door. The house music blared forth but I could hear faint sounds of an argument.

Janet shrugged her shoulders. 'You see how it is. They claim adult status yet people like you expect us to keep a track on them as if they were school children.'

I refrained from saying that if I'd had the late Lee Marvin with me we would have kicked the door in, got Lank-Hair by the ankles and hung him upside-down outside the window until he told us all he knew. Come to think of it, that still might not be a bad idea . . .

On the way out I gave Janet one of my postcards for the notice board. She told me that Lank-Hair's name was Kevin Spragg. I asked if I could come back later and catch Lisa Goody when she was on her own. Janet explained that the girl was entwined with Spragg during all her sleeping and waking hours. He was a resident as well, studying sociology in the brief intervals of separation from Lisa.

Before I left Rushford said, 'Will you be coming back?' She was smiling warmly, her eyes shining. I shook my head but it was comforting to see that the old charm was still working. 'Do pop in if you're passing. I'd love to know if you find her,' Janet persisted as I walked towards my car.

'If I can find the time, I will,' I promised her. I was really glib today, perhaps I should have gone into politics after all.

So, not having made much progress at Abbotsford apart from having brought a taste of intrigue to Janet Rushford's life, I went on a tour of the local newsagents, supermarkets and delicatessens. The shopkeepers were happy to display my notice about Rachel on their boards along with the requests to find stray cats or flatmates for non-smoking vegetarians.

The bright day had become dull. The air was warm and motionless and my throat was dry from too many explanations. I hobbled along the main street in Didsbury village for a pint at the Beeches, a pub renowned for its bitter and the ferocity of its landlord. I showed the barmaid a photo of Rachel. She didn't know Rachel but passed the photo to the staff round the bar.

One of them, a man of about fifty, recognised Rachel: 'Yes, I've seen her before. She hasn't got the sort of face you forget in a hurry, has she?' he said. 'She's not a regular here but she comes in with a crowd who drink in the Barley-Mow, he continued in a bored tone, mentioning a pub not far from Abbotsford.

I put a tenner down on the bar and he became more interested.

'Yeah, I remember her quite well, actually. She stands out in a crowd. Goes round with a bunch from the Metropolitan University.' He peered at the photo again and rapped it with his knuckles, then he leaned forward to impart his information more confidentially and incidentally put himself in a position to trouser my cash without attracting the attention of his colleagues. 'Yes, she's quite a young lady, talks proper you know. Got a bit of class – not like some of them. Always a pleasure to serve her.'

This didn't fit with what I'd heard from Rushford and Sylvia.

But then he was giving the male point of view . . . Or was he just ingratiating himself with an eye on the cash?

His next remark convinced me that he was genuine.

'What's your interest then, Chief? You're not from page three of the *Planet* are you? Because I said to Mavis,' he whispered, indicating with a nod the barmaid who'd passed him the photo, 'I wouldn't mind a closer look at that young lady's attractions myself.'

I gave him a cool look and covered up the note. With his five o'clock shadow and dirty fingernails, he looked like the type who got eye-strain peering at pictures of naked girls. It was significant in light of Mr Elsworth's fears for Rachel that the first positive identification of her should be from a self-admitted lecher.

'Sorry, no offence Chief. You're not family are you? It's just that with her being so pretty I thought . . .'

'You thought anyone else who had an interest in her must be a dirty old man like you,' I said, looking straight into his greedy, red-rimmed little eyes. He wasn't embarrassed in the least. I handed him the tenner which he deftly pocketed. 'Is there anything else you can tell me about her?' I asked.

'Well, like I said, she seemed a bit different from your usual run-of-the-mill student type – you know – dirty jeans and mucky underwear. Always well turned-out she was. I can't say that I liked the look of some of her friends, though. She seemed to get an awful lot of drinks in for them. They looked like a bunch of spongers if you ask me.'

I left him the photo and my number to ring if Rachel showed up again. He was a miserable creep but if I was to get information I couldn't afford to be too choosy. Things might be more urgent than I'd thought at first. It looked as if the idea that Rachel was a property to be exploited had occurred to more than one mind. I'd better press on.

At the Barley-Mow I had to shove in painfully to reach the bar. The staff were too busy to look at Rachel's photo even when I put a tenner next to it. The place was jammed to the doors with students, they were even drinking out in the street. For all its popularity it had a seedy air and the pint they served me was nothing to write home about. I went from group to group with the photo, getting little reaction. Some asked me if

I was a journalist. Some recognised Rachel but didn't know where she was now.

Stumbling round the pub, I was making quite a stir. I didn't care. I was determined to locate Rachel Elsworth and find out why her stepfather was willing to pay so much to have her back. I was so preoccupied that I didn't notice that Lank-Hair Spragg had come into the pub until he grabbed my left wrist.

Twice in one day was quite enough. Placing my right hand over his grip I pulled free and whipped round so that the surprised Spragg found himself standing with his right arm twisted up his back. I put my right instep against his shin-bone.

'Make a move "Whack" and I'll break your arm and your leg,' I whispered menacingly in his ear. He gasped in pain, which I took to be submission. Still holding his thumb in a hard grip, I released his arm. 'Come over here,' I said pulling him through the struggling mob into the street. Lisa was with him. She was wearing a floppy t-shirt and the black leggings I'd seen her pulling on earlier. No one noticed as I kept grinning and patting Spragg on the back. He was goggling all over the place, red-faced, trying to spot someone to help him, so I kept things brief.

'Well lover boy, what do you really know about Rachel?' I asked.

He curled his lip in a surly grin. 'Depends who wants to know, doesn't it?'

I took out a £20 note and waved it under his blackhead-pitted nose.

'Are you from the press, then?' he asked, piggy eyes shining at the sight of the note.

'Never you mind who I am. If you want the money tell me about Rachel and Thwaite.'

'Well Rachel's his girlfriend . . . was his girlfriend. She's a toffee-nosed piece, has loads of money but she'll never lend you anything. Daddy's some high mucketty-muck in a bank.' As he explained the vowel-swallowing Scouse accent he'd assumed earlier gave way to a more standard educated accent.

'What do you know about this cannabis in her room, then?'

'It was just a joke, we didn't think anything would happen.' he whined.

'You mean you're the berk who left it in her room? You

know she protected you?' I didn't hide my disgust when I spoke to him.

'Look man, how were we supposed to know that dozy cleaner would recognise a cannabis plant? Andy said it would give Rachel a laugh,' he snarled back.

'Do you know where she's gone?'

'I know,' piped Lisa, her unsupported front wobbling. 'Andy came round with his van. There was nearly a ton of DJ equipment in her room. You could hardly move in there. It was stacked up to the ceiling. They loaded the van and Andy said he'd have to take it to Southport because his flat was too easy to break into. So they put all her things in as well and set off. She must be in Southport.'

'But they didn't say that Rachel was going to stop in Southport did they?' said Spragg, nodding his head and shaking his greasy hair about.

'You're a great help,' I said, putting back the £20 note and taking out £5. 'Buy yourself some shampoo.' I tucked the note down the front of his t-shirt.

'Hold on mate, you promised £20,' he whinged.

'I promised nothing. The money I've given you is more than enough for the information you've supplied.'

Kevin paused to work this one out, then he said 'I can tell you more than that about Rachel.'

Lisa looked at him with a confused expression. 'Mind what you say Kevin,' she whispered. She looked frightened.

He grimaced at her. 'Well we don't owe her anything. She never did anything for us.' Turning to me, he said 'Rachel's a dependent personality, she's very immature, like.'

'What's this? . . . First-year psychology?' I sneered. 'You're so mature yourself, aren't you?'

'It's true! She needed Thwaite to tell her what to do. They paired up as soon as she arrived at the Metropolitan University. Thwaite's been here years. He must have been looking for fresh talent. She had a good effect on him. As soon as they started going out he began to get top-class gigs at places like the Paloma. He never amounted to much before she started with him.'

'Oh Kevin, you shouldn't speak ill of the dead,' wailed Lisa, her big bosom heaving as she pouted indignantly.

'Shut up you,' said lover boy affectionately.

This was all interesting enough so I gave Spragg another fiver.

'Use this to put down a deposit on a bra for Lisa.'

He gave me an aggressive look and I got ready with the Moss Side kiss.

'Look lover boy, if you want some more dosh ask around Rachel's friends and find out where she's gone. I'm working for her parents. You can phone me on this number. Just leave a message and I'll get back to you.' I could see that by mentioning parents I'd pressed the wrong button. Spragg, just like the dirty barman at the Beeches, would have preferred me to be working for a tabloid.

I shook him off, made my way to the car and headed for home. There was no point in going back to the office now that Delise had vacated it. The roads were jammed with mums driving their children home from school so it was some time before I arrived. To negotiate the entrance to my block of flats it's necessary to turn right across the path of the oncoming traffic, the entrance is too oblique to the road to turn into from the left with traffic behind you.

There was a gap in the traffic and I was on the point of turning when a battered old Cortina, parked half on the pavement, rocketed into my path. I got an impression of a scruffily-dressed man with long yellow hair and a moustache making a V-sign at me as he roared past.

5

When I got in I checked the answering service. There was a message from Charlie Sims: he was willing to wait two weeks for me to start in Middlesbrough if I promised to take a contract and go on his pay-roll for three months. I'd have to work under cover all over the country. I got out my diary and started working out the dates. It meant I'd be working for Happyways up to the end of September. That was great, the summer months are the quietest in the private enquiry trade. I didn't want to seem too eager so I didn't phone Sims right away, first thing in the morning would do.

Before I forgot I got out a bottle of Bell's whisky and took it down to Fiona Salway's flat as thanks for her help that morning. Fiona wasn't in but her twin was. He wanted to know what I'd been up to on the Meadows. He thought I'd been mugged. I wouldn't have been the first to be beaten up on a lonely stretch of the Meadows.

Finbar wanted to boost my confidence. He was willing to come out with me as my minder. The crazy old soldier was after a bit of excitement. Retirement was cruel for people like him. He was involved in every kind of charitable work but it wasn't enough to fill the void in his life. Like a bored teenager he wanted to be involved in something with the spice of danger to it. It was a shame they'd abolished the Home Guard. I discouraged him as gently as I could.

Back upstairs I looked round the flat. Everything was in order but I felt the place could do with a vacuuming so I went into the bedroom, hung up my business suit and put on a green Adidas track suit. Then I got the Hoover Aquamaster out and set to work. The action of moving my shoulder set the pain in my back off again but I didn't mind suffering in the interests of cleanliness. My next household chore was to put the morning's clothes wash into the dryer, then I got out the ironing board and ironed my shirts.

My mother finds it hard to believe how domesticated I've become. It's a pity I've no one to share it with now that Elenki isn't here. Delise never came near being a substitute. It wasn't that I hadn't loved Delise, just that we'd neither of us been willing to make the commitment to the other that a permanent relationship requires. My marriage to Elenki, though brief in duration, had been much more intense than my on–off relationship with Delise. To be fair there might have been fault on both sides, I'd never let Denise get really close.

To stop myself getting maudlin I went to look at what I had in the fridge. There were a few cans of Webster's Yorkshire Bitter, one of the finest things ever to come out of Yorkshire. I poured a can into a pint glass, and was rewarded with a fine foaming head on the bitter.

I took the drink into the lounge and lay on the settee. I picked up Thwaite's diary and read it through carefully. I wasn't in a panic this time.

His career as a DJ had only begun to take off in the few months before his death. He had bookings at clubs in Liverpool and Warrington as well as at Dyer's.

I studied the photograph of Rachel and Andy again. It was a seaside photo, there was a pier in the background. That tied in with the mention of Southport but there were hundreds of piers round the coast. Thwaite, a slim figure with his hair in a ponytail, had his arm round Rachel. She had raven black hair like me. Oddly she wasn't smiling in the photo, unlike Thwaite who had a pleased-looking grin all over his face. Her face was expressionless, as if she was concentrating on something in the distance. As I studied the picture closely the ache in my shoulders began to revive.

I ran a hot bath with the remaining half of the box of Radox in it. I wearily climbed in and fuddled by the beer and the running around earlier I fell asleep.

I woke with a jerk. The bath water had gone quite cold. I'd been dreaming. One of those horrible waking nightmares where the same incident seems to repeat itself endlessly . . .

I was carrying my bike through a deep sea of mud, I was flailing my way through the mud, up to the waist. I couldn't get clear of the mud, it was creeping higher and higher up my body. To escape from it I'd have to let my bike go yet I couldn't leave it. There were men pursuing me. The men were riding on hover-bikes which skimmed above the surface of the mud, they came closer to me, whirling heavy chains around their heads. I couldn't escape . . .

With a shudder I heaved myself out of the bath and quickly towelled myself down. I must have been asleep in the bath for at least an hour. My skin was all wrinkled up, but as I dried myself I realised that my back was feeling much better. I could move my shoulders freely.

I dressed in the bedroom. I chose a pair of cotton boxer shorts; a white, long sleeved, turtle-neck and a pair of light brown trousers. My favourite dark-green, bomber jacket and a pair of Dr Marten's brown derby shoes completed the outfit.

Then I phoned Ted Blake at the Alhambra newsdesk. I knew he was on split shifts and was coming up for a break. I needed to know as much as there was to know about the death in Clydesdale Road and Ted was my best contact with the press. He was likely to know something about Mike Dyer as well.

Ted was just coming to the end of his early evening session when I reached him. Like me, Ted's an enforced bachelor. But his wife didn't die, she ran off with a sports reporter. Her defection was understandable because Ted's been fighting a losing battle with the bottle for years. Although he's only thirty-four he gets taken for a much older man. He has a square-shaped face with a chin like the ski jump on the end of an aircraft carrier's runway. He's also fighting a losing battle with flab.

'Hello Ted, it's your friendly local crime-buster Dave Cunane here.'

'Uh, oh . . . It's you, you barm-pot! What are you after this time?' he scoffed.

'Now Ted, what would you say to me buying you an Italian meal? It's happy hour at Leonardos in Chorlton from six-thirty. You know Italian food is so much better for you than meat pie and chips.' Although I didn't mind a bit of banter from Ted, he owed me plenty of favours, and he knew it . . . Many's the time I'd followed up stories for him when he was in no fit state to. Yes, and typed up the copy for him as well.

'You're going to pay? Incredible . . . sounds better than the Alhambra staff canteen . . . I'll see you in fifteen minutes in the car park at the Evans' Hotel,' he said.

Leonardos is a friendly Italian restaurant. It's small and the tables are jammed together. Marco, the head waiter, met us at the door and seated us at a table for two right in the window. He ran his hand appreciatively over my bomber jacket and turning round to the restaurant announced, 'This is the best dressed man in Chorlton.'

This earned me a round of ironic applause from the patrons. Marco's always playing to the gallery, he loves making Anglo-Saxons blush with announcements of engagements, birthdays, anniversaries and pregnancies.

My stock had been high with him since the occasion I had been dining a Dutch client when there were rumours going around that Ajax were looking to buy some of United's best players. The client had been wearing a blazer with a club crest, and when he paid for the meal with an American Express gold card, nothing would convince Marco that I wasn't a high powered wheeler-dealer in the football transfer market.

Seated under a reproduction of *The Last Supper* Ted and I chose our meal. I had spaghetti bolognese with a prawn cocktail starter, Ted had lasagne verde with a melon starter. We had a carafe of the house sweet white wine. We shared common tastes.

'This is living,' said Ted as he shovelled the food away. A big man, he was as greedy with food as with drink. 'Now what was it that you wanted to find out about?' I was used to his ironic comments shouted out at megaphone volume. He'd got us both ejected from many a pub that way.

'You'd better keep your voice down,' I cautioned, 'I don't want half of Manchester to know my business.' Ted gave me a serious look.

'Like that is it? Tell me more.'

'Did you find out any more about the Thwaite case?' I queried.

'I don't know why you're so interested but I found out what I could . . . Apparently the poor kid was on speed, the police found him with a knife in one hand and a king-sized bottle of amphetamines in the other. He was trying to make the grade as a DJ and just couldn't take the strain. Of course, there'll have to be an inquest and his parents have been informed. He came from Hebden Bridge, a little town in the Pennines. There's nothing in it for the press, just a domestic tragedy.'

Ted wasn't being callous; he sees things from a reporter's point of view.

I didn't enlighten him about my part but I couldn't keep an expression of surprise from my face. There'd been neither knife nor amphetamines in that room, just eight pints of blood sloshing about on the floor. How could anyone fake a suicide well enough to satisfy the police surgeon or the investigation unit that no crime had been committed? I was so anxious to be up and going that I could hardly sit still in my chair.

I asked Ted what he knew about Dyer.

'Interesting you should ask about him, he's been in the news a lot lately. You know that he started out as a boxing promoter on the northern Working Men's Clubs circuit don't you? He arranged exhibition matches between has-been champs and never-happened local heroes. Made quite a good living at it apparently.'

He paused to fork food down his gullet.

'During the late seventies the club scene took off. All over this area they were opening night clubs like soup kitchens in a depression. They couldn't start them up fast enough, packing in the late teens and early twenties. These new customers weren't peaceable either. A lot of them thought brawling was part of the night out. Clubs were screaming for security. That's where your friend came in. He had the contacts in the gyms and the muscle clubs, he could supply all the doormen anyone needed.'

I looked at Ted impatiently as he scooped up more food. He was pacing his eating and talking well, though too slowly for my convenience.

'Later he came into money, or at least got money, and set up his own clubs. It was a case of the right man, at the right time, with the right idea. So far as I know he's never looked back. Should be at least a millionaire by now.'

'It all happened just like that did it? Nothing's ever put a spoke in his wheel?' I asked.

'You don't like him, do you David?' countered Ted. 'When he was on the club circuit he was able to build up his contacts in the pop world. So when he opened his clubs he was able to attract the best performers. That's his formula: good performers and DJs – big audiences, night after night. It's helped him that we've got some of the best pop groups right here in Alhambra-land. Look at the Bee Gees, they started out in Chorlton, one of them went to Oswald Road School just round the corner.'

'Yeah, they probably came in here for their lunch. Thanks very much Ted. You're a mine of useless information. Isn't there any threat from the police that they're going to close Dyer's clubs because kiddies keep dropping dead from drugs in the middle of his dance floors?'

'Don't exaggerate, only a couple have died from Ecstasy cocktails. The police have challenged his licences but nothing ever happens. Some say they only go through the motions for public relations purposes. You know, so they can say they're doing something when the next kiddy hits the deck. More people go to his clubs each week than go to watch United and City put together. This guy was the sensation of the eighties and it looks like he's going strong right through the nineties.' He was looking at his watch. 'I'll have to go. Can I give you a word of advice Dave? Don't tangle with Dyer, he's right out of your league. The word is that he's got some really heavy money behind him. So leave well alone. Whatever this kid was to Dyer, he's out of it now. Are you listening Dave? I know you when you get that look in your eye.'

Marco came over and I paid our bill. There had to be some link between Elsworth, Thwaite and Dyer which would explain what had happened. I walked down to the Evans' Hotel car park with Ted. Bands of elderly bowls enthusiasts were gathering for a tournament on the green attached to the hotel.

I watched Ted amble off towards his car. He hadn't got my looks, charm or intelligence yet he was a rising star in the television news world. No wonder Delise had got tired of me, I needed to smarten up my act.

I got into the Bluebird, switched off the alarm and phoned the Elsworth residence. Mrs Elsworth answered, as cool and upper-class as she'd been on our last encounter. She sounded a bit more anxious when I asked for Harold and she twigged who I was. She still said nothing about Rachel. Harold wasn't back from Brussels and there was no message . . . She'd told him my news.

She suggested I meet Elsworth at the airport. His plane was due in at lunchtime. This all seemed satisfactory, if you could accept the fact that the man running the biggest bank in the North-west spent most of his time out of the country, and that he preferred to keep his wife in ignorance while he had their daughter's disappearance investigated on the side. It must be convenient for him to be away just at present.

I started up the Bluebird and drove to the pleasant tree-lined street where my friend Jim McNeil lived. He lived in an unusually designed, detached house on the corner. The house had been built in the thirties for a *Manchester Guardian* reporter who fancied himself as a disciple of Frank Lloyd Wright. Jim was always having to have the flat section of his roof repaired.

When I rang the doorbell the door frame was nearly knocked out into the street by the impact of massive bodies. The McNeils own two huge German Shepherd dogs. Margaret claims they're still puppies. God help their visitors when the dogs are full grown. After a prolonged struggle to subdue them Margaret let me in.

'Go on through,' she said, beckoning me forward. She was as quick moving and lively as ever. 'Jim's in the front room.' Margaret's full of energy and tension which she passes on to others like an electric charge. She's a nurse and patients on her ward aren't allowed to suffer from depression.

I went in. Jim was sitting at his desk in the corner poring over a heavy tome as usual.

Jim's played a big part in my life over the last few years, he's acted like an anchor helping to keep me in harbour when storms have been blowing me astray. He looks the part of an authority figure. He's heavily built, with shoulders like a coal heaver and a penetrating way of looking at you. Not much gets past him.

His father came from Jamaica, one of those believers in the British Empire who volunteered for service in the RAF during the war. After the war he brought his family to Britain, settled in Glasgow, and against all the odds put Jim through medical school. Jim did well, he's highly qualified, a real 'doctor' with both a Ph.D. and an M.D.. This hasn't stood him in good stead in his profession. He tried working as a GP but the great British public found his Caribbean ancestry too much to cope with so he went back into the University world. Born in Kingston, Jamaica in 1941, he's lived in Britain since he was eight and has a Glaswegian accent. Having to get used to being treated as a 'foreigner' by people half his age has made him very patient.

He's now a medical scientist and university lecturer – neither of them highly regarded career choices these days. He's a warm-hearted man who will go to any lengths to help someone. As kindness and outspokenness are his main qualities he's popular with students but he's never had recognition from the academic establishment, who have him typecast as the token black.

'Well, come in man,' he said in his Glaswegian-Caribbean accent. 'Would you like a drink?' The question was rhetorical because he was already pouring me a stiff slug of Famous Grouse whisky. 'Sit yourself down.'

As I took the glass and sat, I favoured my left side. My right was still very painful. Jim immediately noticed. 'What's up with you man?' he demanded and in a few minutes he was examining my back. 'You were lucky there,' he said.

'Lucky? What d'you mean?' I replied, as I buttoned up my shirt. 'I've been in agony all day.'

'If he'd caught you a few inches lower the chain could have crushed your vertebrae, you might have been paralysed for life, lad. As it is, those big muscles in your shoulders have absorbed the blow. You'll feel like hell for two or three days but then you'll be fine.'

'That's your considered opinion is it?' I said.

I told him everything that had happened in the last two days. I'd promised Elsworth confidentiality but that was before I knew there was bloodshed involved.

'Look Dave, how much blood would you say there was? If the corpse was almost totally exsanguinated, rigor might not have set in for some considerable time. It was a cool day, wasn't it?'

'What do you mean by exsanguinated?' I queried.

'Massive blood loss, more than fifty per cent loss of body fluids.'

'Yes, there was blood everywhere. It had soaked right through the bed into the carpet. I could actually see my own footprints in the blood.' I said.

'In that case death could have taken place any time up to

twelve hours before you found the body. What was the hypostatic lividity like?'

'Pass that by me again Jim?'

'Oh come on Dave! What did the cadaver's complexion look like?'

'Well it was very pale, dead white.'

'Yes, but was there a bluish or greenish tinge?'

I thought for a moment, I hadn't spent too much time staring at Thwaite. Just enough of a glance to identify that it was him and what had happened. 'The lips were still pale red, but the complexion wasn't, it was a flat white colour,' I replied.

'All right, that suggests that not all the blood had completely drained from the deceased when you found him. The face of a bloodless corpse changes to an alabaster shade depending on the arrangement of adipose tissues. That's why embalmers inject straw coloured liquid to restore life-like pallor. If there was still some colour in the lips then death might not have been more than three or four hours before your visit. On the other hand if the corpse had been turned onto its face for a time you'd expect blood to pool in the face giving a bluish, bruised look.

'Well man, he must have been dead for a minimum of four hours and a maximum of twelve from the time you found him. That's the best I can do for you without rectal temperatures and a precise chart of the ambient temperatures for the previous day. So when you found him he might not have been dead all that long. What was the wound like? Was it a big incision?'

'Jim, I haven't studied anatomy. For God's sake, I'm a private investigator not a medical student.'

'Yeah, I know you are. That means you're supposed to be a trained observer – I hope you can do a better job than some of my students manage,' Jim replied with some sharpness.

He fixed me with that piercing gaze of his. 'Just imagine yourself back in that room; look down at the corpse on the bed and tell me what you see.'

'I'm sorry.'

'Look man, you don't need to apologise to me. I can see this thing has really shaken you up. Just relax and try to remember what you saw. Concentrate on the throat lesion.'

'When I opened the door I was standing at the foot of the bed, it was in front of me and his face was turned towards me. His right hand side was towards the window and the cut was on the right side of his throat; it went about halfway round but the left side definitely wasn't cut. The wound was gaping open – full of blood. God, I can't remember when I've had as big a shock.'

Jim refilled my glass. 'It must have been a rough experience for you. What about the blood, where was it?'

'It had sprayed up on to the wall behind the bed and on to the curtain.' I said.

'That would be the arterial pressure. You're sure the cut started on the right ventral aspect of the throat?' he asked.

I nodded.

'Good, from what I can remember from my forensic medicine days that means Thwaite must have been a left-hander if he cut his own throat from right to left, and the knife should also have been in his left hand.'

'I've told you, there was no knife, there was nothing in either of his hands or near them or dropped on the floor. That's why it's so weird. The police say it's an open and shut case of suicide. They're not treating it as a suspicious death.'

Jim gave me a very studious and thoughtful look. 'Can you think back to what the neck looked like? Were there any other cuts besides the fatal one?'

'No, I've told you. Nothing but a great big gash on the right side of his throat.'

'. . . and there was a spray of blood above the right side of the body. You can get it all over the ceiling when an artery is cut, especially with a younger person.'

I nodded in confirmation.

'So we can deduce several things: the arterial blood stains couldn't be easily faked, so death took place in situ . . . Absence of trial slashes indicates, but by no means confirms, that the subject didn't slash his own throat because throat slashers nearly always give themselves a few trial nicks to make sure they've got the blade in the right place.

'If your recollection is correct, and I'm assuming it is, then one of two things is possible. Either the police are deliberately claiming this is a suicide when they know it isn't, or someone came in after you and put the knife and bottle in the dead man's hands. In either case you could be in big trouble.'

'Is that possible?' I asked. 'Would the corpse's hands hold onto things so long after death?'

'They might, if the objects were put in the hands just as rigor was setting in. Then the fingers would set solid and the next person to see the corpse would have to prise them loose. But you shouldn't be worrying about playing detective. Somebody thinks you know more about this killing than is healthy for them. That must be why they're trying to knock lumps out of you. You'd better drop out of sight for a while, take yourself off on holiday with that little girl of yours.'

'You must be joking, Jim. I've split up with Delise and I'm well rid of her,' I said harshly. I had come for medical information, not for a lonely hearts conference. 'She was starting to get very serious. She thought she was going to run my life for me. As for lying low, if I don't find out who really did this I might find the police looking for me. Don't forget my banker client might be trying to set me up to take the rap for him. No, I've got to stick with it.'

Elsworth seemed to be in the clear if he'd really been on a flight at 10.15 p.m. but I'd only his wife's word that he had been.

I could see Jim was annoyed at my stupidity, but before he could start hassling me Margaret swept into the room like a chirpy little sparrow, bright and eager to find out all my news as always.

Margaret's a white girl, the same age as Jim. She married Jim in the days before mixed race marriages were as acceptable as they are now. She's a ward sister in Wythenshawe Hospital and hails from Manchester. Margaret sees her mission in life as being to arrange unions for all her unmarried friends. Like many happily married people she wants everybody to have their share of nuptual bliss.

'How's Delise then? It's quite a while since we had you two round for a meal,' she said. As usual Margaret had immediately homed in on the one topic I didn't want to talk about. Her years in nursing have given her a kind of mental radar for detecting whatever it is people want to talk about least. The only way of dealing with her when she gets the bit between her teeth is by direct frontal counter-attack.

Jim started grinning and held his hands up to signal to her to change tack but I wasn't at all embarrassed.

'Delise has slung her hook, Margaret. She's flown the coop, skipped town, abandoned me, gone off to London with someone else. However you want to put it, she's blown, vamoosed; she doesn't want to see me ever again. It's all over and it has been for a while.'

'All right, all right! You don't need to go on. I never really thought you were suited. Delise Delaney's a very ambitious woman you know. I could see that straight away,' Margaret replied.

'Thanks a bunch! So that means you think I'm a total failure and no-hoper then?'

'No I didn't mean it that way! She wants a man she can manipulate while she's on the way up and you'll never be like that Dave. You know your friends want what's best for you. There's a very attractive staff nurse on my ward. She never seems to have much to do in her spare time. I could invite you both round for a meal if you'd like.'

'Margaret do leave off, will you!' bellowed Jim. 'I'll swear Dave is blushing. Give the chap a chance to get over his last love affair before you fix him up again.'

Turning to me he said, 'I'm sorry Dave, Margaret's turning into a one-woman dating agency. I think she expects commission on every marriage she arranges. Come on, have another drink.'

'No, I really must be going. I've got somebody to see in town,' I replied.

'You're going to have another drink and tell us why you've split up with Delise Delaney, so just sit down there and don't give me that look David Cunane,' Margaret commanded.

Margaret's a small and very contained lady. Determination's her middle name. Her eyes are always very bright and clear. When she starts ordering people about for their own good she's used to being obeyed. She takes no nonsense from anyone, either on her hospital ward or in her home. Against my better judgement I found myself sinking back into the settee and accepting another glass from Jim. She fixed me with her deep blue eyes while Jim also gazed soulfully at me. I squirmed in my seat.

'Look folks, I know you mean well but there's nothing you or I can do about Delise. She's just decided to take off. We haven't had a row or anything. Even if I wanted to get back with her she hasn't left me any way to contact her,' I explained.

'You've been neglecting her, haven't you?' Margaret accused.

'I suppose that could be one way of looking at it, but I've got to make a living,' I said.

'Of course he has. Look Margaret, you're not being very consistent, one minute you're telling Dave he isn't suited to Delise and you can fix him up with a staff nurse. Then the next you're giving him the third degree and accusing him of neglecting Delise,' said Jim, assuming the role of prisoner's friend.

'I know, love. It's just that I remember how many people took me on one side and advised me against marrying you but we went ahead and have been happy. Maybe there are people telling Delise that she should marry "one of her own kind" too,' Margaret countered.

'I can't follow your logic there Margaret. Delise is a coloured girl, her mother's Irish!' said Jim.

Margaret gave me a startled glance. Her husband was no racist but he used the word 'coloured' in the Caribbean sense to describe those like Delise, who were of mixed race. It was a distinction that was important to him.

'Neither of us has ever talked about marriage,' I butted in to what was becoming a purely matrimonial wrangle, 'anyway I really do have to go.'

'There you go Jim! That's just what I mean,' Margaret carried on ignoring my contribution, 'to a black man she's just a coloured girl, and the white man she's been practically living with won't raise a little finger to find her when she drops out of his life. The poor girl, she must feel nobody wants her. Jim, you know Molly Delaney well enough to get on the phone and find out where Delise is . . . Do it now!'

During the period when he'd been a GP Jim had got to know Delise's Irish mother, Molly Delaney. Molly had been abandoned by Delise's father, Zuse McKitty, when Delise was three. Molly had got herself qualified as a teacher and had supported her child on her own. During the difficult period when she was struggling to pass exams Jim and Margaret had often looked after Delise.

Jim gave me an embarrassed look but he made no sign that he was going to disobey his wife's orders. I had a sinking feeling in the pit of my stomach.

'You come into the kitchen while he phones. I've one or two things to tell you in private,' she said turning to me.

I got up and Jim picked up the phone, giving me a wistful look as I followed Margaret into the kitchen. Fortunately the dogs were in the back garden so I was in no danger of having my throat ripped out.

To my surprise, instead of tearing a strip off me Margaret gave me a peck on the cheek and said 'I'm sorry, Dave. I'm an interfering old besom, but I think you should at least speak to her again.'

'I was waiting for her to get in touch, but she said she'd found someone else so . . .'

'She would, wouldn't she? Let the girl have a bit of pride. Can't make any concessions to the male ego, can she? I'm sorry, I get too involved, but one of the things all those wise people told me when I married Jim was that our children would never be happy because they'd never know quite who they were. Well, we never had any children,' she said with a sigh, 'but I still have strong feelings. Delise could be the daughter I never had.'

'That's all right, Margaret, I understand. Don't forget I was married to an African girl for three years. Let's go and see if Jim's had any success.'

'Dave, you're a great bloke and Jim and I will never forget how you nursed Elenki through her last illness, but you only see things from the male point of view. You just shrug off the hostile looks a mixed couple attract in some quarters but it's harder on the woman. There are a lot of people who think a woman must be immoral if she's with a man who's a different colour.'

Margaret spoke with great feeling but I hadn't come round here for a session with an agony aunt. I wasn't convinced that it was outside pressure which had upset Delise, she could be moody and difficult enough when we were on our own. If she wanted us to get back together, she had my phone number. Until she did I was my own man.

When we went back into the lounge Jim was just putting the phone down.

'I got through to Molly. She wouldn't tell me where Delise is but she'll get her to phone you,' he said.

'Great, well if she does phone maybe things will happen. Anyway, thanks both of you for the medical and personal advice but I must dash now, I'm meeting someone and she'll think I've stood her up.

'Aha, fixed yourself up already, haven't you? What's her name?' asked Margaret with a grin on her face.

'No it's not like that. I'm seeing her about a job I'm on,' I replied.

'So it is a female then? You're a fast worker Dave!' Margaret exchanged a meaningful look with Jim. 'Bring her out to see us if things get serious.'

'Look Margaret, it really is in connection with work so don't let your romantic imagination go into overdrive.'

Jim got up to show me to the door and also to keep his monster hounds from chewing me up on the way out. 'Seriously, David, I think you could be in considerable danger,' he said as soon as we were out of Margaret's hearing. 'If you won't get out of town why don't you let me lend you one of the dogs for a while? It'll at least stop someone having a clear run at hitting you over the back of the skull again.'

I shook my head.

'Well take care someone doesn't hand you your arse in a sling, man,' he said, squeezing my shoulder until I winced.

As I thanked him for his offer and got in the car I couldn't help feeling nervous. Jim was probably right, there might well be a connection between the mugging this morning and my discovery of yesterday. On the other hand there was plenty of motiveless violence going on all the time and I might just be jumping to conclusions.

Margaret meant well but she was wrong about Delise. We'd never signed on for a permanent relationship and as for 'practically living' with Delise she couldn't be more wrong. Her comment about Delise being too ambitious had stung a little. Delise had worked hard at Pimpernel Investigations, she'd brought in a lot of business by going round to firms that were having crime problems and offering my services. There was no doubt that she was a go-getter, but it had been a fifty/fifty partnership.

I drove towards town.

6

Princess Parkway, the main road into town from the south, was crammed with in-bound vehicles. Some of the driving was wild: great surges of acceleration from traffic lights followed by equally fierce braking as the next set of lights came up.

Although it was a Friday night I didn't have any trouble parking quite close to the Prohibition Club. It was situated in a small street off Stevenson Square in what had once been a large electrical goods shop. I had never been in the club before and I was wondering how I was going to get in when Sylvia shouted to me from across the road. She was standing in the doorway of the club talking to a large black dude with dreadlocks and a snazzy Italian suit.

On seeing Sylvia I felt another twinge of the unease I'd had when Jim McNeil warned me against coming into town. If this morning's mugging wasn't a purely random event then Sylvia Mather might be involved right up to her pretty neck.

When I got across the street I asked her who the dude was.

'Oh, it's only Leon, he's just a business acquaintance of Mike's,' she said.

We went in to the club. Above the entrance there was a picture of a chubby-featured Mediterranean type wearing a fedora hat and smoking a big cigar. 'Who's he, one of Mike's relatives?' I joked.

'You know very well who he is,' replied Sylvia as we went into the club. The whole place was covered in pictures of other 'Roaring Twenties' gangsters and front pages from the *Chicago Tribune* and other papers with banner headlines shrieking about the St Valentine's Day massacre. The bar staff were kitted out in gangster suits.

Dyer's choice of theme for his club was significant. Was it intended as a sly dig at the Establishment? In the days of Prohibition Capone had shared control of the 'Windy City' with the corrupt politicians and police. It could be that the decor was just some smart designer's whimsy, but knowing Dyer's

Mephistophelian pretensions he could be sending an unsubtle message to someone.

'I don't see any pictures of Elliot Ness though, doesn't Mike like him?' I asked innocently.

'Oh you're incorrigible,' she laughed, picking up my reference to the agent who boasted that he sent Capone to Alcatraz. 'Let me get you a drink?'

I pushed her money back in her bag and made my way to the bar. The place wasn't exactly packed. The same dreary house music that deafened the customers at the Paloma droned away here as well, though not so loudly.

We took our drinks to the back of the room, and sat against the wall like a pair of Wild West gunfighters waiting for the opposition to show up. I sunk three large whiskies before I brought the subject of Thwaite up. Sylvia hadn't managed to find anything about the Southport address but she said Mike Dyer had seemed upset about the death, Andy would have had a great future in the business, Andy reminded Dyer of himself at the same age, etc, etc. Sylvia's report of Dyer's reaction didn't fit with what I'd seen at the Paloma.

'Sylvia, did Mike have a girl with him when he went home last night?' I asked.

'What do you mean? Mike's a happily married man. He's got two children.' She paused for a moment, 'I see, you think he might have had Rachel with him . . . No, no way!. . . How do you know who he went home with?'

'Would you know if he had Rachel with him, perhaps staying with him while she gets over the bad news about Andy?' I persisted.

'He would have told me if he had,' she said indignantly.

'Suppose Rachel was in some sort of danger, he might want to keep quiet about it.'

'You couldn't be more wrong! Mike has no secrets from me,' Sylvia said, her eyes flashing. 'I'm the one who really runs that club you know.'

'I'm sure you are, but if there was something going on Mike might not want to get you involved. After all, you told me how desperate he is to shake off these drug pushers who keep trying to muscle in on him. Maybe Thwaite and Rachel got involved with them in some way and Mike's trying to sort it out quietly.'

Sylvia nodded her head while I said this, she was considering it. The expression on her face was unreadable, it might have been 'That shows how much *you* know mate!' or it might have been genuine puzzlement.

'Let's lighten up a bit,' she said. 'Why don't we go on somewhere and have a bop?'

I was surprised at the invitation, but if Sylvia wanted to mix business with pleasure why should I complain? It was obvious that I wasn't going to get any more information out of her in these surroundings.

'OK let's go on somewhere . . . as long as it's not one of Mike Dyer's clubs,' I agreed.

'We could go to the Casino at the Midland, I'm a member,' she offered.

Although Elsworth was paying me well, he wasn't paying me so well that I could happily go and throw away money at a casino. 'I'd like to but I can't afford to risk losing my shirt on the random turn of a card,' I said.

'That's heresy Dave! No true card player believes that the cards are ever entirely random. When you're lucky they run for you. There's nothing to match it when the right card turns up time after time. Only free-fall parachuting comes close to it,' she enthused. 'Look, I've got an account there if you want to try your luck. Come on let's try it.'

'No, I don't think so. I've never had any luck with cards. I only learned the difference between clubs and spades a few years ago,' I said.

'Ooh Dave Cunane! I think I'm going to like you. You're so direct. You suggest somewhere then.'

Sylvia had never been to Silversmiths, a little jazz club in a side street near Chorlton Street Bus Station. She raised her eyes at the mention of Chorlton Street, the red light district of Central Manchester.

'Do you go down there often?' she said cheekily.

'Of course I don't. Silversmiths is a respectable club. Jerry Silversmith and his wife used to have their own band, now they sing in their own club. They don't need to employ squads of goons there either. Their clientele know how to behave themselves.'

We were moving towards the door while this little exchange

was going on. I sensed that Sylvia had recovered her friendly feelings for me. We drove the short distance from Stevenson Square down to Chorlton Street, passing through busy Piccadilly on the way. Turning into Chorlton Street I took a left up Thatcher Street, and then a right and another left past the entrance to the club. I found a vacant space to park. There were a few saplings growing in a small garden laid out on the end of the block and through the trees I could see the Atwood building in the distance. There were no lights on near my office.

Lots of the ladies of the town who gave Chorlton Street its notorious reputation were hanging about in the lighted area near the club. There were quite a few GMP constables standing around too. Neither police nor prostitutes bothered us.

The club was in the cellar of an office block. I paid for two tickets at the cloakroom-reception area and we pushed our way in.

It was packed with male and female swingers of every age, from twenty-five up to seventy, all out to enjoy themselves. There was a friendly boozy atmosphere about the place which made it a hundred times more welcoming than the Paloma. Although we had to push our way in, the crowd let us through without any unpleasantness. This may have been because my partner was so attractive.

She was wearing a dusky blue culotte suit which set off her golden hair well. From the way some of the men were staring at her it wouldn't have mattered if she had been dressed in sackcloth. We barged our way right through the crowd round the bar and out on to the dance floor.

The DJ was playing sixties and seventies rock music, a bit before my time but easier on the ear than the pounding of the house music on offer in Dyer's clubs. We started dancing separately, but later as the floor became more crowded we clinched. Jerry and his group came on for a couple of jazz riffs, then his wife did her singing.

Sylvia and I were getting quite passionate by this time. I asked her if she wanted a drink and we both had a cooling beer, then back to the dancing. The music was slow-paced and smoochy. Sylvia held me close. 'Your place or mine,' she whispered – a cliché, and I thought she was sending me up. She wasn't.

I didn't have too much time to speculate about Sylvia's motives in propositioning me as we bustled out of the club. I have a high enough opinion of my own attractiveness to the opposite sex but it was still flattering to find that a lady like Sylvia was anxious to share my couch, especially after being dumped by Delise.

Still, I felt it would be a wise move to head for my place rather than hers. If she was trying to set me up for something I'd rather she tried it on my turf than on hers, besides which there was the germ of a naughty idea at the back of my mind.

I drove the car down Portland Street and round the back of the G-Mex Centre towards Deansgate, Chester Road and my home in South Manchester. Sylvia was leaning on my arm. I parked the car some distance from the flat and scanned the street to see if the coast was clear. There didn't seem to be any surveillance so I drove in and garaged the car. Leaving the car on the street would tell any snooper too much about my movements, so I prefer to garage it when I can.

I opened the door of the flat and showed Sylvia into the living room. I didn't say anything as we went in and when she turned to speak to me I put my finger to my lips. She looked mystified as I turned the CD player on and put in a disc.

I left her for a minute and went to rummage among the shoes in the bottom of my wardrobe for what I needed. Sylvia looked even more puzzled when I returned and began to sweep the room with an anti-bugging monitor. I swept the living room, kitchen, hall and bedroom. She followed me with a fascinated expression on her face. There were no indications of electronic bugging, no heterodyne howl from a hidden mike.

'Is this a little eccentricity put on for my benefit or do you check your flat out every time you come in?' she asked, a sceptical but tolerant expression on her face. She offered me her handbag but I'd already surreptitiously checked it. She wasn't carrying any bugs. I put the monitor down.

'Come on Sylvia, anyone who works for Mike Dyer must be used to eccentricity,' I said.

'Yes, that's true but I thought you were normal,' she responded. I had no answer for that. I couldn't tell her that I was suspicious because I thought her boss might have tried to kill me.

If she had come to spy on me her methods made a refreshing change from the usual knuckle-sandwich and kick up the testicles approach practised by seekers after enlightenment in Manchester.

'What's the idea, David?' she said as I gave her a whisky.

'Someone seems to know every move I make. I sometimes do electronic surveillance work for other people. So I thought I'd better check that no one's bugging me. No one is.'

Sylvia laughed heartily, so heartily that she nearly fell out of her chair. She spilled whisky on her culottes. I got up to get a cloth from the kitchen so she wouldn't see how silly I felt. When I came back Sylvia was in the bedroom wearing nothing in particular.

'Now it's my turn to do something silly,' she murmured. 'I wasn't laughing at you. It's just that the thought of bugs is so funny. I thought I might as well change into something more comfortable,' she said as she put her arms round my neck. 'I hope you don't think we're rushing things, but I fancied you as soon as I saw you, you big hunk.'

I wouldn't have been human if I hadn't wanted Sylvia at that moment, bugger my conscience, Delise and Margaret McNeil. If Sylvia really had hooked onto me just to find out what I was up to, her *modus operandi* was a superb example of double bluff. She'd upped the ante after my implied challenge about her motives by cutting out the kiss-and-cuddle introductory stage and going straight to the main course. As I looked into her smiling and eager face, I thought, 'You're a clever lady, and I'm your man if this is the game you want to play.'

While I undressed Sylvia lay on the bed. When I took off my white crew neck sweater she gave a shriek. 'My God! What have you been doing to your back?' She jumped up and came over to me. She ran her fingertips over the livid blue and green bruises on my shoulders. 'Come to momma,' she said as she hugged me.

Afterwards we lay quietly on the bed, Sylvia with her arms round me. I told her about the attack by the chain-swinging maniacs.

'You take all this private eye stuff too seriously, David. You could get hurt even more than you have been already. Promise you'll drop this silly investigation or at least leave it to the police?'

'I've done nothing dangerous, I haven't said a cross word to anyone. All I've done is to ask a few questions about a missing girl. This thing with the chain might just have been a coincidence. If I'd been a doctor or a school teacher I wouldn't have connected it to my job.'

I started to disengage. I wanted to make a cup of coffee.

'Don't get up darling, stay here with me.' Sylvia stroked me with her long fingers. 'It's been so long since I acted on impulse and did just what I want. Do you think I'm a loose woman?'

''Course you are. I spotted it as soon as we met.'

She giggled. 'You're right about Mike in one way you know. He got a lot of the money he needed to start up from some very dubious people. People who'd never get a licence to operate a club in a million years but needed someone well known and respectable like Mike to front for them.'

'Well known and respectable! I bet he's kind to animals and helps old ladies across the road as well,' I mocked.

'He's been kind to me, that I can say. I don't know about the old ladies, and as for animals I'm sure he likes them, but he's allergic to cats and dogs: can't stand them near him,' she murmured defensively.

The flow of information from Sylvia was punctuated by little groans of pleasure as I caressed her. We made love again.

Pillow talk resumed after a while. I renewed my offer of a cup of coffee. This time she wanted one. I nipped into the kitchen and made us both a cup of instant. I put three sugars in mine and two ground-up Mogadon pills in hers. I felt she needed her rest. When I returned she drained her cup without comment.

'I know everything about Mike, he's straight really. I even know the code for the security system at his house. It's the reverse of the year he was born,' Sylvia murmured drowsily.

Before I could ask her how old Mike was she fell asleep . . .

This was working out better than I'd hoped. I had intended to borrow her keys and check out her office for those clues about Thwaite's address in Southport which had so suddenly vanished. Now I might be able to confirm once and for all if Dyer had Rachel at his home.

Mike's fat face wasn't very lined. He could be a raddled thirty-five or a youthful fifty for all I knew.

There would be no better time than now to go and give the Dyer household the once-over. Surprise is the most powerful weapon an understaffed little private enquiry agency like mine has. If there was somebody keeping an eye on me they'd be expecting me to remain tucked up with the lovely lady and I'd never have a better alibi as far as Sylvia was concerned, that is if she was closer to her boss than she'd pretended so far. I looked at her again, she was sleeping soundly, her breathing deep and regular.

I gave her a shake but she remained deeply asleep.

I slipped out of bed, being careful to pull the duvet over Sylvia, and went to the wardrobe, then quickly dressed in black jeans, black polo neck sweater and dark trainers. Casting a regretful eye over the clothes so carelessly strewn on my bedroom floor I blew the sleeping Sylvia a kiss and left.

I drove away as quietly as I could, accelerating gently. After a few minutes I stopped the car on the main road through Chorlton, picked up the phone and dialled Ted Blake's home number. The phone rang twelve times before Ted answered.

'How old is Mike Dyer?' I asked him.

I cut through his cursing and spluttering to remind him not to use bad language on a car phone. You never know who's listening. He gagged with rage again, then groaned 'He's forty one! Do you know what time it is?'

Younger than I'd guessed. For once the journalistic custom of listing celebrities' ages after their names had served a purpose. Ted knew most prominent people's ages as well as he knew the alcoholic strength of his favourite lager.

I drove to the leafy street that ran by the park at the end of the Esplanade and checked the street for signs of movement. Nothing was stirring and there was still half an hour of darkness before first light. I swung over the railings into the park and trotted along until I came to the tennis courts. I could see the lights as I came up to the boundary of the park. Sheltering in the bushes I surveyed the Esplanade, a wide enclosed avenue.

Counting carefully, I worked out that Dyer's house was the

sixth one on my right, and sure enough there was the white Mercedes in the drive. I remained motionless for several minutes. Nothing was stirring so in for a penny, in for a pound. I clambered over the fence and dropped lightly into the Esplanade. I felt very exposed as I ran. I was gambling on two counts: first, that the last thing Dyer and his buddies would be expecting was someone breaking into his house. Second, that his birth year was exactly forty one years ago.

I hesitated for a moment, thinking I must be crazy to act on impulse like this – but then nothing ventured, nothing gained. I blacked up my face with camouflage cream and put on rubber gloves and a black woolly hat.

Dyer had had a girl with him last night. If he had Rachel stashed away I'd be able to bring Mummy and Daddy here in the morning, accompanied by the law, and my part in the case would be over.

When I padded up the drive to his front door no security lights came on. I crossed my fingers and walked straight up to the entrance.

There were two locks; one a rimlock type that would give me no trouble, the other a six lever mortise. I gave the door a gentle shake. It didn't have that firmly shut feeling that you get when the deadlock is on. Yes, I was in luck. The deadbolt wasn't fastened. There was a slight give at the place where the deadlock should have secured the door.

Ten to one the same careless person who had neglected to turn the key in the mortise lock had just left the other lock on the latch without clicking the retainer shut. It soon yielded to my plastic. I was in. Amazing how people neglect their locks when they have an electronic alarm.

I now had a few seconds to find the electronic security console and punch the numbers in. It wasn't beside the door, but by the light switch there was a small painting in a heavy frame, flush against the wall. I strode up to it and ran my hands round the frame and was rewarded with a click. It swung open revealing a small electronic console. A red light was pulsing. Hardly daring to breathe I touched the reversed numbers of Dyer's birth year and stood poised to run.

The red light went out. I left the door of the console slightly open and took stock of my surroundings.

There was no sound. Praying that switching the console off had immobilised all the electronic alarms in the house I opened the first door on my right. Nothing of interest, just a reception room. I swiftly checked all the doors. There was nobody in any of the ground floor rooms, including the kitchen. The last door I tried was locked. I took my picklocks out of the pouch at my waist. It was just a simple double lever lock, easy to spring. It was Dyer's study. Leaving the study door open, I crept upstairs.

This wasn't as risky as it seemed. At 4 a.m. most people really are dead to the world. I already knew that Dyer wasn't likely to have a savage Rottweiler on the premises. He relied on passive security, just like everyone else. The tricky thing about burglary is getting in and out without rousing anyone. That's my theory. Why else would so many dead-beats, who hardly know which end of a crowbar is which, take it up for a living if it wasn't easy?

Eight rooms opened onto a wide landing and listening intently I could make out Dyer's voice behind one of the doors, talking to someone. It sounded as if they were playing cards. There was an occasional chink of glasses but no female voice, so unless they had Rachel trussed up and gagged under the card table she wasn't here. I'd better move before one of them decided to step out for a leak.

I slunk downstairs. There had to be some pay-off for the risk I'd taken. I went back into the study; maybe there would be some scrap of information about Rachel in there. He might have an address book or diary with Andy Thwaite's Southport phone number in it. He had to have some way of contacting Thwaite when he was out of Manchester. I'd already checked all listed Thwaites in Southport. Dyer had to have Thwaite's unlisted number.

A massive steel safe occupied one corner of the room. It was locked. Absolutely no chance of getting in there without a thermic lance.

Cheek and good luck had got me so far. I'd better make the most of my chance. I decided to allow myself two or three minutes. I looked round the room.

Apart from the safe, there was a big desk piled high with papers, a glass fronted display cupboard full of boxing trophies, and one wall entirely covered in framed vanity photos showing a smiling Mike posing with various celebrities, including I noted in surprise, our own Chief Constable 'Wild' Bill Benson. Wild Bill was draining a glass in salute to Mike.

I looked through the photographs carefully: Dyer with the Happy Mondays, Dyer with Madonna, Dyer with Inspiral Carpets, Dyer with Popeye, Jock, other hard cases and respectable types. The thugs seemed out of place somehow like the players in a 1930s 'Gentlemen and Players' cricket photo. I took it off the wall, along with the shot of Benson's ugly mug. I slipped the frames down the back of the safe and the photos into my pockets.

I rearranged the remaining photos. There were so many on the wall that the ones I'd taken might not be missed. They might come in handy. I went over to the desk – there must be something which would link Dyer to Rachel.

The desk wasn't locked; it contained two ledgers in the top drawer and a pile of bank statements in the lower. I looked through one of the ledgers. Each double page contained expenditures and returns from the club business. What caught my eye were the payments to individual DJs, each named separately with VAT number listed. A cash balance for each day was carried over to the next day. The second ledger was the same except that it had the letters NMP written on it.

Could NMP be the initials of Dyer's silent partner of dubious reputation whom Sylvia had hinted about . . . the person who'd supplied Dyer with his start-up cash? If Dyer wasn't hiding or harbouring Rachel himself maybe NMP was. Presumably the second ledger was a duplicate of the first but I would need hours to study them both.

Luckily I'd come fully equipped. I switched the desk lamp on and arranged it to shine on the double pages and then whipped out the trusty Minox miniature 'spy' camera which has earned me many a fee by providing visual evidence of documents crooks would rather keep secret. With practised ease I photographed a considerable number of pages in each ledger.

Why did I bother? Well I'd failed to find Rachel but there might be something in those pages which might tell me something about Dyer and NMP's business in the days before Rachel disappeared and Thwaite got his throat cut. I'd nothing to lose and it only took me a moment. I photographed the bank statements for good measure.

Then I picked up a black leather Filofax from the desk. Flicking through it I saw to my surprise that Harold Elsworth's name and home phone number were listed. A chill ran down my spine but I hadn't time to consider the implications.

I was desperate to get on and get out. A few pages further on in the Filofax there was a phone number for NMP. Thwaite featured at the Clydesdale address but there was nothing to do with Southport or Rachel. I looked at the appointments for the last week. Dyer had had a meeting at the Northern Pioneers' Bank last Monday – two days before Thwaite was killed!

I looked at my watch, my felonious visit had only lasted eleven minutes so far. There must be some connection here between Dyer and Rachel Elsworth! I scrabbled desperately through the papers on the desk. Bills galore, contracts between Dyer and various well-known Manchester groups, a profusion of fliers for different groups. A few papers slipped on the floor.

There was nothing about Rachel.

I hurriedly tried to replace everything I'd touched and as I did so I heard a noise outside. Someone was coming towards the door. I switched the light off and flattened myself along the wall.

Popeye cautiously poked his head round the study door, his hand snaking towards the light switch as he pushed his head into the room. He saw the papers on the floor, gasped and took a step forward. The back of his head was fully exposed to me, so trusting that a bruiser like him would have a thick skull I gave him a gentle rap with the torch. He groaned, sank to his knees and then stretched out in front of the safe.

I kept my wits about me. I dragged him in and checked he was breathing, put him in the recovery position, then left the room. He was only mildly concussed and in that position he couldn't choke. I had a few seconds to get clear. Popeye may even have caught a glimpse of me. I closed up the electronic security console, hoping that Dyer would think it had never been turned on in the first place rather than that his code had been betrayed by Sylvia, and made a swift exit.

I flew down the street and over the fence into the park, looking back down the street as I went. No sign of pursuit,

Popeye must still be unconscious. I could get five years for assault committed during the course of a burglary and a lot worse than that if Dyer caught me. Jim McNeil was right, this morning's blow from the chain-swinging loony must have scrambled my wits. As I was thinking this a patrol car turned into the Esplanade and slowly cruised down the street to the turning place at the end. I slowed down and flattened myself against a tree.

I was close enough to see the men inside. Then it turned round and drove out. I crossed the park, got into my car and allowed myself to breathe for a moment. Then I rubbed cold cream on my face, carefully wiped it off with a wad of kitchen roll, started up and sped back to the flat.

Driving along the deserted streets gave me time to get my thoughts in order. 'Wild Bill' had got his nickname during his service with the East Anglia police, before his surprise promotion as Chief Constable of the Manchester Police force. 'Spiteful Bill' or 'Mean Bill' would have been a more appropriate name by all accounts but they didn't have the same ring to them. Benson was noted and widely feared for his skilful practice of administrative revenge. He had a detailed knowledge of the minutiae of police procedure which gave him a tremendous advantage over ninety-nine per cent of other coppers. He used this lore to make life miserable for anyone who crossed him.

My father and his cronies, some of them still in the job, spent hours dissecting Benson's character. Of course they were bound to take a jaundiced view of any outsider arriving in Manchester, especially with two such popular men preceding him in the Chief Constable's chair; what they deduced was that at the heart and core of Bill Benson, where there should be feelings and emotions, there was just fierce ambition: a never-ending quest for personal advantage.

To be fair, Benson had been put in the job by the Home Office precisely so that he would rein in those individualistic and human qualities that my father and his mates so admired in his predecessors. Still, he was more unpopular than other outsiders had been. Not every southerner venturing into the northern fastness gets eaten for breakfast. It was noted that few of Bill's subordinates ever seemed to do well. A particular one would be flavour of the month for some time, then fault would be found. The favoured one would disappear into limbo, never to be mentioned again.

Wherever there was credit to be gleaned, there would be Bill Benson – determined to reap the benefit. In cases where there was any kind of difficulty he'd find an excuse to be well out of the frame. With his little twitching moustache he seemed to have a rat-like ability to sniff out those areas which gave maximum career advantage. The constant stream of advice circulars emanating from the desks of constipated civil servants in the Home Office provided him with a particularly fruitful opportunity to display his talents.

'Spoken of very highly in official circles' was our Bill, unlike so many of his colleagues who went out of their way to ignore or ridicule any advice from the men from the Ministry. When one of these Home Office geniuses penned a circular recommending some worthy but impractical initiative, Benson made sure it was implemented by the GMP. He'd have his underlings working their nuts off to operate the latest airy-fairy scheme and then appear centre stage to take the credit if there was any. Ideas that died in infancy joined those involved with them in limbo, never mentioned again. Bill was only associated with success. It was widely understood that he was the coming man in the British police service, an administrator's administrator.

No one was in any doubt that he saw his chief-constableship as the launching pad to higher things; not just Commissioner of the Met., but head of a national police force – Britain's first J. Edgar Hoover. The British Bureau of Investigation. The BBI – it was coming, some said it had already arrived – and nothing was going to mess up Wild Bill's chance of being at the head of it when the time came.

So how did a smooth operator like Benson allow himself to be photographed with a reptile like Mike Dyer? Where was the career advantage in that? I ruminated confusedly on these puzzles as I steered the car back into the drive at Thornleigh Court.

Reaction was setting in when I got into my bedroom. I felt drained as I stripped and slipped into bed beside Sylvia. She hadn't moved from the position I'd left her in. I put the Minox in my bedside drawer and fell into a deep sleep.

7

I woke up with weak sunlight shining in my eyes and felt for Sylvia. There was a warm place where she'd been. I could glimpse her through the open living room door wearing my white crew neck which just covered her vital areas. She looked a lot more sexy wearing it than I did.

'What would Monsieur like for breakfast?' Sylvia asked with a smile.

'Come here Goldilocks,' I said, reaching out for her, but she slipped away.

'Later, just you keep yourself under control,' she laughed. 'Would you like a cup of coffee? I had a really deep sleep, I still feel drowsy.'

I told Sylvia where to find things in the kitchen and lay back on the bed, luxuriating in the unusual situation of being waited on. I looked at the clock. It was nine-fifteen. I flexed my shoulder muscles – only a faint twinge. My back seemed to have recovered well.

Sylvia came back into the bedroom with two cups of coffee.

'Are you sure this is all right or would you prefer to begin the day with a couple of shots of Red-Eye?' she joked while slipping out of the crew neck and back into bed beside me. She yawned and stretched her shoulders. In the pale morning sunlight I could see that she had been wearing a bikini when she got her tan.

The coffee was stone cold by the time we got round to drinking it. As we sat up sipping it Sylvia was unable to hold back her curiosity.

'Your flat looks very neat. I've never seen a man's kitchen so clean and tidy. Are you sure you're not married?'

'It's because I'm not married that the place *is* so neat. When I was married I never could keep the place so clean. That kitchen is my operating theatre.'

'What was your wife like?'

Normally I wouldn't have satisfied her curiosity but I was feeling pleased with myself and very benevolent. Perhaps I was light headed from lack of sleep. Whatever the reason was, I was in an unusually confiding mood.

'She was as different from you as it's possible to imagine. She came to Manchester as a student from Sierra Leone and I met her and then we got married. I only knew her for ten months before we married.'

'So you fell in love with a beautiful African girl. What happened – or would you rather not talk about it?' Sylvia asked quietly. She could see that my expression had changed.

I wasn't offended by Sylvia's directness. My mood of benevolence continued.

'Elenki and I were married for just under four years and then she died of a disease that only West Africans suffer from. Nature's little joke on me for marrying an African.'

Sylvia said nothing. She gave me a hug. In two minutes Sylvia had shown more feeling than Delise had done in two years. Despite my efforts to maintain some detachment towards her, Sylvia Mather was succeeding in getting under my skin.

'How long ago was this Dave, you're not very old now, are you?' she asked gently.

'It was just two years ago this February, and before you ask: yes, there has been someone else since. I've had a long, hot and cold affair with my secretary Delise Delaney, which now seems to have reached the terminal phase,' I said curtly, not wanting to be reminded that I'd been thinking about getting back in touch with Delise. I was surprised at how much I was telling Sylvia about my private life, but in the intimate circumstances I found it hard to hold back. What I was telling her wasn't a secret or in any way related to the Elsworth case.

Sylvia didn't say anything in reply, she just draped herself on top of me ready for some more activity. But the talk about Elenki and Delise had ruined my mood. I shivered as I thought about Elenki lying in the ground, so far away from her home.

I turned on the bedside clock radio before the silence could stretch out too long and because I have an incurable habit of listening to the news whenever I can.

'*. . . There are more reports of violence from Manchester's Moss Side district. A car drove into Charlton Close, scene of several previous violent incidents involving firearms this year, at 6 a.m. this morning and opened fire with shotgun blasts. There are no reports of any* *injuries to people but there was extensive damage to property. There is informed speculation that the raid was intended as retaliation by other local gangs in response to incidents involving the so-called Charlton Youth Group, or Charlies . . .'*

As the news was coming through I could feel Sylvia becoming more and more tense and stiff beside me. I wondered what was going on in her head and was tempted to ask her but that wouldn't be playing the game by the rules. Still, if she had come round here just to snoop she hadn't found out much. Her reaction to the news about the violence in Moss Side showed that she probably knew far more about what was going on behind the scenes than I did.

'Does this mean trouble for you, love?' I asked.

'I'll have to go right away. I've got to be in work by twelve usually. Mike's sure to want extra security staff on duty at all the clubs tonight and I'm the one who'll have to organise it.' Sylvia slipped out of bed and began dressing in that quick neat way women have that men can never seem to match.

'I'll give you a call about six and let you know what I'm doing this weekend if you're still interested,' she said with a smile as she straightened her hair with my brush. 'What are you going to be doing today, are you still working on that Thwaite thing?' she asked casually.

'Yeah, I'm still looking for Rachel, if that's what you mean. I'm going to the airport to meet someone who may be able to throw more light on things.'

I got up quickly and darted into the bathroom as Sylvia came out. I brushed my teeth and showered. I started thinking about what I was going to wear and decided to put on a charcoal-coloured suit, white shirt, and striped tie. I wanted to look the part of a thrusting young executive when I met Elsworth. I knew he regarded me as a tiresome lower-class nerk and I was keen to confuse him.

My rapid ablutions were cut short. I heard a key being sharply inserted into the door lock and the door opening. I felt a sudden twisting sensation in my guts.

It could only be Delise; she was the only person, apart from myself, with a key to the door. Feeling like a man who's just heard that there's fifty pounds of semtex under his bed, primed and ready to blow, I waited for the inevitable explosion when Delise met Sylvia.

Nothing happened.

There was silence from the living room, or at least I couldn't hear anything being said. Maybe it wasn't Delise, or maybe she was on tranquillisers. Then there was a quiet tap on the bathroom door and Sylvia spoke in a very small and subdued voice . . .

'Dave, you'll have to come our right away. There's a woman here to see you,' she said, almost whispering.

I hurriedly took shorts and a shirt from the airing cupboard, slipped them on, and stepped out to face the music. Trouserless as I was, I must have looked wet as I poked my head round the living room door, half expecting to be met by a well-aimed ornament thrown by Delise. There were no flying ornaments, but there was saltpetre in the air: an explosion seemed imminent.

Sylvia was standing by the door almost next to me and opposite her, silhouetted against the window, was the figure of Delise Delaney. My former lover and near-partner in detection had taken up a position as far away from Sylvia as she could get and still be in the same room.

Slightly built and gracile, Delise often seemed tense even when in repose, but now she was obviously full of nervous energy. Dressed as she was in her tight-fitting black body suit, flowery leggings and stacker boots she seemed to be of a very different generation from Sylvia, who was still wearing her expensive, smoky blue evening outfit. The boots lent inches to Delise and emphasised her slender build.

It would be an understatement to say there was a feeling of tension; I think both Sylvia and I were keyed up for some swift and violent action from Delise. The angular planes of her face had been sharpened, or perhaps it was just her position standing by the strong light from the window. She looked like a predatory cat getting ready to pounce.

'Hello Delise, come to bring your key back, have you?' I said brazenly, in an attempt to pre-empt her wrath.

Delise was unaffected by my feeble wit.

'Come in Dave, come right into the room. Not shy are you? I believe both this lady and I have had the pleasure of seeing you without your trousers on before now. Come in and let's have a look at the great lover.'

I cautiously remained where I was, poised for flight to the bedroom. There was a prickling sensation on the surface of my bare legs and on my face. My skin suddenly seemed two sizes too small to contain my body.

'I said you were an oversized Chippendale reject didn't I? How right I was,' Delise continued scornfully.

'Now Delise. This isn't what you think. Don't go leaping to any conclusions, Sylvia is helping me out on an investigation. Anyway, be fair! It was you who said you were leaving me,' I argued to cover my confusion.

'Well you haven't exactly let the grass grow under your feet, have you?' she said trenchantly, reverting to the ominous calm she'd maintained before.

'I didn't know I was supposed to be celibate,' I mumbled, hard pressed to justify myself. I couldn't work out what Delise was thinking: knowing her temperament I'd expected a physical attack on myself or Sylvia before now. I didn't say anything else. I couldn't think of much to say.

'Aren't you going to introduce me to your new friend, or should I say playmate, Dave? Not too tongue-tied, I hope?' Delise said tartly.

'Delise Delaney, this is Sylvia Mather,' I said glumly.

'Well, is Dave working hard on your case, Miss, Ms or Mrs Mather? I hope he's giving you good service. You look as if you've been serviced,' she said to Sylvia.

'It's Mrs Mather actually, not Ms; and Dave isn't on my case or doing me a service, as you so elegantly put it Miss Delaney, but I'm sure his performance will improve now he's working under better conditions,' Sylvia replied equally sarcastically.

Delise had discovered more about Sylvia's status in their brief exchange than I had to date. I must find out what Sylvia's maiden name was.

With the claws being unsheathed in earnest I felt it was time to beat a retreat before I got myself scratched. I nipped into the bedroom for my robe which Sylvia had discarded there.

When I came back Delise and Sylvia weren't speaking, but at least they weren't attacking each other and Delise had taken a seat. The threat of an immediate violent eruption had apparently receded.

'I only came round to tell you something but now there isn't much point – you seem to have found a replacement for me already,' Delise said plaintively. Her voice was pitched low and, as always when she was under tension, the sharp Cockney speech patterns of her childhood began to break through the overlay of perfect elocution.

Delise had lived in Hanwell until she was seven and then been shuttled between London and Manchester as her mother pursued her own education and career.

'Look, I can go. I have to be going anyway,' interjected Sylvia.

'Wait Sylvia, I was going to give you a lift,' I said hastily.

'He's so considerate isn't he?' intoned Delise. 'I don't have much to say. Shouldn't keep you long.'

Contradicting her previous statement that there wasn't much point in speaking to me, Delise was determined to say her piece. She hadn't got herself dolled up and come out at such an early hour on Saturday morning for nothing. Perhaps it was to spite Sylvia that she stayed but Delise definitely isn't the shrinking violet type: if she'd come here to tell me something, tell me she would.

'Well in that case I'll just go and gather up one or two things,' said Sylvia, her face set. For the first time in the whole exchange I sensed that Sylvia was slightly out of sorts with me. As a determined character she matched Delise: it was flattering to my self-esteem that she hadn't decided to make a rapid exit.

'Yes, you do that Mrs Mather. I expect you've lots of things you want to collect in the bedroom,' said Delise enigmatically. Sylvia stood up and looked at Delise as if considering her response, but said nothing. At five foot four she was taller than Delise, but the smart money would have to be on Delise if it came to a punch-up. Delise was far leaner and fitter looking. A real mean machine.

Sylvia turned, gave me a very warm smile and went into the bedroom. I heard the door shut.

'This is all fine and dandy isn't it Dave? Aren't we civilised? You've always had a liking for busty blonds haven't you? So she's ideal for you; you with your pectorals and her with her chest, at least a 40D cup. I should think she's had silicone implants, wouldn't you Dave?' Angry words poured out of Delise.

Delise has always been self-conscious about her own equipment in that department: which is perfectly in proportion with the rest of her. Her breasts were like two round little apples.

'Don't be silly Delise. I don't know what gives you the right to complain. It was you who left me the "Dear John" letter saying you'd met someone else.'

'Well I was only trying to wake you up and help you to make your mind up. You're so literal minded Dave. You believe anything anyone tells you . . .'

I snorted, still at a loss for words.

'I came to tell you that I've applied for a supervisor's job at a site on Jersey and they've taken up my references. I was going to ask you if you'd like to come with me for the season. We've enough put by to keep up the payments on this flat and the office. I thought a long break would do you good.'

Delise trained as an archaeologist at Manchester University. She's worked on sites in Britain and Pakistan, but full-time or even well-paid seasonal jobs for archaeologists are as rare as hen's teeth, which is why Pimpernel Investigations has had the benefit of her services for so long.

'So you weren't happy working for me then?' I asked peevishly.

'Dave, you left me on my own for weeks on end with nothing to do but type up your everlasting reports and answer the phone. I've got a mind of my own . . . there isn't really anyone else, just the chance of a job that'll get both of us out of a rut.'

'God Delise, you're contrary. One week you're telling me you never want to see me again, the next you're inviting me to go away with you. I never know where I'm up to with you. Jersey sounds a lot better than Middlesbrough, which is where Sims and Happyways want me to go, but I'm committed to the job I'm on now. I can't just drop everything and walk off the case.'

'Are you sure that's what you mean Dave? Are you sure that you just don't want to walk away from Mrs Bouncy-boobs in there?' she said, getting up to go.

'Delise, you haven't even got the job yet. I'll be in touch in a few days' time.'

'Don't bother Dave, I won't be here.' She slammed the door as she left.

She still hadn't returned my key. I was thoroughly confused. I was relieved that she hadn't found someone else, yet annoyed that she'd turned up to complicate things again.

I went back into the bedroom to complete my interrupted dressing. Sylvia was sitting on the side of the bed putting a gold chain back round her neck. I couldn't help wondering just what she was thinking.

I noticed now what I should have noticed last night: what an extraordinary amount of jewellery Sylvia was wearing. How had Delise been able to guess that Sylvia had brought the contents of a fair-sized jeweller's window with her? A diamond tiara was the only thing missing. She had heavy gold ear-rings, an expensive gold watch, an opal brooch to match her suit, rings on both hands and a bangle on each wrist. Maybe I'd mingled with larcenous shop assistants for too long if I was missing such obvious details, which Delise could sense intuitively.

'Sharp, isn't she? That one, she'll cut herself if she isn't careful,' Sylvia commented. 'If things were cold between you before, I should think they're downright glacial by now,' she added laughingly. 'I can recommend you a good secretary, she's fat and forty-five, with five kids and an out-of-work husband to set on you if you start feeling flirtatious.'

I hurried to get dressed. She sat on the bed watching me choose my clothes.

'You're certainly a fastidious dresser Dave,' was her only comment, 'you must be meeting somebody important.'

Did she really think of me as just a slab of meat as Delise had implied, a good lay to pass the night with? Was she only interested in me for sex? Well it had certainly been good for both of us. Look how blinded I'd been last night.

I decided to stop worrying about whether Sylvia or Delise had the more genuine interest in me. You can hurt your brain like that.

When we got in the car Sylvia didn't have much more to say for herself. I thought she must be worried about the danger of violence in the clubs tonight. I dropped her off at her flat in Heaton Mersey and drove back down through Didsbury, turning down Palatine Road towards the airport.

The weather had changed for the worse. The few weak gleams of sunlight had gone. It had clouded over and there was a steady drizzle. This hadn't deterred the Saturday morning golfers: a steady stream of them was turning into the golf courses as I crossed the bridge over the Mersey at Northenden. Turning out onto the M56 I raced the last few miles to the airport. The motorway was crowded with citizens escaping to the pastures of Cheshire or the hills of Wales.

I hit the approach road, drove past the new terminal building and got into the lane for Terminal B – International Arrivals. Although the holiday rush hadn't yet peaked there were plenty of people about. Weaving through the maze of roundabouts I looped into the short-stay car park. As usual there had been another complicated rearrangement of the entrance to the twelve-level multi-storey. The airport authorities are always fiddling about with it in the interests of so-called efficiency. I had to go to Level 8 before I found a space.

At the International Arrivals lounge I positioned myself in front of the information screens at the Meeting Point. I needn't have bothered to hurry, there was a delay on the arrival of the flight from Brussels. Meanwhile a wide-bodied jet had arrived from Lahore. The immigration authorities must have been scrupulously checking each passenger because they were only emerging through the gate at long intervals. Relatives were summoned from the waiting groups to go and interpret. The mainly Asian crowd was growing in size as more joined groups and then settled down to wait until their travelling companions made it through.

For the first time in two days I didn't have to hustle myself somewhere in a hurry. I went over to the news-stand and bought the heaviest paper I could find, but I couldn't settle to read it. The PA system announced repeatedly and monotonously that unattended baggage would be destroyed.

Another delay was announced on the Brussels flight. I was going to be here for a while. Through the windows I could see that the damp weather had really set in. Rain was streaming down, a typical June in Manchester. Water was cascading down the windows of the terminal. After sitting for a few minutes more watching the friendly Asian families looking anxiously towards the Arrivals gate I'd had enough. I decided to phone from the car to see if anyone had responded to my postcard campaign in Didsbury.

The families making their way back to the car park were all happy, they'd been reunited. I passed them as they trudged, heavily encumbered, towards the high speed lifts taking them to the car park.

My car was right at the end of the bay. As I walked towards it I spotted a white, current-year registration BMW with one-way mirror glass windows cruising along very slowly: a real drugger's buggy. It wasn't looking for a space. I paused for a moment.

The BMW slowed to a halt by my Nissan. The rear doors opened and two tall young black men stepped out. They were neatly dressed in grey business suits. Both of them were wearing the same kind of shades as the car windows. They looked weird, which I suppose was their intention. Then as one of the young men moved I felt a thrill of fear. There was something familiar about him.

I looked again, as if unconsciously expecting him to disappear. Was I losing my bottle, jumping back in fear at the first young black man I saw?

It was my friend the biker. He and his partner were walking round my car, then he took a phone out of his hip pocket and spoke to someone.

I felt hot and cold at the same time. All the clichés about fear came true; the bottom had dropped out of my stomach; my hair was standing on end. It was all happening. The biker was the taller of the two, his mate was shorter and stockier. He was wearing a navy blue shirt and a silver tie, the thicker set man a white shirt and striped tie.

Luckily a family piling cases into an old Volvo gave me cover for a moment. I dodged into the lift and back to the ground floor.

What a joke. Here I was in one of the most heavily policed airports in the world, that very same Manchester Airport that Benson used as a dumping ground for all those coppers he deemed failures, and I couldn't get any help. I couldn't go running to the police making accusations. There's no law about wearing shades to make yourself look sinister.

I could always catch the bus into town and try to phone Elsworth later. A safe but feeble way out.

I needed to find somewhere I could observe from without being observed. Everything was against me. The arrivals area was so small, there was nowhere to hide without the certainty of being spotted immediately. The rows of seats were too low to duck behind unless I lay full length on the ground. That would make me look even dafter than dodging round the pillars in the middle of the hall.

The newspaper shop was just an open bay. The enquiry desk and car rental booths were all fully staffed and no doubt supplied with panic buttons. The coffee shop was on a dais in everyone's view and it was tiny. There was a show car on display but I could hardly hide inside it. I had to face it, this place had been designed with the express purpose of stopping people from hiding.

In the few seconds remaining I made a decision. I pushed up to the barrier and joined a family group who were looking at the arrivals. The crowd around the gate had thickened. The Asian throng had been joined by many more people waiting for the Brussels passengers to come in. I pushed right in among them and sat on one of the seats backing onto the barrier. It was the best I could do. I was screened from view.

The Brussels passengers finally arrived. I was going to have to break cover soon to meet Elsworth. I bobbed up in my seat.

There they were, bold as brass. The one in the white shirt covering the exit to the lifts, the other one further back in the hall ready to go to the exits on either side of the Terminal. They were glancing at each other from time to time, watching themselves in their reflective shades. They were pros.

The passengers from Brussels were coming out now, far more quickly than the Asians had done; they were pressing forward to meet up with those waiting to receive them.

I ducked down and began wedging a way through the crowd towards the men's toilet, which was over on my right, away from my own reception committee. I ran inside. It was empty.

I pulled out the newspaper I'd bought earlier and in frantic haste shredded it and pushed it into the large basket full of used paper towels. I lit it in three places, checked it was burning and made a rapid exit, praying there was a smoke detector in range.

I stood in the recess by the loo door but no alarm sounded. I looked across the hall.

They'd spotted me. My biker was beckoning to the one in the white shirt, pointing me out.

I needed a distraction. There must be an alarm near. High on the wall about six feet further along was a large aluminium button. Screening it with my body, as best I could, I bashed it with my fist.

Instant loud shattering noise burst out from alarm bells.

After a few seconds of shocked pause the clatter of the bells was joined by uproar from hundreds of people shouting to each other in Asian languages and English. Going back the way I'd come, I tapped the arm of a prosperous looking Asian professional and pointed back at my two pursuers who had now joined forces not far from the loo door.

'It was them! I saw them set that alarm off!' I went on deeper into the crowd, shouting and pointing 'It was them! It was those two!' I couldn't have picked a better moment, everyone was looking round in response to the alarms. The choreography was perfect, my pursuers slowed in mid-stride as if they'd hit an invisible barrier. Their sinister sun glasses convicted them in the eyes of the crowd. I pressed on, pointing and yelling to make myself heard above the bells.

By this time fire engines were rolling up to the exit doors and firemen and airport staff were calmly walking towards the crowd. I yelled again, 'False alarm! Those two, they set it off!' Other people took up the cry, 'It was them! It was them!' Fingers pointed them out, angry fists were raised. Police were converging from corners of the building. The pair were being surrounded.

The chaos I had orchestrated so far now spiralled away out of my control. The airport staff and firemen were trying to separate people from their luggage . . . 'Leave your luggage, proceed calmly to the exits.'

It was ready to go but no one else was. None of the people near me took any notice of the pleas of the staff. Their instinct, like a herd of buffalo, was to mill together when under attack.

I think some of them didn't understand English and the rest had no intention of leaving their far-travelled luggage for the attention of thieves.

The public address system began booming out the same orders as the staff, appeals interspersed with chiming musical tones which added a surrealistic element to the confusion . . . 'Leave your luggage, proceed calmly to the exits.'

Angry hoots of disbelief greeted these orders. Some were moving; snatching up small children, shouldering bulging cases, moving to the exits. But the majority were hesitating; havering while the staff tried to cajole them. There were even some who had previously moved towards the exits now trying to make their way back to where they'd left property. In any case, the instruction to leave baggage conflicted with the earlier threats that unattended baggage would be destroyed.

As I was caught up in the terrible confusion I looked towards the centre of the hall. My pursuers had turned on their heels and were running for the exit. It was the worst thing they could have done. Every exit was jammed with people and there were now uniformed and armed police all over the place. By running they'd confirmed their guilt. Police, sensing that they were up to no good, began converging on them. I felt no guilt at arousing a mob against them, only a fierce sense of satisfaction.

At this point someone flung the door of the men's loo open. Billows of white smoke swept out into the lounge. There were shrieks of panic. Groups who had been delaying to defend their baggage turned to flee from the smoke. Blasts of cold air were coming in from the wide open exits as the automatic door-closing system was switched off.

Outside there was a cloudburst, solid rods of rain coming straight down and bouncing off the pavements. The people who'd reached the open air hesitated before moving out into the downpour. Behind them the crowd bunched up and then pushed forward, urged on by firemen. I was moving forward in the general scrum when I saw Harold Elsworth just ahead of me. I forced my way forward through the throng until I was at his side. I grabbed his arm as we went through the exit into the torrential rain.

As soon as we were through the door Elsworth turned and angrily shook off my grip.

'What the hell do you think you're doing? Have you found Rachel?' he bawled at me, in a much broader Yorkshire accent than he had had on Wednesday.

'Getting soaked like you by the looks of it, and as for Rachel I'll tell you in a minute,' I replied.

It was true enough about getting soaked. The whole crowd of people milling about outside Terminal B were drenched, Asians with loose saris and robes clinging to them. To my astonishment as I looked round I could see that every building in the whole airport was emptying out into the wind and rain.

I felt quite nervous for a moment, until I remembered that the police had their culprits and there were no video cameras inside the loo.

The fire brigade were now present in force and they were barring the way back into the building. There was nothing to do but stand and get wet. Ambulances, police cars and Black Marias were joining the fire engines blocking all the approach roads to Terminal B and the car park.

We weren't going to be able to leave in a hurry, however much I wanted to make a quick getaway. I kept in step beside Elsworth as we moved farther away from the buildings.

'I came to meet you and report on my progress. Your wife told me that you were arriving on this flight,' I explained to Elsworth.

He shook his head and looked at me with distaste, then turned away. His thin sandy hair was plastered to his head and small rivulets were running down it onto his beaky nose.

'If you haven't found her, what are you doing here? I'm paying you for progress, not reports. You should have gone round to Thwaite's flat straight away instead of giving him time to clear off. Dee said nothing about you being here when I spoke to her this morning.' He spoke slowly, without the sharpness he had at our last meeting. Being pitched out into a rainstorm was obviously a shock to his system. He didn't know what had happened.

'Haven't you found anything at all about Rachel's whereabouts?' he asked again. He didn't look directly at me. I got the strong impression he didn't want anyone to see him talking to me.

'Haven't you heard about Thwaite?' I countered.

I still had that old feeling that I hadn't got his complete attention, because he didn't answer. 'Hasn't your wife told you anything? I asked her to tell you there had been an important development.' This produced a sort of grunting sound from Elsworth, or maybe he was just clearing his throat but no further utterance came from him.

'Look Mr Elsworth, I told you before. You can't expect me to find your daughter for you unless you give me something more to go on. Something's happened to Thwaite. I'll tell you about it later,' I said. He didn't look as if he could take any more shocks at the moment.

'Was Rachel with him? Has she been hurt? Is there something wrong with her?' For the first time since I'd met him he was listening to something I said, rather than just reacting. He obviously didn't give a damn about Thwaite.

'No she wasn't with him, but don't worry. I haven't actually found her yet but I've a good idea where to look for her. I need to talk to you about what's been going on and it had better be somewhere more private than here,' I said.

Elsworth made a very tiny movement of his head which I took to be a nod of agreement.

Now that everyone had been thoroughly soaked the weather began to improve, the sun breaking through the gloom. We were standing near the Olympic building, the sharp angle of its corner wall like the edge of a sword looming up above us.

Whether it was the building or someone walking over my grave I don't know but I felt a sudden icy feeling of fear come over me again. I looked through the crowds milling about.

I couldn't see anyone looking for me. It was probably just reaction to my narrow escape, or contact with the chilling personality of Harold Elsworth on top of getting a soaking.

8

I could see that our experiences had knocked Elsworth back. The cold and rain and apprehension of my impending news had deflated him, temporarily at least. He'd lost the lordly air which had grated on me at our first meeting. He insisted on carrying his own cases from the lift to the car. I was relieved to see that the Nissan was still in one piece.

'Why don't you phone your wife and let her know that you're en-route? The phone's just there.' I said, when we had driven clear of the airport.

He alerted his wife, Dee, about his imminent arrival with the fewest possible words. He gave the impression of a man who was too weary to make the effort to speak. That suited me. I didn't feel like making small talk either. I had a lot of questions to ask Elsworth but they would have to keep for now.

With its usual contrariness the weather was clearing up. There were still signs of the recent cloudburst everywhere but the sun was struggling to shine through.

In what seemed a very short time I turned off the M56 and took the road towards the London motorway. Before reaching it we turned off towards Elsworth's home at Tarn. It was handily placed for a dash down the motorway to London, or for the airport, or Manchester; the area was popular with rich executive types such as my client.

The winding road on which he lived looked out onto open fields in one direction; the other side backed onto a small lake which gave the place its name.

It was this right-hand side which was lined with large villas. There was a wide verge with mature beech trees growing in it. Behind this, well screened from the road, nestled the homes of Manchester's commercial aristocracy. Each house was set in its own grounds. Some were enclosed with high fences and conifer hedges; others were more open, content to flaunt themselves to those passing along the road.

'Turn in here.' Elsworth grated, pointing with a quick flap of his hand to the gold-painted wrought iron gates of one of the bigger villas. The Nissan crunched over a thick gravel drive towards the porched entrance where a tall woman stood waiting for us.

The house itself was a Betjemanesque wonder with projecting bays, balconies, half timbering and pointed gables all combined with modern features such as a built-on garage which could take at least four Rolls-Royces. There seemed to be about half an acre of garden attached to it at the front and more land behind, sloping down to the lake. Before the car came to a halt Elsworth, showing signs of life for the first time since I had confronted him at the airport, was opening the door and getting out.

While Elsworth was greeting his wife I got his two large suitcases out of the boot. Neither had much in, he could have managed with one much smaller case.

'Leave those alone,' Elsworth said sharply when he saw what I was doing.

Putting the cases down on the gravel I took the opportunity to give Mrs Elsworth the once-over. She was built like a can-can dancer; tall, with good legs and a full figure. She was as tall as Elsworth himself although she was wearing low heeled slip-on shoes. Her face was well structured rather than beautiful, with an expression of determination being its dominating feature. There was a trace of well-controlled anxiety also in her expression. She looked like a person you'd rather have as a friend than as an enemy. She gave an impression of strength and direction which was lacking in her husband. It would have been flattery to call her beautiful but she certainly had lots of presence.

She was younger than him, much younger than I expected – plenty of mileage left on her clock. Despite her height and regular features there was nothing 'horsey' about her, she wasn't a member of the green-welly brigade. She was far more robust and normal looking than I had imagined from speaking to her on the phone. I'd been judging her by the impression I'd formed of Harold Elsworth.

Sensing my inspection she turned to me when her husband released her.

'This is Cunane, he's doing some research for me,' Elsworth

introduced me grudgingly. She immediately offered her hand to be shaken. She had a firm grip too.

'I know all about Mr Cunane. You're a private detective aren't you?' she said as she turned to lead us into the interior of her home. I made no move to pick up Elsworth's cases until he started for them himself. I picked up one. He pulled it off me. 'You won't be told, will you?' he grunted.

Before I had a chance to say anything to him Mrs Elsworth barked 'Don't be so rude Harold', as if she was speaking to a seven-year-old. 'Have you found out anything about Rachel? Is there any news?'

I wasn't sure whether she was speaking to her husband or to me. In view of Harold's request for secrecy I kept quiet. I could see he was angry. Mrs Elsworth obviously knew more than she was supposed to and he thought I was to blame.

'Don't look at him like that Harold, he didn't tell me. Have you heard anything about Rachel?' she asked again.

By way of reply Harold turned his watery eyes on her and gave a shrug of his shoulders. He looked a lot older with his hopeless expression and bedraggled clothes.

She advanced on him, and for a second I thought she was going to take him by the scruff of the neck and give him a good shaking, but she merely put her arm round him and drew him into the house. She gathered me up on the way and pulled me along by my sleeve.

I got the strong impression that Elsworth wasn't pleased to have me entering his home and meeting his wife. I'm sure he would have sent me off with a flea in my ear if his wife hadn't been there, but I was determined to hang around until I found out more about what had been going on.

As I crossed the Elsworth threshold Dee remarked to us both, 'You look like two drowned rats. Look at your clothes, your suits look as if they're made of muslin. You'll both have to bathe and change right away. Then I want to hear what's been going on.'

Taking advantage of this humane concession, Harold obediently scampered up the stairs leaving me alone with Dee. She obviously knew how to handle him.

'If you'll follow me I'll show you to the guest bedroom. I

don't suppose you've got any dry clothes with you, have you? I'll see if I can find something for you,' she said.

I thanked her as she showed me into a room off the main hall on the ground floor which turned out to be a bedroom with attached bathroom.

'Go ahead, you'll find everything you need in there. I'll find you something dry to change into, though I'm not sure we've got anything so wide across the shoulders that it would fit you.'

I went into the bathroom; it was supplied with everything I could need. Stripping away the remains of my suit I remembered that this was the second change of clothes I'd destroyed while working for Elsworth. Even if I had the suit dry-cleaned and pressed it would look like a sack. It was only fit for the Oxfam shop. At this rate I should be out of clothes entirely by next weekend. I took my time in the shower, and felt refreshed when I stepped into the bedroom.

There was a new tracksuit laid out on the bed, also socks and size ten trainers. I dressed. The bedroom was well furnished with new, modern furniture. Four watercolours of scenes around the lake at Tarn hung on the walls. I was no judge but they seemed to catch the quality of the light on the lake and trees very well.

There was a tap on the door.

'Come through into the lounge as soon as you're ready, I'm dying to hear what you've got to tell us,' Dee called through from the corridor.

Feeling awkward in the tracksuit and tight-fitting trainers I went out into the hall. There was an open door on my right which presumably led to the lounge.

I entered a wide pleasant room looking out on to beautiful gardens and the same lakeside scene which I'd just been admiring in the paintings in the bedroom. To someone as used as I was to being hemmed in by bricks and mortar on all sides this beautiful scene, adjacent to the living room, was luxury indeed.

'Come in and have some hot soup, I've just made it,' said Dee. She and Elsworth were seated in front of a low table in the middle of the room.

'I've just been listening to the radio – what on earth was

going on at the airport?' she asked. Now that she'd stopped bustling around and bossing Harold about she looked much more anxious, but the stiff upper lip was still firmly in place.

'Well there was some kind of bomb scare or fire which led to a mass evacuation just at the very moment your husband was coming into the Arrivals Lounge. To cap all that there was the same major cloudburst you've had here and the people going out tried to come back in again,' I guardedly explained, trying to put the best gloss I could on the mischief I'd caused.

'Four blacks were arrested,' Elsworth interrupted me to supply some details of his own. 'We saw four young blacks being led off in handcuffs. I've never seen such a shambles in all my life. We were standing for hours before they let us back in to claim our baggage.'

'And what's all this about you telling Cunane to meet me at the airport? He says you told him to meet me there.' Elsworth was doing his old trick of eye rolling and blinking up at the ceiling as he spoke reproachfully to Dee, but she soon showed him a touch of the whip.

'You can take that tone out of your voice, Harold,' she snapped right back at him. 'If you think you can keep it secret from me when you're hiring private detectives to do what you should be doing yourself you'd better think again. You underlined Mr Cunane's name in the Yellow Pages and it didn't take Hercule Poirot to work out what you were up to.'

This all came as a shock to Harold. Dee must normally give him his dressing-downs in private. I concentrated on my soup during this matrimonial interchange. It was delicious lentil and barley broth and I could feel myself reviving with every mouthful.

Looking round the lounge again my eye was drawn not to the luxurious furniture nor to the Delft pottery in the antique Welsh dresser but to the pictures on the walls. Hanging there were two L.S. Lowrys. I was so used to seeing reproduction of his paintings that I goggled at the real thing. They must have held my attention for some seconds because I became aware that both Elsworths had fallen silent and were watching me.

'Yes, they are genuine,' said Dee with a proud smile, 'but I want to know what progress you've made in finding my daughter.'

'Well considering I only started on Thursday morning and that your husband was most unwilling to give me even the simplest information, or half an hour of his time, I've found out quite a lot. She's been mixed up with some hard cases – although I found that the boyfriend described by your husband as living in a drug-infested ghetto was actually just an ordinary Jack-the-lad on the make. He couldn't tell me anything about Rachel.'

'I thought you were incompetent. This proves it! He must know where she is,' Elsworth butted in.

'Thwaite can't tell us anything because he's dead. He's had his throat cut.'

'Here, hold on! Just watch what you're saying,' interjected Elsworth. He recoiled in genuine surprise and put his arm round his wife. They both looked shocked. Dee sagged against him and gave a low moan. She looked as if all the starch had drained out of her.

'No, you hold on Mr E! You sent me hot-foot round to his flat. You're the one who was so anxious for me to find him and it seems to me that you've got quite a few questions to answer yourself. You've really landed me in it. Thanks to you I could be charged with interfering with the evidence in a murder case.'

'You'd better explain to us exactly what you mean,' said Dee in her commanding tones, recovering quickly from her shock about Thwaite's death. No wonder the British built up such a big empire with women like these gingering them up.

'Certainly. I found the man whom Mr Elsworth claimed had virtually kidnapped your daughter lying in a pool of blood. He'd been murdered. It wasn't suicide. His throat was well and truly cut and there was no knife, or anything there. I removed evidence linking him and Rachel from the scene. Then I made an anonymous report about the death to the police, expecting them to start a full-scale murder hunt.

'Only, surprise, surprise! They say it's an open and shut suicide case with no doubt about it . . . Although police blunders are routine this isn't the sort of mistake they ever make. Someone must have been back into that flat and stuck a bottle of uppers and a knife in the corpse's hands.'

'Are you quite sure it was Andrew? I just can't take it in,' Dee said, breathing heavily.

I nodded. 'There's no doubt! It's been in the papers, though only a few lines. I'm amazed you haven't read about it. The police say it was suicide but I know for certain it wasn't.' I was getting angry. What did the woman need before she took it in? A visit from Thwaite's ghost?

'Calm down Mr Cunane,' she said tersely. 'Lashing about and blaming people won't get us anywhere. Why did you remove evidence and why did you think Harold was involved?'

'Anybody in their right mind would've suspected him. He was so anxious for me to go round to the flat. I took the material linking Rachel and Thwaite not for Harold's sake but for my own. I had to be able to prove that Rachel really existed and that she really was connected with Thwaite as Harold had said. I realised that if Harold was fitting me up for the murder I'd hardly a scrap of proof that I was making legitimate enquiries about Rachel. I didn't have any proof that he was who he said he was, or that Rachel was his daughter. He was in such a hurry for me to find Rachel yet he hardly gave me any details about her.' I explained. 'It seemed suspicious enough at the time . . .' I concluded lamely.

It sounded thin but I wasn't going to admit that I'd panicked at the murder scene.

'I'm sure the police would have treated his death a great deal more seriously if they had known a wealthy banker was sending private detectives after him,' I said.

Elsworth seemed to be taking all this seriously himself. He drew himself up to reply, probably in the same way he addressed his Board of Directors, but in this case limiting his audience to his wife.

'It has been ten days now since we've heard anything from Rachel. She's never been out of touch with us for so long before. I thought Cunane could find her while I was in Brussels. I realise now that I was in error in not giving him more information to act on. It seems that he has found out something entirely different from what I expected.'

Elsworth was obviously good at committee work. This was an excellent attempt to deflect attention onto me. Perhaps he had been trying to get me to take the rap for him after all.

However, before I could start justifying myself again, his wife intervened. She was obviously used to his little ways.

'Harold, you sent Mr Cunane down there to do your dirty work. You knew very well there was something wrong.' Dee sounded like a blood hound in full cry, denouncing her husband with her upper-class vowel sounds.

Elsworth frowned, and, with what I realised was his typical gesture, raised his eyes to the ceiling and began reading his lines off an invisible screen.

'I knew, or thought I knew, that Rachel was in Didsbury with her young man. I didn't wish to get involved in any unseemly incident which might have jeopardised the position I hold; a position, I might remind you, that brings us both a very good living. I had to fly to Brussels that night. It was perfectly reasonable for me to employ an agent to perform a simple task without having to give him our entire family history.'

He sounded like the judge at the Nuremburg trials summing up the case for the prosecution.

'You should have told me, she's *my* daughter. I would have gone,' shot back Dee.

'That's exactly why I didn't want you to get involved. You're too excitable. You would have driven Rachel away from us forever.'

Dee Elsworth looked surprised. She looked at her husband, then they both looked at me. There was a silence. I didn't like what was going on here. The behaviour of these two raised more questions than it answered. Elsworth's remark implied that Rachel was staying out of touch because of her mother, yet he'd claimed to be employing me because his wife was out of her mind with worry – so much so that I wasn't to speak to her.

Was Dee Elsworth capable of murdering her daughter's lover? Was that why Elsworth had wanted me to get Rachel away from her lover so urgently? Had he suspected that Dee was ready to kill to protect her precious daughter from a potentially dangerous boyfriend?

She was a tough cookie, but from what I had seen of her so far she wouldn't have needed to resort to violence to deal with

Thwaite. There was something else going on that Elsworth didn't want his wife to know about.

Could he have done the job himself, after all? Maybe he needed to keep Dee in ignorance as part of his cover. Did he fly to Brussels, then back on the next flight, kill Thwaite and fly away again?

If Dee had discovered that her husband had hired me as a detective and then told me about the cash arrangements on her own initiative that would explain why Elsworth was so annoyed to see me at the airport. After all, he had been so anxious to keep our arrangements secret that he'd paid me in cash. He hadn't wanted any contact in public, least of all at the bank.

He was an odious creep but so concerned with his precious job that it was hard to imagine him saying boo to a goose, let alone murdering someone if there was the tiniest chance of discovery.

Finally he spoke again. 'What you did, Cunane, was very stupid; but good may have come of it. The police must have found nothing to connect Thwaite with Rachel, or they would have been round here by now. So there is nothing to tarnish her reputation or ours. I'm grateful to you for that, and it's worth the money I've paid you so far.

'The original reasons I hired you haven't changed. I'd still like you to find Rachel and bring her back to us with as little fuss as possible. If you need to extricate her from some problem it's better you do it than us. Don't tell me about it. Just do it! If you need money, even large amounts of money, ask for it. I can get it. Just get on with it and do what I hired you for in the first place!'

Having delivered himself of this major speech Elsworth resumed his characteristic pose. I was supposed to tug my forelock and gratefully depart on my mission.

'You're very good at putting your own actions in the most favourable light, aren't you Mr E.?' I said. 'What you're not taking on board is that someone out there rearranged a murder so it looked like suicide, and they did it so professionally that the police accepted it without question. So there is someone out there who deliberately harmed Thwaite and he or she may mean to harm your daughter.'

Elsworth wasn't having any of this.

'You're not suggesting that Rachel had anything to do with this alleged crime I hope? We've only your word for it that he was murdered. Probably you were mistaken. The shock of finding the body . . . or perhaps you have another motive. It could be that you removed evidence yourself with a view to squeezing more money out of us.'

'No Harold, Mr Cunane didn't try to squeeze money out of us. It was me who pressed more money on him. Can't you see that we must find Rachel? She might be in terrible danger. Please tell us David . . . can I call you David? You must have some theory about what's happened. Where do you think she might be?' Dee Elsworth came as close to pleading with me as she was capable of.

'I told your husband that he was tying my hands behind my back by not letting me start here with a search of Rachel's room, but I've made some progress. I think Thwaite must have had some place in Southport where he kept his gear.

'He got involved way out of his depth with some very nasty people, probably about something drug-related, and I think he told Rachel to lie low there till he got in touch with her. He was probably hoping to sort out whatever it was but someone found it more convenient to sort him out instead. So my best guess is that your daughter's lying low in Southport waiting to hear from him.'

'We've a connection with Southport. Harold's sister lives there. We often went there when Rachel was younger, she knows her way round Southport very well. Harold, why don't you phone Helen and ask her whether she's seen Rachel?'

Elsworth got up and went out into the hall to phone. Dee went into the kitchen to make a drink. I examined the pictures on the walls. As well as the two by Lowry there were other paintings by local artists. I recognised a Harold Riley.

'He gets them through the bank,' commented Dee when she came back in with a tray. I pulled out a small table for her and she put down a silver coffee pot and china cups.

Elsworth returned to the lounge.

'Helen's not seen Rachel, she's definitely not staying with her. I'd know if Helen was trying to hide something,' he said.

Dee poured out coffee. There was a strained silence in the

room again. Across the end of the garden the lake seemed to merge with the rain which was once more descending in sheets. The weather matched my mood.

'Why don't you let me have a look through Rachel's room. Perhaps I could find some fresh clues,' I offered helpfully. 'Mrs Elsworth could phone round Rachel's friends to ask if they've heard anything from her.'

'Thanks very much Cunane. Don't you think we've tried that already?' said Elsworth sarcastically.

'No he's right,' said Dee. 'Let him look through her rooms, a fresh pair of eyes might see something I've missed. I'll phone round again, someone may have heard something from her.' Elsworth glowered at his wife but said nothing. It was clear that whatever his position at the bank, she wore the trousers in the home.

Dee led me up the wide staircase to a pleasant suite of rooms.

'This is Rachel's study,' she said, showing me into a large wainscoted room bigger than most Oxbridge students' study-bedrooms. The room was tricked out with framed photographs of teams and sports trophies hanging from the grained oak panels. For all its apparent Englishness, there was something very American about this expensive recreation of a nineteenth-century room. The interior designer they'd employed must have had a Ralph Lauren catalogue in mind. Anyway, no expense had been spared. Looking again at the team photographs I wasn't sure whether they related to Rachel or had been bought with the decor as part of a set.

Rachel must have found her room in Manchester very tiny. This room looked out over the lawns down to the lake, the view from the window being framed by rich royal blue velvet curtains.

'Then through here is her bedroom, her bathroom and her guest bedroom,' Dee continued, conducting me round the suite. The floor space available to Rachel Elsworth was far bigger than my entire flat in South Manchester. Something in the way I was looking at the rooms must have made my thoughts obvious to Dee, perhaps I had raised my eyebrows when she said 'Rachel's guest bedroom'.

'She is our only child you know. We like her to have someone to stay for the weekend.'

'Oh I'm not being critical, Mrs Elsworth, everyone should live like this. I just wonder that Rachel could bring herself to leave here. Did Thwaite every come to stay?'

'Andrew came for one weekend before Christmas, and he didn't use this guest bedroom. There's another one on the ground floor, the one you used to change in. We may be old-fashioned but we didn't want our teenage daughter to have her boyfriend in the next room.'

'Of course not, I didn't mean to imply that you would. I was just wondering if you had seen much of him.'

'Harold didn't like him and he told Rachel not to bring him again,' she replied.

I looked at her quizzically.

'It's no use asking me what Harold's got against Andrew . . . I mean, had against Andrew. Harold hasn't liked any of Rachel's boyfriends, you'll have to ask him why not. I'll leave you to look through here now, I'll go and phone her friends again.'

When she left I got down to work. I'd whinged to both of the Elsworths that by being denied the chance to search Rachel's room I was being prevented from doing my job. At the time I hadn't realised what I was letting myself in for. A thorough search would take several hours. I started with the study. I knelt down on the thickly carpeted floor and checked for anything which might have been dropped or discarded recently, young girls being notoriously careless and slovenly. But there was nothing. Either Rachel was exceptionally tidy, or Dee must employ an efficient cleaning lady.

There were several expensive-looking cuddly toys scattered about and an antique rocking horse standing in the corner. The horse looked as if it belonged in the nursery of one of the National Trust's well-preserved stately homes: there was even a faded crest on the saddle. It was early Victorian, but still in a usable condition. Remembering my own heedless childhood, I wondered at the mentality of parents who provided their children with museum-quality antiques to play with. Had Rachel really been allowed to have high jinks on this?

More up-to-date entertainments hadn't been neglected. A television and VCR stood in the corner, with video recordings neatly shelved underneath. The videos were a very tame selection of recent children's films and comedies. I didn't see any pop videos or anything reflecting a teenager's personal taste. There were four unlabelled cassettes. Hoping for a revelation, I put one of these into the VCR and pressed Play. It was a recording of a gymkhana showing Rachel putting her pony over the jumps. She looked very determined for a thirteen-year-old. The recording also featured Dee, looking very chuffed as Rachel collected a rosette.

Ponies also played a large part in Rachel's reading material. An oak book case was filled with Pony Annuals and Pony stories, all well-thumbed and neatly labelled 'Property of Rachel Elsworth'. Next to them there were a large number of dog-eared Enid Blyton books, mostly Famous Five and Secret Seven adventures. The inscription in these read 'Dee Pemberton', so they must have been books Dee had handed down to Rachel. This was good, so far I was learning more about Dee than about Rachel. A new set of the complete plays of Shakespeare and a complete *Encyclopaedia Britannica* took up the remaining shelf space. Neither looked as if they had ever been opened.

To satisfy my naturally suspicious nature I plucked out the encyclopaedia volume for 'R' and riffled through the pages. There was no hidden piece of paper tucked away. Having started, I checked the rest. Also negative. Nor was there anything tucked down the sides of the two leather armchairs.

On the oak desk there was a BBC 'Master' computer with a disc drive and container of floppy discs. I looked through the titles on the discs. They were all commercially produced; either games or educational programmes with the 'read only' flaps sealed – nothing personal of Rachel's. Similarly in the desk drawer, just a few old ball points; no junk, no clutter. It was beginning to look as if my search for clues about Rachel was doomed to frustration. Then I noticed a piece of card under the computer monitor.

I pounced on it. It was a ticket for the rock festival at Glastonbury, dated June last year. Rachel had obviously wanted to keep the ticket but why had she hidden it? Was it something Mummy didn't approve of?

I went into the bedroom hoping it would yield a better harvest of information than I'd gathered so far. This room was decorated with pretty, flowery wallpaper. The curtains had frills and tie-backs, and there were frilly pillows on the large single bed. There was no flotsam and jetsam on the floor in here either, but what did catch my eye was the china doll in Victorian costume on a shelf above the bed. A headless teddy bear sitting next to the doll added a rather gruesome note to the scene.

Next to them, on the same shelf, were two old riding hats. Judging from the size of the smaller, Rachel must have been under four years old when she first rode. There was an empty space on the corner of the shelf.

After staring dubiously at the shelf for a while I went to examine the contents of the wardrobe.

As I expected the fitted wardrobe was well stocked with costly clothes. There were plenty of outfits with expensive labels; Next suits, and brightly coloured Benetton leisure wear. There was a black leather jacket, fancy looking denims and denim jackets, mini skirts, tights, leggings, a couple of silk shirts, several pairs of shoes – all from Bally – and a pair of black boots. It was clear that there were two types of clothing in the wardrobe, classic clothes chosen by Mummy for formal occasions and things Rachel had chosen herself, some of them with Miss Selfridge labels.

I pulled out one of the classic smart suits, a black watch tartan skirt with matching boxy jacket. To my surprise it still had the shop labels on it. It must have cost several hundred pounds but Rachel had never worn it. I put it back next to the white bridesmaid dress that she'd worn in the photo Elsworth had given me. The only clothes which showed signs of use were her riding things.

Pictures of ponies, pictures of Rachel at gymkhanas – her fringe of straight dark hair poking out under her helmet, Pony Club trophies and rosettes dominated the bedroom. It seemed as if Andrew Thwaite had been a straight replacement for horses in Rachel's affections. There were no pictures of other boys or even the inevitable pop groups.

Rachel was like a mirage, she seemed to lose reality and definition the closer I got to her. As she passed through adolescence she hadn't bought much which reflected her own tastes. There wasn't a single book or film that would have taxed a fourteen-year-old.

In the dressing-table drawer there was a very expensive Cartier gold watch inscribed 'All Our Love – Mummy and Daddy', presumably an eighteenth-birthday present. There was also a gold chain and matching bracelet, and a dainty pair of diamond ear-rings. These were all still in their Boodle and Dunthorne's boxes. Not in a box there was a little gold bracelet inscribed 'Rachel' which she must have worn as a baby. One interesting piece was a signet ring with the same crest that was on the rocking horse.

As well as these parental gifts there was a large chocolate box full of cheap costume jewellery that Rachel had bought herself: leather strips with wooden beads on, brightly coloured enamel dangly ear-rings, large chunky plastic rings, enamel rings. It was reassuring to see that left to herself Rachel had some normal tastes.

There were no diaries wedged under the mattress or under the bed. The water tank in the toilet was a sealed unit. There was nothing stuck to the underside of any of the drawers. There were no loose floorboards: the rooms had fitted carpets anyway.

Rachel must be an excessively neat person, there was no trace of spillages on the carpets, no sign of chewing gum, no spilt make-up. The place was immaculate, like an exhibition in a furniture store.

There was an audio system, but I didn't have a screwdriver to dismantle it so I contented myself with looking at it. There didn't seem to be anything tucked away in the loudspeakers or internal spaces. I couldn't find out what her taste in music was because, as with the books and films, there was nothing that looked recently bought. It looked as if Rachel had cleared all her more recent acquisitions from the suite, leaving it as a shrine to her early childhood. Perhaps there was nothing personal here because she didn't intend coming back.

Going back into the study I checked out the computer and television. Again there was no evidence of tampering.

I was getting desperate. I thought about her school career; might there be a clue there? Maybe the girl was slightly retarded. After all, Elsworth had raved about her beauty, not her intelligence, when he hired me. However, evidence was better than guesswork – in the back of the wardrobe there was a box containing her old exercise books. The writing was extremely tiny, about thirty words to a line compared to the normal eight to ten. I knew this signified something, probably that Rachel was repressed. The marks and teachers' comments were uniformly good – 'Well done Rachel!', '10/10'; the earlier books were plastered with gold stars.

I also spotted some academic certificates among the Pony Club trophies – 'Best Girl in Fourth Year', 'Governors' Prize for French', and some music certificates. She played the flute. She hadn't taken it with her, it was still in its box, so she wasn't busking for her living in some shopping arcade.

I was getting a picture of Rachel in my mind and it wasn't a picture I liked. A girl smothered in wealth unable to express her own personality, repressed by over-caring parents who'd given her everything except the freedom to be herself.

I sat on the bed to think for a moment. No human being, particularly a teenager, leaves so little trace of their personality in a room they'd occupied for years as Rachel seemed to have done. Even a Trappist monk must mark the passing of the years by scoring a line with his finger nail on the wood of his hard bed. I just wasn't searching thoroughly enough.

I stared at a sampler on the wall with the name 'RACHEL' embroidered in red silk.

So far as these rooms were concerned Rachel might as well be a creature of her parents' imagination, a phantom child they'd dreamed up and conjured into reality with their money.

She was real though, I had plenty of evidence of that from independent sources.

The only thing in the room that was less than perfect was the headless old teddy. I picked it off the shelf and gave it a squeeze.

Bingo! There was something in it. Inserting two fingers in the neck I prised a flat box and a softish lump of some substance from the torso. The box was an opened 12-pack of Durex Elite condoms with one missing. The softish substance was a block of cannabis; good quality stuff too, still fresh. It looked as if Rachel's misadventure with the cannabis plant at the hall of residence had a less innocent explanation than had been claimed. A girl who hid the weed in her teddy bear must have known what the plant was.

I pushed them back into the bear and replaced it as I'd found it. I gave the china doll an experimental rattle but it wasn't concealing anything. There may have been other things hidden but it would take more time than I had to find them. It was a relief to have found something that indicated that Rachel had an existence independent of her parents.

Given the fact that Rachel had moved into a hall of residence it wasn't surprising that there were so few personal things in her rooms, but there should have been a few letters, postcards from friends, something with a few names and addresses on. It was almost as if some one had been through the rooms with a fine tooth-comb removing anything which might have given me a lead.

Dee Elsworth came back upstairs. 'There's nothing from any of her friends, they've not seen her or heard from her for weeks. Most of them are away at college or university. Some of their parents are going to get in touch later.'

'Well I didn't expect much, she'd have probably got in touch with you first if she was going to get in touch with anyone,' I said, more to comfort her than because I believed it.

'Can you tell me more about Rachel yourself? What's her main interest in life at the moment? Your husband said she gets enthusiasms.'

'Yes, she does. Rachel's an unusual girl in some ways. She gets totally absorbed in what she's doing . . .'

'Well isn't that a good thing?' I suggested.

'In a way it is, but Harold and I feel that Rachel would have benefited if we'd had other children. That's why we've always encouraged her to have friends to stay for weekends.'

I began to be puzzled. What was Dee hinting at?

'Look Mrs Elsworth, er. . . . Dee, I'm sorry but you'll have to speak more plainly, you're not getting through to me. Are you saying there's something wrong with Rachel?'

'No, no. She's perfectly normal. It's just that she takes things a bit too seriously at times . . . Well, there were one or two little things . . . She's a bit more success-orientated than the normal nineteen-year-old. She's very self-possessed, wants to be the best at everything she turns her hand to . . . very competitive.'

'All right, but aren't lots of teenagers competitive? Surely that's not a cause for concern?' I still couldn't see what the problem was. Rachel's mother was obviously not prepared to explain.

'My husband said you have no children of your own . . . I'm not saying I'm an expert myself . . .' Dee hesitated. 'Look come back to the lounge and I'll try to explain.'

She led me back downstairs. I wondered what there was about Rachel which needed such explanation. At every stage of this enquiry complications increased. Once again I was being reproached for not having children and not being able to understand teenagers yet I was a lot closer in age to Rachel than her father was. The problem was that they were both so absorbed in her life that they couldn't see the wood for the trees. They didn't see that she needed space to grow apart from them. Rachel's situation didn't seem very different from my own at that age. It could be that I was understanding her a lot better than her parents were.

When we reached the lounge Elsworth had made himself scarce, not difficult in a house this size. This case was definitely a breakthrough for Pimpernel Investigations – most of my previous customers lived in council flats or suburban semis. Dee really put herself out to explain her missing daughter to me. She brought us tea and biscuits and tried to put me at my ease. Her treatment of me was a great deal better than the disdainful way in which her husband had dealt with me.

'I'm sorry David,' she said, 'I realise that it was rather crass of me to suggest you didn't understand. It might be better if you tell me what impression you've formed about Rachel and then I can try to give you some perspective.'

'Don't apologize, the customer is always right!' I said with a smile. 'You're right. Well what do I think about Rachel?. . . She seems rather impersonal, as if her life was a blank page until Andy Thwaite came along . . .' I could see that this wasn't going down too well, so I struggled to re-phrase what I'd said.

'By "impersonal" I mean, she seems repressed. There's not much sign of other interests apart from horses . . .' I knew what I meant but I was floundering for a way to say that Dee's daughter appeared to be totally characterless, a cipher cocooned by wealth against the normal troubles of day to day living.

'Teenagers usually leave lots of traces of their existence, lots of mess . . .'

Dee looked at me sharply. I thought she was going to order me out of her home.

'I think you're on the right track. What I was trying to say is that Rachel's very contemptuous of the idea of failure. She's always determined to achieve perfection in what she does. I don't know whether you noticed that most of those rosettes were for first place. She's got no tolerance of failure, in herself or other people. It's as if she's always got to be perfect . . . There's only one broken thing in her bedroom – I expect you noticed . . .'

'The teddy,' I said.

'Yes, she ripped its head off in a tantrum when I wouldn't let her have her own way. She was only seven, but she grieved for that bear as if it was a real person. I thought she'd forget about it and let me get rid of it but she never has. There haven't been many tantrums since either. I think Harold and I have been afraid of provoking her.'

I nodded encouragingly and Dee continued with her revelations.

'Rachel isn't Harold's daughter but she's more like him in many ways than if she was his natural daughter. They're both perfectionists, both get embarrassed by failure in others. I sometimes think that in some ways I've been a disappointment to the pair of them. Anyway Harold believes in Rachel's future. He thinks she's going to amount to something and I do too. We've both believed in her, from an early age,' she said firmly, as if to deny the impression that she did not share one hundred per cent her husband's faith in Rachel's destiny.

'At one stage I thought she was going to follow my interests. You know, ballet and things . . . I was a dancer myself before I met my first husband, Rachel's real father. She was quite good but then it just petered out. Her main interest lately has been Andy Thwaite, he's the only thing she ever talks about. Harold hates it . . .'

She paused for a moment to gather her thoughts.

'What we both hate most of all is when she goes up into her room and shuts herself away for long periods. She just sits up there for hours and ignores us. She lives inside her head too much. Harold says he's read about some girls of Rachel's age who sever all contact with their parents. They just disappear and find a life of their own. I thought a boyfriend like Andy would be good for her, that he'd help to bring her down to earth. Harold doesn't agree with me. That's why I'm so worried now Andy's dead. He might have been the anchor fastening her to Manchester and us.'

Dee's explanation of her daughter's personality didn't entirely convince me that she was telling everything she knew. If Rachel had been such a paragon, a child revered by her own parents, why had she cleared off now? There had to be an objective reason for cutting her parents off at this moment.

'How long have you and Mr Elsworth been married then?' I asked.

'You know that Harold isn't her real father. Harold was a university friend of my first husband's older brother.'

This seemed to be an involved story so I settled myself patiently to listen and she went on to explain.

'Rachel's real father was an army officer. He was in the Guards and I'm afraid it's the old story of a well-connected young man marrying the chorus girl. I was on the chorus line in a revue in London, all perfectly respectable despite what some people think. I met Richard Rankine and got married to him at nineteen. His family weren't very pleased but they'd have come round in time. I took elocution lessons and started to become quite the little Sloane Ranger myself, but then Richard had to go and get himself blown up in Northern Ireland. He was an impetuous character.

'I was pregnant with Rachel at the time. Richard's family didn't want much to do with me after his death, they seemed to blame me somehow. I'd hardly known their son for more than six months. They paid me off, gave me a small allowance. That's how I met Harold. He came round with the brother to sort out the financial arrangements. He was already well on his way to the top in the banking world.

'He kept finding excuses to come round to see me. I had a little flat in South Kensington. It was "Sign this, read that . . ." He seemed to be round every few days. Then he helped me to move back up here. I come from Cheshire originally.

'One thing led to another and we got married not long after

Rachel was born. It was so odd him courting a pregnant woman that I think most people thought he must be Rachel's father. Certainly his own parents did, and he never told them otherwise. They gave me a lovely bracelet for Rachel and all kinds of other gifts, some of them quite unsuitable. Then they made Rachel their heir; he was their only child, so she got the lot, and not just from his parents either. There were titled connections of the family through Harold's mother – an earl's granddaughter. Naturally we didn't broadcast the fact that Harold isn't Rachel's father, but his parents have been dead for some time now. It isn't really a secret. Rachel herself has always known the truth. Harold's the only father she's ever known and I'm sure he feels for her just as much as her natural father would have done.'

I didn't tell Dee that she'd shattered my faith in my ability to detect the nuances of the English social classes, but she had. I'd been so certain that she was an upper class lady, 'to the manor born'.

'You're not disappointed in me are you?' she said. 'I do believe you're a snob!'

'No, nothing like that, I just had you placed in a social class above Harold!'

'Well you couldn't be more wrong, Harold's family have been in banking for generations. He's descended from one of those old Quaker families. His grandparents used to say "thee" and "thou". That's why he's so scared of anything which might affect his precious reputation,' she said sadly.

She can't have had a very exciting life married to Harold, I thought.

'But this is all beside the point. Have you found anything out? I want my daughter back, and I don't care if she hasn't a penny to her name!' This was said with much more spirit.

'Yes I have. I feel I know a great deal more about Rachel now and that I can find her. I think she's hiding in Southport. Tell me, how is she off for money? Does she have a credit card or an allowance?'

'Yes she does – both – and that's one of the first things Harold did when we didn't hear from her . . .'

'What? He hasn't cut off her allowance?' I interrupted.

'No, will you let me finish? He checked to see if she was

spending money. I think that's what got him so worried . . . that she isn't. Mind you, she's always been very careful with money, something she's learnt from Harold I suppose. Since she's been with Andy she's never asked for much money from us.'

'I was going to suggest that you cancel her credit cards as a way of making her get in touch with you, but if she isn't using them anyway there doesn't seem much point. I think I'll call it a day now . . . I've done all I can here. Can I ask you to persuade Harold that he'll have to get in touch with the police if I can't find anything, say by Wednesday of next week?'

Dee looked doubtful about her ability to persuade Harold, but I was confident she would. What had started out as a simple missing daughter case was becoming too complicated for me. As I was leaving I did my best to reassure Dee that I believed Rachel had come to no harm, that she was simply lying low waiting for Andy to get in touch. Elsworth reappeared as I was departing. He said nothing. I took this as agreement for me to stay with the case.

As I drove back into Manchester the weather had closed in again and although it was only five in the afternoon it looked like dusk on a winter's day. There was no cricket played at Old Trafford.

I decided to go home for the Minox camera and then into the office to develop the photos I'd taken of Dyer's accounts in what remained of the peace and quiet of a Saturday afternoon in central Manchester.

9

The heavy rain and the recession were keeping the shoppers out of town. I'd no trouble parking on the street outside my office. There was no sign of anyone following me either. I couldn't help feeling a sneaking pleasure over my efforts at the airport. There's something of the hooligan in all of us. Even highly respectable types, like Harold Elsworth, get a kick out of slapstick comedy – though thinking about it, he probably wouldn't. I smiled to myself as I walked up the dark stairway to my gloomy little office.

Developing the photographs in the little cubby hole I used as a studio gave me time to think over the day's events: if there hadn't been that providential downpour I might have been arrested at the airport along with my pursuers. I used the largest size of photographic paper I had for developing the prints. They came out very well. I hung them up to dry and made myself a cup of coffee.

Dyer's finances showed a degree of obscurity. My work on fraud in business over the years has given me some experience. He was banking a lot less than he was taking in, and in the NMP book he was claiming much greater expenses on fees for groups, staff wages, bar staff etc, all paid cash-in-hand, than he was in the first set of books.

Daily costs in each of his six clubs were listed against initials of the club: Pal. for the Paloma, B.P. for the Blue Parrot, Pro. for the Prohibition, C. for the Circus, S.T. for the Sad Thursday, S.J. for Soapy Joe's. In all his clubs the expenditures for damage to fixtures and fittings, sweeteners to bruised bouncers and battered customers were through the roof. A tax inspector would have a field day with these accounts, but that was fine by me. He could fiddle the tax man all he wanted.

There were payments listed to Andy Thwaite, one of his best-paid DJs. He must have had plenty of cash. There was no mention of Rachel and all of Dyer's six clubs were in Manchester, nothing as far away as Southport. Dyer certainly had all his eggs in one basket. One of the clubs, Soapy Joe's, had been closed for two weeks following a riot.

I turned from the accounts to the photos I'd taken from Dyer's vanity collection. Wild Bill Benson's thin face and wobbly moustache leered out. He was raising a glass and smiling at Dyer. This could be interesting to certain people: the picture was probably innocent but the knowing look on Benson's face would take some explaining. Given the speed the press moved these days, from the first smear to the certain proof of guilt by association, Benson's credibility was going to take a battering if this ever came out. Was Dyer blackmailing him?

Why would a smooth operator like Benson let a photographer get near enough to photograph him with Dyer? What was Benson doing in Dyer's company in the first place?

The photo of Dyer with his band of roughs was also interesting. Apart from the pimply Scot and the bouncer with the massive forearms whom I'd christened Spotty Jock and Popeye and who seemed to be Dyer's leading henchmen, I didn't recognise any of them, but they were a rare collection of uglies, oddly mixed up with respectable types. Two of them were displaying tattoos on their muscular arms, one was holding up a clenched fist with letters tattooed on the knuckles. Some of this collection looked as if they'd done plenty of time at the Strangeways Hotel. Probably they were just the rougher end of Dyer's crew of bouncers – but the really weird ones were the businessmen. Why were these impeccably dressed types mingling with Dyer's crew? I put the photos in the pocket of the tracksuit I was still wearing and filed the other information I'd found under 'R' for Rachel. I decided to write a brief summary of events to date and include it in the file. It might come in handy if someone arranged another little accident for me.

When I left the office to drive home it was quite dark although it was still not midsummer and the days were supposed to be lengthening. There were wide pools of water in the streets. Manchester was going to revert to the swamp it had once been unless the local economy improved soon and the council started unblocking the drains, not that that would improve the weather. The early rush of pleasure seekers was just getting underway. I turned under the Mancunian Way past the John Dalton building, and then onto Princess Road. I'd just turned into Mauldeth Road when the car phone rang. I pulled over.

'Hello Dave is that you? It's Sylvia here. Where have you been? I've been trying to get in touch with you all afternoon. I thought the idea of having a car phone was so that people could contact you easily.'

'Well sorry to disappoint you love, but the car phone is for me to get in touch with people. I have an answering service for business calls. I've been busy all afternoon with this and that.' I'd no intention of reporting on my movements to Sylvia. She wasn't my wife or mother and I didn't owe her any explanations. Having escaped from one overbearing female I wasn't anxious to attach myself to another.

'Enough said, sorry I asked,' she said tartly. 'I didn't know you were so touchy. How did you get on at the airport? There was a riot down there I hear.'

'Yeah, there was a fire or some sort of emergency drill. My friend and I spent hours standing in the rain waiting to get back in the terminal,' I answered.

'Haven't you been listening to the news? Four men were arrested on drugs charges. No matter, that isn't what I wanted to talk to you about. Would you like to meet me for a drink somewhere, I want to ask you something,' she said.

'Do you mean right away? I need to get changed before I go out again, I'm only wearing a tracksuit,' I wasn't anxious to return to town.

'Don't be so fussy. I only want to talk to you for a few minutes. We could go to the Masons' Arms on Shudehill. Lots of people go in there after playing squash. Say you'll come. I'll buy the drinks, but I've only got a short time off work before I need to be back at the club.'

'Now Sylvia, you know I can't refuse a lady. I'll be there in about ten minutes. Can you make that? OK. See you.' I drove on to the next break in the central reservation and did a U-turn which took me back into town.

The drive to the Masons took me longer than ten minutes and Sylvia was waiting in the lounge with a pint of Boddington's ready for me when I met her. She was looking luscious in a long red jacket and skirt. She was wearing pearls, big gold ear-rings and a bracelet. Her hair was tied back with a red bow. I felt distinctly underdressed in her company.

She was reading the *Financial Times* when I spotted her. She quickly put it down when I went over.

'Honest love, I would have got in touch with you later,' I said as I gave her a quick kiss. 'I'm a really faithful type.'

'Well I don't exactly jump into bed with every handsome hunk I meet either, but I didn't ask to meet you for more pillow talk; this is business,' she said, all hard and brittle. 'You said you saw Mike taking a young girl home, well I asked him if he'd a girl with him on Thursday night and he's very upset. He thinks you're trying to break his marriage up.'

'What are you talking about, I haven't the least interest —'

'Just shut up a minute, will you? Mike's paranoid at the moment. There's something going on I don't know about, but he's always been sensitive about his marriage. He thinks either his wife or one of his rivals has hired you to dig up some dirt about him.'

'Well I'm sure that wouldn't be difficult,' I sneered, 'but I told you both I was looking for a missing girl and I still am. In fact I'm thinking of going over to Southport tomorrow or Monday to see if I can turn her up. If I can't then her parents will just have to bring the police into it. They've got a lot more resources than I have. Her father will just have to put up with the publicity.'

'Oh Dave, don't go to the police.'

She was actually pleading with me. I didn't feel too delighted that she'd played my questions back to Dyer and now she was trying to interfere with my work.

'Don't you see what this will do to Mike? The press will make a meal out of it. They'll connect Rachel to his clubs. It's just the sort of publicity we don't need right now,' she said.

I didn't see how it was going to affect Dyer directly and was about to tell her so, but her blue eyes looked ready to fill up with tears. She was really devoted to her work for Dyer. I supped the creamy head off my pint of ale and thought about it.

'Look lover, I appreciate that you have to do the best you can for your boss, but I have to think of myself too. Suppose this little rich girl turns up dead somewhere and then it comes out that I'd discouraged her parents from getting in touch with the fuzz earlier. I'd never get work in this town again and the police would bust me on some technicality. In any case I don't see why the press should make waves for Dyer. Thwaite was the romantic interest and he worked in clubs all over the place. Or is there something you haven't been telling me?'

Sylvia looked angry at this suggestion. She was either giving me all she knew or she was a very good actress. I didn't want to upset her. She was the best thing that had happened to me in a long time, a real change after the moody Delise.

She sighed. At that moment I would've believed her if she'd said Mike Dyer was a lay preacher.

'I know you can't stand Mike because he threatened you at the Paloma but he's not like that normally,' she said earnestly. 'He's terrified he's going to lose all he's built up. There are a lot of people waiting to see him take a tumble, then they'll all rub their fat hands and say "I told you so". He's always been a good boss to me.'

'All right darling, I'll stop being boring about Dyer, if you'll just lighten up a bit yourself. I don't need to look for trouble.' As I spoke I could see the tension fade out of her eyes, and she smiled.

'Would you agree to meet him, just for a chat to sort things out. I think he does know something more about Thwaite and Rachel.' Sylvia had the pleading tone in her voice again.

'Proper little peace ambassador aren't you? But I haven't forgotten that he told me his boyos would hammer me into the ground last time we met. I'll meet him somewhere neutral and he's got to be on his own.'

'Thanks Dave, I'm sure Mike will agree. You won't thump him or anything will you?'

''Course I won't – what do you take me for? Do you know Ardwick Green? There's a pub next to St Luke's church, well it used to be a church, it's some sort of social centre now. If Mike goes and parks in the car park at eight o'clock tonight, I'll go and see what he has to say. I'll cruise up and down the green a few times just to see the coast is clear.'

Sylvia held up her hand and I slapped it in confirmation of the deal.

I finished my drink. It went down well but as I'd had nothing to eat since Mrs Elsworth's soup I didn't want to start doing any serious drinking on an empty stomach. I needed ballast.

Sylvia said she didn't have to work on Monday, how did I feel about her coming to Southport with me. We could book into a nice hotel on Sunday night and come back on Tuesday. Sounded all right to me.

I told Sylvia I would have to love her and leave her as I wanted to go home for a quick bite to eat and change before meeting Manchester's own Mr Nightlife. I didn't tell her that I also wanted to pick up some 'sports' equipment', namely my baseball bat, in case things didn't work out as nicely as she thought they would.

I drove home for the second time that day, taking a different route to the one I'd followed before, along Deansgate and Chester Road. When I got in I put some pasta on to boil for ten minutes while I showered and changed.

I put my black leather jacket and dark Bloggs jeans on with a dark t-shirt. If I needed to hold the baseball bat behind my back the floppy jeans would give me maximum cover.

The pasta was tender when I came back into the kitchen. I took it off the boil and emptied a can of tomatoes, olive oil, mozzarella cheese, basil and black pepper into a frying pan. It only took a few minutes until the cheese was runny then I poured the whole lot over the pasta and put it in the oven for a few minutes. While it was cooking I went to give Ted Blake a ring.

He was at home. He hadn't started his usual Saturday evening pub crawl. I asked him if he'd like to come to Old Trafford to see Lancashire play Yorkshire the next day, weather permitting. It would mean him having to get up before eleven o'clock but he would be able to carry on drinking if he brought his own freezer box full of canned lager. Ted was more than willing. He also wanted to know why I'd woken him up in the middle of the night to ask how old Mike Dyer was. I promised to reveal all at Old Trafford.

When I went to the oven and took the pasta out it was done to perfection. There as far too much for one person to eat. I did my best, and then washed the meal down with a strong cup of instant coffee.

All seemed above board with Dyer but I knew more about

him than Sylvia did. A man who could be so devious in his financial dealings was capable of any sly trick. Should I phone Jim McNeil and take him up on the offer of one of his giant German shepherds? Not a good idea, I'd be worrying more about the dog than about myself if push turned to shove.

It might be a good idea to phone Jim anyway and let him know where I was going. Twice in the last two days someone had been out to get me, and the odds were on Dyer as the mastermind. Most likely he wanted to scare me off an enquiry that might embarrass him in ways even Sylvia couldn't guess.

Getting sexually entwined with somebody involved in the course of an enquiry didn't come under the 'highly recommended procedures' column in the detectives handbook but sometimes I thought that old book needed rewriting. It was designed to make the world grey and boring.

Life with Sylvia certainly wasn't that. Poor old Delise seemed very dull and domestic in comparison. She must have been horrified when a female opened the door to her at my flat. It served her right, she'd been happy enough to tell me she'd replaced me. She wouldn't be able to rest now until she'd altered the script back to the original ending. I'd be hearing from Delise again.

I phoned Jim. He asked me how my back was. I told him I heal rapidly and that I was going to meet the man who might be responsible at Ardwick Green tonight. When he offered to come with me I told him the meet was intended to be a peace conference.

He told me to be sure to phone him when I got back or neither he nor Margaret would be able to sleep. I tried again to reassure him that the meeting was just routine.

As I took my sports bag out of the wardrobe I could feel the pasta sitting heavily on my stomach. I might have been better with just a sandwich after all. I checked the bag to see that everything was there. The baseball bat lay on top of my sports kit. I'm licensed to carry firearms and own a Beretta 92SB-C which holds thirteen 9mm parabellum rounds in its compact, double column magazine. I would only wear it in public if I was on official body-guarding duty and if a nosy copper found me carrying a concealed weapon on my way into Manchester on a Saturday night I might find myself looking for another line of work. So the bat in the sports kit was the best thing I could do. If anyone objected to me having it in the car I could say I'd left it there after a game with one of my nephews. It was a lot more explainable than a loaded automatic in a shoulder holster.

When I got to Ardwick Green I was nice and early. I'd chosen the location because it was handy for the end of the Mancunian Way. There was a pale-coloured contractor's van parked close to the church, quite some way from the deserted pub. The churchyard had been annexed by the pub. Notices warned that anyone using it who wasn't a customer was liable to be wheel-clamped. There were three old cars and no one moving about.

Apart from the flats round the corner this area of Manchester, once a teeming district, was now de-populated. The pavements were broken. There were areas of waste ground where streets had been bulldozed. Some elegant Georgian houses remained further up the street. The waste lands were barricaded by earth-works to obstruct the travelling people.

The desolate environment was eerie. I felt a twinge of nerves. Sylvia had to be on the level, she wouldn't be setting me up. Anyway, I'd chosen the spot for the meet. My eyes kept straying back to the contractor's van. I stopped behind it and peered through the dirty rear window. I could make out some bundled up shapes, they looked like piles of old canvas. Satisfied, I drove on.

I kept circling until bang on eight Dyer's big white Mercedes pulled into the car park. I got out of my car, slipped up the narrow path beside the church and looked over the wall into the car park. There was no one with Dyer. He was lighting a big cigar. I slipped back to the car and drove in next to him. I gave him a friendly wave as I got out, concealing the bat held loosely between two fingers behind my back. I walked crab-wise to his side of the car, carefully shielding myself from the fading light filtering into the gloomy space.

He opened his window and blew a lungful of cigar smoke at me, part of his Mr Big act. Not a very friendly way to begin a peace conference. I tightened my grip on the bat. His first words to me weren't very friendly either.

'Right you sickening little pimp, how much is it going to cost me to get you off my back?' he snarled. His face was twisted with anger. I took a step back.

'Who are you calling a pimp, that's your trade not mine,' I shouted back at him. Nothing like putting your cards on the table.

'Do you deny that you're trying to squeeze money out of me like that worm Thwaite?' he growled.

'So it was you who murdered him then! I thought you didn't show any surprise when I told you he was dead.' I was watching his right hand in case he tried to go for a weapon, but he was gripping the fat cigar, so I felt safe. My accusation seemed to shock Dyer. It struck me that he thought I was a friend of Thwaite's.

'What are you on about? You crazy fool. The police have said it was suicide. He was trying to involve me in a deal with his future father-in-law, only it didn't come off, did it? Elsworth wasn't having any of it. He was only prepared to lend me money on normal commercial terms,' Dyer rasped away at me, his tone less hostile.

'What was the deal then?' I asked.

'He was supposed to use Rachel to get her Daddy to put money into the business. Strung me along for months. Then when I go to see Daddy he doesn't know me from Adam, only prepared to advance money if I give the bank a controlling interest and a preferential claim on my assets if anything goes wrong.' Dyer was incensed by the injustice done to him. I could imagine the scene with him trying to tip the wink to Elsworth that he was the man who knew his daughter's boyfriend. Elsworth must have thought he was dealing with a loony.

'Well I'm really, really sorry for you Dyer. It couldn't have happened to a nicer guy, but it doesn't explain why you set the Afro-Caribbean heavy squad onto me,' I countered.

'What the fuck are you on about?' he demanded.

I explained this mornings events at the airport.

'God! You're a real knobhead, Cunane!' he exploded. 'Don't you know who's been trying to close me down for months? Don't you ever read the papers? The last people in the world I'd send after you would be our inner-city friends from Moss Side, they're the buggers who're trying to put me out of business. Hell'll freeze over before I employ any of those bastards to scrub the loos out in my clubs, let alone tidy up a nasty piece of work like you.'

He seemed to be getting amusement out of our meeting now.

'You're telling me you know nothing about the fake suicide or the disappearance of Rachel Elsworth, but in that case who was the girl you took home with you on Thursday night?' This was a stab in the dark but it might help to keep Dyer barking up the wrong tree. So far he'd given me quite a bit of information I hadn't known before, but still nothing on Rachel.

'What the hell's it got to do with you? That was Jock's bit of fluff . . . Bob Lane thought someone was following us. It was you wasn't it?'

I didn't see much point in disagreeing so I nodded my head. Bob Lane must be the character I'd labelled as Popeye. Shoving his fat cigar back in his ugly mouth Elsworth took out a wad of notes from his top pocket. He riffled through the thick wad and then put it back.

'I was going to offer you money to get you to stop pestering me,' he said with the cigar clenched between his teeth. 'I know nothing about this bloody Elsworth girl except that she doesn't have much influence with her Daddy.' As he spoke he threw the partly smoked cigar down on the ground, raising a shower of sparks. 'All you've earned yourself now is a bloody good hiding.'

He wound his window up.

I turned towards the street to follow his glance. Three men were leaping from the back of the contractor's van.

It was a set up after all.

I looked at Dyer. He was smiling broadly, licking his fat lips at the prospect of fun. The cigar must have been the signal.

There was nowhere to run to. In my cleverness at choosing a meeting place I'd boxed myself in, well and truly. The only point in my favour was that in the narrow space between the cars where I stood the three of them would have to come at me one at a time unless Dyer joined in. I kept the bat behind my back and retreated a couple of feet further back so Dyer couldn't catch me by slamming his door into my legs.

As the first man came within range, arms extended to grab me, I swung the bat round and taking a two handed grip stabbed at his beer-belly where it flopped out at the top of his low-slung belt. He folded like a deck-chair and slammed into the ground in a heap.

The other two, rushing forward, were unable to stop; or at least the first of them was. Stumbling over his prone partner, and cursing vilely, Popeye lashed out with his right fist in a wild attempt to make contact.

These boys had been used to intimidating teenagers and old ladies for too long. I swung the bat down on Popeye's wrist with all my strength. There was an audible crack and he started screaming.

This had all only taken a few seconds but it was enough for Dyer, he revved his motor and started backing out as fast as he could, just missing the thug on the ground. I ran forward and smashed the end of my bat into his windscreen; the glass shattered but he was going too fast for me to make contact with him.

He roared off down the street leaving his deflated bouncers to their fate.

Jock, the last of the trio, stepped forward holding the palms of both hands towards me. My heart sank, I thought he must have a black belt in kung-fu. Holding his hands palm outwards, he bent down, got hold of the beer-bellied character, and dragged the groaning slob to the van.

No one had come out of the pub during this encounter. It wasn't the sort of neighbourhood where you came out to look when you heard screaming in the streets.

Jock came back for Popeye, or Bob Lane, as I now supposed he was called. I was on my guard but Jock circled me warily, he'd no intention of adding lumps to his collection of spots. He'd no stomach for tackling someone who might thump him back.

Using his full vocabulary of Anglo-Saxon, Bob 'Popeye' Lane indicated exactly what he thought of Jock's performance. With a friendly 'Fuck you too then, you wee hairy wally!' Jock abandoned his mate with the same speed that his boss had shown in abandoning him.

I was left alone in the car park with a weeping and cursing thug at my feet.

I should have become a doctor as my mother used to hope

and pray I would. When I looked at the cringing figure of Popeye at my feet I felt a twinge of pity which was mixed with calculation. Perhaps he might let slip one or two little extra details.

'Come on, I'll give you a lift to the casualty department at M.R.I. You've got a broken wrist there.'

Popeye responded to me with the same terms of fondness he's used to his partner, if anything a little more colourfully, adding the s-word to the c-word and the f-word and inviting me to retreat up my own anus.

'Come on,' I said soothingly. 'You don't want to hang around here until the police arrive. Come on Popeye.' This use of the nickname I'd invented seemed to galavanize him.

'How do you know my nickname?' he gritted between clenched teeth. 'Who are you?'

'Come on, get in the car. It's only a couple of minutes drive to the hospital.' I waved the bat to show him the way, and he stumbled to his feet. I showed him round to the passenger side and, pushing the seat as far forward as it would go, shoved him into the front seat. He hardly had room to breathe by the time I got the seat belt round him. He'd no room to get at me with his unbroken left arm and anyway he'd already shown he wasn't left-handed.

I took my time as I headed through the city centre towards Oxford Road. 'Where did you get those black eyes then?' I asked. 'Did you fall out with a little old lady?' He explained between bouts of cursing that Jock had given them to him because he'd left the burglar alarm off and let one of those Moss Side hooligans into the boss's house early this morning.

'They've got rough ways of showing their disapproval in your mob then,' I commiserated.

'Aye, they're a rough bunch of lads that work for NMP,' he admitted.

'What work do they do then?'

'Club doormen, what do you think? Bunch of bloody nursery nurses?'

'Well your friend with the big gut performed better as a doormat than as a doorman,' I said.

'That wanker's no friend of mine!'

'Did you catch the guy who broke in?' I asked innocently.

'No, but we knew where he came from and some of the boys went round and taught them a lesson they won't forget in a hurry.' Self-pity and pain had made him incautious but when I asked him if he knew anything about Rachel and Thwaite he clammed up. I dropped him at Nelson Street just a few yards from the entrance to the Casualty Department.

Just out of curiosity I turned off Oxford Road and drove through Moss Side on my way home. I turned up Alexandra Road a short distance from the dreaded Charlton Close with its gang of thugs, the Charlton Youth Group – Charlies for short.

The word gang was too strong to describe the Charlies; sellers of crack-cocaine and heroin, they were more of a loose federation of deadly rivals, fiercely independent capitalists to a man. None of them would hesitate to shoot at a fellow 'gang member' who invaded his pitch. They had absolutely no loyalty to each other. I hadn't the faintest proof that the men who'd been after me at the airport were connected to the Charlies, except that they were the biggest band of drug dealers in the area and that many of them were black: the only predominantly black gang in Manchester.

There was nothing unusual happening apart from the number of patrol cars around. The houses were all new and looked a lot better than the derelict streets round Ardwick Green.

When I arrived back at my flat the first thing I saw was the McNeil's battered old VW Beetle parked outside. They both got out and scurried over to me. They had the bigger of the two German Shepherds, Esau, with them. Jacob must be back at home guarding the ranch. I invited them in for a drink, but Jim insisted that they weren't stopping, they only wanted to see that I was all right and leave the dog with me. They wouldn't take any argument from me, so in the end I accepted the loan of Esau. He trotted after me and I bedded him down outside my bedroom.

With the heavy cheese pasta and the Boddington's bitter swilling around in my stomach I felt unsettled. It was too early for bed even though I hadn't had much sleep last night. I sat in my living room and looked at the blank wall.

The events of the day milled around in my head. Sylvia

hadn't set me up, had she? If I'd said the right words to Dyer I'd have just come away with a handful of money and no bruises. That was her scenario – peace talks. She was just acting like a loyal employee and guarding her boss's back. It seemed like he'd wanted to pay me off to avoid bad publicity.

In that case, why had he turned up with a trio of heavies? They must have been hiding in that van for at least half an hour. So assume that everything Dyer had said was a load of lies. He'd used Sylvia to get me in position for the threatened hammering. Why? He objected on principle to being asked questions by a small-time private investigator and he probably had lots of things to hide. He'd lied when he said he knew nothing about the brothers at the airport this morning. He'd lied about Rachel and Andy. He'd lied to Sylvia about a peace meeting.

I concluded that I needed to know more about Dyer and his methods if I was to come through this job with nothing worse than a few bruises on my back. Reluctantly, I picked up the phone and dialled my parents' number.

'Dad I need a bit of help, I need the answers to some questions,' I said, biting my lip. The old man's always ready enough to help but not in a subordinate capacity. He likes to be in charge.

'Yes, that's the only time I hear from you David, when you want something.' As usual Dad's reply was unfair. I'm a dutiful son and always keep in touch. He was the one who liked to break things off when he wanted to register disapproval at something I'd done.

'Well anyway Dad, could you ask your friends about Mike Dyer? I need to know everything I can about him,' I continued.

'You mean the club owner? Out of your usual league aren't you?' There was a pause while he considered. 'All right, I'll see what I can do. I'll phone you back as soon as I can.'

We exchanged the usual barbed pleasantries about our mutual health and about Mother and then he hung up. Dad could be relied on. Although he made a fuss about it, he enjoyed being involved.

Feeling more relaxed now that I'd set the wheels in motion against Dyer I went to bed, but just as sleep was about to descend a nasty thought struck me. What if it had been Sylvia who'd sent those men after me this morning?

Before sleep finally came I convinced myself it couldn't have been her. Dee Elsworth had also known I was going to the airport, did I suspect her? My movements weren't exactly conducted in secret. If I was able to follow Dyer home what was to stop him posting someone outside my flat?

It had to be him, with his threats of hammerings and good hidings. His account books showed he had something to hide. Once I'd mentioned Thwaite to him the alarm bell must have started ringing. Perhaps Andy Thwaite had got himself too involved in Dyer's crooked finances for his own good. Until I turned up Dyer must have been priding himself on having neatly erased Thwaite from the record.

10

Shadowy figures were chasing me across a grey landscape. I was trying to run but every time I put my foot down it stuck to the ground and I had to struggle to move it. Trapped and waiting for the blow to fall I had an intense feeling of dread.

Waking in a cold sweat, I opened my eyes and there was Esau lying like a log across my legs. I kicked off the duvet and jumped out of bed.

He followed me into the kitchen. I took the bag of ground up meat, offal and God knows what else Jim had left as food for his monster hound and slopped out a dollop, then poured myself a glass of orange juice.

Esau made sickeningly short work of his breakfast, the meat and gristle going down in rapid, jerky swallows.

The day didn't look very promising, there were banks of cloud rolling in from the west. Regardless of the weather, the dog needed exercise so I put on my cycling shorts and vest. I improvised a lead from an old clothes line plaited into a thick rope about twelve feet long. One end went round his chain collar.

The dog trotted down to the garage behind me with pathetic eagerness. I tied him up to a drain pipe while I got the bike out. It had survived unchained for two days, still covered in mud.

I set off towards the Meadows. This was going to be an adventure. Esau padded along beside me, easily keeping pace. When we reached the Meadows I let him off the lead. I was going to need all my attention to circumvent the pools of water and mud left by yesterday's downpour.

When we arrived at the footbridge at Jackson's Boat the river was still in full spate, churning angrily between its banks. I decided not to risk riding along the bank with the dog so I crossed the bridge and passed the lonely inn, also called Jackson's Boat, which was once the haunt of Jacobites and smugglers.

Esau was covered in mud but he was enjoying himself. There

was no sign of ambushers this morning. There were joggers and early morning dog walkers but no bikers. The dog loping along with me roused an unaccustomed feeling of companionship. I decided to leave the river bank before I started getting sentimental about him.

When we got back to the flats I had been out for about forty minutes.

I got the hose out and washed the mud off my bike, then feeling brave sprayed Esau as well. He submitted cheerfully to a drenching in cold water and shook himself off all over me. Back in the flat I rubbed him down with an old bath towel and then had a shower myself. He tried to get in the shower with me, he must have thought it was a great game. I dried him and myself off again.

Dressed in grey casual cotton trousers, a polo shirt and a cotton crew necked Aran sweater, I made myself my Sunday morning breakfast of bacon, two eggs, fried tomato and three slices of thickly buttered toast. The dog watched me while I ate, his eyes moving from plate to mouth and back to plate with the regularity of a metronome. I might have been the first human being Esau had ever seen eating.

I rounded up my dirty clothes and put them in the washer and then vacuumed round; lots of dog hair everywhere. The cooker hob was still gleaming from my assault of three days ago so it didn't need any attention. I took out my coolbox and loaded up eight chilled cans of Yorkshire bitter. Ted Blake was up and active when I phoned to check. We arranged to meet outside Statham House at the entrance to the Lancashire County ground.

The McNeils were also in when I phoned them to say I was bringing Esau back.

As I left the flats clutching my coolbox of beer in one hand and the German shepherd's lead in the other I bumped into Fiona and Finbar Salway going out to church. The twins spend quite a lot of time doing that. Whatever you might think about their religion it hasn't made them glum. They were both far too cheery for that time of day. I nearly made them late by stopping to chat for ten minutes.

They admired Esau, though I could see that Fiona was terrified that he was going to jump her. I heard myself saying all the usual things which owners of savage-looking dogs say about how harmless their pets are. I explained that friends had lent him to me so that I could go down on the Meadows unmolested by lunatics on motor bikes.

Finbar found plenty to say about my unwise comment. 'I knew it wasn't an accident. You should have let me get the police, or at least come with you next time you go down there.'

He's a combative character. Despite a military career in which he'd been wounded several times, he's always ready for violent action; yet he's the kindest of men.

I mumbled an affirmative reply. I was anxious to get on my way but Finbar's indignation on my behalf was not easily assuaged. He seemed more upset about it all than I was.

'It's a disgrace if able-bodied men like you have to equip themselves with a big dog before they can go out . . . and don't think the dog is going to protect you. I know someone who was burgled even though they had a German shepherd in the house.'

I smiled at the idea of burglars stepping over sleeping shepherds.

'It's all right for you to laugh, but mark my words we're going back to the days when every man had to carry weapons in public,' he commented.

'Take no notice of him. He's got a bee in his bonnet,' laughed his twin. Then looking at her watch Fiona realised that they were going to be late for church and the pair of them scuttled off.

On my way into Chorlton I took advantage of the car wash at the Jet garage. I tied Esau up to a fence where he sat barking fiercely while I stripped some of grime from the Nissan. When I was finished we both hopped in the car and I was round at NcNeil's in a few minutes. Jacob greeted the return of his brother by barking loudly even before I had crossed the threshold.

Jim opened the door and a reunion took place. Big and solid as Jim was the dog got its paws on his shoulders and was pushing him back down the hall as it licked his face. I don't think I could cope with so much canine affection.

When I approached the cricket ground there was already a jam even though I was early. I parked in the Stretford Grammar

School playing fields and crossed to the corner of Greatstone Road. There were hundreds of others with all sizes of coolboxes heading in the same direction. As I scanned the crowd I picked out the burly figure of Ted Blake ploughing his way through the crowd like a battleship at a regatta. He was hard to miss in his bright red anorak. I met up with him and we went into the ground.

Lancashire won the toss and put themselves in to bat. All around us cans were being opened and a day's serious drinking begun. Ted like lager spiked with occasional shots of whisky from his hip flask. I preferred bitter, so we each stuck to our own.

'How are things on the Dyer front then, Dave? You don't seem to be the worse for wear.' Ted started a long slow-paced conversation which matched the slow pace of the over rate. I didn't tell him how close I had come to being hospitalized by Dyer.

'Do you know if Dyer is tied in with the Moss Side gangs?' I asked as a ripple of applause greeted a Lancashire boundary.

'You must be joking, they're trying to put him out of business,' he replied scornfully. I could tell from his tone that he was already getting quite a buzz from the booze.

'Just who is trying to put him out of business and why?' I asked.

'Look Dave, don't you read the papers? Everyone knows that these drug pushers would like to move their act from Moss Side right into the town centre and that they want to take over the club scene.' His face was almost as red as his jacket. What he said confirmed Dyer's story.

'Well I didn't know it. Anyway which Moss Side gang is it? There's more than one you know,' I said.

'They say it's this Charlton Youth Group. You know, a group of young men with something to sell. They're tired of being contained in Moss Side. If they could get control of even one of the big clubs in town they could really begin to shift their goods, and I don't just mean a few Ecstasy pills,' he said. 'There's no chance that Dyer's involved with them.'

Ted stated his conclusion with such an air of conviction that I hesitated to challenge him, but it didn't fit with what had happened in the last few days.

'I wouldn't be so sure about that. I think that's what he wants everyone to believe, but that he's really tied up with them in some way. Think about it, what's the biggest profit generator among the 18 to 25 age group, bigger than music, bigger than clothes? It's got to be drugs. The overheads are so low.'

'That's true Sport. But, where the profit is high, the risk is great. Dyer's a legitimate businessman now, whatever he may have been. He'd lose his clubs and everything he's got if a link could be proved between him and one of these drug gangs. You're going to need hard evidence before you get people to believe Dyer is a big wheel in the drug scene,' Ted said sceptically.

'Do the letters NMP mean anything to you then?' I asked.

'North Mercia Proprietary, my old cock, they're a group of developers who have their fingers in half the property deals in the city. They haven't been doing to well recently. There's a big mob of them: solicitors, estate agents, speculators, planning officers. All very respectable on the surface but if you get between them and their chance of early retirement to the Costa del Crime, heaven help you.

'They build up packages of old property like redundant churches, terraced streets, derelict factories then clear the whole site and sell it to some multi-national retailer,' he said.

'Well what's naughty about that? Sounds quite public spirited.'

'For a private detective you're very innocent,' he remarked. 'The naughty bit is that parts of their package might not want to sell. You might get two derelict industrial sites separated by streets of privately owned houses. Each site on its own is too small to be worth much, so they get them cheap. Then they lean on the householders to sell up and the council to re-zone the area as commercial. Usually the council's only too keen to cooperate. They generate much more income from a retail park than they do from a derelict slum.'

'I see, and if you have a whole derelict city it must help if you have advance noticed about which particular parts the City Council is willing to re-zone,' I said.

Raucous shouts of 'Howzat, howzat!' followed by groans interrupted our conversation just as it was getting interesting.

The information I was getting from Ted, while it was useful, was not going to be helpful in bringing Dyer to grief. I felt my lip curl as I thought of him sitting in his Mercedes licking his lips in anticipation of me being beaten to jelly.

Ted must have seen me pulling faces.

'You don't want to take it so hard Dave. If Dyer's doing something wrong you can be sure he'll eventually over-reach himself and come to a nasty end,' Ted said.

'You shouldn't be so complacent. How many lives is he going to wreck before he's stopped? I'm certain he killed Andrew Thwaite but it isn't convenient for some people to accept that.'

'I thought that was it, I should've known when you phoned me in the middle of the night to ask what year Dyer was born. Dave, you must be a brick short of a load if you think the police would deliberately cover up a murder. They don't like Dyer much either,' Ted said.

'Suppose I told you I had a picture of him and Wild Bill Benson grinning at each other like a reunion of long lost brothers?' I said.

'So what, Dave? You can't make a connection between the police treating Thwaite's death as suicide and Benson smiling at someone at a public relations jaunt. Wild Bill might not even have known it was Dyer he was smiling at. But if you can show me concrete evidence linking Dyer with NMP and the drugs scene I might be interested in telling the *It's Your World* team about it. Most of them are as cracked as you, always ready to make a mountain out of a molehill.'

'Right Ted, now you're talking. If you get an anonymous letter showing a link between our friend and the NMP you'll show it to the team?' I asked. 'Is that a promise? I think your station has a public duty to show just what is going on in this town.'

'Fine, whatever you want Dave. Now, would you mind letting me watch the cricket? You can be very boring when you get these obsessions.'

We sat and watched Lancashire pile up an impressive score against feeble Yorkshire bowling. All around us people were supping away. So I let my concerns with Dyer and his machinations go and joined them in trying to subside into an alcoholic haze.

It didn't work very well. I could feel a slow burn of anger building up inside me. In my present mood I was either going to quarrel with Ted or end up thumping some unlucky Yorkshire supporter.

When the interval came I'd managed to sit quietly for nearly two hours without blowing a fuse. Maybe I was improving. Ted and I were chatting to our neighbours about what was turning out to be a very dull match. There's a much wider social mix of spectators at a cricket match than at most other spectator sports. I was chatting to an elderly military man who was expressing his disgust at the decline of Yorkshire cricket in an eloquent way; judging from his beautifully cut tweed suit he was probably a retired general. When I turned back to Ted he was deep in conversation about Wasim Akram with another spectator. I decided it was not a good idea to spoil his day with more questions about the criminal scene in Manchester so I kept my thoughts to myself and carried on being an attentive audience to my military friend.

Just as the Lancashire fielders emerged there was a squall of rain. Ted, of course, had brought his umbrella with him, but I hadn't. This gave me all the excuse I needed to leave. I told Ted I'd send him the letter about NMP.

He looked at me doubtfully, saying 'I'll believe it when I see it', but did agree he'd show it to his investigative colleagues on *It's Your World* when and if it arrived. We parted on a fairly friendly note.

When I got to the large playing field car park I scanned the area for some time but there was no one lying in wait so I got in. I drove down Chester Road and turned up Seymour Grove and then along King's Road into Moss Side. Auntie Lovena lived at Bert Gibson Close, one of the many new housing developments in Moss Side. The close was part of a warren of new streets confronting older terraced properties across a busy road.

Lovena Anderson is famous in the neighbourhood. She's a district midwife working out of St Mary's hospital but my wife and I had got to know her not as clients but because of sickle cell anaemia, the crippling blood disease which strikes those of West African descent.

Lovena's son Carleton and Elenki had both had it at the

same time and we met at the clinic on Monsall Street. Elenki and I had often been for meals in her home. There wasn't much going on in Moss Side that she didn't know about, not that she was a gossip but she was so friendly and hardworking that people liked to tell her their troubles. Hence the nickname 'Auntie'.

I wanted to know if she'd heard anything about links between Dyer and the Charlies, whose headquarters were only half a mile away on the edge of Alexandra Park.

Jay, Lovena's eldest son, let me in. He's seventeen and still at sixth-form college. Jay's inclined to be surly and I knew his mother had battled every inch of the way to force him to stay in school. She'd even had me along to give Jay fatherly advice, which showed how desperate she was. While outsiders leaned on Lovena for helpful advice her own son paid no heed to her pleas that he should work and go to university. He was wasting his time at sixth-form college although he had a good brain when he wanted to use it.

I went into the small living room and gave Lovena a kiss.

'Hello David, you're looking peaky, have you been feeding yourself? When you going to get yourself a wife? I can find you a nice girl you know, if you ain't going to make an honest woman of Delise. You come and sit here by me.' Lovena greeted me with her usual warmth. Her years in Manchester have not wiped out her West Indian accent.

Lovena herself was looking anything but peaky. The nickname 'Auntie' was something of a misnomer: testimony to the extreme youth of so many of her customers rather than to her own age. At thirty-seven years of age she retained a youthful figure and appearance. The only jarring note was that she'd had her hair straightened. That did nothing for her but otherwise she was highly attractive. She wasn't very big, about five foot one, but made up for lack of inches with an outsized personality. Her cackling laugh usually heralded her arrival in a room. Lovena's sunny character was the product of a deep self-assurance about her value in the scheme of things. Her gift was to be able to pass this feeling for life and happiness on to other people. As a midwife she'd found an ideal vocation, with the sight of her enough to reassure any mum-to-be that everything was fine. Lovena usually put out a great feeling of cheerfulness. Only her renegade son could succeed in dampening down her high spirits, and the only time I had seen her really downcast was after Carleton's death.

Out of the corner of my eye I could see Jay shuffling away to the kitchen in embarrassment, but her younger son, fourteen-year-old Douglas, was as friendly and outgoing as his mum.

'Touch', he said raising his fist to me.

'Douglas you go and see David's car's all right. Keep them Thompson kiddies from playing on it.' While Lovena still retained the musical brogue of St Kitts, both her sons spoke with the nasal Manchester 'black' accent. The obedient Douglas went out on guard duty without a murmur of dissent.

'How you been keeping then?' Lovena asked. 'You're looking tired.'

'Well I'm in trouble Auntie, I'm in bad trouble,' I said.

She raised both her hands, slapped her knees and gave a cackling laugh. 'Well you came to the right place, David. I'm just on my way to the Sunday afternoon service, and you're welcome to come with me and lay your troubles before the Lord.' Lovena was an extremely devout Pentecostalist. She attended at least three services on Sunday.

She listened in silence as I told her what had happened to me since Wednesday evening. I didn't tell her anything about Sylvia.

'You got a problem, boy, didn't I tell you that them drug dealing leeches weren't all black boys? There's just as many Asians and whites trying to get rich quick as there is blacks. More. You can see them walking up and down round here with their phones in their pockets. They're ruining this place and no mistake.'

'I just wondered if you might have any idea who might be working for Dyer round here?' I said.

'David, you be careful what questions you ask, there's people round here go for you with a machete, you look at them out of the wrong side of your face.'

Then she lowered her voice to a whisper, 'I've been having trouble with Jay, he knows some of them Charlies. Not all of them boys are bad, they're easily influenced. They're frightened someone's going to say they're not men if they don't help their mates, but there's people using them. There's people making a lot of money from those boys. They is the ones should be in the paper, not the youth, but the police don't seem interested in catching them.'

'Who do you mean Lovena, who are these people who use the Charlies?' I asked hopefully.

'Every penny that ever come into this house I've worked for it but there's people round here that don't seem to work but have lots of money.' She turned to the kitchen and yelled to Jay who was still lurking there –

'Jay you come through here and tell David about the African man.'

Jay slunk back into the room. He was a tall youth, easily six foot two in height but not strongly built. As a younger boy he'd always been full of fun, always doing impressions of Lenny Henry or Desmond but lately he had become morose and glum.

'Don't you get me mixed up in this. I'm not going up the Charlton with you, man!' he said defensively.

'No, Jay. I want you to take David to have a chat with Sese Manteh, you know the man you admire so much because he's got them tribal marks,' his mother explained with a grin.

'What good will that do?' demanded Jay.

'He be able to tell David if there's someone after him. He can tell him if this Dyer has hired some of the youth to hurt David,' Lovena replied.

'This Sese come from Ghana, first he work for the church then he's a community leader. He wears a white suit and drives roun' in a big car all the time and all the youth think the sun shines out of his behind because he's got the tribal marks and he tells them black people invent everything. He says black men built the Egyptian pyramids, that them Pharaohs was black men, that a whole lot of white people is really black men.' Lovena stopped her tirade when she saw me looking in surprise at her.

'I thought it was Irish navvies that built the Pyramids,' I said.

'It's not me that's mad, this is what they believe, he say black youth don't have "good role models" so he's giving them some.' Lovena gave her cackling laugh. 'He even says Beethoven was black, that his grand-daddy was a black man from Belgium or some such place. Anyways I was never brought up to think much o' them Pharaohs of Egypt. Didn't they enslave the Children of Israel? Somethin' fishy 'about that man, if you goin' ax me.'

'You're always scorning us, Mum. Sese is trying to raise us up, that's why the youth likes him. He don't put us down all the time. Anyway why should I take David to see him?' Jay asked.

'You do it because your mother is asking you and this man can tell David if there is someone after him,' she said. When he didn't move she repeated her instructions in patois.

With a sour expression on his face Jay obeyed. He put on a new mustard and black bomber jacket over his t-shirt. He was wearing wide bell-bottomed jeans also made from two different colours of cloth and Reebok 'pump' trainers. When we got outside his clothes made quite a contrast with his brother's. Douglas was just wearing ordinary jeans and trainers, nothing fancy. Seeing me examining the state of his clothes Jay said 'What you looking at man!' in a half funny, half cheeky sort of way.

'I was admiring your trainers, they look great,' I replied.

When we got in the car Jay directed me along Claremont Road and for a while I thought he was taking me 'Up the Charlton', but at the junction with Alexandra Road we carried on past the Chinese church and community centre and soon turned into a very different kind of close.

Here on the edge of Whalley Range there was a development of luxury flats which had been built in the early eighties. Jay directed me to park near one block and I managed to find a space between a Jaguar and a red BMW. The parking area was in the centre of the close with the blocks all round looking down onto it like a Roman amphitheatre.

'What's this Sese Manteh like then?' I asked but Jay wasn't being communicative.

'You'll find out soon enough, man,' he said, pressing the intercom button. He spoke into it and there was a click as the electronic bolt was withdrawn on the front door to give us access. Sese's flat was on the second floor and as we walked along the carpeted and glazed balcony I could see why these were known as luxury flats. The passageway was twice as wide as in my own block.

When we got to Sese's apartment the door was open.

'So, Auntie Lovena sent you to see me?' Sese said in a deep bass voice. He had an educated American accent which sounded somehow out of place coming from a smiling African wearing the robes of his country. We had sat down on new leather chairs in a richly carpeted room. The walls were hung with souvenirs of Africa. There was a framed photograph of Marcus Garvey looking down at me.

As soon as Sese Manteh had spoken my intuition for rogues, which had served me so well in detecting frauds in the Happy-ways Hypermarkets, had begun to give a warning twitch.

The man in front of me was a tall, slim figure not unlike Jay in build except that in some indefinable way he looked more African. They both had dark complexions, both black, but Jay had some Carib Indian or white blood in his family tree way back which gave him a subtle difference in looks from the African.

'Yeah, I'm having bother with some of the youth,' I replied cautiously, 'and Lovena thinks you might be able to mediate for me.' I explained about the commission I had received to find Rachel Elsworth and how following a visit to Dyer I'd been set upon and how the same man had apparently followed me to Manchester Airport. I noticed that Manteh scowled when I mentioned Dyer's name.

'I hope you aren't stereotyping all black youth as violent drug peddlers Mr Cunane. Your name wouldn't be Jewish would it?' he asked.

'What's that got to do with it? My mother's a Catholic,' I said.

'Oh, no matter,' he said mysteriously. 'Well it seems to me that this Dyer may have employed some ill-disposed youth to do you harm. I heard about the trouble at the airport, four young men were arrested and charged with possession of cannabis and released on bail. I was called to stand surety for them. Those boys said they were just down there to meet a friend, it looks as if I'll have to question them more closely.'

'So you do know who they are, then? Would you like to tell me their names?' I asked.

Smiling broadly, Sese shook his head. 'Oh no man, I can't do that. That would indeed be a breach of confidence. But I can ask these young men if they have been so misguided as to take money from that sewer Dyer. I don't think those boys will be bothering you again.'

'Well can you tell me if they belong to this Charlton Close gang?'

'There you go again, stereotyping us. There isn't a Charlton Close gang. That's just got up by the racist media. Sometimes the youth round here feel they must defend themselves against racist attacks and they may band together. Isn't that right, Jay?' He turned to Jay for support. Jay nodded his head vigorously.

Gradually Sese was losing the geniality with which he had greeted us at first. He was wearing rimless glasses and they seemed to catch the light coming into the room and reflect it back at me.

'Mr Manteh, I'd be willing to make a very substantial contribution to any good cause you care to name if you can help me to find Rachel or to establish a link between Dyer and people who sell drugs,' I said.

Manteh jumped to his feet angrily and hitched his robe over his shoulder, 'You think that because I'm an African I'll sell out my friends for a bit of cash from a rich white man's pocket. You are insulting me!' he shouted. He stood in the pose of an ancient Roman senator, wounded nobility personified.

I stood up too. 'I'm not insulting you, I want to find out why some young man you say you know is going round trying to bash my head in. There's nothing insulting about that. I'm only after information. I'm not the police. This man Dyer is dangerous and it's time someone stopped him.'

'Your meddling could cost you dear, Mr Cunane, a lot more than a contribution.' Manteh had recovered self-control and was speaking calmly.

'I suggest you drop this investigation before you cause yourself real pain,' he continued calmly, giving his robe another swish and looking me in the eye. 'Have you got a family? Well then, think about who would be upset if anything happened to you. I believe there's already one young fellow who has come to a bad end.'

There was a deep arrogance in the way he spoke. I was being warned off again, my fate at every stage of this investigation.

I hadn't mentioned Thwaite and the fake suicide to Manteh.

I mustn't have looked too impressed by his veiled threats because he went on.

'I know where you live Mr Cunane and I can tell you it's going to take more than a big dog to guard you if you keep on sticking your nose into other people's business.'

I felt chilled by his words, not because of the threat, which I'd heard more often than I cared to remember, but because someone must have told him about the German shepherd.

'But that's my job, Chief,' I said. 'I just exist to uncover things people don't want me to know.' This seemed to provoke him again. The tribal marks, three parallel scars high on each cheekbone, stood out vividly against his dark skin. He turned from me and faced young Jay who had also stood up and was twiddling his thumbs in agitated embarrassment. Jay was taller than Manteh and slightly more muscular, but it was clear who was doing the dominating.

They could have been father and son from the way Manteh spoke to him. Which is precisely where Manteh got his power over such as Jay, I thought.

'You're going to have to choose your friends more carefully Jay, and decide whose side you're on,' he said.

'That's exactly what I was going to say,' I said, moving over to Jay and grabbing his wrist. 'Come on Jay, let's get out of here,' and without ceremony I took Jay by the elbow and drew him towards the door.

He came with great reluctance and when we got in the car he sat in silence. I thought he was on the point of tears.

'Jay, that guy is a con-man, your mother knows it and you know it.' Jay didn't respond but when we stopped at the traffic lights at the corner of Alex Park he wrenched the car door open, got out and strode off towards the park.

The only thing I seemed to be succeeding at today was making enemies.

11

After Jay's unexpected departure I debated carrying on down Alex Road and having a drink in the Little Alex – I might be able to dig something up about Sese Manteh – but I decided not to. I'd already had a skinful at Old Trafford and I was driving to Southport in the evening. I didn't want to lose any more points off my licence, so I did a neat U-turn and headed back up Alex Road.

Even on a Sunday afternoon the ladies of the town were on display at their customary spots. A hundred years ago this had been one of the fashionable suburbs of Manchester. Now the big houses were all institutions and the woman on the pavements were hookers looking for trade. Despite the chance of being taken for a kerb crawler I kept my speed down as I drove along the wide straight road – a favourite spot for radar traps.

As I thought about traps I glanced in my mirror. A battered old Cortina with a male driver was overtaking me. He pulled right alongside me and pointed to the kerb. I pulled over. The baseball bat was back in its place in the sports bag but I didn't get it out. There was only one man in the car. He walked over to me. I recognised him, it was the scruffy individual who had nearly crashed into me outside my flat on Friday afternoon, a man in his late twenties with designer stubble, long blond hair and a moustache.

When he reached the door he took a small card out of his pocket, a police warrant card.

'D. S. Rice, Mr Cunane,' he said, holding the card for inspection. 'Mr Sinclair would like a few words with you. If you'd like to get in the car and come with me. I don't want to hang about in the street round here for any longer than is necessary.' He spoke in a perfectly courteous way with an unexpectedly non-regional, educated accent.

'Right, I will,' I replied weakly, 'but there's no way I'm leaving the car here. A friend lives nearby so let me park it outside his house.'

As an undercover cop his disguise was perfect. Wearing a

scuffed old brown leather jacket, faded purple t-shirt, jeans that bagged and went into holes at the knees, dirty white trainers with matching holes at the toes, the impression he successfully created was of a hippy down on his luck. Dirt under his nails, unwashed hair, and a personal odour that wasn't exactly fresh added to the grainy realism of the disguise.

What wasn't part of his disguise was the expression on his face, which would have frightened any small child. His red-rimmed, bloodshot eyes, along with the stubble and untrimmed moustache, gave him a fierce warrior-like aspect, like a combat veteran just on leave from the battlefield. Definitely a hard case.

I drove round to the McNeils and left the car under the tree outside their house. Jim came to the door and looked dubiously at the scruffy undercover copper. He had the dogs with him; it only needed a word from him and they would be on top of Rice.

'It's all right, Jim. Do you mind if I leave the car here for an hour? I have to go and sort something out.'

'What do you mean "sort something out"? I can call the police if you want,' Jim shouted.

'No don't do that. Really, it's all right. I'll be back in an hour or if not I'll phone you and let you know what's going on.'

I got into the battered Cortina. Rice drove up to the traffic lights, indicating a left turn along Wilbraham Road. We went down Wilbraham, left at the Parkway past the empty new Science Park built on the YMCA playing fields, down towards town. I thought he must be taking me to Bootle Street, the old Manchester Police HQ but we carried on through Albert Square and out of the town centre up Bury New Road.

Eventually we turned into the Police Training Centre: formerly a female teacher training college until the state decided it needed policemen more than teachers. We parked at an administration building next to the former chapel.

Rice showed me into the building. He already looked smarter and more like a policeman as he squared his shoulders and shed his street character.

He knocked on the internal door of the office and a light flashed up 'Wait', so we waited where generations of trainee teachers had trembled at their summons to see the college principal. Burly desk-bound coppers with large bottoms trundled to and fro bearing pieces of paper. The light flashed 'Enter' and, with a deferential tap on the door from Rice, we went in.

'Come away in, David. How are you?' was the greeting I received. Mr Sinclair, a Lowland Scot, with one of those ever so 'refeened' Edinburgh accents was standing at his desk, offering me his hand which I shook cautiously. I made a show of counting my fingers when he released my grip. Sinclair is Detective Chief Superintendent in charge of operations, normally based at Boyer Street, the GMP headquarters in Stretford.

He's in his late forties, moving towards retirement from the force, and had been a close friend of my father's. Dad had nicknamed him 'Svengali' because he seemed able to mesmerise villains into making admissions. With his lean frame, the kind on which clothes always hang well, he's an impressive looking man. Dad, whenever he mentions him, expresses surprise that Sinclair hasn't made it to chief constable rank. Many people regard him as the grey eminence behind our current head copper, Wild Bill Benson.

Caution's the operative word in dealing with Sinclair. Beneath a show of mateyness he's only ever interested in one thing: solving the current case. It's this reserve in dealing with his colleagues which has prevented him from reaching the highest rank, so far. He gives the impression of being too clever for a copper.

I had ever reason to be worried. If he found anything out about my recent tricks no friendship with my father would prevent him from prosecuting me; on the other hand if he thought I could 'assist him in his enquiries' he might be able to supply me with lots of useful information and save me days of trekking back and forth over a cold trail in Didsbury.

'Sit down, would you like a cup of coffee?' he said with great geniality. 'I know you're partial to something a wee bit stronger but the sun's not sunk below the yard arm yet. Michael, would you like to step outside and see if you can rustle up three coffees for us?' Rice, who had been clipping his security pass to his top pocket, nipped out smartly.

'Bright young man that, he'll go far. You would have done well here too, you know.' He shook his head as he spoke, he knew well enough how it irritated me to hear him or my father going on about what a wonderful career the police offered.

'You'll not mind if I light up my old pipe will you?'

Now I knew I was going to get the third degree. He uses the smoke from the pipe to soften up his victims before he tricks a damaging admission out of them. Speaking to him, even when he's being outwardly friendly, I always get the impression that he's mentally tape-recording my statement.

'Well, what have you been up to?' he asked with an undertone of menace.

'Oh this and that, you know,' I replied vaguely. 'I've been working undercover in Rochdale for several weeks. There was a team of rip-off artists operating out of Happyways Hypermarket's big warehouse there. They were taking their share of every load that went out of the bonded warehouse and altering invoices with the help of a crooked computer expert.'

'You'd be working with Charlie Sims then. He's a good man is Charlie. You'll not go far wrong working for him.' Charlie Sims was a fellow Lowland Scot and had worked on the old pre-amalgamation Manchester force with Sinclair.

'And are you still working for Charlie?' he asked slyly.

'Well, he has offered me a short-term contract,' I said.

'Your mother and father will be delighted to hear you're working regularly. You won't mind if I give Charlie a call to ask him about the case you're working on for him now? I have his home number here somewhere.' He made a limp gesture as if to pick up the phone.

He was an absolute master at wrong-footing people.

'No, I'm not working for him now. You know very well I've got my own office and I don't have a boss, not Charlie Sims nor Wild Bill Benson, nor my Dad,' I said sharply.

'Calm down laddie. Ah, here comes the coffee.' Michael Rice bustled in holding a tray with all the aplomb of a high-class butler. My grilling was adjourned for a moment while we sorted out the coffee, sugar and milk. Police canteen coffee hadn't improved since the last time I'd tried it.

'I'm just a bit concerned about you. I've known you since you were in short pants you know. When Michael here got in touch with me on Friday morning to say that you'd been interfering in one of the most important investigations we've had for months I could hardly believe my ears. Then, when I hear today that you've been spotted coming out of the home of one of our targets accompanied by a member of the Charlies I want to know just what the hell the son of my old friend thinks he's up to.' As Sinclair spoke the pretended warmth he'd started off with gradually cooled to a temperature a few degrees above absolute zero.

'I haven't a clue what you're talking about Mr Sinclair,' I said, trying to annoy him with a line he must have heard ten thousand times.

He fixed me with his watery blue eyes, I glared right back at him. He started to get angry.

'Don't play games with me sonny, this isn't an American TV series. I can and will nick you for obstructing the police in the execution of their duties if you don't come clean.'

As he made his routine threat I breathed a mental sigh of relief. If he'd had anything on me regarding the break-in at Dyer's house or the bother at the airport he wouldn't be threatening me so early in the proceedings. This must be just a trawling expedition on his part.

'Now Mr Sinclair you know I wouldn't do anything to obstruct the police. Just tell me how I can help you and I will. Have I ever given you any bother before? You know I haven't.'

Sinclair greeted this comment by blowing an immense cloud of blue smoke in my direction. He was too old a hand to have the wool pulled over his eyes.

He let the silence lengthen for a while, and then asked 'What are you messing about with Mike Dyer for? Don't you know the Chief's determined to close him down? He says Dyer's a source of moral pollution in this fair city. If you've taken a job for Dyer drop it right away laddie; however much he's paying you it'll not be worth it in the long run.'

I almost fell out of my seat laughing.

'Dyer paying me! He might pay for some flowers for my funeral if he was allowed to choose the method of my departure from this world. Otherwise I can tell you there's no way he'll be paying me any money.'

'Well David, Michael here thinks Dyer may have paid you to act as a go-between for him and Sese Manteh. His theory is that Dyer wants to make some kind of compromise deal with the Charlie Boys; they stop smashing his clubs up in exchange for a piece of the action in the drugs racket.'

'Come on Mr Sinclair, you know as well as I do that if you could definitely link Dyer with the drugs trade Wild Bill would never have let him have a licence for any of his clubs. The reason I went to see Dyer is confidential. I'm making confidential enquiries for a client. Dyer's only marginally involved,' I said.

'You've no right to claim confidentiality but that's by the by. Michael saw you follow Dyer to his home all the way from the Paloma Club in the early hours of Friday morning and today he saw you coming out of Manteh's flat. I told him to pull you in. If you start fooling around you'll snarl up our investigation. Dyer'll start claiming police harassment. Anyway what were you doing at Manteh's house?'

'Same thing, confidential enquiries,' I said.

'No laddie, that's not good enough. You're going to have to tell me a lot more than that.'

'Well I've an important client and his daughter has run off and I thought Dyer and Manteh might know where she's gone.'

It sounded thin but why should I break my bargain with the Elsworths? The police had had years to deal with Dyer and my feeble efforts weren't likely to deflect them. My worry was that Sinclair and his head prefect, Rice, might use me as a convenient scapegoat to take the blame for any failure on their part. Modern police work is all about minding your back.

I decided to play the one good card I had in a poor hand.

'According to you the Chief is determined to stop Dyer, but I have a photograph which shows them together in a very pally pose. The *Evening Banner* might be interested in publishing it on the day when Wild Bill "ever-so-reluctantly" renews Dyer's licences.'

'What! What are you talking about? Be very careful what you say! . . . Michael, step out of the office for a moment, go and buy me some tobacco will you?' He glared at me while his underling got himself out of earshot.

'What is this photograph?' he demanded.

'I've got a photo showing Benson raising a glass to Dyer. It'll look nice across the front of the *Evening Banner* on the day that the Chief decides he can't close down the Paloma.'

A look of intense calculation crossed the face of the chief superintendent. I could hear the wheels whirring round in that cunning Caledonian brain.

'Now David there's no need for anyone to go to extremes. I wonder if you know how your father and I felt when you started up as a private enquiry agent instead of joining the police. Your dad thought you'd only stick it a few months then you'd quit. In a way we're proud of you for doing so well but you mustn't let things go to your head. Just think of the resources we've got here and compare them to your own and have a bit of sense.

'I'm prepared to help you if you're willing to be frank and co-operative with me. What is it these Americans say? "One hand washes the other"; or as your dad and me would say "You scratch my back and I'll scratch yours".' He gave a creepy laugh and rolled his eyes back.

If this was what thirty-odd years in the police force reduced a man to I was glad I'd never let Dad push me into it.

While Sinclair was attempting to bargain with me I began to feel tired of the whole business. Sinclair's well-cut dark suit looked dressy, the ghastly attempt at a chummy grin was like the smile on the face of a week-old corpse. I was sickened by his assumption that I would trade with him, but if you sup with the devil you need a long spoon. I couldn't afford to be too scrupulous if I was going to get a result by Tuesday.

'Fair enough Mr Sinclair. That's the way the world goes I'm sure. My problem is that a young lady's got herself tangled up with a certain young man who turned up dead the other day. His name was Thwaite and he worked for Dyer as a DJ.

'She's done a bunk. Having met her father I can't say I blame her, but the mother's all right. They both want the darling daughter returned but they don't want Mr Plod involved. According to your lot, Thwaite was into drugs in a big way and died clutching a bottle of uppers. Dyer claims he knows nothing about the murder. Manteh poses as a friend to inner city youth, so I went to ask him if he'd heard Thwaite was dealing.'

Sinclair listened to this edited version of events keenly and jotted down Thwaite's name.

'I don't suppose you're going to tell me the name of this girl are you, David?' he said. 'It must have been a crooked path that led you from the girl to the photo, and I don't want to find out how you came by it. The photo could be unwelcome publicity for Mr Benson for all kinds of reasons. Now, how can I help you?'

'Can you let me have some information on the late Thwaite and fill me in on what's going on between Dyer and these gangs he's involved with?' There was a lot more I would have liked to ask but I was sticking my neck out a long way already.

'Right, on your feet then. I can't leave you in here. Have you got Thwaite's date of birth?' He was smiling again and showing his well preserved teeth.

How many villains must have seen those pearly snappers and thought what a friendly copper he was until they heard the cell door slamming behind them?

We went out of the office. Sinclair headed for a computer terminal and I sat on a chair outside looking at a poster of the local Aids advisory offices. He returned in a few minutes with a printout in his hand. We returned to the room. He wouldn't let me keep the printout but allowed me to take a few notes.

Andy had been a naughty boy. He had received two Inspector's Cautions for shoplifting before he was fourteen and at the age of sixteen had been involved in receiving stolen goods. Two fines for possession of category A drugs followed. Altogether Andrew was lucky that his youthful liking for wacky baccy hadn't landed him in jail. What interested me was that he'd run away from home twice and on each occasion had been found working on fairgrounds. Maybe Rachel had also headed for a fairground when she cleared off.

Sinclair then filled me in about Dyer.

'I can't tell you much about Dyer and Manteh because it's part of an ongoing operation which I don't want to compromise but the outlines should be known to anyone who reads the papers. Dyer is the big wheel behind teenage entertainment in this town.

'Thousands of punters go to his clubs and although drugs are sold he keeps it to a minimum mainly by excluding your inner city friends. They'd like to smash up his clubs so that they can deal to their hearts' content.'

'We've made mistakes. We tried to contain the drug problem in Moss Side, but instead of being localized it's flourished. Now it's coming out of Moss Side. The dealers want to expand their trade. Control of half a dozen clubs in the centre of Manchester, perhaps operating behind a respectable front, would give them the base they need for expansion. Don't forget most of the punters who use these clubs have votes. Once the dealers were established, we'd find it very hard to persuade the politicians to close all the clubs down. Manchester would become another Amsterdam,' he said.

'I see, but why have they got to have Dyer's clubs? Surely he's no push over?' I asked.

'Precisely, David. But if they can roll him over then they'll have no problems with anyone else. It's like the two biggest kids in the street having a scrap to see who's going to be "cock o' the walk". Dyer's the king pin. Knock him out and everyone else will fall into line. Much as I hate to say it, keeping Mike Dyer healthy is a big priority with this police force. That's why your attentions are unwelcome.'

'What about Manteh? Where does he fit in?' I asked.

'That's just what we're trying to find out. He seems to have great influence over the lads and no visible means of support. Some of our people think he's trying to build himself a power base in Moss Side. It's also been suggested that he's some sort of obeah-man trying to start a new religion. A new blend of Christianity and African religions which will have him as a wee Popie on top.'

On the face of it this was ridiculous, Auntie Lovena would take her yard brush to anyone trying to convert her, or her sons, to a new religion; particularly someone trying to revive fear of spooks and duppies. But how to explain the reaction of Jay? He had seemed very impressed by the charlatan to me.

Sinclair probably knew a great deal more about Sese Manteh than he was letting on.

I decided to push my luck a little.

'Have either of them been involved in any sort of property deals Mr Sinclair?' I asked.

'Just stop right there David. You said you were trying to trace a missing girl not set the city to rights. What the hell do you know about property deals?' he said angrily. I'd struck another exposed nerve.

'Say no more, say no more . . . Forget I mentioned NMP.' I raised my hands in a mock surrender.

'Damn and blast you to hell David Cunane! I don't know how much you've found out about what doesn't concern you, but I'm telling you you're fishing in very muddy waters. You'd better mind your own business. We're investigating all aspects of this scene and we don't want some private investigator grandstanding all over the case.'

Sinclair got up and went over to the filing cabinet and took out a bottle of Bell's whisky and two glasses. He poured out two glasses and pushed one over to me. We both sipped our drams in silence. He was annoyed because he hadn't been able to manipulate me to his own satisfaction.

He was a copper's copper, married to the job – he'd never had a wife. It must gall him to see a paper-shuffler like Benson in command of the force in which he had passed his entire working life. Equally, it must break him up to think that an amateur was making guesses about links between the drug world, the entertainment scene and property speculators – accurate guesses.

He gave a heavy sigh, 'Things have got very complicated since the days when I was skippering for your Dad. Let me warn you David, some of the people you're mixing with have their ways of making people disappear. You have a gun licence don't you? Well make sure you don't go out without your gun for the next few days. If you get any trouble from anyone on the force tell them to call me on this number.'

He scribbled his number on a scrap of paper and pushed it over to me.

'Can I ask you one more question?' I said.

'Go on then, try me.'

'Does Dyer have anything to do with a fancy-looking black guy called Leon, who wears dreadlocks and Italian suits?'

Sinclair took a file out of his desk marked 'Known Associates' and looked through it.

'No, no Leons in here. Anyway I told you, although Dyer isn't exactly race-prejudiced, he's keeping the black community at arm's length.'

Sinclair drained his whisky. 'I'm going to give you thirty-six hours to find this girl and then I'm going to pull you in. It's for your own good. I've been at too many funerals of friends lately and I don't want to start going to my friends' children's funerals.'

There was a knock on the door and Rice came in. The man had timed his return well, or the old fox had summoned him with a hidden bell. He fawned over his superintendent, a yes man to the threadbare tips of his size ten trainers.

'Now Michael you go into David's flat with him and he'll give you a photo which he'll seal up in this envelope. Under no circumstances are you to look at it. Do you understand, Michael?' Sinclair opened his desk drawer, took out a large envelope, wrote his name on it and handed it to me.

The interview was over so I stood up. 'Why don't you give me forty-eight hours, give me till Tuesday evening and if I haven't got anywhere I'll jack the case in and go and work for Charlie Sims in Middlesbrough,' I said.

'All right, forty-eight hours and then I'll be sending Michael here to pick you up again. Understood?'

I accepted his orders as cockily as I dared, smiling broadly and shaking Sinclair's hand. I wanted to leave the impression that I couldn't care less about letting the police hustle me off the case. I must have succeeded as far as Rice was concerned because as we drove down the steep hill away from the training college Rice turned to me and said, 'You seem very pleased with yourself for a man who's just been to have his bottom smacked.' He had a smirk on his unshaven face.

'Oh I wouldn't say that, I've known Sinclair since I was a kid. His bark's worse than his bite.' I was trying to look laid back. I must have succeeded again because he decided he needed to reinforce his boss's advice by giving me a not-so-playful punch on the leg.

'Just stay out of my hair Cunane. You trailed Dyer and his entourage from the Paloma on Friday morning. Luckily they weren't on their guard, or they would have spotted you, and then they might have got onto me. This isn't a game for amateurs, so stay away! Get it?'

My impulse was to give him a punch back but it's never a good idea to give someone in Rice's position any excuse for having a grudge against you, so I gave him a weak grin and kept my lips buttoned.

We took a different route back to South Manchester through Miles Platting and along Grey Mare Lane. Despite some efforts at improvement, there were acres and acres of derelict land where steel mills, diesel engines factories and locomotive works had stood. Was it all going to be turned into retail parks, I wondered? This was where twenty thousand men had once earned a living. All now a wasteland waiting for some smart lads with Michael Douglas haircuts to 're-develop' it for a percentage.

When we reached the leafier lanes of South Manchester I gave Detective Sergeant Rice directions to the McNeil's house. Once again he took a roundabout route. On arrival at the house he was unable to stop himself getting out of his car and give a last piece of advice. It was a mistake. The McNeil's front door opened and a brown and gold thunderbolt shot out and launched itself at Rice.

Esau's forepaws struck Rice on the shoulders and he went down. A perfect tackle by the dog which picked itself up before Rice could move and crouched on his chest growling but making no further move.

'Get the bugger off me! You lunatic!' he panted.

A shocked Jim McNeil came running out. He hauled the dog off Rice, gasping 'Margaret's phoning the police.'

'I am the police, you bloody fool!' shouted Rice, as he climbed shakily to his feet.

I ducked into the front door to tell Margaret to call the police off but she hadn't been able to get through anyway.

When I got out again Jim was still apologising to Rice but I didn't feel too much sympathy for him myself. I got into my own car and he had to follow me down to my flat. In five minutes I was opening the door for him.

'Well Sergeant, I'm sorry about the dog, and I'm sorry you blew your cover,' I said, twisting the knife in the wound.

He scowled at me and gritted his teeth but didn't speak.

I sealed the photo inside the envelope Sinclair had given me and handed it over. He took it, showing no pleasure that his chief had such little confidence in his discretion as to not let him see it. I could see he was dying to ask me what it was all about. It pleased me that Sinclair and I were now the only people with copies of the photo. I was sure that Sinclair didn't think I was so naive that I would give away my only one. Rice looked round the flat with a sniffy expression, if he'd had a list of stolen furnishings on him I'm sure he would have pulled it out and started checking my goods over.

When he saw that I wasn't going to strain myself on the hospitality front he growled, 'I don't believe amateurs should get involved in police work' and left.

He was the sort of copper who leaves you thinking well of the criminal fraternity. However, I had no time to worry about his likes and dislikes as I got myself ready to meet Sylvia for our trip to Southport.

Before leaving I gave my father a bell to see if he'd gleaned any useful titbits about Dyer from the retired detectives fraternity.

He was taking his afternoon kip and was grumpy about being interrupted but didn't mind being roused when I filled him in about my enforced meeting with Sinclair. He seemed to think it was very significant that Sinclair had shifted his headquarters to North Manchester, that Sinclair must be up to something big involving South Manchester which he didn't want found out.

He reminded me that it was a former Chief Constable, not the present incumbent, who'd been obsessed with moral objections to people enjoying themselves in the ways so profitably provided by the likes of Dyer. Benson had maintained the policy of being sticky about granting club licences but so far none had been refused and none had been revoked.

The version of Dyer's rise to fame and fortune which my Dad's cronies had heard differed sharply from the yuppyish, eighties-capitalist success story which Ted Blake had relayed to me.

According to Dad's friends Dyer had put together his team of bouncers and thugs before he'd ever become an impresario on the club circuit and long before he'd owned a club himself. He had been in the business of supplying 'protection' in the form of club doormen. He used his team to intimidate club owners into hiring his men as bouncers by threatening to wreck their clubs unless they took his men on in return for a share of the profits.

Apart from wrecking clubs Dyer's main methods of intimidation involved boots, broken bottles and beer glasses in the face. I'd nearly had a taste last night of his standard operating procedure when dealing with awkward customers: a well-honed routine.

Dyer also had a profitable sideline in debt collecting and loan sharking. He was a lovely boy.

There was a strong rumour that one club owner who'd resisted Dyer too strenuously now formed part of the supporting foundations for a pier under a section of the M61. Nothing had ever been found out, however, despite the efforts of Manchester's finest. Nobody could ever decide which pier it was.

Everyone, including the scores of people who'd been beaten up or cut or defrauded, was determined to keep silent where Dyer was concerned.

In recent years police vigilance over Dyer's activities had slackened as he seemed to be going more or less straight. That is, his legit profits were now greater than his criminal earnings and he was able to afford the services of one of the best PR firms in the North of England to tart up his image.

Dad's coppers' old boy network was a mine of information and I was tempted to put him on to sniffing out any juicy material about Manteh but thinking of the price that would have to be paid for putting myself under too deep an obligation to my father I refrained. I'd have to find out what I could about Manteh using my own resources.

As I put my case in the boot of the car I wondered if Sylvia's employment with Dyer dated from the time he'd employed the image enhancers or from before. It had to be the former I guessed.

It was interesting how confident Ted Blake had been that he was well informed and on the inside track compared with a small-timer like myself when all he was doing was recycling the guff about Dyer put out by Dyer's own PR team. I remembered Ted's comment in Leonardos about how Dyer's formula for success included drawing on the musical talents of the Manchester area. Dyer had really based his rise to prominence on the existence of a quite different pool of local talent: the endless supply of mindless thugs of the 'Popeye' Bob Lane sort.

12

Sylvia wasn't as welcoming as I'd expected her to be when I called for her at her flat in Heaton Mersey.

'Dave, have you spent the whole day drinking at Old Trafford?' she asked.

I couldn't deny it without telling her where else I'd been, so I just gave a nod of agreement.

'There's no way you're going to drive me to Southport in that state. You ought to think of your licence. Change seats, I'll drive.' At least she was still willing to come to Southport with me. She was wearing black leggings and a white cotton shirt, her hair was tied back and she had small sleeper earrings in her ears. She looked desirable.

'I hope you packed a suit,' she said as I put her suitcase beside mine in the boot. 'I've booked us into a good hotel and I want to dress up for dinner.'

'Whooee! A good hotel in Southport; must be really something else! I hope they're not charging us too much,' I said.

'Don't be sarcastic, Dave. It doesn't suit you,' she replied, giving me a kiss as I handed her the keys. 'Now what's the best way to get to Southport?'

'Up the M61 and turn off past Chorley, then follow the sign posts,' I said.

Sylvia was a suicidal driver. She kept creeping up close behind vehicles in front then overtaking sharply. I had trouble repressing signs of nervousness. Fortunately the M61 wasn't crowded and there were no convoys of lorries going to Scotland. She was worked up about something.

'Did Dyer tell you what happened at our meeting on Saturday?' I asked.

'He phoned to say that you turned nasty and tried to beat him up,' she said huffily.

'Do you want to hear my side of it?' I said. She didn't reply, so I told her that the Ardwick Green 'peace talks' had failed. She drove on in silence for a while, then as the sign for Rivington Services came up she pulled over.

We went for a coffee.

'I hope you don't think I knew he wasn't going to settle, do you?' she asked.

I shook my head.

'Mike's been in a funny mood for some time. He seems desperate about the business yet we're making a good profit every night of the week at all our clubs. I thought his marriage was on the rocks and that was why he was so worried about you knowing Jock took a girl home with him on Thursday. But there must be something else. I think someone's blackmailing him and he thinks you're involved with it. That must be why he doesn't trust you.'

I looked round the café; parents were fattening up their children on chips and beefburgers. A party of old age pensioners was complaining about prices and in the background was the constant roar of traffic from the motorway.

I didn't know how to explain to Sylvia that her boss was a shit. Dyer had gone out of his way to treat Sylvia well because she was such an attractive woman, but also because she was such a good front for him and his obnoxious activities. As long as she believed in him she'd project a positive image of him.

I looked into her blue eyes.

'You're going to have to face something about Mike Dyer. Whatever you thought about him in the past, he's a thug. He may have told you that he was going to pay me to stop bothering him but the only pay-offs he's used to making involve shoving broken beer glasses into people's faces. He came with three hard cases to put me in the hospital.'

Sylvia's face clouded as I told her about her charming boss and his 'funny moods'. My revelation didn't seem to be having the intended effect so I went on:

'I put one of them in the hospital instead and Dyer was lucky to get away before I could give him what he was asking for. He isn't being blackmailed. He was trying, courtesy of Andy Thwaite, to use Rachel Elsworth to extort money or a soft loan from her father. Rachel's boyfriend crawled out from under the same stone as Dyer. He was using his position with Rachel to con Dyer into giving him favourable treatment as as DJ—'

'No, that can't be right. Mike would never hurt anyone and

the clubs have never made such good money. He doesn't need any loans,' Sylvia interrupted. She was on the point of tears.

'Have you heard of something called NMP?' I asked.

'Yes, they supply a lot of the security staff Mike uses,' she replied.

'Well did you know that Dyer's paying them a hefty slice of the profits from the clubs? Are they the people who gave him the capital to start up in the first place?'

Sylvia nodded her head slowly.

'As far as I can see they're bleeding him dry. They're higher up the food chain than him, they're feeding on him just as he fed on others. That's why he's desperate for loans. If he can start up other clubs he might be able to make enough to pay them off; then he'd be free and clear. That's why he had Thwaite killed, because he failed to get the loan from Elsworth.'

Sylvia began to weep. Quietly, without any fuss, streams of tears began rolling down her face. I offered her a handkerchief. We left the coffee bar and walked back to the car. She carried on crying and got in the passenger seat. We turned back on to the motorway and sped on our way.

The Southport cut-off was the next one after the service area and we turned onto a winding country road which was labelled as an A-road but wasn't much better than a country lane. It wound round picturesque villages and retirement cottages with roses round the door. In places it ran on an embankment above the low-lying fields. It required all my attention.

I kept glancing at the rear-view mirror and although I was doing a good speed there was a white Transit van keeping station with me about two hundred yards behind.

As I curled into the sharp bends I kept glancing at the mirror to see if it had turned off but there it was, nosing round the bend. It was impossible to see who was driving. Sylvia noticed me glancing at the mirror.

'We've picked up some company,' I said. She'd stopped crying and now turned round to study the road behind us.

'It might just be going to the same place as us. This is a narrow road, after all,' she said reasonably.

I hoped she was right.

We came up to a T-junction, joining the major road from Liverpool to Preston. The right turn went on to Preston, the left to Southport and Rufford Old Hall, a National Trust property. I pulled over to the centre of the road and indicated a right turn. The traffic was heavy and I had to wait for a gap but when one came I turned sharp left instead, pushing through a line of traffic, and raced towards the entrance of Rufford Old Hall.

The hall was closed but the car park was still open and I drove in and parked among the pine trees. For a moment I regretted not taking Mr Sinclair's advice and bringing the Beretta 92 with me, but I knew Sinclair was crafty. He was easily capable of advising me to carry the gun and then having me arrested. Not that it was illegal for me to carry it but since Hungerford the police have been touchy about anyone with a gun.

The excitement was having a good effect on Sylvia. She'd freshened herself up and was back to normal.

'What can we do if they are after us?' she asked.

'That's a good question. We'll just have to try and shake them off. Maybe they're completely harmless. How are you feeling now?'

'I'm all right. We'll have a talk later. I still think you're wrong about Mike Dyer. I just can't see him as a murderer. He's always so scared that he's under police observation. That swine Benson is determined to get something on him.'

We pulled out of the car park and continued towards Southport. After a short time we passed the white van going in the opposite direction. It was driven by a black man, and he had a companion but I couldn't see whether he was black too. Sylvia gripped my arm. I put my foot down and we drove on to Southport in a state of tension but with no further sighting of the van.

When we arrived at the resort I left the Nissan in the remotest part of the King Edward Hotel car park. It wasn't visible from the road but anyone searching round the hotels would soon find it. My alternative was to hide the car away somewhere but that would leave me on foot while I collected it and I preferred to have it where I could get at it quickly.

Sylvia had reserved a room for us under the name of Mr and Mrs Jones and it felt strange to be part of a married couple after the years on my own. I hadn't stayed in any hotels with Delise. Maybe if I had she'd still be around. The hotel was luxurious, lots of signed photographs of famous Royal Birkdale golfers on the walls. Our room had a big en-suite bathroom as well as a king-sized double bed.

We changed for dinner. I put on a white shirt, silk paisley tie, grey gabardine trousers and navy double breasted blazer. Sylvia changed in the bathroom and emerged in an emerald green, ballerina-length, taffeta evening dress.

We were a fit-looking pair when we strolled into the dining room. I got through a steak and the best part of two bottles of wine. Over the meal Sylvia asked me what made me think Thwaite had been murdered. I didn't go into details but told her I was certain that it was murder, not suicide. I was more interested in hearing what she had to say about the Dyer empire.

I wanted to believe in Sylvia. Sometimes she was too ready to give her boss the benefit of the doubt. On the surface everything was pleasant: beautiful meal, beautiful woman, fine wine. Everything should have been perfect but it wasn't quite.

There was just that question mark. She'd said she had no interest in Dyer sexually, so what was her interest? Why was she such a loyal employee? I tried to shake the mood by changing the subject and asking Sylvia about her background.

'I'm from Barrow-in-Furness originally,' she said. 'My father had a good job at Vicker's.'

I knew what they made at Vicker's but I let Sylvia do the talking. I didn't want her to think I was giving her the third degree.

'My father was a manager,' she went on. 'He built nuclear submarines and my sister and I went to a convent school. When we were there it was very international, lots of South Americans.

'Mike Harding, the folk singer, says Barrow's at the end of the longest cul-de-sac in the world,' I joked. 'Don't they all talk slow and broad up there.'

'Well I didn't. What about you? You've got an accent yourself,' she said.

'No I haven't. I speak perfect BBC English.' I changed the subject. 'Do they have a lot of seagulls in Barrow? In this survival book I'm reading it tells you how to survive if you're lost in a wilderness and one of the ways is by eating seagulls.'

'Go on,' she said, 'it sounds revolting.'

'You wrap a stone up inside some food and toss it into the air. The seagull swallows it and overbalances because of the heavy stone in its crop. Then you kill it and eat it,' I explained.

'That doesn't sound right, if you had so much food that you could afford to toss it into the air to seagulls then you wouldn't want to eat them,' Sylvia argued.

'I thought of trying something similar with your friend Dyer. I bet he's a greedy gannet. If I was to toss him some nice juicy piece of bait he'd be certain to try and swallow it.'

'Oh Dave, you've got a one-track mind! Let's go up before you get too drunk to stand.'

We went to our bedroom and Sylvia disappeared into the bathroom, from which she soon emerged in a satin nightdress. The sight of her banished all lingering thoughts of Delise Delaney.

We woke up early, I felt refreshed and ready to find Rachel Elsworth and wrap the case up. I'd returned her to her parents, take the job in Middlesbrough and let the police sort out Dyer, Manteh and the Charlies. Everything seemed less complicated this morning. From Middlesbrough I'd be able to keep in touch with Sylvia and things would develop.

I looked out of the window. It was a clear day with a strong wind blowing across the front. The tide was as far in as it ever comes at Southport. I could see the waves two miles away across the wide flat sands. To the north Blackpool Tower was clearly visible and the Lake District hills further to the north beyond Morecambe Bay.

Sylvia and I dressed in jeans and casual pullovers. We went down for breakfast holding hands like a pair of honeymooners. Over a slow breakfast we made our plans for the day. I wanted to look round the shops and seaside attractions. Rachel must be working somewhere. On a bank holiday Monday all places of entertainment were sure to be fully manned. I walked out to the car park and checked the car. It was intact, but that was no proof that it hadn't been spotted. None of the posse were in view.

We decided not to start our search until the shops opened so we sat and read the papers. I asked Sylvia to stay and let me do the search on my own but she was eager so shortly after nine our two-person dragnet hit the streets of Southport. I should have asked Sinclair not to count the Bank Holiday, but I had been pushing my luck in getting an extra twelve hours.

There were a lot of people about, mostly Liverpudlians out for the day. There were queues at the cash dispensers outside the banks so they were here to spend their money. Lord Street, once the Mecca of the local mega-rich, was now in decline. There were still some good furniture stores and tobacconists but cheap novelty shops had taken over most of the street.

We soon found our search was a waste of time. The regular shops and cafés along Lord Street didn't have many casual employees and the staff weren't willing to answer questions on the busiest shopping day of the year. For purposes of elimination I checked all the shops in Lord Street and the stores in the streets behind it. There was no sign of Rachel or of anyone following me.

I began to relax my vigilance. We spent a full three hours going into every shop and restaurant that was open and by lunch-time we were both ready for a break. The crowds on the streets had increased. It was difficult to move.

We walked back to the hotel and decided to do the amusement park and seafront in the afternoon. If nothing turned up I'd have to spend tomorrow checking the poll tax list to see if Thwaite was listed as paying tax in Southport. I was still convinced that this was where Rachel had gone to ground. After a short meal we went out again, heading for the Fun Park which was at one end of the extensive garden and lake which formed the sea-front.

There were men on water scooters roaring round the tiny lake watched by a crowd of thousands. The small amusement park was bursting at the seams with people.

There weren't many black faces in the crowd but I was still jumpy.

We looked everywhere; we went in everywhere, but no sign of Rachel. Quite a lot of the attractions were manned by temporary staff but they weren't student types – they were hard-faced Merseysiders with shaven heads and rings through their noses. Answering questions was against their principles. Both of us were getting irritable. The last thing I needed was a public quarrel with some doped-up Scouser. They thought we were either the drugs squad or the vice squad.

A huge ramshackle pub faced the sea behind the funfair. Sylvia didn't want to go in but the walk back to Lord Street without a stiff drink was more than either of us could face. The wind was still belting in from the sea and the crowds were edgy and jumpy. The Merseysiders moved differently from Mancunians and their eyes were sharp and watchful.

Leather-jacketed bikers had taken over the pub but we found a corner seat. I got a gin and tonic for Sylvia and a pint for myself. We sat and planned our next move, grateful to be out of the breeze. I was conscious that Sinclair's deadline was getting closer.

The casual search was clearly hopeless so we'd have a drive on to the beach, a quick look round and then on to Birkdale to see if Rachel was lurking among the natterjack toads. Sylvia didn't want to walk back to the King Edward car park. She said she'd wait for me on the beach near where the hovercraft was picking up people for rides.

I set off through the crowds of bored adults, whining children and booted teenagers. I was so absorbed in the passing scene that I got halfway before I remembered that Sylvia had the car keys in her handbag. I went back towards where I'd left her, but this time cut round to the right of the funfair towards the pier and along the front.

Out on the sands, well away from the roaring hovercraft, there was a long line of ponies. Children were queueing for rides and a young woman in white breeches was giving them riding helmets. My eye was caught by her figure – it was certainly worth a second glance. There was something familiar about her face. It couldn't be. I stopped and looked. I stood quite still in the middle of the promenade for several minutes. I must have been gaping at her, open-mouthed. Several passing children were trying to see what I was looking at so intently, then giving me curious looks as they were pulled along by their parents.

I climbed over the concrete barrier and strode down the marram-grass covered slope on to the beach for a closer look. I had the sense to stop before my interest was noticed. The young woman at the pony ride was Rachel Elsworth, her dark hair tied in a bun. There could be no mistake. Even at this distance I could see that her father had not been exaggerating when he said that she had stunning good looks. I took out the photo I carried with me to make quite certain. The girl in tight white breeches was definitely Rachel Elsworth. She was putting her own riding helmet on now.

While I watched she went into the back of the canvas booth where the proprietor was issuing tickets for rides. A few moments later she emerged, brushing something off her nose. She was obviously concerned about her appearance if she had to powder her nose before every ride, I thought. Unless of course the powder wasn't just a beauty aid?

What a fool I'd been! Seeing two riding helmets in Rachel's bedroom had put me off asking Dee if Rachel had more riding kit with her. I'd missed the obvious clue of the empty space next to her other helmets. I ought to have realised that a devoted horsewoman like Rachel would always have her riding stuff with her and that a holiday riding school would be an obvious place to look for her.

Well, at least I could console myself that I had correctly followed the clues leading to Southport. Still, Southport's a big place and if I hadn't decided to walk back along the prom to Sylvia I would never have spotted Rachel. The vast empty expanse of beach was the last place anybody would have thought of looking for her. She was riding now, leading out a line of eight small ponies.

It looked as if my hopes for a quick solution were about to be realised. Sinclair wouldn't have the satisfaction of taking me off the case. As Rachel rode away I went over to the man who was taking the money. He had beetling black eyebrows which met in the middle of his forehead.

'Are you here every day?' I asked.

'Every day, barring high tides,' Beetling-brows replied. He looked more like a racecourse tipster than a riding school proprietor, but he was obliging enough.

'Is that girl over there working tomorrow?' I inquired. He gave me an old-fashioned look, with brows curling and uncurling like a file of seasick caterpillars.

'She seems so good with the kiddies and my six-year-old's always nagging me to start her on lessons,' I explained.

'Yes, we're here from eleven till three. Shouldn't be a queue tomorrow. Just bring your kid along, we've lots of nice ponies. We'll soon get her sorted out.' He didn't mind enquires about his beautiful assistant as long as they were accompanied by offers to increase his trade.

I offered to pay him in advance but he said there was no need to bother. I squinted across the sand to see where Rachel had got to now. Her string of ponies was disappearing under the pier.

I hurried on to tell Sylvia. I could see her by the hovercraft stand. Something was wrong. She was talking to a tall black man. It was Leon. The man she'd claimed was a business acquaintance of Dyer's when I saw her speaking to him outside the Prohibition Club. She was pointing something out to him. She was showing him my route through the funfair back to the hotel.

Leon was in bike leathers and just past him in the beach car park two youths were unloading scramble bikes from the white Transit. He had a portable phone in a holster at his hip and there was a public phone box not twenty yards away which Sylvia must have used to reach him.

Things began to fall into place. An hour after I told Sylvia that I was heading for the airport on Saturday a gang of drug dealers had arrived there looking for me. I couldn't know for sure that they were Charlies. That might be a personal fantasy but their homicidal intention had been real enough. It must have been Sylvia who had tipped them off.

Sylvia must be the link between Dyer and the drug gangs. Perhaps they'd already made the deal Sinclair feared so much. What if, instead of resisting the dealers as everyone claimed he would, Dyer had got into bed with them? It might make a lot more sense for him to go along with them for a share in the profits. It would also make more sense for Dyer to go to great lengths to keep such a deal secret for as long as possible. Had the unfortunate Thwaite had his throat cut because he had stumbled onto the truth and then tried to blackmail Dyer? That certainly gave Dyer a stronger motive for murder than annoyance at being conned by Thwaite with his tales of loans. An operator like Dyer must be used to being turned down by bank managers.

I must have presented a deadly danger when I came along trying to find Thwaite's girlfriend, the only person who might know the truth. They'd even been ready to provide me with Sylvia as a companion to extract any information I might let slip after I survived their efforts to relegate me to the hospital or the cemetery.

If they were trying to find Rachel on their own account they must have decided I was a rival muscling in on their act. The newspapers carried nightly stories about how the Charlies dealt with competition.

Sylvia had used my vanity against me to discover my moves in advance. No wonder she found me attractive. My ears were burning. I'd been a bloody fool. The one good thing I could find in my favour was that Sylvia didn't know I'd found out and she didn't know that I'd found Rachel.

I stood and watched from my vantage behind the funfair wall until their conference came to an end. Leon headed back to the car park where both bikes had been unloaded. Two masked figures mounted the bikes and roared across the beach towards the sea where there were people racing around in cars and motorbikes. Leon drove the white Transit out of the car park and on to the road to Birkdale. Very clever, when I got back there would be no sign of any pursuit. Sylvia would be able to summon any help she needed if we found Rachel.

I scrambled over the wall back into the funfair and hurried towards Sylvia through the funfair gate with its throng of harassed parents. To disguise my feelings I pretended to be out of breath. Sylvia seemed delighted to see me. She offered to come back with me this time to see I didn't get lost.

Back at the room she was out of her jeans and pullover before I'd had time to lock the door. I couldn't just stand there gawping at her like a novice monk as she peeled her bra off. One thing followed another and we spent the next hour strenuously. The sea air was very bracing.

Afterwards as we lay on the bed I rationalised that sex with Sylvia was now a commercial activity – strictly business – nothing personal. I told myself that Rachel's safety depended on deceiving Sylvia: I couldn't dump her without revealing what I knew.

'Do you still want to drive along the beach?' I asked. It was quarter past four. There was still time for plenty to happen.

'All right, the sea air'll re-charge our batteries,' she laughed.

We dressed and went out. Something of my mood must have shown because Sylvia said, 'Are you worried about Rachel? Don't – I'm sure you'll find her. At least we've found each other, however this works out. I just want to go on being with you. How do you feel about that?' I had to give Sylvia top marks as an all-round performer. I gave her a squeeze on the arm as a reply.

We drove down Lord Street to the roundabout and then straight out on to the sands. The hard sand at Southport stretches for miles. There's an aircraft landing-strip to the left of the beach entrance. Away down towards the sea there was a confused mêlée of scramble bikes and four-wheeled-drive vehicles cruising up and down.

'It looks dangerous down here,' I said as I drove slowly down towards the sea. 'I hope everyone keeps a safe distance.'

Cars and bikes were racing along in all directions and I steered in a wide circle. Eventually two particular bikes began to keep pace with us. The feeling of danger and excitement was increased because, as well as moving vehicles, there were parked ones and pedestrians to weave around. I increased my speed experimentally and then slowed down again. The two bikers kept pace with us. The sand was uneven, in most places firmly packed but there were spots where it had been churned up and was much softer.

I chose a course parallel to the sea where the little ridges left by the waves caused us less vibration and put my foot pedal to the metal hard.

'Dave,' shrieked Sylvia, 'be careful, we want to get home in one piece.' I laughed, I wasn't too sure if she did deserve to keep a whole skin. The Nissan roared away as I twisted and turned out of the paths of moving vehicles and round stationary ones. In the mirror I could see that the bikers were following closely, they must have been under orders to keep me in sight.

Choosing my moment with great care I waited until I was almost up to a patch of soft sand then I slammed the hand brake on and did the sharpest possible turn to the right. The pair of trackers shot past me and, moving as one, tried to do an equally showy turn but in the soft sand.

They both shot off their bikes at least twenty feet up into the air and then hit the sand with bone jarring and very satisfactory smacks, audible even inside the car.

Sylvia looked at me in shocked surprise but I played it completely straight. I stopped the car and got out and walked back to where a crowd was gathering around the prone pair.

A red-faced individual with an officious manner was already ministering to them. Against all First Aid advice he was moving them, quite possibly causing more injury. I didn't rush in to stop him. They seemed to be gasping for breath.

'They're all right, just winded that's all. It's their own fault. I saw it all. They should never have tried to turn there at that speed.' He started slapping one of the black youths hard on the back. Unfortunately no necks seemed to be broken.

'There you are lad, come on, get your breath. I've seen worse before now. At least you only hit soft sand.'

Among the fraternity of bikers and beach motorists who had gathered round us no one was blaming me, or thought things were serious enough to summon an ambulance. Collisions and falls were an everyday happening. The bikes were in a bad way. One had a twisted front fork, the other was half buried in soft sand.

The Good Samaritan in the oiled jacket continued slapping and smacking the breathless pair. I don't know what they found worse, being thrown through the air or being revived by him.

'We get this every holiday, you know. Lads who don't know the sands go over the top of their bikes when they hit a soft patch. There's nothing you can do, they'll be as right as rain when they get their breath back,' he said.

I made the excuse that my girlfriend was upset to slip away.

Sylvia was looking white and shaken when I got to her. I drove back to the sea-front very sedately. I wanted to draw things out as much as possible. We sat in the car for a while.

'Do you mind telling me what that was all about?' Sylvia asked eventually.

'What do you mean? It was an accident. Two young fools getting too close. That man in the waxed jacket said it happens all the time. They were only shaken up.'

'It's a miracle they weren't killed. You want to be more careful,' she said.

'I'm sorry. It wasn't my fault, but I can see you're upset. To make it up to you how would you like a flight over Southport?' I said, pointing to where the single-engined Beechcraft monoplane was taking off.

'Dave you must be mad! Are you serious?'

'Of course I am. Come, fly with me! Unless you'd rather do the experiment on the seagull I was telling you about last night. We might be able to see Barrow-in-Furness from up there.'

She took me at my word and we joined the short queue for the aircraft. There were two alternatives on offer and I opted for the longer one. There were only five seats in the plane. Sylvia and I sat at the back.

As the plane climbed steeply into the air I could see the whole scene on the beach. Someone must have gone to fetch Leon and his white van because he was already on his way to collect his friends. Sylvia was peering forward. At the extreme end of Morecambe Bay we could see the massive new nuclear submarine fabrication sheds at Barrow, and nearer to us the nuclear power station at Heysham Head.

The trip was brief, more of a hop than a flight. We looped round Southport then back towards the landing beach. In the foreground I could see the ponies jogging along with Rachel leading them. To distract Sylvia I pointed out Formby Head and the Seaforth Container Terminal beyond. The huge bulk of the Atlantic Conveyor II loomed out of the docks, like a pig in a rat-hole. A glance to my right as we arrowed in to land confirmed that Leon was still ministering to his mates.

I bustled Sylvia back to the hotel when we landed. She was ready for more horizontal activity and she wanted to continue the hunt for Rachel. I told her it was hopeless and that I'd find better clues back in Manchester. I didn't care whether she guessed that I knew what was gcing on but I was determined to go back. Finally I told her I was working to a deadline: I had to find Rachel by tomorrow or lose my fee. In the end she agreed. We checked out and I paid the bill with my plastic.

We joined the masses heading away from the coast. I got lost and we drove right into the crumbling suburbs of Liverpool before we found the end of the M58 and the route back to Manchester. I dropped Sylvia off at her flat in Heaton Mersey and went home for an early night.

I was in bed by ten o'clock. My last thought before dozing off was that if luck had been on my side in finding Rachel, I'd made my own luck by surviving long enough to be in the right place.

13

I slept for under an hour before waking suddenly. I wasn't tired. Walking round Southport and bed with Sylvia weren't enough to exhaust me. The revelation of her apparent treachery had excited me, my brain was seething. I had to find someone to talk to. The brief sleep had refreshed me.

I got up, made a cup of coffee and dressed, putting on black jeans, a white crew-necked sweater and the green bomber jacket that Marco had admired so much at Leonardos. As I left the flat I was on auto-pilot; it was as if the brief sleep had made up my mind for me. I drove round to Delise's mother's house just a short distance away in the terraced streets of the old part of Chorlton.

Although it was now engulfed in the encroaching suburbs of Manchester, the aspect of the streets in this area belonged more to the Dickensian epoch at the start of the last century than to the dominant Edwardian style found elsewhere. Just enough houses of character had been built at a time when Chorlton was a remote village in Lancashire, not joined on to Manchester. They were in a medley of styles, a fact which gave Chorlton village its air of quaintness. There was nothing mass-produced or planned about Chorlton Green and the village street running off it I thought, as I turned the corner of the little street where Molly Delaney lived.

Molly's house stood in a neat terrace opposite a pocket-handkerchief-sized park mainly used for pooping by the local canine population. As their human partners refrained from scooping, there was usually a powerful odour in hot weather. This hadn't turned Molly against animals or the street. Her car, a 2CV festooned with labels in favour of whales and against nuclear power and racism, was outside the house and, as there was no space on that side of the street, I left the car outside the park, crossed the road and rang the bell.

She wasn't in. I guessed she must be at the Animal Rights club, whose HQ was only a few streets away. I looked at my watch, it was still only 11.15. I decided to wait until she came back so I strolled back to the car. My discovery about Sylvia left me feeling a lot older, which, I suppose, is why I found myself staking out the Delaney establishment.

Although she hadn't said anything, I guessed Delise had given up the flat she'd had in Fallowfield and moved back to her Mum's. When I'd called her at the flat earlier the phone had been disconnected.

As a veteran of many evenings spent waiting for villains to show, doorstepping Molly was no hardship. Patience was part of the job specification. Eventually I spotted her bike coming along the pavement. She prefers the bike to the car for short trips, not because it's more environmentally friendly, but because it's safer when she's a drop taken.

I didn't get out to confront her on the pavement. Molly was perfectly capable of tackling me as a potential mugger if I surprised her. I waited until she'd manoeuvred the bike into her front door before approaching.

Molly Delaney's built like a strongman's daughter – her arms as thick as the average man's thigh, her face like a map of Ireland with all the mountains and bogs shaded in. Maintaining discipline in a comprehensive classroom has never been a problem for her. One piercing shriek and a suggestion of forward motion is usually enough to cow the fiercest juvenile.

For dealing with me she has refined and sharpened her classroom techniques.

Usually dressed in sweater and dark jeans, her fixation on saving large animals is understandable: she looks like a killer whale herself. Molly's face always registers an expression of sympathetic understanding gone slightly wrong. She has shelves of books proving mutually contradictory ideas, all of which she's believed in passionately at one time or another.

It's always dangerous to raise any current topic with Molly. Even a casual comment about the weather can give rise to a twenty-minute rundown on the latest theories about global warming. Anything openly political provokes a far more searching inquisition. Disagreement, or even a mild suggestion of shades of grey, could lead her to making angry denunciations of crypto-fascism or racism on the part of the person foolish enough to dispute with her: usually a mild-mannered social worker or charity organiser. Few try it twice.

Hard to credit though it was, this was the character who had given birth to Delise. Nature must have been working by opposites. Of course, I'd never met the late and unlamented Zuse McKitty, whose brief but hardly divine role had been to fertilise the young Miss Delaney. Sensibly enough on his part, he hadn't married her. He must have been a very handsome man I've often thought, but that's only guesswork. Delise herself is the only visible reminder of the part he'd played in Molly's life.

'Oh, it's you,' she said, blocking her doorway. 'I might have known it would only be a wastrel calling on me at this time of night.' Her arms were folded and she looked in formidable fettle. From the slight flush on her face I could tell she'd been hitting the organic wine with her animal-loving pals. She isn't the sort you try to push past.

'Can I come in?' I asked mildly. 'I need to see Delise.'

'You do, do you? Pity you didn't arrange to see her at a decent hour of the day, like any decent man would.' Molly spoke with a standard, non-regional educated accent; the only traces of her Irish origin were revealed when she pronounced the word 'any' as 'annie' but, although never made much of, the Irish background is the bottom line in Molly's life story. The woes of Ireland are always the final, clinching argument she wheels out when all other verbal or physical weapons fail her.

'You're looking very well, Molly. All this rain we've been having agrees with your complexion. You know, you're a hard woman to get in touch with,' I wheedled. 'Won't you let me in for a chat? I know Delise isn't at her flat.'

'I suppose you'd better come in. I don't want the neighbours complaining that I've been brawling in the street again, but you're just to state your business and then go.'

I hurriedly entered before she changed her mind, stumbling over the stack of back copies of the *Guardian* which she kept as a kind of reference library by the front door. She'd had the downstairs rooms made into one long living area, with the kitchen at the far end, away from the street.

'Before you ask, Delise isn't in. I'm expecting her back shortly. She's been out with some of her university friends. She's got to be in early because she's to make the arrangements to get herself to Jersey tomorrow,' Molly said and then went into the kitchen. I followed her and sat down near the kitchen entrance. I could hear cups being clattered about but Molly was in no hurry to re-emerge.

I didn't have long to wait before Delise herself arrived.

She entered the long living room and walked towards me, the movement of her arms and legs so casual that the fact that she went in a particular direction seemed purely by chance. She was wearing red hotpants on top of flowery leggings and a short blue denim waistcoat over a yellow long sleeved blouse. Favouring me with a scornful glance she went into the kitchen for a conference with her mother.

'I'm going to bed, if you want to make a mess of your life, then get on with it,' was Molly's unpromising comment to her daughter as she swept past me. I heard her heavy tread on the stairs, then there was silence.

Delise came out and sat on the settee at the other end of the room. As in my flat previously, she was maintaining her distance. I stood up and went over but didn't sit down next to her. If she wanted personal space I had to give it to her.

'So you're going to Jersey then?' I said.

'Only for an interview. I haven't got the job yet.'

'But you must stand a good chance if they've asked you for interview,' I insisted.

'Yes, but they haven't seen me yet. I've heard they're very prejudiced on these small islands. Somebody said they all speak with a kind of South African accent in Jersey,' she said nervously.

'Don't be silly, Delise. They've people going to Jersey from all over the world, just because the Jersey accent sounds South African doesn't mean they are South Africans. Anyway you're well qualified or they wouldn't have sent for you.'

'Yes, it's excavating a Neolithic tumulus and I've had experience with the British Neolithic and in Pakistan. I'm ready to supervise. They want two supervisors under a local man as Director. This could be a big break for me.'

There was a pause as we both considered the implications of this.

'Sit down Dave. You're making me nervous standing there

like a prehistoric dolmen!' I sat at the end of the settee, still some distance away from her.

'Hadn't you better tell me why you've come round. We didn't exactly part as friends,' she continued.

'Well I wanted to explain about that. It wasn't quite what it seemed to you. This woman has some information . . .'

'Just a minute Dave, it wasn't "this woman" the other morning. It was Sylvia, and you can't disguise the self-satisfied smirk you get on your silly face when you've just had your ashes raked out, so don't play your games with me!' she said with a flash of the Delaney temper.

'It's true, she knows something about this missing daughter of Harold Elsworth – and it was Elsworth, not Ellington, by the way. You nearly lost me the commission.'

'Marvellous, I spend twenty minutes persuading this weird character who seems to have ants in his pants and a twitch in his eyeballs to see you, and not go elsewhere, and this is what I get thrown back at me! I had one hell of a job getting him to open up at all. I thought he said his name was Wellington and then Ellington, it was hard to tell what he was saying. His upper lip didn't move at all. He was like a ventriloquist.'

I had to smile at this description of Harold Elsworth. Delise visibly relaxed. The atmosphere improved.

'You're right about him, but his wife and daughter aren't so bad. I've found the daughter, she's in hiding in Southport and I need help to get her into safekeeping.'

'So you've given your new playmate the brush-off have you?'

'Well, more or less. I could see she knew more than she was ever going to let on.'

'Dave, you're hopeless with women. You may have some intuition with men but your over-active libido sends you haywire with women. I could tell straight away that Mrs Mather was only after one thing. You can spot that sort of woman coming a mile away if you know what to look for. I guessed she'd be covered in jewellery and the clothes, talk about power dressing! She was only after you for a bit of recreational sex, Dave!'

'I wouldn't go as far as that, Delise. Anyway she's history and I just wanted you to know,' I said.

'She's done something to you hasn't she? Dented your male pride? I can tell. Chewed you up and spat you out did she? You can't hide these things from me, can you?' She moved closer to me, smiling ruefully. 'Well we did say Pimpernel Investigations always get their man, or in this case girl, but I'm sorry. I can't do anything for you. I've got to be in the Channel Islands for this interview, unless you think I should give up the best chance I've had in years of working in my own field?'

I shook my head.

'No, I don't think even you were that self-centred Dave. You'll have to find someone else.'

'Honestly Delise I don't know why I came to see you. You've told me I'm a bastard, look like a Chippendale reject, let myself get taken in by a nymphomaniac in a load of jewellery and now I'm self-centred,' I said resignedly. She took hold of my hand.

'Aw diddums!' she mocked.

'How are you getting to Jersey? Are you all right for cash?' I countered solicitously.

'I'm going to try to get a lift down to Poole in Dorset and then catch the ferry from there.'

'Look, our tight-lipped client Elsworth may be mean with the words, but he's generous with the cash. Why don't you let me sub you for the airfare? British Airways fly direct from Manchester.'

'No Dave, thanks but I don't want to go back to being your kept woman.'

'When were you ever that? If it hadn't been for you I'd be sleeping in Cardboard City now, scrabbling about for a swig of meths.'

'Go on! You were never that bad.'

'Please Delise, take it. No strings attached,' I said, getting £300 out of my wallet. 'I'll only spend it on clothes. It isn't as if I don't owe you.'

'It's not conscience money is it? No, well let me have £100, then I'll not leave you short.'

In the end she settled for £200. At least she'd be able to buy a return air ticket. She went to put the money in a jar in the kitchen cupboard. When she came back she sat close to me.

'Do you want to stay tonight? Mum won't mind, I know

she's gruff and grumpy but she's no prude. As long as we don't make too much noise and you don't mind us squeezing into a single bed.'

Despite Delise's belief in my over-active libido and the brief sleep I'd had earlier I wasn't certain I'd be firing on all cylinders. Still, if that was the way things were trending, never let it be said that I didn't attempt to please a lady in any reasonable request. Delise's invitation was a challenge to my stamina; now I would see if all those bike rides were going to pay off.

Delise slipped off the denim jacket and put her arms round my neck. She kissed me, but then I felt her stiffen.

'You bastard!' she shrieked. 'Since when have you taken to wearing Chanel Number 5? You've been with that bitch all day and then you've the cheek to come here pawing at me.'

Before I could do anything, or invent a plausible lie, there was a violent rumbling sound as Molly Delaney charged down the stairs and entered her living room like a twenty-metre yacht with sails at full stretch before a Force 8 gale.

'You damned peeler's get! You're raping my daughter!' she howled as she advanced on me with a bundle of rolled-up newspapers in her hand. She must have been lying on the floor above, with her ear jammed to a crack, listening for the slightest sound of disturbance.

Delise and I stood paralysed by fright, but it was Delise who snapped out of it first. She must have had a less strenuous day than me. She gave me a sharp push and I leaped over the settee, putting that between me and her furious mother.

'What are you playing at! Let me get at him! If he's laid a finger on you I'll break every bone in his body. This is what you get for messing about with a copper's son.' It was one of Molly's obsessions that because of my remote connection with the law I was personally responsible for every misdeed by any police force from Los Angeles to Lhasa.

'Leave off Mother. I'm perfectly capable of dealing with the two-timing rat myself,' shouted Delise.

I tried edging towards the door before Molly could give me a rap over the nose with her rolled-up liberal newspapers. She moved to block me.

'Leave me alone mother, he's not worth it,' Delise intervened.

'None of them are! What have I always told you? We're better off without them,' she said to Delise. Then she continued advancing round the settee towards me. I could see I was going to be made to pay the price of Zuse McKitty's neglect if I didn't make a break for it. Before I could jump over the settee again Delise grabbed her mother and pulled her back.

'Get out you bloody fool, and take a shower before you come to see me again! That's if I'm ever available again! Next time you need a shoulder to cry on go round to Mrs Mather,' Delise ordered.

I made good my escape.

On the whole it hadn't been a good day for my relations with the opposite sex. The encounter with Sylvia, while satisfying physically, had scarred me mentally. I was sentimental enough to be displeased with the idea that Sylvia hadn't been attracted by my manly good looks alone. No wonder the vengeful French military establishment had had Mata Hari shot.

I winced again at the thought of being seduced by a beautiful woman merely after information. This was why Russian spy masters had been ready to use the sexual 'honey trap' on diplomats visiting Moscow: male egos were so bruised by the experience that many of the men concerned never revealed that they'd been a victim of sexual entrapment. They preferred to spy against their own country rather than let it be known.

I really had needed a shoulder to cry on.

Sylvia had temporarily unhinged me. I'd rushed round to Delise like a moonstruck calf, fresh from Sylvia's arms. The resulting kick in the groin from Delise and her mother had been just what I needed to restore my sense of reality. For me the alternatives when in distress were rushing round to Delise or trying to get comfort out of a whisky bottle. I was glad in a way that I'd chosen to go to Delise. It proved that I was still basically sane.

Delise's parting words didn't sound like total finality and she hadn't thought my money was so tainted that she needed to throw it back at me. If her mother hadn't had an evening on the sauce I might have been able to repair things between us. There was a strong mutual attraction pulling us together.

I had needed Delise tonight and, despite what her mother had said, I thought she needed a man in her life. There had only been one real love in my life and that was Elenki. She was lying in Southern Cemetery, and part of me was with her. Something had broken, or perhaps just frozen, when she died. I'd never been able to develop a full emotional relationship with Delise. What had happened to me with Elenki had crippled me in some way.

But there was fault on Delise's side too. It was she who had said she'd found someone else. She'd made the first move to split up. Admittedly, I'd let myself get too obsessed by my job, but there'd been nothing apart from that cursed mother of hers to stop her coming to Rochdale herself. If I was suffering from the effects of grief then Delise was also something of a casualty. Growing up without a father, palmed off on one unwilling child-minder after another, and then constantly catechized about the evils of the entire male sex, it was a wonder that Delise was as normal as she was.

As I went to bed for the second time that night I resolved to get the Elsworth case out of the way as quickly as possible so I could get back to having a private life.

14

I was up at six and out on the bike, sticking to main roads all the way. Riding helped to clear my head. Despite what I'd been told I was still certain that it was the Charlies who were in a secret alliance with Dyer. They didn't have Sylvia to report my movements any longer. So they'd be watching me by other means. Rachel must know something very damaging about Dyer and his secrets. If I just drove over and picked her up they were capable of any kind of stunt to snatch her. They were bound to have the heavy mob on my tail. I had to think of some way to confuse them, and I'd to reckon on being watched all the time. It could be that my sudden parting from Sylvia had aroused suspicions that I had found Rachel.

Why hadn't Rachel just run off to the Glastonbury Rock Festival again like a nice sensible girl? Extricating her from the tangle of deceit surrounding her was going to take both cunning and luck.

I still felt sore about Sylvia, like a fool I'd been ready to hop into bed with the first attractive woman who'd shown an interest in my boring activities. What really made me wince with embarrassment every time I thought about Sylvia Mather was the thought that but for a chance sighting I might have led her and her associates straight to Rachel.

My only excuse was that after Delise, with her complications and her mother, Sylvia had been like a breath of fresh air. I must have been rebounding from Delise's letter harder than I'd thought to have been so stupid as to let my emotions get involved with Sylvia at all. Maybe I didn't understand my own feelings about Delise.

Even giving Sylvia the benefit of the doubt, and allowing that she wasn't completely in Dyer's confidence, she must have been working as his liaison with the drug peddlers.

But was that credible? Was there anything in Dyer's history to say he'd trust anyone with such an important job? Perhaps she'd found herself drawn in deeper than she'd intended. She might have been too anxious to please her boss. She'd said she was the one who ran the clubs, maybe he'd delegated more and more to her. I could believe he was lazy.

When I had seen her talking to Leon in Southport it could have been perfectly innocent. Dyer could have sent Leon over to tell her to keep away from me. No, that couldn't be it. She must have got in touch with Leon herself, not once but several times, to report my movements. How could she be so sly? How could a girl from a straight-up place like Barrow in Furness get to be be so devious. Must have been the convent education.

Perhaps Dyer had a hold over her and she was being blackmailed. That could be it. What could she have done? Helped herself to the petty cash? More likely he'd involved her in some crime and was using the threat of exposure to keep her in line.

The weather was cold, more like February than June. It looked as if it would rain later. I pushed hard and peddled back through Chorlton to the flat. I had a shower, dressed in a warm pullover, slacks and black leather jacket, and then snatched a quick bite of muesli.

While eating I listened to Radio 4. Brian Redhead was trying to get a government minister to admit that his department might have made a mistake but however cunningly Brian phrased the questions the minister wriggled out of a straight answer. I knew how Redhead felt.

I drove to my office on empty early-morning roads. There were a few executives in their BMWs heading in alongside me but I was beating the main rush by an hour. The homeless teenagers and derelicts were making their ways to vantage points with their placards at the ready. When I got to my building Fred Lumsden was already on duty. He seemed to haunt the place. I couldn't fault the old vampire for availability.

He gave me a packet of mail.

'I kept this for you Boss, seeing as Delise isn't around. When will she be back?' he asked nosily.

'I don't know Fred. She'll suit herself like she always does,' I answered.

'There was a middle-aged couple round here looking for you yesterday afternoon, Boss. They came back twice and then left you this letter. They didn't seem best pleased with themselves either, in a right state they were, the woman was crying.'

'Thanks Fred, did they say what it was about?' I asked. Fred was following me to the lift. His poached egg eyes were fixed on the letter and he was drooling at the prospect of a piece of interesting tittle-tattle.

'No Boss, I reckoned it was their business. Anyway they left you the letter, like.' He looked at me expectantly. I was supposed to open it to satisfy his curiosity. He came even closer to me. I was able to focus on individual hairs on his unshaven lantern jaw. It was like a horror film gone wrong but to keep on the right side of him I quickly opened the envelope and looked at the signature . . . George Thwaite.

I must have stood in the lift with a startled look on my face for a minute before Fred spoke, 'Everything all right Boss? You look as if someone's just walked over your grave.' References to graves from a Dracula look-alike were something I could do without at that time in the morning.

'Thanks Drac . . . er Fred, it's just from someone I didn't expect to hear from. That's all.'

Fred pulled the lift door shut and I enjoyed the privilege of a powered ascent to my floor as I read the letter carefully.

George and Hilda Thwaite, parents of Andrew Thwaite, had seen my notices in the shops in Didsbury when they came to make arrangements for their son's funeral and because I claimed to be a friend of their son they would like to see me. They left their phone number and had been sent to my office by my answering service.

I went into the office and sat at the desk to ponder this. I looked through the other mail, as usual mostly rubbish adverts for personal computers and yet more life insurance and pension schemes. The last envelope had a cheque for £3,000 from Happyways. It included my fee and a bonus for recovery of stolen goods. I was solvent at last.

Glowing with the buzz of this news I decided to do the decent thing regarding the Thwaites. I owed them nothing but I'd been the one who'd discovered the corpse and I'd advertised myself as a friend. It was still before seven-thirty when I phoned them.

The call was answered immediately by a man speaking with a Yorkshire accent. It was George Thwaite. I explained who I was.

'We're very sorry we missed you yesterday Mr Cunane. I was going to phone you later this morning. My wife and I are very anxious to speak to you, we know you're a private detective and get paid for your time. We'd be willing to pay you whatever the going rate is.' He sounded humble but I detected a fierce pride there as well.

'There's no need to talk about money, Mr Thwaite,' I said, but I was well aware of the old Northern proverb, 'Folk who'll do owt for nowt, 'll steal' . . . If it made them feel more comfortable to pay me I could set a nominal fee.

'I could see you this morning if you can tell me how to get over to your place,' I said.

Thwaite gave me directions to get to Hebden Bridge via Todmorden. Their house was hard to find so if I turned right past a pub called the 'Shoulder of Mutton' and into the car park then they could meet me outside the pub. I promised to get to them at about ten or soon after.

While talking to Mr Thwaite I thought a visit to Yorkshire would be a cunning diversion. If I was going to be followed wherever I went I might as well lead Leon and his cronies a merry dance.

The next call required some consideration. I needed help from Dee Elsworth but was she likely to give it? I had to try. She seemed a much more resolute person than her husband. I phoned and Dee answered. She explained that Harold had already set off for work and I wouldn't be able to reach him for a while, but I told her that it was her I wanted.

'I'm going to ask you to do some things. They may sound crazy but I want you to hear me out before you slam the phone down. Will you do that?' I asked.

'Is it something to do with getting Rachel back?' she queried, the old upper-crust accent back in place. She was paying me enough to be as condescending as she pleased and if everything went well I would soon be shot of her, and all the Elsworths.

'Certainly, why else would I be ringing you?' I replied coolly. 'Look Mrs Elsworth, I need a horse-box and Land Rover. Also a pony about sixteen hands high. Can you handle that?'

'What do you mean! I've put more ponies in horse-boxes than you've had hot dinners!' she said indignantly.

'Right then, no problem! You should be in your riding gear

and meet me at about twelve thirty at the Evans' Hotel in Chorlton,' I requested.

'Just a minute! What on earth is all this for? What are you up to?' she replied angrily.

'Look, I told you what I wanted would sound crazy but if I have to explain exactly what I'm intending to do it might put Rachel in even greater danger than she is in already.'

'Where are you ringing from Mr Cunane? I'm getting in my car this minute to come and see you. If Rachel's in danger I've not the slightest intention of messing about with ponies and horse-boxes. Are you trying to prepare me for bad news? This is all much too much!' She was shouting and I had to hold the phone away from my ear for a moment until she fell silent. She was furious.

I tried to put every once of smarm and charm into my reply. If I couldn't get Dee's help I'd be in serious difficulties with any alternative rescue plan. 'Mrs Elsworth – Dee – I wouldn't be asking for your help in this way unless I honestly thought it was absolutely essential in order to get Rachel back safely. She isn't in great danger at the moment but you remember that I said the people who killed Andy might not have good will towards Rachel? Well, they're sniffing around looking for her and I need the pony so I can spirit her away as inconspicuously as possible.'

There was a long pause before she replied. 'It all sounds very odd to me, but I suppose I have to trust that you know what you're doing. I'm warning you now that if I find that you've been wasting my time my husband and I will see to it that there are unpleasant consequences for you, many unpleasant consequences! Is that clear!' she snapped in clipped and aggressive tones. I was right about her being resolute. She sounded like one of the officers in a 1940s British war film.

It was my turn to pause now. I felt like putting the phone down and walking off the case. I'd only to tell her where Rachel was. She'd go and pick her up, and then after a day or so Rachel would be found dead. It might be an overdose, it might be something more violent, but Rachel Elsworth would be out of the picture for keeps.

No, I couldn't let Rachel pay such a price just because her mother had put me down. At whatever personal cost I was determined that this girl, to whom I'd never even spoken, was going to escape the clutches of Dyer, Mather, Leon and whoever else was out to get her.

'Thanks for trusting me Mrs Elsworth,' I said bitterly. 'You're going to need to pack some of Rachel's clothes in a small case. Smallest you've got, right? Last, but not least, write a note to Rachel telling her that she's in danger and to trust the man who gives her the note. Oh, and can you bring some cash?'

'Yes, certainly I can. Can you repeat it all?' she answered, speaking in a very impersonal way.

I had to give her directions to Evans' Hotel but otherwise getting a horse-box and pony was easy for her. She wanted to know what was going to happen but I told her I'd give her the details when I met her.

Next I phoned my Dad. He'd a part to play in my scheme. After a lot of explanation he was willing to drive to Southport and do his thing. I could tell he was excited at the prospect of some action, especially when I told him to pack his gun.

My last call was to Detective Chief Superintendent Sinclair. As usual I had to leave a guarded message for him, saying I hoped to collect the parcel I'd discussed with him so no action on his part was necessary. I hoped that was enough to keep him off my back until I got everything sorted. With luck everything should be coming to a conclusion by nightfall and then I could shake the dust of Manchester off my feet for a few weeks. Dyer and Manteh and Sylvia could stew in their own juices and forget about me. Delise would know how to get in touch if she wanted to.

I needed to move quickly to get the show on the road. I left the office. It was just before 8 a.m. when I arrived back in Chorlton. Back at the flat I strapped on my shoulder holster. Then I stripped down and oiled my Beretta 92 and tested the action. It was smooth. Outside the flat I looked up and down before setting off for Hebden Bridge. I couldn't see any surveillance but that didn't mean it wasn't there, just that it was good.

I rolled through Stretford with the rush-hour flow and then out onto the M61. I kept an eye on the mirror but the heavy traffic made it easy for a tail to lie well back. When I came to the turn-off for Bolton and Preston I signalled that I was turning left and kept in the left-hand lane, only turning back at the last moment onto the M62. Horns screamed out at me as I forced my way back into the stream. I probably hadn't tricked anyone but it was worth a chance.

'Death Valley', the familiar motorway to Rochdale, saw me surging along, nose to tail with the rest. I passed the turn-off for Rochdale and took the next turn for Milnrow and Littleborough. The road was good as far as Littleborough but then I turned towards Todmorden.

I thought parts of Manchester were grim, but this journey was like travelling through a time-warp. The road ran between green hillsides, but the jumble of houses and factories along the valley bottom showed how the proverb 'Where there's muck, there's brass' had started.

Short rows of neat stone-built cottages alternated with untidy factories built right up to the main road. The factories were old textile mills now put to other uses. Their poorly printed signs, piles of materials dumped any old how and scruffiness didn't give an impression of profitable industry.

There were 'chapels of rest' and undertakers shops every few hundred yards. If things went on this way there wouldn't be anyone living here in a generation. There weren't even many Asian shopkeepers trying to scratch a meagre living.

From Todmorden the road wound uphill along the Calder Valley and the hillsides got even steeper. I came to a picnic area and pulled over for a few minutes. Among the vehicles behind me I caught a glimpse of Sergeant Rice in an old Escort. How did he explain this! Far from me interfering with his investigations he was pushing his snout into mine! I felt angry. He had another man with him. Behind him there was an Afro-Caribbean in a VW estate.

There was an unpleasant quality about Rice. He radiated the smug certainty that the police in general and himself in particular were better and brighter than any civilian could be.

When I pulled out, the Escort was parked further up the road. The Passat had disappeared. I gave no sign to Rice that I'd clocked him. Soon the valley widened slightly and I was coming into Hebden Bridge. It's a clapped-out mill town now making its living as a tourist centre. Book, antique and souvenir shops lined the main street. I turned left at the end of it.

Straight ahead was the 'Shoulder of Mutton'. I turned right, into the small car park.

The car park opened on to a small square. There were two rows of weavers' cottages facing each other, converted into shops. Across the street stood the pub. I took my time before moving. My fellow travellers arrived and drove on past me without any sign of recognition.

The Thwaites were sitting on the benches outside the pub. I sized them up and walked over. Seeing me bearing down on them they stood up.

'Mr Cunane is it?' said Thwaite as he extended his hand to me. He was thin and grey-haired in a well cut suit. He moved like a man who'd earned his living by manual labour. His complexion was well tanned as if he'd worked out of doors for a long time.

'It's kind of you to come all the way here to meet us. I would have given you directions to our house but it's right up there,' he said, pointing to the warren of two- and four-storied homes and chapels built into the hillside. 'An off-comer would never find his way up there.'

He then introduced me to his wife, a sad lady wearing a Laura Ashley dress. She had a defeated look about her; the effects of grief I supposed. She seemed older and more care-worn than Thwaite. Neither of them looked like your typical impoverished Pennine hill dwellers. I decided they might be immigrants who'd made their pile in a nearby town, or maybe they'd a flourishing business here.

They invited me for coffee in a nearby ristorante called 'Il Mulino'. As the name implied it was built into the upper storey of a converted mill. There was an awkward silence while the coffee was being served. I wanted them to ask the questions. George started talking first. He wore the trousers in his family.

'Mr Cunane, I don't know how well you knew our Andrew, but the police tell us he killed himself through drugs. Now, that's not our Andrew. It's like they're talking about a different person. Every time me or his mother say something they come back to drugs . . . drugs, it must be drugs that sent him crazy. He were caught with cannabis when he were at school and the police picked on him for a while after that, but Andrew never were a drug addict and I'll not have it said . . . Do you think he was a drug addict?'

'I'm sure he wasn't,' I said tactfully. 'I didn't know your son when he was alive but I've found out plenty about him since. I'm sure your son wasn't on drugs.' I wasn't sure of any such thing, but why should I add to their grief?

'Eeeeh, it's a comfort to hear you say that. You're the first one that's agreed with us. But you wouldn't be saying it just to make us feel better, would you?' George asked sharply.

'Look, I'll be frank with you. I'm being paid to find your Andrew's girlfriend, Rachel Elsworth. She's gone missing. While doing that I've met a lot of the people who were with Andrew right up to the day before he was found. No one but the police thinks he was on drugs.' When I said the name Elsworth it evidently meant something to the Thwaites. They exchanged startled glances.

'Did you say Elsworth? Andrew introduced his girlfriend to us as Rachel Rankine,' George said.

I took the small photo of Rachel from my wallet. The Thwaites studied it.

'Aye, that's the lass all right. Elsworth you say, that's a well known name in these parts. There used to be Elsworths owned mills all round this area. They're in banking now.'

I nodded my head. 'It's the same lot, her stepfather's the boss of the Northern Pioneers' Bank in Manchester. Rankine's her real name, but she goes by her stepfather's name.'

Thwaite didn't actually say 'Well I'll go to the foot of our stairs' but from the way his eyes were bulging I could see he was thinking it.

'Eeeeh well, I'm sure it's as you say Mr Cunane, but that gives me one more reason for thinking our Andrew would never do away with himself if he were seeing a grand lass like that,' he said.

I interrupted his flow, 'Before you go on, Mr Thwaite, would you like to give me your reasons for thinking that your son didn't kill himself?'

'Well, like I said, he were no junkie, we might not be as sharp as you townies but any road, I could tell he were no druggie. He had his head screwed on too well for that. You know he were making money hand over fist as a DJ?'

I nodded.

'He used to send me hundreds of pounds to invest for him every month and lately it's been thousands of pounds. You tell me why someone worth thousands would cut his own throat after taking a few pills.'

He spoke with real anger. I noticed that neither he nor his wife recoiled from the words 'cutting his own throat', they weren't using euphemisms. They were as hard as the mill stone grit their houses were made of.

I took Andrew's diary from my inside pocket and laid it on the table. 'This is Andrew's and if you look through it you'll see that he was getting top engagements through a man called Mike Dyer. There isn't any way to put this nicely. I believe that your son found something out about Dyer, perhaps that Dyer wasn't Mr Clean on the drugs scene. Perhaps Andrew had something on Dyer . . . I don't know for certain but that could be it.

'I think Andrew put the squeeze on Dyer to get gigs. I'm not saying Andrew wasn't a good DJ but there's loads of hype in that line and if you get the right people behind you the punters think you're good – and anyone doing a top spot at the Paloma must be good by definition. So he got more bookings all over the place.'

Thwaite hadn't blinked at my unflattering explanation of his son's rise to eminence in the Manchester music world but his wife was dabbing her eyes with her handkerchief.

'He were always ambitious, our Andy, right from a bairn. You see how it is round here. A hundred years ago a lad like Andy would have got on and had his own mill but that's all gone now. There's nowt much round here for an ambitious lad. Them that made their brass here, like the Elsworths, never put anything back, tha knows.'

Before he could go into an elegy about the textile industry I cut him off. 'Was Andrew right handed?'

Thwaite looked puzzled at the question but nodded his head.

'You could get the police to tell you how a right-hander managed to cut his throat from right to left.'

There was a long silence. Then Mr Thwaite said, 'You seem to know a lot about this . . .' and let the statement trail off into the silence.

'Maybe I do,' I replied, 'but I'm not asking you to trust me or take what I say as gospel. You can look through the diary yourself and you can insist on a second post-mortem at your own expense, if necessary. I know it's gruesome but I think it will show that your son didn't kill himself. He may not have taken any drugs before he died.'

We finished our coffee and walked down the steps to the little square. There were some youths larking about. One of them on a skateboard had a shaven head with a bandana round it and was wearing black leggings and high boots. He had rings attached to all his orifices. His mate, dressed in a khaki camouflage version of the same costume, was hawking up phlegm which he was spitting over parked cars. I gave them a hard look.

'Some of their own mothers won't have 'em in,' said Mrs Thwaite sadly. We walked over to where my car was parked. The small part Mrs Thwaite had played in our discussion prompted me to wonder what kind of role model she'd been to Andrew in his dealings with women. She was probably one of those Yorkshire women who addresses her husband as Mister even in rare moments of passion.

'Look Mr Cunane, would you like to take this case on and find out who did kill our son? The police don't seem interested in catching the bugger. We're not without money. We can pay as much as your fancy Elsworths,' said Mr Thwaite.

He looked at me hopefully and I felt a spurt of sympathy for both of them. They were the real victims now – robbed of the son who'd had such promising prospects. Mrs Thwaite had tears in her eyes and her husband put his arm around her. It was hard to pull myself away but I'd already suffered because of emotional involvement with Sylvia Mather. Realistically, there was nothing I could do to get their son back for them. I had to direct my efforts towards helping the person I might be able to save.

'I would like to help you but I've got to sort out Rachel first. I think the police might take more notice of you now. I'd be grateful if you could keep my name out of it, tell them you found the diary stuck down the back of his bookcase or that he sent it you in the post.' I shook hands with them again and walked over to the car.

It would be all to the good if they could stir the police up and get some action. I didn't know who'd killed Thwaite Junior but somebody had, and Dyer hadn't blinked once when I told him about Andrew's death. At our last meeting he'd denied murder but he'd been lying about everything else. If it was my client Elsworth who'd done the job I wasn't going to cover up for him either.

It would all come out. What was amazing was how quickly the police had discounted a sinister scenario. Almost like sex discrimination. If some attractive bimbo had turned up dead it would be all over the tabloids in hours with press-men besieging her parents and friends for photographs. The death of a DJ only rated a couple of lines on an inside page and a few hours of a copper's time. No wonder Thwaite Senior was angry.

I was in a thoughtful mood as I drove out of the little town. I looked in the mirror for my faithful shadow, Rice, and was rewarded instead with the sight of the old couple trudging off up the hillside with their heads bent. I ground my fingernails into my palms. There was nothing I could do for them. It might not be Dyer who had killed their son. The chances were that I would soon know who was responsible, one way or another. Now I was involved up to my own neck in the same malicious world that had brought Andy Thwaite and his parents to grief.

Neither of my trackers was visible but I couldn't doubt that they were on the move. The weather had worsened. There was low-lying cloud in the valley. I glanced at my watch. It was 11.10. I had to get to Southport with the horse-box before two.

I drove in and out of patches of mist. I thought of dodging off the road and hiding in a mill yard but discarded the idea. It was important I get the timing right. If I was lucky I might be able to get to Chorlton and slip away with the horse-box before being spotted.

I put my foot down, winding round the narrow road at seventy. There wasn't much traffic. Speeding towards Todmorden I thought about George Thwaite. Definitely of the old school, no nonsense about 'call me George' with him, and he did all the talking too. Presumably he would inherit the capital which Andrew had been able to amass, I hoped it might help to make up for the loss of his ambitious son.

He hadn't told me what he did for a living but both of them looked such respectable chapel-going folk it must be something honest. Perhaps he was an undertaker.

I rejoined the M62 and despite the cameras stuck on posts to catch speeders did ninety all the way into Stretford and on to Chorlton. I kept going over various aspects of my plan but I couldn't see any way to improve it. All I knew was I was longing for this case to be over. I must be the only person in the country who was anxious to visit Middlesbrough.

Roll on chemical factories, acid rain and giant hypermarkets. I couldn't wait to get there and start mixing with ordinary criminals again.

15

By the time I reached Chorlton the weather had improved. I left the car at the back of the massive Department of Social Security building and walked past its entrance. Disappointed-looking claimants were coming out clutching their giros and walking into the drab shopping precinct which lay alongside.

I joined the throng and walked through the precinct to the main road and towards my rendezvous at the Evans' Hotel. Buskers and beggars competed for my small change. The sunshine added little colour to the twenty-year-old development with its peeling white paint and garish shop signs. On the other side of the street the pre-war buildings kept an air of dignity despite the changes of use they'd undergone.

I took the pedestrian crossing and hurried along the broken pavement, jinking between the displays of pot plants and garden ornaments. I didn't want to be spotted but almost as soon as that thought crossed my mind I bumped into the Salway twins, on their way to the shops. There was something youthful about the way they were bowling along the pavement. Dressed in their matching bright summer outfits, they were confidently threading their way through the sad crowd heading away from the DSS offices. Their good humour was infectious and just meeting them raised my spirits after the difficult morning I'd had so far.

'Hello David. Goodness you're popular today. Your doorbell hasn't stopped ringing.' I was already halfway past Fiona but this cheery greeting stopped me in my tracks.

'What do you mean? Who's after me?' I asked suspiciously.

Finbar beamed at me. He repeated what his twin had said. 'All morning, they've been ringing on your bell, all morning. Rough-looking characters some of them too.'

Torn between desire for a speedy getaway to Southport and the need for information. I decided to listen to what they had to say.

'The first one was a muscular little man with his arm in

plaster, he didn't want to go away at all. Claimed he was a club doorman and you knew him,' said Finbar.

'He was on the doorstep just after eight o'clock and kept trying to push into the building but Finbar threatened him with the police,' Fiona interrupted her brother. 'Makes you realise why they call them bouncers,' she giggled.

I must have just missed him.

'The next lot were a whole deputation. There must have been about six of them, led by this chap wearing a sort of silver disk at his throat. It looked like an eighteenth-century British Army officer's neck armour,' Finbar said knowledgeably. To my surprise he was describing Dyer. If Dyer was willing to take the risk of a personal appearance, then things must be serious. The fact that his henchmen hadn't done the job on Saturday night must have peeved him.

'What happened to them?' I asked him. I was anxious that the twins might have come to harm as they briskly despatched Dyer and his minions on their way.

'They rang your bell for about twenty minutes until I went down and told them to bugger off. The fancy chap was quite nasty about it. He said to tell you they know where you live and they'll be back.' Finbar spoke in a jaunty, matter-of-fact way which suggested that dealing with a mob of thugs was all in a day's work. Not long after they'd gone a nice-looking woman came round. She left a letter for you.'

That could only be Sylvia, Delise still had her key. If only I'd phoned Sylvia while I was in the car, but Rice had distracted me. I looked at my watch. Dee was sure to be waiting for me. There was no way I could go home and find out what Sylvia wanted now, not that I cared much anyway.

When I thanked Finbar and Fiona, I asked them if they liked dogs.

'What do you mean, to look after one for you?' replied Finbar.

'No, I could get one that would look after you and Fiona. You know that dog I had the other day? Would you like to borrow it for a while and keep it in the flat with you?'

'Don't be silly, David, I've got quite enough to do looking after *him* without having another huge animal moulting hairs all over my carpet,' Fiona joked as she pointed at her bald-headed twin. 'No seriously, we'll be all right. It's you that needs to look out. Give us a ring before you come back to the flat and we'll take a look round outside and tell you if the coast is clear. Do you owe them money?' she asked, laughing again.

'We'll be fine,' agreed Finbar, 'they don't know we're friends of yours. I haven't had so much fun since I left the Army. If you like I can get some of my friends round and we can arrange a proper reception.'

'Oh don't be daft, Finbar. I don't know, you men! You're like school boys.' With that remark from Fiona, they went on their way and I scurried off towards the Evans' Hotel.

As I watched them disappear round the corner I wondered whether their calmness was due to their naive optimism or to a lifelong refusal to be intimidated by anyone or anything. Whatever their secret was, I envied them.

Chorlton lies under the Manchester Airport flight path and people don't look up when they hear aircraft, but the distinctive clatter of a helicopter caught my attention as I hurried towards my rendezvous with Dee Elsworth.

I looked up to see the police helicopter circling overhead.

There was no way they could spot me walking along the crowded street. Then I remembered that they were equipped with television cameras which gave them a telescopic view of what was happening on the ground. I hurried along, trying to keep the trees between myself and the helicopter and crossed the road to the Evans' Hotel – a rambling, red-brick pub with brewery slogans draped over its architectural features like a Victorian lady's crinolines.

The 'County' Land-Rover with its horse-box took up two bays of the adjoining car park. I walked to the open window. Dee looked at me but made no move. 'Aren't you going to let me in?' I asked. Her expression reflected anxiety, eagerness and hostility in equal amounts.

I was aware of her attractiveness as I stepped forward but rule number one in the private detective's manual states don't mess about with a client's wife if you want to get paid. Well, it might not be number one, but it's high on the list.

Her shoulder-length dark hair was set off by a folded purple scarf, knotted under her hair at the back. She was wearing a white blouse undone as far as the third button – revealing two inches of cleavage, and very faded blue jeans. I detected the fragrance of perfume as I leaned towards her and said, 'Come on. Let me in. I don't want to be seen hanging round here.'

She managed to overcome her evident distrust and open the passenger door.

'Is something wrong? Has someone been annoying you?' I queried. She looked at me coolly with her wide-set blue eyes, like a farmer's wife appraising a frisky bullock – would I jump over the farm gate and tear up her garden or not? I felt like grabbing her arm and telling her not to be frightened, but I knew that would be the wrong move. I tried to smile reassuringly but I was tense myself. It didn't come out right and I don't think the effect on her was much better than trying my first idea would have been.

'No, nothing's wrong,' she said. 'I've just been wondering what on earth I'm doing here. I'm not going to drive an inch until you tell me what's going on. If you think I'm just a passive little housewife who's willing to do your bidding, you couldn't be more wrong. I only came because you said it would help Rachel.'

'Look Dee, I'm sorry I couldn't tell you more over the phone this morning but I was in a hurry. I've been to Hebden Bridge to speak to Andrew Thwaite's parents. Now we're going to go and get your daughter. She's working on the beach at Southport giving kids pony rides. I think she's in danger from the same people who killed Andrew. That's why we've got the horse-box, so we can sneak her out. If you'll get us moving I'll tell you the rest on the way.'

This did the trick. With grinding of gears and manoeuvring we got on our way. We took the M62 towards Liverpool. Dee said the straight roads would be better for the pony than the winding route Sylvia and I had taken – ponies get travel sick. I looked out of the windows, scanning both the sky and the road behind, but I couldn't spot any surveillance. Not that Dee gave me much chance to look. She plied me with questions about her daughter, her cool reserve forgotten now.

I told Dee that Rachel had been in the best of health when I saw her yesterday; that she was gainfully employed in a legal activity; that she'd been working for several days and that she wasn't in the clutches of some sinister character. She found it hard to accept that I hadn't just gone up to Rachel and told her to come home. She was eventually prepared to believe that such an approach might have made her daughter hide herself even more thoroughly than before.

I didn't like to tell Dee that I had adopted a very cautious approach at least partly because I couldn't trust my travelling companion. I also didn't feel that it was straining the truth too much to imply that my discovery of Rachel had been the result of following up the clues from her bedroom. After all, I had probably been subconsciously alert for signs of horsey activity in connection with Rachel. It was just that I spotted her by chance, before I had actually made the mental connection. Detectives, like politicians, have to be ready to make the most of whatever credit comes their way.

Dee seemed relieved but still very tense. The fact that I kept peering into the extended wing mirrors trying to see who was behind the horse-box must have heightened her feeling of insecurity and nervousness. I assured her that we weren't being followed and that no one but us knew where Rachel was. I stressed that she would only be in danger if Thwaite's killers found out her whereabouts through our carelessness.

There was no visible pursuit. That didn't mean much. If Sinclair was interested enough in my activities to order the helicopter to keep tabs on me he could have half a dozen cars tailing me. Perhaps I was becoming paranoid; but the events of the last few days gave me an ample excuse for that. I could only hope that my deception plan – to be played with two ponies and a car – was going to work. I told Dee her part of the plan. She seemed to accept it.

I asked her how Harold was. This released the tension which had gripped her since I'd joined her. She obviously had far more on her mind than an errant daughter.

'He's away again this week, off to Brussels again today. I can't understand it. He's supposed to be the chief executive of a bank here in Manchester, yet he's been going abroad almost every week for the last three months,' she said in the plaintive tones of a wronged woman.

'I thought you told me he's helping the European Commission to draft new banking laws?'

'Yes, that's his excuse. He certainly goes to Brussels. I've seen him on to his plane often enough. He books a hotel room in Brussels but when I phone him he's never available, even late at night.' Dee spoke with acid bitterness yet she seemed relieved to be telling someone, even a stranger. I listened with professional skill.

'What do you think he's up to then?' I murmured.

'I think he's found someone else, some woman he met in Brussels and that he's going through an elaborate game of making trips over there on behalf of the bank and one fine day he's going to come waltzing back with a foreign piece.'

'Are we talking about the same man?' I exclaimed. 'It takes Harold all his time to make a simple request. He'd never fix himself up with a bit of fluff. The girl would die of boredom. If I hadn't already met him I might credit your story. He's more likely to be carrying on with a set of dictionaries than with some tart in a see-through nightie!'

My unflattering comments about Harold couldn't have been much comfort to Dee but didn't seem to upset her. Her own explanation for Harold's mysterious absences was still the most plausible.

Harold was likely to be going through this elaborate deception because he was too embarrassed to tell his wife that she was off the team. My experience was that husbands got up to all kinds of tricks when away from wifey in foreign parts. I didn't think he was carrying on with a foreign floozy; probably some designing Mancunian minx from his own office had got her hooks into him, perhaps even the little cutie at his reception desk.

'He's changed in other ways too,' Dee continued. I was used to personal revelations by now but I was surprised that Dee Elsworth would go in for this kind of soul-baring.

'No, not that way,' she said, blushing slightly. She must have seen something in my expression.

'He's always been secretive but now he's worse. At first I thought he was in trouble at the bank. He keeps getting phone calls at all hours of the night. Not women, men with local accents, they shut up when they hear it's me answering. Harold won't let me listen to what they say. He says it's better if I don't know anything.'

'When exactly did all this start, then?' I asked gently. I didn't want to shatter any illusions about Harold's sexual leanings.

'Over three months ago; he started his visits to Brussels right after these late night calls began. The other odd thing I've noticed is that he's started taking his luggage to work with him the day before he's due to fly out, always two big suitcases, yet he never seems to have that many clothes with him. I thought he was picking someone up in Manchester and that the space was so that she could put her things in his cases but I've watched him getting on the plane several times and each time the flight consisted entirely of businessmen.'

'At least we know he's not smuggling drugs from Manchester to Brussels. That would be carrying coals to Newcastle,' I joked. She looked at me blankly, so I explained, 'Brussels is notorious as one of the centres of the drug trade.' A whole new can of worms was opening up where Harold Elsworth was concerned.

Dee had been driving steadily up to now, keeping in the inside lane at fifty; when I mentioned drugs she swerved into the centre lane. There was a violent fanfare of horns from a lorry which had been about to pass us. She swung back into the slow lane as the lorry swept past, its driver glaring and tapping his forehead with a finger in contempt. I hastily pushed the pistol back into the shoulder holster from which I'd drawn it by reflex action – not that a gun would have helped us in a road accident, but it could have been the opposition, trying to force us off the road. Dee hadn't noticed. I was jumpy and nervous.

'Hold on,' I said when she'd recovered. 'I only meant that as a joke. A wealthy businessman like Harold is hardly likely to be mixed up in petty crime. He's got too much to lose from exposure.' Even as I spoke I realised that I'd said the wrong thing again.

'What a fool I am,' Dee wailed, no longer so aloof. 'I thought he was messing about with another woman and you've made me realise that it could be something much worse.'

'Dee, there could be a thousand explanations of why your husband likes to carry two suitcases. He may be like one of these men who wears both belt and braces, nervous that he's going to lose a suitcase so he packs a suit in each case.'

'*No*, you don't understand, the cases are light coming back but going out they're so heavy that he pays excess baggage on them.'

'There could still be a perfectly innocent explanation. He might take a lot of paperwork out with him,' I suggested.

It didn't sound very convincing to me. The more I tried to get Harold off the hook the more I ended up playing devil's advocate. If a high-powered executive like Elsworth wanted to take large amounts of paperwork to Brussels surely he could fax it there more cheaply? He'd hardly be taking multiple copies of documents with him.

The simplest explanation was that he *was* up to something. Possibly, as Dee suspected, he was playing away from home and had set himself up with a fancy piece in Brussels. Maybe he filled the suitcases up with English groceries to fortify himself against the starchy Belgian diet. He might be teaching his bit of fluff how to make Yorkshire puddings . . . unlikely. I couldn't see Harold Elsworth in the role of sugar daddy.

We were now approaching the outskirts of Liverpool, a city left high and dry by the ebbing of prosperity from the North-west. Passing many boarded-up houses and derelict factories we left the M57 for Southport. The wife of the head of the region's largest home-grown financial institution suspected her husband of treachery and the two largest cities in the area were both crumbling. Was there any connection I wondered?

'Do you understand what you've to do?' I asked. 'Drop me at the funfair and then drive on past the pier and the Marine Lake to the next turn-off leading to the beach – which is the Sand Works track. Leave the horse-box out on its own and my father will come and park right next to you. You saddle up and ride down to the pier, then you know what to do next.'

'I think I've got all that but are you sure all this deception is really necessary? It seems so silly.'

'How can I be sure? I know that since I started looking for your daughter I've been followed and mugged by half the criminals in Manchester. So if you want her back safe and sound we'd better do it this way.'

As I spoke we both heard a loud clicking noise from behind us. Once again my hand shot nervously to the pistol in my shoulder holster but without a word from me Dee pulled over on to the hard shoulder. We got out and walked round the box. The pony was kicking against the door. Did he have a premonition of disaster? There was nothing we could do. After a few minutes he stopped and we drove on in silence.

Suddenly she lashed out at me: 'I want to know why Rachel can't just come home with me. Why has there got to be this big mystery about hiding her away somewhere?'

'You've got to realise, Rachel's safe at this moment. She's gone to a lot of trouble to hide herself away not just from you, but from anyone else who might be looking for her. She's done that for a reason, and until the Thwaite killing is sorted out it's best to keep her in hiding. When Harold comes home we can arrange to send her abroad, somewhere nice and remote. But, she's really in danger. I spent the morning with Andy's parents and they can't get the police to believe he was murdered. Lots of powerful people in Manchester want to keep their eyes tight shut to what's going on. They wouldn't give a toss if Rachel was to disappear permanently.'

Dee didn't like my plan. She may have suspected me of some obscure swindle but we were committed to go on just as much as the pony in his box. We came to the end of the motorway near Aintree and at least driving along with a horse-box behind us wouldn't seem as unusual as Dee feared. We were in character with the neighbourhood.

We reached the coast road and drove along the A565 through Formby. The daylight had a hard quality to it which brought out the defects in the brick-work and the buildings. Although the houses were neat enough the harsh coastal light showed up their red bricks as glaring not glowing: the opposite of mellow.

At Ainsdale we turned off the main road and joined the coastal road taking us along the side of the Nature Reserve with its endangered natterjack toad colony. As far as I was concerned the toads were welcome to the whole wind-blasted region.

Arriving at Southport I could see Dee was very nervous. She kept taking out her handkerchief and twisting it into knots then putting it away again. Things had been simpler back when everyone was allowed to smoke. I felt nervous myself but I was careful not to show it. Was there going to be a reception committee provided by Dyer and his cronies? My hand went to my shoulder holster again. The gun was still there but it wasn't comforting anymore.

I checked that I had Dee's letter and then as she slowed the Land-Rover down for the roundabout on the Marine Drive I jumped out.

There was a fresh breeze blowing of the sea which immediately leached all trace of warmth from my body but it was a bracing day for riding. I had half an hour to kill before Dee got saddled up and into position so I walked towards the funfair past the spot from which I had seen Sylvia talking to Leon.

It seemed an age since yesterday afternoon. Had I been such a fool to fall for the oldest trick in the book? Well I wasn't the first trout to rise for such a well-packaged piece of bait as Sylvia and I wouldn't be the last. What made me angry was the sincerity Sylvia had shown. She'd seemed to feel something for me. Now I knew it had all been for effect, a con.

I had a feeling of unreality. Only by an effort of will did I force myself to pay attention to my surroundings. There were fewer people about than yesterday but Southport was still a holiday resort; people were ambling round the funfair. There were no menacing faces, no hooded motor cyclists. A relaxed and enervated air, despite the breeze, made the thought of violence seem ridiculous.

I could detect no sign of anyone stalking me, neither Michael Rice nor Leon, but the more I looked the more I felt uneasy. I could sense the hairs prickling on the back of my neck. They must be around somewhere. It was getting nearer to two o'clock, the time I had fixed for my imaginary daughter's riding lesson. I didn't want to get close to the pony rides too soon in case I gave the game away to whoever was following me.

The tension increased. Like a hire-wire artist launching himself into space with arms outstretched for the catch I was utterly dependent on my partner swinging the trapeze out on time: Rachel had to be there. A thousand reasons why she might not be present flashed through my mind.

I hoped Dee was having no trouble getting the pony saddled up. I didn't feel any concern about my father. He would perform well, or improvise, whatever the circumstances. In fact, thinking about it, it might have been better to have asked him to haul Rachel off to his moorland cottage on his own without getting involved myself. Still, though I thought of him as being indestructible, he was over sixty and much as he might like helping me out I couldn't expect him to do the job I was being paid for.

At five to two I walked over to the pony ride. I checked the time on my Omega watch twice. I felt very vulnerable and ready for disappointment. 'Beetling-brows', the proprietor, was seated inside a small caravan at an open hatch and Rachel was outside helping a child to mount. I was so relieved to see her that I had to consciously restrain myself from rushing up to her. She was looking round, scanning the horizon. I felt a glow of pleasure at seeing her. So much could have gone wrong – and could still go wrong.

I went up to the caravan, trying to walk at a normal pace, and was immediately recognised. It was only yesterday I had booked the rides after all, but the proprietor was a typical 'New Brit' entrepreneur type – ready to supply anything for the right price. I explained that my daughter couldn't come, was it all right if I took the lesson? I'd always wanted to learn to ride properly. As I'd already shown him that I could pay yesterday, he didn't mind at all, though he did raise his eyebrows once or twice. Nor did he mind adding a small supplement to the child's fee he'd quoted yesterday: 'It's the VAT regulations you see,' he remarked with fluent mendacity.

I went to my mount like an actor stepping on to a stage. There was a sensation of having an audience. I tried to shake it off. Manteh's comments about having me watched were making my imagination work overtime.

Although there were fewer ponies than yesterday, one or two were big enough to take my weight. I must have looked a bit silly standing in the queue with a bunch of young girls. Rachel tried to put me at my ease by giving me a friendly smile and saying hello in the conspiratorial tone in which one speaks to a fellow-adult when surrounded by children. She gave me preferential treatment. She and her boss were quite willing to let adults ride as long as they paid full fare. I was having trouble holding my own face in an ordinary smile. I felt like beaming at her.

Rachel looked like a real country girl, not an inmate of Dyer's clubs. The sea air and riding suited her. Her dark hair was plaited and tied into a bun. Her eyes looked very bright and prominent. With her rosy cheeks and fair skin she could have been taken for a farmer's daughter rather than a banker's. She handed me the reins of a grey pony of about fourteen or fifteen hands height and adjusted the stirrups for me. She treated me as a novice until I walked round to the left side of the horse, put my left foot in the stirrup and swung my right leg over his back.

'Oh, so you know how to ride,' she said. Her Sloane Ranger accent was less pronounced than her mother's but still posh for these parts. She had a wary expression about her, I suppose it was a sharp alertness, like a deer in a game park. She was aware of the space around her. I sensed that she'd run at any moment if I got too close. She turned away from me to help some children to get mounted.

'Excuse me miss, could you have a look at this letter?' I called down to her. Her faintly amused expression told me that she thought this was an elaborate way to arrange a pick up but she took the letter and opened it. She read it quickly, looking from the letter to me and then back to the letter. She turned pale and looked confused.

'Just do what you do normally and everything will be all right,' I said in a low voice.

At least she didn't burst into tears or run away. I glanced over my shoulder at the caravan. The boss was counting a wad of notes. I didn't want him to think I was propositioning his employee.

Dee's letter told Rachel she was in great danger and that she must do exactly what I told her.

We set off. There were only eight of us, not counting Rachel. The other seven were eleven-year-old girls, here on a school outing – 'See the toads, ride on the beach, visit the funfair!'

Rachel rode alongside me.

'Just who are you?' she asked.

'I'm here to help you. Think of me as a bodyguard. Believe me, you really are in danger.' From her expression she didn't need much persuading of that, but I could see that she wasn't sure of me. 'There are people who want to get hold of you. If we ride along for a few more minutes you'll see your mum and she'll tell you what to do.'

She gave a nod, then rode ahead but kept looking back over her shoulder at me. I imagined that she was thinking about all those Pony Stories she used to read, not so long ago. It only needed the slightest false move by me and she'd be away across the sands.

The line of ponies trotted towards the pier at a steady pace. I looked but there were no motorcyclists converging on us. The coast was clear: literally only a few cars here and there in the distance and the hovercraft still grinding back and forth to the water's edge. But my irritating sixth sense told me something was wrong: the tiny cloud on the horizon no bigger than a man's hand.

The sand was firm and the air fresh. Looking along the coast I could make out Blackpool Tower easily and the outline of Black Combe beyond Barrow in Furness. It was a perfect day for anyone observing us with a pair of binoculars but there was no point in worrying about that as we reached the pier.

The ponies were used to stopping there to turn round and as they slowed down Dee emerged from the shadows under the pier.

I was observing Rachel closely. She certainly didn't show any enthusiasm at the sight of her mother. 'Hello Mummy,' she said without any inflection. 'Thank God it's really you. I read your note but I couldn't believe it was from you. I was getting ready to make a break for it.'

'It's me all right and if you knew the trouble I've been through finding you, you wouldn't find it hard to believe.' Dee bent across and kissed her. Rachel certainly didn't seem to be over the moon with joy at the surprise reunion. Mother and daughter made a striking pair, like a skin cream advert. The only flaw in Rachel's complexion was her slightly red nose – did she have a cold or had she been snorting coke as I thought yesterday? If she had, it was her business.

By this time the girls had gathered around on their mounts and an observer would have had trouble spotting what happened next. Rachel and Dee swapped mounts and jackets. It took only a few seconds. I held Rachel's bridle, while Dee adjusted the stirrup length for her longer legs.

'Right Rachel. If you want to disappear again you must do exactly what I say . . . Follow the tracks to the next car park along. You'll see a horse-box there. Load the pony, take the suitcase which you'll find and then get into the blue car which is next to the horse-box.

'The driver's an ex-copper. He'll take you to a cottage where his wife will look after you. You can trust them.

'Have you got it? Instead of hiding yourself we'll be hiding you. You'll have protection.'

Thank God she didn't start arguing. She must have been smart enough to work out that if her mother could find her, then so could anyone else. She set off, and the rest of us, led by Dee, started in the opposite direction. The children accepted the switch in leaders without question. They thought it was laid on for their benefit.

Dee even corrected the riding posture of two of the children.

In fifteen minutes we were approaching the caravan where another little group of pony-trekkers stood around waiting for their turn. Rachel should already be on her way to safe refuge with my parents. Their home is hidden in a fold in the west Pennine moors of central Lancashire. It's a renovated weaver's cottage attached to a run-down farm.

When we reached the caravan Beetling-brows, the boss-man, was waiting, and looking at Dee suspiciously. His bushy eyebrows, sharp brown eyes and sunburned face suggested a Romany ancestry.

'Here, what're you doing with Rachel's pony? You didn't pay for a ride. What have you done with Rachel?' he started up aggressively.

I dismounted and stepped forward. 'Can I have a word with you in private?' I asked.

Not wanting to frighten off his customers, he nodded his head and began gathering the ponies up and tying them to the picket line strung out behind the caravan. The children had dismounted by themselves and were talking to friends waiting their turn in the queue. Everything must have looked normal to someone watching from a distance.

'I know it must seem odd, but Rachel had to go away in a hurry. It's a family problem about divorce and custody. Rachel's father is after her, this is her mother.' I looked at Dee and she took £40 out of her purse. Beetling-brows' eyes lit up but knowing when he was on to a good thing he milked the situation for all it was worth.

'Well, it's very inconvenient, I must say. How am I expected to sit here and collect money while there's kids expecting to be taken out for a ride?'

'Look don't get stroppy, or I'll go and make a complaint that you've been employing a thirteen-year-old for full time work,' I said.

'She said she was nineteen!'

I took the money from Dee and waved it under his nose. 'Why don't you just take the money and forget you've ever seen us or Rachel? You don't need to worry about paying her what you owe her either. We don't want her father nosing around, her mother might lose custody if he found she'd run away from home.'

Dee joined in before things went further. 'Why don't I take the next couple of rides out for you? That'll give you a chance to phone for someone to replace Rachel while my friend here watches the caravan.' He may have seen the glint in my eye, or Dee's suggestion was just too sensible for him to ignore, because he snatched the money from my hand and went off to the phone box, but not before locking his till and taking it with him.

I didn't think there was any danger of him phoning the police. He was only too ready to accept our unlikely story as long as it was backed by cash.

All this messing around was delaying us. I'd wanted to get away quickly. On the other hand the longer we hung around, the more chance it gave us to decoy pursuit from Rachel and my father. The sensation of hidden eyes watching had never left me.

Dee went out and began getting the children mounted. She was experienced. They were all up in their saddles in no time and off along the beach. Beetling-brows bustled back in to his caravan and after checking that I hadn't nicked anything dismissed me with a wave. I went over to phone for a taxi and settled down for a wait.

I couldn't help thinking about Sylvia. What were her motives? It was hard to think she was acting out of love for Mike Dyer. What was it Mrs Thwaite had said about the punks this morning – 'Their own mothers wouldn't have 'em in.' Dyer was such a horrible mess that Sylvia couldn't be acting simply out of love for his endearing personality. That left a lot of other motives available. I wondered what was in the letter she'd left me back at the flat.

Dee finally appeared just as the taxi I'd ordered was circling the roundabout. We reached the Sand Works track in five minutes. The pony was waiting patiently in his box, none the worse for being left standing for nearly an hour. I hoped the seaside trip had done him good. My dad's car was gone. It looked like the deception plan had worked. Rachel should get on well with my parents. Mum would like someone as 'well spoken' as Rachel.

We drove back off the beach and took the road for Manchester. We were both more relaxed. I answered her questions about Rachel's destination and about her protector in very general terms. There was no point in going to all this bother to hide Rachel and then telling her mother all about it. For all I knew Dee might be the champion clatter-gob of Cheshire. Dee was pleased with herself after seeing Rachel.

She kept chuckling, smiling and going over and over the day's events. I was gratified by her pleasure at our success but I thought she was going over the top. I'm sure she'd have burst into song if I hadn't been there – a Wagnerian song of triumph, no doubt.

16

I phoned the Salways from the Evans' Hotel to check if anyone was snooping round Thornleigh Court. Finbar did a quick recce and reported all quiet, so I made my way home.

As soon as I got in I rang Dad. He'd arrived safely. Then I ran a hot bath and had a long soak. There was a letter from Sylvia waiting behind the door but I decided to postpone reading it until I'd eaten. I soaked in the bath, thinking my way through the day's events. It looked as if Dyer was determined to do me grievous bodily harm. If I hadn't started my day early he and his thugs would have caught up with me. I felt a surge of hatred for Dyer. Who did the pie-faced freak think he was? Al Capone?

The surge of rage didn't last long. Dyer would be in trouble if the Thwaites succeeded in convincing the police that their son hadn't topped himself. He'd have to explain why he had suddenly started upping the fees paid to Andrew. He might find himself having to answer some awkward questions. I thought of him choking in the thick blue smoke from Sinclair's pipe. Serve him right.

Apart from Dyer the rest of my day had gone well. Rachel Elsworth wasn't quite restored to her family but as near as made no difference. Until the police put Dyer away she could stay in hiding, or her parents could send her abroad for a while. Her father had said he'd wanted to put her in finishing school.

The hard part of my job was done. My back was a little bruised, I'd got closer to the seamy side of life in Manchester than I cared to but otherwise I'd come through the week well. My finances had improved and would improve again when I got into town tomorrow.

The only cloud on the horizon was Delise Delaney. Now that the alternative of Sylvia wasn't available, was I feeling a return of affection for Delise? Or was the explanation that I needed a shoulder to cry on, as Delise had said?

I got out of the bath and dried off. There were still dog hairs all over the place from Esau's visit; I would have to get back into domestic routine. I put on jeans and a polo shirt and ambled towards the kitchen, having already poured myself a tumbler of Famous Grouse. I couldn't bring myself to read Sylvia's letter. Whether it was hurt pride at being tricked by her, embarrassment at having slept with her after finding out what she was up to, or a wish to avoid reading an explanation from her I couldn't decide. Anyway, I left the letter on the hall table. When I got in the kitchen I could see there were one or two spots of grease on the cooker hob. I got out the Scotchbrite and set to work.

Something wasn't right, there were too many loose ends in this case. I couldn't just hop off to Middlesbrough and forget everything. What about Sylvia, didn't I owe her something? What about Manteh? Would he be prepared to let bygones be bygones when I came back to Manchester in a few month's time? Somehow I doubted it.

I carried on scouring and sipping my whisky, waiting for inspiration. I'd made a lot of enemies in a very short time: Dyer and his gang, Manteh and the Charlies, Michael Rice. Perhaps it was time I tried to make a friend or at least repair a relationship.

When I phoned Molly Delaney she wasn't in. She's one of these people who're never available on the phone and never in when you want them. She was probably out at some rally for nut-eaters or on an expedition to put superglue in butchers' keyholes. I left a message on her answerphone asking her to ask Delise to get in touch. It would be nice to know how she'd got on in Jersey.

Disappointed, I started to make myself a meal: a bacon sandwich with HP sauce. The bacon was sizzling away nicely when my reverie was interrupted. Someone was trying to knock the door down, hammering on it with all their strength. I felt the hair on the back of my neck standing up. I rushed to the safe where I'd put the Beretta, got it out and chambered a round.

Bang, bang, bang, the hammering on the door continued.

'Who the hell is it?' I yelled.

'Open up, you pillock. It's Michael Rice.'

'Show me your warrant card. Push it under the door.' He

still hadn't stopped banging and I didn't know him well enough not to be taken in by someone imitating his voice.

The banging stopped and I heard muffled cursing. Eventually a warrant card appeared under the door. Rice's.

Should I assume it really was Rice, put the gun away and open the door? Should I assume that the Charlies or Dyer had somehow got hold of Rice's warrant card and were trying to bluff their way in?

Thinking 'Better safe than sorry', I was tempted to shove it back and tell him to bugger off but that might lead to complications. I kept hold of the gun and, with it in my right hand, cautiously opened the door with my left and jumped back into a firing position.

The light was out in the hall, confirming my worst fears. My finger tightened on the trigger and I could feel the blood pounding in my temples.

'Get back against the wall where I can see you,' I shouted hoarsely.

It was Rice. He saw the gun and stood against the wall in the area of light coming from my doorway.

'I hope you've got the safety on that cannon,' he muttered as he sidled towards me. I lowered the gun and clicked the safety on at the same time.

'How the hell did you get in?' I snapped. 'There's supposed to be an intercom and security-locked double doors to get past before you can come up here.'

Rice laughed. 'I showed my warrant card to an old dear as she was coming out and she let me in. Simple!' He held out his hand for the warrant card.

'Sinclair sent me round to see how you are. Pretty nervous by the look of you. Do you mind letting me have a look at your Gatling gun?'

I ejected the chambered round and removed the magazine before handing him the heavy Beretta.

'It's licensed. I've every right to have it, particularly when uninvited visitors start trying to knock the door down.'

Rice, who was in his scruffy street clothes – brown leather jacket, crumpled shirt and jeans – nodded his head tolerantly. Something must have turned up to change his attitude. He looked spaced out. The guy was either working too hard or he was well-oiled.

'Oh, yeah! That's OK. Mr Sinclair said you might be armed. Just thought I'd try and test your security.' He sniggered again and took a light bulb out of his pocket. He must have removed the passage light.

'You can put that back on your way out, then,' I said, holding out my hand for the gun.

'Stop trying to be a hard case, Cunane. He carried on playing with the Beretta and then walked into the living room and sat down. 'Interesting name these things have, at one time *biretta* meant a priest's hat not a 9mm handgun.' He gave me back the Beretta and then putting his foot on the coffee table rolled his trouser leg up.

'What's this then, a Masonic initiation?' I asked. Rice grinned and revealed a small automatic pistol strapped to his leg. He removed it and taking out the mag handed it over to me.

'A Detonics Pocket 9, only half the weight of that cannon you carry yet it holds six 9mm rounds.'

'Very nice,' I replied, admiring the chromium-plated ladies' gun, 'but my Beretta holds thirteen rounds.'

I laughed. It was hard to imagine a situation where I would need to fire a baker's dozen of bullets. Rice laughed too. Mutual weapon inspection must act as a sort of friendship test for him. Maybe he was up to the 'good cop – bad cop' routines in his jumbo *Teach Yourself Detective Skills* book.

'You did well this morning. You lost me a couple of times on the way back from Hebden Bridge. Have you had training in shaking off pursuit?'

More public relations. I didn't say anything. He needed to do more than pay a back-handed compliment to get a friendly reception from me.

'Where did you go after you got back to Chorlton then? Mr Sinclair's interested in your mystery client all of a sudden. He was very pleased to get that photo. I think he feels he owes you one. He sent me round to keep an eye on you but you don't seem to need a nursemaid.'

He was speaking in a friendly and relaxed way and my coldness towards him began to thaw slightly. I had to mentally caution myself. Behind his smooth patter there must be some hidden purpose. Honey baits a trap better than vitriol. He'd obviously kissed the Blarney Stone at some time.

'I was just fixing a meal when you tried to bash the door in, only a bacon butty. Do you fancy one?' I asked.

'Not half, that's my stomach you can hear rumbling, not the drains.'

He followed me into the kitchen, 'You like them with HP sauce, great.' I got the rest of the bacon out of the fridge and put it on the grill. He looked like a man with a healthy appetite.

'Are you married?' I asked, just to make conversation. He was wearing a wedding ring.

'I'm separated now. The wife went back to her mum. She couldn't stand the hours I work.'

'Sounds familiar,' I said ruefully, pointing to the bottle of Famous Grouse. 'Pour us a drink, will you?' I was turning the bacon over. 'Do you like your bread thickly buttered?'

'Yeah, I love it, and with lashings of HP sauce too. Great!'

We went back into the living room to eat. I waited for him to put whatever proposition he or Sinclair had in mind. We talked about nothing in particular for a few minutes then he got round to the topic of his boss.

What a fine man he was. What a pity it was that he had never had the recognition he deserved. How the lads in uniform always seemed to get the top jobs while brilliant jacks like Mr Sinclair were passed over because you can't always be scrupulous if you want to put some of the really bad boys in the slammer.

He went on and on about how wonderful Sinclair was. If I'd had a violin I could have accompanied him but as I hadn't, I made a receptive audience, agreeing and nodding my head in all the right places. I'd heard this litany many times before from my father and his cronies. Still, I'd nothing much to do with my evening and I might as well let him put whatever proposition he'd come to deliver in his own time.

I poured him another stiff jolt, taking less for myself.

'Take your friend Mike Dyer, we're never going to put him away. He's far too cute to be caught by simple Plods like us. Mr Sinclair's convinced there's something going on between him and these Moss Side gangs. He's had me trailing first Dyer, then the other lot for months. We've tried to infiltrate but he always seems to spot our blokes. Then you come along and the whole place is buzzing. You've got under Dyer's skin. He's taken more chances trying to do you a mischief than he's done in months. It's an amazing effect you have on people.'

Very flattering I thought, but I'd no intention of telling him my business. If Sinclair had sent Rice round here on a snooping expedition they were both going to be disappointed.

'You see the thing is, David, Mr Sinclair wondered if you might be willing to help us set Dyer up. We need to arrest him for actual commission of some criminal offence, then we can search his premises and find some evidence on what he's been up to with these Charlies.'

It crossed my mind that Sinclair's enthusiasm to arrest Dyer was a very recent one. After all, he'd had years to get something on the guy. Perhaps the cause of his sudden enthusiasm was not a million miles away from that photo of his boss sharing a glass with Dyer. The police put far more time, effort and dedication into their internal politics than they do into banging up the likes of Dyer.

'What did you have in mind?' I asked truculently.

'Well, you could arrange a meet with him. Say you want him to call off all the rough stuff. Ten to one he'll come round mob-handed and start putting a little pressure on you, then we turn up and arrest him.'

'Sounds simple, I suppose you'd take my statement at my bedside in the Infirmary in the form of a dying declaration.'

'Mr S. thought you'd say that. He said you could take me along for protection, as it were. If we arranged the meet in the right place we could have people just waiting for him to start something. How about that office of yours in town? We could have it wired up. Then the minute he threatens you our lads'd be in there doing him for breach of the peace. He wouldn't have time to stroke your head before we'd be there, and I'd be in the room with you anyway.'

I was annoyed by this nonsense. 'Talk sense! As soon as I gave Dyer a place and a time he'd have his thugs round there. It would be a crime convention, your lads and his bumping into each other all over the place. He'd smell a rat straight away, and then he'd arrange for some of the Charlies to beat me to a pulp some dark night when the heat had died down.

I'm sorry, much as I revere Mr Sinclair, I'm not going to leave my nuts in the mincer while he sorts out his office politics.'

I didn't voice my suspicion that Dyer somehow knew exactly what was going on at the Boyer Street headquarters. Hadn't Sinclair guessed why they'd never been able to infiltrate Dyer?

Rice sat up so sharply that he almost spilled the whisky he was clutching. 'What do you mean – office politics? We've been looking to catch these drug pushers for years.'

'Yes, you've been trying to catch them – the little guys, the small fry. But what about the real sharks? Don't you know that Dyer's financed by property developers – the NMP – and that they're in bed with half the politicians and even policemen in Manchester? They're desperate to increase their profits since the bottom dropped out of property.

'You're ready to pick up the distributors but what about the people who make it happen? Do you think it's teenagers in Moss Side who finance shipments of drugs? The NMP'll just have a field day with you,' I said self-righteously.

'Get off your soap-box Cunane! I've no idea what you're talking about. All we want is to sort out as many villains as we can. You might be right about catching Dyer but you're where the action is at the moment and I'm going to tag along with you until something turns up involving Dyer.'

A few breadcrumbs and a trace of HP sauce clung to Rice's long moustache. I concentrated my attention on these rather than on his words. If I needed an assistant I could recruit someone from the ranks of the unemployed. If I'd ever wanted to be someone else's assistant I could have joined the police force. There was no way I was going to work with Michael Rice . . .

I filled up his glass. We were coming towards the end of the Famous Grouse. It was aptly titled. I asked him who'd been with him in the car this morning. The change of subject took him by surprise.

'What do you mean, with me this morning?' he spluttered.

'When you were tailing me, on the road to Hebden Bridge; there was someone in the car with you and there was someone else in a second car behind you.'

'Oh, I just took a trainee detective along for the ride. Mr

Sinclair likes to train as many in his methods as he can. There was no second car, I was on my own.'

'No you weren't. There was an Afro-Caribbean in a VW Passat behind you. He was definitely tailing me as well.'

Rice looked at me and shook his head, 'Not one of ours.'

'When we were at the Training Centre on Sunday, Sinclair said you had a theory that Dyer is working with the Charlies. I think so too. Could you give me your reasons?' I said.

'It's only a theory. Dyer's had clubs wrecked by gangs steaming in from Moss Side, they've even stabbed his bouncers. Right. Everybody knows he doesn't like blacks from Moss Side. He tells everyone he meets it's business, not racial prejudice.

'Suppose he did a deal with Manteh, "keep the Charlies off my back and I'll turn a blind eye to some of your pushers in my clubs in return for a piece of the action" . . .

'If they're caught they're on their own and he can point to all the precautions he's taken and he'll get sympathy not blame. Mr Sinclair thinks I'm wrong, that Dyer has too much to lose, but when I saw you first with Dyer, then with Manteh I thought I'd struck lucky.'

He gave me a hard look, 'But wrong again . . . the boss says you're as pure as the driven snow, Davy boy.'

'It's nice to know where I stand. I can't afford you trailing round with me. I'm a private detective, not CID, but I need to nail Dyer as much as you do. He must be connected with the Charlies whatever he says. So all I can do for you is carry on and get in touch with you if I think Dyer's going to do something you can bust him for,' I said.

I got up and went into the kitchen for another bottle. Rice seemed to have hollow legs. When I came back the phone rang. I shut the living room door and went into my narrow entrance hall to take the call. It was Dee Elsworth.

Despite her precise elocution and modulated tones, she sounded breathless.

'Look Mr Cunane, er . . . David, I don't like bothering you but there seem to be some strange men hanging round the house. They keep driving past along the main road. I wouldn't have noticed them but I got another one of those phone calls earlier. You know what I told you when we were going to

Southport, rough-spoken characters asking for Harold. Like a fool, I told them he wasn't in . . .'

'Now don't panic. They may just be double-glazing salesmen. Check that all your doors and windows are locked. Have you got any firearms in the house? No . . . Well why not phone the police? They can be with you before I get there,' I said.

'I don't want the police, I want you. Everything's gone so well so far. We've got Rachel back, or at least we know she's in safe hands. If they're connected with Rachel or Thwaite it means everything will come out into the open . . .'

There was a long pause on both sides of the line.

'Can't you come down? I'll feel safe then and Harold should be back tomorrow evening,' she pleaded.

Further involvement with the Elsworth family hadn't been part of my plan for the evening. Still, they'd paid me plenty and a spot of body-guarding shouldn't be too difficult. If she was imagining things I could check the place out and set her mind at rest. If she really was in danger I could take her somewhere safe or leave her with one of her friends for the night.

I told her I was on my way and put the phone down.

That left me with the problem of what to do with Rice. Should I take him with me or should I leave him? At least three-quarters drunk, he'd found his way into the second bottle of whisky. He raised a cheery glass to me as I came back in.

'Cheers mate, I've got to go. That was my ex-girlfriend,' I lied, 'she wants me to feed her cat. If you'd like to make yourself at home here for a while until I get back please feel free. The telly's over there.'

Rice gave me a glazed look and nodded affirmatively. Whether he went or stayed made no odds to me. I put on my brown leather jacket and after hesitating a moment put the Beretta and a spare magazine into the large right hand pocket. On the way out I noticed the unread letter from Sylvia so I shoved that in my pocket as well.

I came out of the flats in a hurry, if anyone was waiting to mug me they'd have to be quick. I got the Nissan out of the garage and on the road in record time. It crossed my mind to phone Sinclair and tell him to come and pick up his detective. I decided not to, the poor bugger looked as if he deserted a night off.

I hurried through Sale and Altrincham, driving fast but carefully. I didn't want to be picked up for speeding or drunken driving. I was pretty safe, there were two hours to go before the pubs started chucking out and there weren't many police about.

I was through Altrincham, and on the London road doing about 60 mph in the direction of Tarn, when the car phone started warbling. My first thought was that it was Rice phoning to demand that I come back and entertain him. When I came to red lights at an intersection I picked the phone up. It was Bob Lane, Popeye to his friends.

'Is that you, Mr Cunane? I've got some news for you. Dyer and his mates are on their way round to your place to work you over. I've tried your home number but there was no answer and I got the car phone number when you gave me that ride to the hospital. Wherever you are I'd keep on driving if I was you.'

'Thanks Popeye, can you just hold on for second?' The lights changed and I turned left towards Tarn and pulled into the parking area behind the Swan Hotel. I picked the phone up again.

'Was that you who came round this morning, were you trying to warn me then?'

'Correct squire, I reckoned I owed you that one. Dyer was hopping mad this morning but he's a damn sight madder now. He's had the police round asking about Thwaite. He blames you and he wants to take it out on your hide, so stay away from Chorlton if you don't want to wake up in hospital.' Popeye's flat, North Manchester accent made the threats seem more real.

'I'm grateful to you Mr Lane, you must excuse me calling you Popeye but you did say your friends called you that. I'd like to show you how grateful I am and give you something for your trouble. Have you got a phone number I can reach you at so that I can arrange a private meeting?'

After a pause he replied, 'I wasn't trying to tap you for money. I'm sick of the way they treated me and I don't like what they want to do to you. Call me old-fashioned if you like, but ten against one doesn't seem very brave.

'If you want to keep in touch I'll give you my mother's

number, then I'll phone you back when she tells me you've phoned. It's better that way.' He gave me the number.

Popeye was certainly doing me a favour. He must have taken umbrage in a big way when Spotty Jock and Dyer abandoned him on Saturday night.

When I'd got the number down I phoned home to warn Rice that Dyer was on his way round to commit a breach of the peace but there was no reply. He must be asleep.

While I sat here phoning, Dee might be in trouble. The weather had worsened; although it was still only 9 p.m. the skies had darkened and it was raining heavily. There were flashes of lightning away in the hills as the cold air coming from the east met the warm moisture-laden air from the Atlantic. I sat looking at the sky and the road.

I phoned Sinclair but as usual it took so long to get through to him that I almost put the phone down in despair. Eventually, I left a message that he was to be contacted urgently because Detective Sergeant Michael Rice might be in trouble at my flat in Thornleigh Court.

This was where Delise had come in so handy, I thought. When she was around I could have handled all this hassle with one call to her.

Then I phoned Ted Blake at the Alhambra Television newsdesk.

I got through immediately. I told Ted that the Thwaite murder case was going to break wide open at any moment, that he ought to get in touch with George Thwaite at Hebden Bridge to find out the full story of police negligence and that Dyer had already been questioned.

Ted drank in the news. Police cover-ups and bungling were 'a highly topical current issue' at the newsdesk. He also told me that the *It's Your World* team were interested in doing the story about corruption and drugs in the Manchester nightclub scene. He'd try to include an update about developments in the 10.30 p.m. local news and would pass the story on to the national press.

When I started moving again I was feeling 'charged up'; adrenalin and booze were having their effects. Two lucky escapes from Dyer in a single day robbed me of caution. I drove rapidly along the road to Tarn and turned into the Elsworth's drive. There were lights on in the house and no cars parked outside so I guessed that there were no unwelcome visitors there yet.

I jumped out of the Nissan and rang the porch door bell. The door was flung open revealing Dee, white-faced and trembling. When I got in the hall I saw the reason why.

Leon, Sylvia's mysterious friend, was standing there. He was grinning all over his face and pointing a shotgun at me. A mean-faced white man was sitting on the stairs, also with grin and shotgun.

It looked like my luck had run out. With a sick feeling in the pit of my stomach I realised that I hadn't told anyone where I was going. I'd been in such a hurry to get here that I hadn't even phoned Jim McNeil.

17

Leon didn't waste breath on any of the usual clichés, he just used the shotgun to beckon me into the hall. When I got close to him he smashed me in the face with the butt of his gun.

'That's for Wayne and Errol!' I heard him say as I crashed to the deck. My last conscious thought was to wonder what he was talking about dead Hollywood film stars for. I felt the breath forced out of my lungs as he kicked me in the ribs, then I blacked out.

When I came round I was slumped forward in a chair. They were throwing water over me and through a wave of pain and red lights I could feel myself gasping and spluttering. The left side of my face was on fire. I must have cried out because the water throwing ceased.

'Back in the land of the living are you, smart-arse? It'll not be for long.' This must have been Leon because I heard the other man laughing from across the room. My head was being pushed back by something hard, as my eyes focused I realised that it was the muzzle of the shotgun. I could hear the sound of Dee sobbing.

'Right lady. You're going to tell us what we want to know. Where's your bitch of a daughter? Tell me or I'll blow the local hero's brains out right here and now – all over your nice carpet. He's going to get it anyway, it might as well be here as somewhere else.' I felt too sore and concussed to be frightened but I could tell from the weight in my jacket that they hadn't removed my gun.

I wanted to be sick and when I moaned Leon gave me another rap with his gun barrel. I tried to concentrate and get some feeling in my muscles but there was nothing there. I couldn't have stood up to save my life.

I heard Dee telling them that Rachel had been taken to stay in a country cottage somewhere north of Manchester and that I hadn't told her exactly where and with whom Rachel had gone. Then I must have blacked out again. When I came to I was lying on the floor with my face jammed into a pool of sticky stuff which the smell told me was vomit. I didn't move or groan.

I could hear Leon talking loudly on the phone. He was agreeing emphatically with someone. 'OK I got that, man. Bring Cunane in and you'll have him singing like a canary. Well he ain't goin' be talking to anyone for a while . . . I owed him one after what he done to Wayne and Errol . . . OK Trevor's looking after him now . . . No, we got in clean as a whistle, left the Volvo in a neighbour's drive . . . They're out, man. How do I know when they'll be back? . . . We'll be long gone by then . . . What you want me to do about the woman? . . . OK man . . . Real sad, man . . . Leave it out . . . We'll not harm her.'

Then the phone was put down and Leon went into the lounge.

'OK Trevor, we've got to take Sleeping Beauty back to town with us, the big man wants to have a little chat with him before we put him away.'

'Well what about her then?' piped up a whining Cockney voice. This must be Trevor.

'Boss says to leave her here,' said Leon.

'What, can't we even have a bit of fun with her?' As he spoke I realised Trevor's accent was Strine not Cockney.

'You heard what the Boss said, leave the bitch alone,' said Leon more urgently.

'Well he didn't say we wasn't to have fun with her, did he, sport? He said we wasn't to harm her. We wouldn't harm her, would we? I mean, not harm her, like?' Trevor whinged.

'God I don't know, you white boys! You've got to satisfy your appetites whatever you do. Must be all those steroids you're on.'

'Go on, we won't harm her, just warm her up a bit. She looks like a cold bitch.' Trevor pleaded sickeningly.

'OK then man, take her upstairs and we'll have ourselves a bit of fun. It'll teach her old man not to hire himself a private detective. Haw, haw, haw.' Leon's laugh was like a raven's call: three hard distinct sounds.

I heard a startled shout from Dee then the Strine drawl came on again, 'Hadn't you better check out Sleeping Beauty there, mate?'

I felt a tremendous kick in my side but I didn't do more than grunt. I was biting my lips to stop myself from crying out loud. I knew that if I moved or stirred I might lose my chance to live. A hand gripped my hair roughly and turned me over. Then I felt fingers prising my eyes open. I rolled my eyes as far back as I could. Leon was apparently satisfied.

'He's dead to the world for the time being and he'll be 'bout dead enough when we get him to the Boss. Go on then, get the bitch upstairs.'

I heard them dragging Dee up the stairs. She was resisting but the Aussie was some kind of bodybuilder and there was nothing she could do to stop him.

I risked opening my eyes. The position Leon had left me in meant I could see out of the lounge door into the hall. Dee was bent double as the big Aussie dragged her up the stairs. Leon was right behind them nursing his shotgun and grinning. God knows what they meant by a 'bit of fun' but it wasn't going to do Dee any good. They passed out of my line of sight and I heard further shrieks and whoops of cruel laughter.

I couldn't move my legs. Try as I might I couldn't get my legs under me to lever my body up. I tried again but waves of dizziness threatened to black me out. There was still strength in my arms and using them I crawled on my elbows out of the lounge to the bottom of the stairs. The sounds from above were more piercing now.

There was a phone in the hall but it was on the wall and there was little chance of me even reaching it, still less phoning without being detected. I could probably make it through the door and into the seat of my car, but that meant leaving Dee. I took the Beretta out of my jacket pocket, slipped the safety off and chambered a round. Then I put it back.

Slowly and painfully I started hauling my carcass up the stairs. Red and blue lights flashed before my eyes. My throat felt raw from fumes of whisky and bitter vomit but I kept on slowly going upwards. After an age I reached the top of those grandiose stairs. My elbows felt sore from the friction with the carpet.

I was on the landing. The shrieks and grunts and harsh laughter were coming from the main bedroom on the right-hand side, next to Rachel's rooms. I crawled along and put my head round the open door fully expecting to get it blown off.

Dee was on the bed in the centre of the room with her head towards me. Trevor had ripped most of her clothes off and was straddling her. He was trying to pull her tights off while she fought furiously. Leon was standing by the bed, with his side to me, laughing and enjoying the 'fun', but still clutching his shotgun.

Trevor was licking his lips as he concentrated on his task, his mouth was working first in one direction then the other.

The decision on what to do next was already made for me. I had no options. If I called out, or tried to interrupt, Leon would just bang me on the head again. If I tried to hold them at gunpoint while Dee summoned help I were likely to black out or get blown away by Leon. I had no option.

I took the gun out and very neatly shot Trevor right in the centre of his chest. My perception of time changed so that seconds seemed like minutes. He threw his arms out and rocketed to the back of the bed.

Leon began to swing towards me and I shot him in the head. I suppose I didn't want to mess his suit. He seemed to flick the blow off like a boxer shrugging off a punch and kept turning towards me, his gun coming to bear, so I fired again but missed. Leon's eyes were glaring at me with terrible anger. I looked back at him desperately trying to aim and fire again when he started folding at the knees. He came down in front of me, almost genuflecting. His eyes were still on me, then he pitched forward on his face.

I must have blacked out. The acrid odour of burning nitro-cellulose mingled with the sharp smell of death was the first impression I got when I recovered consciousness. Then I heard a hard, dry, sobbing sound coming from the bed and I tried to lever myself up to see what was going on.

I called or croaked to Dee, 'Get off the bed Dee.'

'What have you done, you murderer!' she yelled.

'Get off the bed.'

'You've killed them both.'

There didn't seem much that I could say at that moment, but Dee did start struggling to get off the bed. Her would-be rapist was spread-eagled against the wall. The bed head was supporting his weight and his arms were draped in a grotesque crucifixion-like pose. Dee was pulling free from his legs which were still pinning her down. She rolled off the side of the bed only to land on top of Leon's corpse.

She gave a drawn-out moan and then stood up, towering over me. 'What have you done? What have you done?' she wailed.

'Shut up, you're repeating yourself,' I said. 'Come here and help me to my feet.' Some of the toughness I had detected earlier must have reasserted itself because she knelt down beside me and supported me as I pulled myself upright.

We stood facing each other. Dee looked at the bodies and shuddered. Then she got a grip on her emotions.

I tried to stand without her help but tottered back against the lintel. Then she bent forward and, to my surprise, kissed me on the lips.

'I'm sorry . . . I've been a fool,' she said quietly and then drew back leaving me to stand unaided. 'What are we going to do? Shall I go and ring the police?'

'That's the last thing you're going to do unless you want to spend several years in jail,' I snapped at her. She started trying to cover herself with the tatters of her blouse.

'The only people allowed to get away with killing in self-defence are the police. If they walk in here now I'm looking at years of porridge, and so are you for aiding and abetting me. That is, if I stay around. There's nothing to stop me getting in my car and clearing off then they'll think you and your husband did it. Pull yourself together woman, and help me clean up this mess!'

'Don't you dare call me "woman" you hooligan! If it hadn't been for you none of this mess would have happened,' she blazed back.

'Of course it would. Why do you think Harold came to me in the first place? You think I don't know why you started throwing money at me? You thought Rachel was in trouble with drug pushers. You people make me sick! You think all you have to do is chuck your money around and then everything'll be all right. Some oily rag'll do your dirty work for you and then you can chuck him back in his box!

'That's why you hated going to Southport with me. You didn't want to get involved yourself.

'These two didn't follow you, they knew where to come.

You as good as told me that your precious Harold's up to his eyeballs in something. If you want to get out of this with no comebacks you're going to get your hands dirty now and start helping me to clean up!'

I didn't care what effect this tirade had on Dee but it did me a power of good. It seemed to loosen my nerves and by taking my mind off my physical troubles had the effect of lessening them.

Dee was looking at me with round eyes, heedless of her appearance.

'Right, tell me what to do,' was her practical response. I knew she had spirit.

'Have you got any old sheets or blankets?' I asked.

'Take the sheets off the bed, I'm not going to be using them again.'

She went over to the linen basket and chucked over a couple of blankets. 'We don't have anything old in this house unless it's a genuine antique.'

There was no dainty way to do what had to be done.

I spread one of the blankets on the floor on the right side of the bed and grabbed Trevor by the arm and heaved him on to the floor. He made a tremendous crash as he landed on his face. Moving carefully without sudden moves which might cause me to relapse I knelt beside him.

My neat shot had got him right in the heart. There wasn't much blood and there was no exit wound so the bullet probably hit the spine and lodged inside. No use worrying about it now.

This was going to be the only post-mortem performed on him if I could help it. Cause of death: shot through the heart while enjoying the act of rape. He probably hadn't known a thing about it.

When I started stripping the body of its few remaining clothes Dee took herself into her bathroom. I could hear her running a shower. It didn't take me long to get Trevor out of his clothes, he'd started the job himself.

Then I went to Leon and did the same. My shot had gone right through his head and as two windows were broken my bullet had probably travelled on and smashed through the window. My wild shot must have broken the other window. I stripped Leon of his Armani suit and his Gucci shoes.

I wasn't going to risk leaving a cadaver with such easily identifiable clothes. I made a pile of their garments. Before long I had the corpses trussed up like a pair of Egyptian mummies.

Dee came back for clothes and got herself a pair of jeans and a pullover.

I tossed her the Volvo keys. 'Go and see where it is, will you? Leon said he left it at a neighbour's. Bring it back and park it in your garage. Keep it out of sight.' Happy to be given a job which took her away from the scene Dee left without comment.

I wasn't capable of shouldering the two corpses so I had to drag them downstairs, through the house and out to the back. The wrappings were stained by the time I got them there but there was no time to be squeamish.

I had to get the corpses underground as quickly as I could. So determined was I that I was in a kind of frenzy. My physical weaknesses took second place to my desire to dispose of the mortal remains.

Dee returned, looking pale but composed, just as I arrived gasping at the back door. 'They left their car in a drive three doors down. The people are on holiday in Bermuda.'

She gave me back the keys and I gave her more orders. It was important to keep moving. If we gave ourselves a rest we might go to pieces.

'Thanks Dee. Can you go to the bedroom and bundle all their stuff up. There mustn't be the smallest trace left.'

'You don't need to talk down to me. I haven't lost the use of my reason,' she said. She was recovering from the shock.

We went our different ways. I got the wheelbarrow from the garden shed and moved the corpses to the bottom of the garden.

Considering it was still before ten and almost midsummer it was a dark night. Just what I needed. There were masses of clouds blotting out what daylight remained and on the Pennines flickers of lightning still illuminated the low hills.

I went back into the shed. There was a pickaxe and spade. I looked round: there was a canister of compost accelerator, a lantern and rolls of black polythene sheeting. I dumped them in the wheelbarrow and trundled out.

I stood in the middle of the garden. It wasn't overlooked. I could dig anywhere I pleased, but I had to choose the spot carefully: I would only get one shot at this. I still felt weak and dizzy. I must get on. No point in looking at the lombardy poplars, or the lawn, or the flowerbeds. I could never hide a grave there.

Then, thinking of the compost accelerator, I remembered the many times I had listened to *Gardeners' Question Time* while clearing up after Sunday lunch. There must be a compost heap somewhere. There it was, in the corner, screened by a hedge of Leylandii. You couldn't spot it from a distance. It was just a break in the hedge. Inside there was ample room to do what I planned.

I brought the bodies over. But there was something holding me back. I stood under the trees and looked up at the sky.

How the hell had I got myself into this mess? Tears of self-pity streamed down my face. It was caused by release of tension and fear of death rather than genuine remorse. I couldn't kid myself that I felt sorry. I struggled to compose myself; I was the one who had been spurring Dee to do what needed to be done.

Well, needs must when the devil drives.

It went into the secluded area and began raking away the compost until I came to bare soil. I needed to think about this carefully, there's a certain skill to grave digging which most random killers aren't masters of.

I remembered an ex-Metropolitan Police sergeant telling me that the nastiest time he'd had, apart from piecing together corpses blown apart in an aircrash, was when he'd had to dig up the remains of a woman whose husband had buried her in bits all over the garden. None of the bits were more than a foot or two deep.

Your spur of the moment killer get his victim underground as quickly as he can. He's usually in a state of panic. But the police have thermal imaging devices which can spot a shallow grave by the heat of decomposition. They weren't going to get me that way. I was going to sink this pair eight feet minimum. I marked the grave out and got to work.

As I laboured I began to sweat the alcohol out of my body and my injuries seemed less painful too. I stripped to the waist and shovelled away. The digging was easy. The soil was very light and peaty. I dug madly, in a kind of rage at myself. The sweat ran into my eyes and blinded me, but I carried on.

I reached a depth of three feet after half an hour and permitted myself to think I'd cracked it. Three feet is the average axe murder's limit. That's when the snags began to become apparent. As I got deeper into the ground it became harder to spade the dirt away. I pondered how to go on as I kept at it.

In my exhaustion I must have fallen into a half-conscious state because I was suddenly started back into wakefulness when Dee spoke, or rather shouted, 'What do you think you're doing, you maniac?I thought you were going to put the bodies in the car and take them away.'

'Keep your voice down.' I gave a hysterical laugh as I tried to gather my wits together. 'Do I look like an undertaker? Do you expect me to break open the crematorium at Southern Cemetery and cremate them? Or do you think I should lug not one, but two, corpses up Saddleworth Moor and start digging?

'I've told you: you're in this as much as me. If we do it right no one'll ever find any trace. Get back in the house and burn everything you can except the cash and credit cards.'

'We've got a solid fuel Aga in the outer kitchen. I could get that going,' she said in a contrite tone.

'And while you're at it get a hammer and smash their watches and pens to bits. Tiny bits. Got it?'

She went.

I solved the problem of shifting the soil by making the hole rounder and shovelling the dirt out clockwise as I rotated, making a shallow mound all round the grave. I seemed to have got my second wind. The hysterical strength with which I'd started the task had evaporated, but I was getting energy from somewhere. When I got to five feet down I ran out of peaty soil and hit heavy boulder clay. Every bite of the spade was hard to lift and the hole began to fill with water.

Soon I was standing up to my knees in water but I went on. I broke the clay layer up with the pick and continued excavating. After an hour I was so deep that I couldn't see out of the hole. I used the pick to cut a step and climbed out. I turned the lantern off.

With the greatest difficulty I dropped the corpses into the grave. I don't know who went in first but Trevor found himself at least eight feet nearer his homeland than he had been when he set out for Tarn. I poured on the compost accelerator and then I quickly began filling the grave; first with the clay, then the peat, pushing it off the slippery polythene sheeting.

Finally I restored the compost heap to its original appearance as well as I could manage. I fought back the sentimental impulse to say a prayer over the grave. Their plans for me hadn't included the burial service.

My emotions and physical feelings were confused and contradictory: triumphant and downcast, tired and refreshed. I knew I needed a few minutes respite.

I stumbled through the back door into the kitchen where Dee was grimly feeding small bits of clothing into the roaring Aga.

I was utterly drained but there was still lots to do. It was a sign of the state I was in that impossibly long lists of further tasks to perform kept flashing up in my mind. I had to get on. This is where impulse killers get caught, they can't be bothered to attend to the post-mortem details. I took Dee's arm and steered her unsteadily to the kitchen table. I could see she'd been weeping, but then so had I. We'd both been through a lot and I'd been hard on her.

'Dee, make us both a cup of hot sweet tea . . . please, Dee. I'd do it myself but I don't know where the things are. We've both got to keep going till we've finished this job.'

She complied silently.

Handing me the drink, she gave me a wan smile, 'Well we're a clever pair, aren't we? Do you think we're going to get away with it?'

'I don't think we've done anything wrong. If we'd buried a dog in the garden we wouldn't expect to be accused of a crime. I saved you from getting raped and myself from being murdered. There was nothing else I could have done. I couldn't have held them at gunpoint, that only happens in films.'

'So you think it's just a waste disposal problem, do you David?'

'You could put it that way – but you must never tell anyone, not even Harold. Speaking of waste disposal, how about cleaning up the bedroom?'

'I've already done all that, slave driver! No wonder you're

not married. You're the most domineering person I've ever met. You had me up at the crack of dawn rounding up horses. You've hidden my daughter somewhere you're not telling. Now I'm sworn to secrecy about two corpses buried under my compost heap.'

'Tough! I thought this case was all over bar the shouting, until you phoned me to come and be your bodyguard. I thought I was well out of it.'

We sat in silence considering the turn of events for a while.

'Right, let's get moving again,' I said briskly. 'Will you drive the Volvo or will I? We'll take it to the airport and leave it in the long stay car park. Then we'll book two flights to Australia.'

'What! I'm not leaving England!' she gasped in shock.

'Not for us! For Trevor and Leon. We've got to lay a false trail so their friends think they've scarpered. Manteh might be suspicious by now, but he's not likely to risk sending anyone else out to look for them in such a heavily policed spot as this. Leon and Trevor were probably his most respectable-looking henchmen. We'll use their plastic to book them on a flight from Manchester to Jersey. Then we book two tickets from Paris to Sydney.

'I see. Well why not book them on a direct flight from Manchester?' Dee asked in a more reasonable tone.

'If we book them from a French airport ten to one any enquiries from this end will stop there. Only about one in a hundred English coppers speaks French and even fewer criminals, so we'll have the language barrier working in our favour.'

'I can see what you're trying to do,' she said wearily, 'but there's no point rushing out of the house at this hour of the night. If you tried to book a flight they'd call the police. You look like a tramp. You'll have to clean up. Come on and I'll find you some clothes.'

Rising from the table she led me out of the room, through the lounge and up the stairs into her bedroom. She'd really done a job on it. Apart from the windows there was no trace of earlier events. She'd replaced the sheets and duvet and moved the bed further away from the window.

Despite my weariness and soreness I was aware of what an attractive woman she was. She was pale, but her eyes were very bright. She seemed to be looking at me in a more direct way than previously. Some sort of barrier had gone down.

'Why don't you go in the bathroom and take a long shower, it'll take some of the pain out of your face and side. Throw your clothes out here and I'll see what I can do with them.' Her voice was much huskier, she'd lost the posh accent.

I went in the bathroom, stripped off, and threw my clothes out. The shower felt great, I could feel warmth and strength returning to my limbs. Standing there luxuriating in the warmth I heard the shower curtain rustle. Dee slipped in next to me.

Events took their course. We didn't speak at first. The only language was physical. She caressed me and I kissed her breasts. Escape from death had sharpened my appetite, overcoming weariness and reserve.

'David we're going to look pretty silly making love in the shower, aren't we? I thought you were so practical, you're going to break your neck on the soap,' she said, restraining me.

Grinning at each other like fools we got out of the shower and dried each other off.

She led me to her bed. Our narrow escape from death or defilement made us both as randy as goats. Every demand each made on the other was satisfied until we both lay exhausted. I knew I didn't love her, or she me, but the heightened emotion of the last few hours had aroused us both.

Afterwards we fell into a deep sleep.

I woke in daylight to find myself alone. I was conscious that I'd broken that rule never to get involved with a client's wife but what the hell! We were both over the age of consent and what we'd done felt right.

I saw that she'd laundered my clothes and left them on the end of the bed. She'd even cleaned the mud off my shoes, something I was sure she didn't do for Harold. I dressed and went downstairs.

Dee was waiting in the kitchen, quite the little housewife with her apron on. She made me breakfast and sat drinking coffee as I consumed five rashers of bacon, two eggs, three sausages and fried tomatoes. We didn't have much to say to each other.

As I got up to go she asked me to wait. I was embarrassed.

'Look Dee, I hope you don't think I made a habit of doing things like . . . last night. I don't make a habit of killing people and I didn't plan what happened afterwards. I don't think I'm a knight errant entitled to the favours of damsels in distress. I hope that doesn't sound pompous.'

'David don't be silly! You didn't do anything to me that I didn't want you to. It was lovely. It just felt like the natural thing to do. It's the first time I've been unfaithful but I don't feel guilty. It's never going to happen again, is it?'

She gave me a long stare and then continued. 'Whatever you may thing about Harold, and whatever he may have been up to, I still love him and I'm going to stay with him.'

'That's all right Dee. I understand. I'll never mention it again,' I answered gratefully. Perhaps my reply was given a shade too quickly: she didn't say anything else. Having cleared the decks of any possible misunderstandings we both got on with preparations for the day.

There was a pile of cash which had come from the wallets of the deceased. I wanted no part of it so we put it in an envelope and sent it to the Hospice in Didsbury. I took the plastic, however, and the bits of jewellery, watches, and pens that Dee had spent half the night hammering into shapelessness.

The two shotguns stamped 'Manufactured by Viking Arms, Harrogate, England' were stacked neatly by the front door. I loaded them into the boot of the Nissan and got on my way after giving Dee a chaste peck on the cheek. She got into the Volvo.

Dee parked it in the long stay car park and took a taxi back to Tarn while I went to the Loganair counter and booked two flights to Jersey using Leon's platinum American Express card. There were no queries but I had his driving licence in case there were. When they didn't show up for the flight there would be no fuss from the airline. You had to check in first, and then disappear, before they got upset.

The beauty of it was, whoever got hold of the monthly statement would see Leon's flight to Jersey dated after his trip to Tarn and draw their own conclusion. I intended to book two flights to Australia at the first travel agency I came to. Then *finis* to the story of Leon and Trevor. Let whoever was interested seek them out.

18

Cruising towards the motorway intersection in heavy traffic I tuned in to the local channel, GMR. As usual a linkman was prattling away. The news came on just as I was turning onto the M56.

'. . . Police were called to an affray at a block of flats in Chorlton last night. Two men were arrested and one man is receiving treatment in hospital.

'More news is coming in about the alleged suicide of popular local DJ Andy Thwaite. Police have stated that they are continuing enquiries into the death, which was previously stated to be a drug-related suicide case.

'Andy's father, George Thwaite, has issued a statement through the well-known local firm of solicitors Nigel Gemelli and Co., denying that it was a drug-related suicide and stating that powerful local interests had involvement in his son's death. All the police will say is that enquiries into the case are continuing . . .'

The use of that little word 'alleged' was very significant.

Gemelli & Co. are a nationally known firm of solicitors renowned for sorting out difficult compensation cases where the authorities are being obstructive. The tenacity of Nigel Gemelli is legendary; if he was on George Thwaite's side there were bound to be developments soon.

I drove straight into town, left the car at the G-Mex building and went to the office. There was a jumbled pile of mail on the desk, so Fred had been in. I was able to pay bills by sending off cheques. Two insurance firms were offering me pension schemes. An honest bookie wouldn't give me short odds on living long enough to draw a pension I thought, as I threw them into the wastebasket.

I got out the file under R for Rachel, looked through the material I'd already included and added a couple of pages of notes. Without being specific as to names and dates, I wrote enough for Sinclair to piece together what'd been going on if need be.

That was how I rationalised it. Keeping files and records

gives a historical depth to my activities. Although I'm only a one-man business and I've only been in operation a few years it's amazing how people and circumstances recur. Also, typing up my records gave Delise something to do during my absences. Thinking about her made me realise that I'd been avoiding the officer because it reminded me of her: I was missing her.

I called Jim McNeil at his office number. He wasn't in. Jim travels all over the country giving talks on his speciality and might be anywhere, so I phoned Margaret to see if she knew anything about the 'affray'. She said Jim was in London and wouldn't be back until late. She agreed to drive past my flat to see if there was any activity. I was to phone her back in half an hour.

Having a few spare minutes for the first time in a week I worked out how much the Elsworths owed me to date and took myself off to see Mr Blomely at the Northern Pioneers branch on Deansgate. He paid up without any question but insisted on a receipt. I noticed he was looking at me rather strangely and as I signed I saw that my hand was shaking slightly.

Coming out of the bank I looked at my reflection in the window of a bookshop. I had a massive purple bruise on the left side of my face where Leon had clouted me. It would take days to disappear. I ought to go and get an X-ray.

Before I could start getting too emotional about my close brush with death it started raining again. We seemed to be having more than our share of rain this June, even for Manchester. I ran back to the office and as I reached the top floor I heard the phone ringing in my little cubby hole. I rushed in and picked up the receiver expecting to hear from Margaret McNeil or even Delise.

It wasn't either, it was Sylvia. She launched into conversation without waiting for me to respond.

While I was wondering whether to hang up Fred Lumsden came in without knocking and plonked a large mug of steaming hot tea on the desk. Fred meant well, but he always made his tea with dollops of sweetened Nestlé's condensed milk, which gave it the stickiness and consistency of syrup. I pointed to the phone and Fred backed out of the room, showing unusual tact for him. I was sure he wasn't out of earshot though.

Dave, why haven't I heard from you?' she continued insistently. 'I've been really worried about you. You shot off from Southport like a scalded cat and I haven't had sight or sound of you since. Haven't you read my letter yet?'

I searched my pockets for the letter. It was still there in my inside pocket, unopened. I gave an affirmative hum.

'What do you think? If you came in with me we'd make a great team. My looks and your muscles . . . there'd be no stopping us, we'd clean up. We might even end up with our own TV chat show. Can we meet soon, I need to talk things over with you?'

I cleared my throat again and took a large gulp of Fred's tea.

'Not very chatty today are you? What's got into you? You couldn't get enough of me last week. Not going off me already are you? Look, the arrangement I proposed can be strictly business if you like. We don't need to have any entanglements if you've cooled off. You're sure you're not married?'

'I told you. My one and only wife died, and that's the truth!' I said.

'Well, if there's somebody else I wouldn't mind having an open relationship. That might be best for both of us.'

That's why I liked Sylvia. She came straight to the point. No beating about the bush. Despite all the reservations I felt I found myself agreeing to meet her for lunch at a Chinese restaurant on Cross Street near the Royal Exchange.

Nosy Fred came back in just as I was opening Sylvia's letter. It looked as though I was fated not to read it.

'Tea all right, Boss? You look as if you've had a rough night. You want to be more careful. I hope the other bugger's bruises are as bad as yours?' I noticed, to my surprise, that I'd actually drunk the whole mug of tea. I must have been more distracted than I thought.

'Yes, that was kind of you Fred. You might say the other two buggers came off worse than I did. How's it going with you?'

Fred raised his eyebrows and bared his toothless gums in a silent cackle.

'OK Boss. Those people on the ground floor were making a stink about someone using their photocopier again.' We both laughed and on an impulse I took out my wallet and gave Fred £20.

He looked startled, as well he might, but he'd handled the Thwaites well for me on Monday and I needed a friendly pair of eyes keeping a lookout for me these days. Fred went on his way rejoicing.

I started to read Sylvia's letter again.

She began by saying that she was upset that I'd cleared off from Southport so abruptly but that she guessed it was something to do with Rachel and that she'd no interest of any sort in Rachel. She was interested in me, she'd so enjoyed (heavily underlined) our two encounters between the sheets and was looking forward to the encore.

She hoped that I wasn't having a fit of morality, she wasn't a loose woman. What did I think about going into business with her as her partner? She knew enough about running clubs to be able to set up on her own. She'd a bit put by, and she was sure her contacts would lend her more. Unfortunately, running a club in inner-city Manchester was still a man's game. However, with me as her full partner (again heavily underlined) she was sure we'd make a go of it.

She now realised that Dyer was a rat and didn't want to go on working for him.

Whether it was the effect of Fred Lumsden's tea, or the events of last night catching up on me I don't know, but after reading the letter I felt quite sick. Did Sylvia want me to be her toyboy, keeping her bed warm while she built up a clubland empire? Or was she still being crafty, trying to allay my suspicions while she found out what was going on? I could feel tension rising and my battered and swollen face began to ache fiercely.

The fact that she'd written and phoned suggested that whatever her dealings with Leon had been, she hadn't been made fully aware of what his plans were. I felt a shiver up my spine. I'd be buried under some road construction now, if Leon hadn't been careless.

I needed someone to care whether I lived or died. Dee Elsworth had made it clear that what had happened between us was a one-off; not even a nine days' wonder, as my relationship with Sylvia was turning out to be, and Delise was maintaining her stubborn silence.

Still, Sylvia was offering me a partnership in a business where she knew all the right buttons to press. What pleasure there'd be in seeing Dyer's face when he found out the news. He'd be spitting feathers when Sylvia deserted him.

I took a couple of paracetamol and washed them down with a glass of water before ringing Margaret. She said she'd been trying to get through to me before. There was a police car parked outside Thornleigh Court and they were measuring things up outside the building. It didn't sound too good.

I remembered that I still had a couple of illegal pump-action shotguns in the boot of my car, not to mention that I'd fired the Beretta and not cleaned or reloaded it yet. I asked Margaret if she'd mind if I left a parcel with her. Before going out I shoved the Beretta down behind the filing cabinet. Ideally I needed a safe in the office to lock it in, but it was probably better to leave it anyway since the police had started shooting firearm carriers first and asking questions later.

The rain had cleared up when I got out on the street again. The air felt fresh for once, and the pavements weren't crowded. I was only approached by beggars twice on my way down through King Street, past the Bank of England.

A bullion delivery was taking place. There were armed police in bullet-proof jackets all around. They carried Heckler and Koch sub machine guns in their hands and .357 Magnum revolvers in their belts. Interesting to imagine the circumstances in which they would need to use both. Perhaps they ought to come in tanks.

I got down to the car in the massive brick vaults under the G-Mex Centre, the converted station hopefully intended to keep Manchester on the map as a centre for exhibitions. The vaults succeeded in blotting out the car phone when I tried to get Ted Blake at his home number. I finally got through to him when I was high in the air on the overpass at the start of Chester Road.

Cradling the phone on my knee, where I hoped my illegal mobile call wouldn't be noticed, I quizzed Ted about developments.

'Any news on the Dyer front, Ted?'

'Bloody Dyer again, you'll be getting diarrhoea when the police get hold of you, mate. Haven't you been home yet?

There was a riot at your place last night, bunch of old age pensioners having a punch up with some yobs.'

'God you're crude Ted! What happened?'

'Not half so crude as what happened last night, I can tell you. A bunch of rowdies broke into your flat and were proceeding to knock hell out of the occupant when they were set on by some crazy pensioners who took them apart. I got round there as soon as I heard it was Thornleigh Court, expecting to find you on your way to Intensive Care.

'Obviously it wasn't you that got clobbered. It was some copper and they'd already carted him off to hospital when I got there.'

'Oh bloody hell! They must have thought Rice was me!'

'Rice, what are you talking about? Can I quote you? Who is this Rice?'

'He is, or was, an undercover cop and if you or I start talking about him you can bet Sinclair will be coming after us with his arse-kicking boots on, so belt up while I think . . . Have you heard anything about whether the police are going to arrest Dyer in connection with you-know-what?'

'They've had him in but he's got a cast-iron alibi and they let him go. I told you that was a pipe dream. People like Mike don't get arrested for murder, but they're definitely treating the case as murder. What I heard is that some people in Police Headquarters think you've a lot of questions to answer yourself. I'm talking about some very high-up people, Dave. One of my sources says that Benson himself was looking very peevish when he heard your name mentioned.'

'What! Damn! I hope I can count on you to put all your "sources" straight, Ted. Thanks a bunch! You know I had nothing to do with it! I'll do the same for you some day.' I gasped for breath for a minute. Then, thinking of the Salway twins, rather than myself for once, I asked Ted if any of the old age pensioners were hospitalized.

'Interesting you should ask, Dave. They all came out of it rather well. That's what pissed Benson off. A crime reporter from the *Daily Reflector* asked him if he was relying on a Senior Citizens' Vigilante Army to keep order in South Manchester. He turned green. You can imagine what his political masters in the Home Office will make of it when the story hits the street.'

I was turning into Seymour Grove when this bombshell was delivered. Trust the boys in blue to fumble when you passed them the ball.

I'd have to have a chat with Sinclair. They probably thought I'd arranged for Rice to be beaten up as well. Why oh why had I ever got involved in this case? God knows what my father would say. Sinclair's boots weren't the only ones likely to be aimed at my already aching backside.

As I passed the Throstle's Nest I was tempted to nip in for a quick one but the last thing I needed was to be smelling of booze when I saw the narrow-lipped Scotsman. So I drove on to Margaret's and parked in her leafy street.

Five seconds after I rang the bell the whole door frame and front wall of the house shook as massive canine bodies impacted against the door. I could hear Margaret struggling to restrain her hounds. What a comment on the state of our fair city when a middle-class housewife in the suburbs didn't feel safe without dogs the size of small ponies.

After a brief wait I was admitted. In the distance I could hear the noise of sirens wailing along Wilbraham Road.

'This whole area of South Manchester is in danger of turning into another Beirut,' I thought as I asked Margaret whether she would mind hiding two pump-action shotguns and a pile of ammo for me.

Or rather I didn't ask her that because I'd wrapped the guns up in a car rug and asked her if I could leave a parcel in her loft for a few days. So she'd no idea what it was.

The police say most petty criminals get caught because they can't bear to get rid of some obvious clue which connects them to the scene of the crime. I was banking that these two shotguns weren't licensed or listed anywhere. So even if I was caught in possession they couldn't be traced to Leon.

Margaret insisted I sit down and tell her what was going on when I came down from the attic.

I couldn't tell her I'd just shot and buried two men. I gave her an edited version of recent events and used the opportunity to rehearse my story. She gave me a very old-fashioned look when I'd finished. My story had as many holes in it as a tinker's socks.

If I'd just been innocently guarding the Elsworth residence all night, what was I hiding in her attic? And why did I have a massive bruise on the side of my face? The material was a bit thin, but Margaret's a good friend. I felt guilty about leaving a parcel of firearms in her loft but it would only be for a few days and the chance of discovery was remote. I was sure Margaret knew what was in the parcel. She was far too intelligent not to have joined up the ragged ends of my story. She preferred not to be told.

'Stay here for a bit,' she said. 'At least wait till Jim gets back and let him have a look at your face. You might have damaged your sinuses. Have you had any ringing in your ears?'

'No more than usual, Margaret. You know me.'

'Yes I do, and I think you're up to something a lot more dangerous than you're letting on. Let me put some make-up on your face to tone down the colour of that bruise. It makes you look really desperate. You're going to give old ladies and children the horrors if they see you like this.'

I submitted quietly while Margaret applied the concealer and liquid foundation to my ugly mug. It was painful but not as bad as when I'd shaved with Harold's Elsworth's razor this morning. I looked at the result in the mirror. My face was still swollen but didn't look half as frightening.

While this was going on I could hear Esau and Jacob howling and scratching furiously at the kitchen door. Margaret explained that although Esau, who knew me, would probably be friendly, Jacob might try to take a piece out of any strange man who was in the house when Jim was away.

Thanking Margaret for her care, I made a hasty exit.

I drove the short distance to my flat, worried about what damage might have been inflicted. I wasn't getting myself into a lather about what had happened to Michael Rice. It was poetic justice that within half an hour of proposing to me that I get myself beaten up in the cause of his career, he'd received the same himself.

Better him than me, and anyway God looks after drunks.

As I pulled into the garage entrance two stout policemen stepped forward. I emerged from the car and they approached.

'David Cunane, you've to come with us. Mr Sinclair and Mr Benson want a word with you.' This was said with such deep feeling that I thought I ought to genuflect.

The speaker was a short, chubby-faced sergeant with a pug nose and prison pallor. He delivered his awesome summons in a slow and deliberate manner, as if newly minting each word. He was peering intently at me as he spoke. His partner was tall and solidly built with a fresh complexion. The pair had a comic effect on me. Whether this was because of the belt on the head from Leon, or because I was hysterical with relief that they weren't putting the cuffs on me, I don't know.

I mentally christened them 'Little and Large'. It was flattering that they'd sent two men for me this time.

'Wow! Mr Benson in person, what an honour! I'm sorry to disappoint you but I'm not coming anywhere until I've seen my flat and changed my clothes,' I said boldly.

I kept the tone of my voice even and friendly. There's nothing more guaranteed to cause the constabulary to react badly than to refuse their little 'requests' in an arrogant or aggressive tone of voice. On the other hand wheedling or feebleness also brings out the worst in them. It's like dealing with Margaret McNeil's dogs. You need a confident and reasonable tone of voice.

The sergeant narrowed his eyes at me and then spoke into his radio. So I hopped back into the open car and picked up my own phone and started dialling.

This had an effect. They thought I was phoning for some legal help because before he'd even received a reply Sergeant Little looked at Constable Large and then poked his head into the Nissan:

'That won't be necessary, Sir. I'm sure we've time to let you change your clothes, after all they've only had us waiting here for four hours so another twenty minutes won't make much difference.'

The door of the flat had been kicked in. The lintel was splintered where the lock had come away from the frame but otherwise the damage was less than I'd feared. The fighting must have taken place outside on the landing. It served Rice right for removing the light bulb.

I asked the sergeant to make himself and his mate a cup of tea or coffee while I changed. He was happy to do that and recommended me to replace the door with a security door. When he was sure Constable Large couldn't overhear he put a proposal to me . . . his brother-in-law had a little firm . . . he could provide a security door at reasonable rates . . .

I took a business card from him and said I'd consider it. It's heartwarming to see how far the entrepreneurial spirit has spread in post-Thatcher Britain.

While he was making the coffee I changed into my best navy blue suit, button-down Oxford shirt and silk tie. With black shoes, the effect was of a slightly battered but definitely respectable character, perhaps a rugby-playing barrister or an executive who'd forgotten to duck when the jib of his yacht swung over. Not at all the impulsive hothead I knew Sinclair thought me to be.

The coppers had served themselves in the kitchen while I groomed myself and we were ready to roll on down to GMP headquarters.

We parked facing the White City shopping precinct and went straight up to Sinclair's office on the tenth floor. My chums handed me over to a detective sergeant who logged me in and then buzzed Sinclair on the intercom.

I heard an abrupt command and was ushered in immediately. Feeling that offence is the best defence against a character like Sinclair, I breezed right in and walked over to the window.

'Hi, how's life at the top of the big greenhouse in the sky?' My own foolhardiness startled me as I asked the question. The place was blue with pipe smoke.

Seated in an armchair set at an oblique angle to the desk was the diminutive figure of the ironically nicknamed 'Wild' Bill Benson. He was adding his share to the haze in the room by smoking a cheroot. The little grey moustache on his lip fairly quivered at the sight of me. His uniform, stiff with shiny insignia, seemed to enclose him like a steel breastplate.

Close up, and without the peaked cap, his face was rather weak. The head was too narrow, almost freakishly so. His upper lip was very wide. That tiny little moustache, nestling under the narrow chisel-shaped nose, did nothing to camouflage the wide expanse of lip. Also his eyes were definitely too close together. Nevertheless, it was the eyes, deeply sunk into the skull, and the prominent cheekbones that gave him the indefinable air of menace which was his stock in trade. There was something reptilian about the way he fixed those eyes on his victim.

With a shiver I realised why many a brave copper, who would have cheerfully faced down a shotgun-wielding maniac, had resigned from the force rather than undergo this experience. To counter the effect of those eyes, drilling into me from behind their bony embrasures, I fixed my gaze on Benson's moustache. That ludicrous wisp of hair was the one comic feature in his grim face.

'Sit down and behave yourself. I want to know everything you know about the Thwaite killing and you'd better be straight with us or you'll find yourself facing a charge of obstruction,' boomed Sinclair.

I directed my attention towards Sinclair and away from his boss. I didn't ask him why, as a master of interrogation, he needed the assistance of the chief constable to ask a few questions.

'Please put another record on Mr Sinclair. You said precisely the same thing last time you had me in for a little chat.'

'That was before I knew the extent of your involvement in the Thwaite case. You told me some story about searching for a missing girl. You didn't mention that you knew all about the Thwaite death before we did.'

'What do you mean? Is it a crime to her bad news?' I protested.

'No Mr Cunane, but it is a crime to interfere with evidence; which is what I suspect you've been up to. Luckily for you I can't prove it or we'd be holding this interview in very different circumstances,' Sinclair replied menacingly.

'How's your Merseyside accent?' he continued. 'We were alerted to the death at 90 Clydesdale Road by a phone call logged at 1915 hours on Thursday by a man with a Merseyside accent who wouldn't give his name. I don't suppose it was you, was it? We were only able to get the first three digits of the caller's number but the call came from South Manchester.'

'Of course not. What do you take me for? I don't go round impersonating people's accents. Anyway, is it such a miracle that a call reporting a death in Didsbury came from South Manchester? Don't you allow Liverpudlians in?'

What he guessed, and what he could prove, were two very different things.

'You still think this is Jackanory don't you?'

'Just a moment Archie,' Benson interrupted, 'ask him why he told Mike Dyer that Thwaite had died by his own hand at 2330 hours that same day, a full six hours before any news was released to the press and well before Thwaite's own parents were told?'

'Leave it out Mr Benson. I'm not the first to know about something before the police do. Not that I'm admitting anything. You know I've got good contacts with the police and press.' Benson's intervention suggested to me that there was some underlying tension between him and Sinclair.

'Well they must be better than my own and I work here. Just let me have the name of the officer who tipped you off then, sonny,' Benson said through tightly clenched teeth.

Bill Benson was very angry.

'Come on! I'm not going to give you a name and then see you crucify somebody who just let slip a useless piece of information. In any case why does it have to be a copper who tipped me off, if I was tipped off? Your mysterious Liverpudlian might have any number of reasons to tell me what he knew.'

'So you admit you're deliberately impeding an inquiry by withholding the name of your informant,' Benson said with a note of triumph in his voice.

'Not at all. I've not admitted anything. I just don't want to see GMP make a serious mistake.'

'Very nobel I'm sure. I see you haven't asked Chief Superintendent Sinclair how Michael Rice is. Suggests that you're very keen on the welfare of the police doesn't it?' Benson scowled at me.

'Well how is he then?' I said, turning to Sinclair.

'They kept him in hospital overnight for observation, he got a right going over.'

'I'm sorry, but pardon me if I don't tear my hair out with worry for a man who conned his way into my flat to suggest I should act as a Judas-goat for trapping Dyer and his thugs. You'd never dream of risking one of your own like that but because I'm a civilian, dependent on police co-operation, I'm expected to volunteer for the suicide squad.'

This put Sinclair on the defensive. Benson raised his eye brows at Sinclair. There was something going on between them that went beyond concern over the fate of Michael Rice.

'I don't know what you're talking about, laddie. I never sent Michael round to see you. He was supposed to be on observation work, checking for any moves Dyer made in your direction. He had a trainee detective constable with him when I sent him out,' Sinclair replied huffily.

'All right, so it was private enterprise. He still works for you. I'm sorry he got hurt but I phoned to tell him to get out as soon as I was tipped off that they were on their way. It wasn't my fault that he was sleeping when I phoned—'

'That's enough Cunane!' Sinclair interrupted me sharply. He could see that his career was poised on a slippery slope.

I wasn't about to let him off the hook.

'Why the hell didn't you do something about it? I phoned you as soon as I knew I wasn't going to rouse him.' For the first time in this grilling I felt that I had the upper hand.

He turned to Benson, 'The lad was officially off duty at 1800. He's been working undercover in Moss Side.'

Looking at me with a wintry expression on his face he said, 'If certain people took advantage of his tiredness and gave him a couple of stiff drinks, it's no wonder he fell asleep.'

Benson gave him a very dubious look but said nothing. No dirty linen was going to be washed but it would be no surprise if Michael Rice's next job was turnkey in the cells at Bootle Street and Sinclair was looking at an airport posting.

My job was hard enough without having to act as nanny to overwrought detectives but there was nothing to be gained by telling Sinclair that Rice had been more than half pissed already when he arrived at my flat. Gratitude that Sinclair apparently knew so little made me cautious about saying any more.

Sinclair paused to paste the smile back on his face, then turned the sly charm on me.

'Fair enough David, you've made your point, all credit to you. But you obviously know more about what's going on than you've let on so far. For instance, why did the Thwaites start making allegations about police incompetence not five minutes after you'd visited them?'

'That's right, there was incompetence – nothing to do with

you Mr Sinclair, you weren't involved, but a child of five could have discovered that Andrew Thwaite hadn't killed himself. There was no forensic investigation at that house until four days after the body was found.

'It'll look nice in the papers won't it? . . . "Police intimidate detective for digging up evidence against Dyer." '

'There you go again with your obsession against Dyer,' Benson burst out angrily. 'If you have any evidence against him that we haven't you're legally obliged to give it to me now! Otherwise leave him alone. He had to be restrained when your name was mentioned during questioning. Practically foaming at the mouth he was. So "put up, or shut up" Cunane!' Benson snorted.

'I know he's guilty.' Commonsense made my choice easy.

'That's not enough for us David. We aren't allowed to lock people up just because you've taken a dislike to them,' Sinclair intervened piously.

'Oh, so you don't lock people up because you dislike them? Not what I've heard. Not what they've heard in Birmingham.'

'Don't be cheeky! You know me better than that. We aren't Lone Rangers dishing out justice to the men in black hats. We work within the laws of evidence.'

Sinclair was breathing hard, there were two purple spots on his withered old cheeks that seemed to be getting brighter by the minute. I couldn't help but feel sorry for the old trout, but I knew he was most dangerous when at bay.

Benson was obviously sniffing around to see if I'd any hard evidence against his mate Dyer. It was hard to be certain, but there also seemed to be some internal conflict going on.

'You're the ones who send out the cowboys,' I said in a quiet tone.

'Yes indeed. Well I'm satisfied you think you know something but that it's mostly in your vivid imagination,' Sinclair replied coolly.

I almost asked him what he'd done with the photograph I'd given him, but caution held me back. Dropping him in it with Benson wouldn't do me any good.

'I'm sorry Michael Rice got too involved,' he continued, like a vicar at a funeral, 'but he's paid a high price for messing about with you. You've got some remarkable neighbours at that flat of yours. They pitched into the men who broke in. If they hadn't, we might have been looking at a murder enquiry. So we should be grateful for small mercies.

'You can go but watch your back, from now on I'll not be able do it for you.'

'Before we let you go,' butted in Benson, his moustache wobbling on his lips, 'I want to make it clear that you'll be sued if there's the slightest suggestion emanating from you that known criminals are being shown favour by this police force.'

Until that moment I had been preparing myself for a long grilling, but it seemed each man had something to hide from the other. Benson didn't want me talking about Dyer and Sinclair didn't want me to talk about Rice and the photo. So that was it. The interview came to an abrupt end.

'Thanks for the reminder Mr Benson, and thank you Mr Sinclair. When you replace Rice why don't you get a female officer. I'm a soft touch for the fair sex.'

Sinclair looked embarrassed but he gave his dry chuckle and his usual gallows grin. Why did he always remind me of a vulture sitting out in the African sun waiting for an antelope to die?

He rang his buzzer and I was accompanied to the front door on Boyer Street. There was no offer of transport so I set off walking through Seymour Grove. I'd reached the Customs and Excise building before I realised that I'd stood Sylvia up. She'd have been waiting for at least an hour. It looked as if a decision on that score was being made for me . . .

19

Seymour Grove is a long, straight street through a tough neighbourhood. If I walked the full mile of it I'd be in Chorlton and then back at my home. I could get in my car and drive away to Middlesbrough and have well-paid employment for three months. Then I could slink back to Manchester, keep a low profile and hope Dyer and Manteh had forgotten me. That's the way it could go.

I felt my anger building up. Benson would have been a lot more pleased if it had been me in he hospital instead of Rice. Why had they wanted to see me? They hadn't really wanted information. The sting had been in the tail, the threat from 'Wild' Bill.

He would sue me if I suggested there were reasons why Dyer hadn't been prosecuted.

Sinclair was a crafty snake, supposed to be a friend of my father. Some friend! He was attempting to shove the blame for the massive cock-up over Thwaite in my direction.

This whole thing started when I asked Dyer if he knew anything about Rachel. The very next morning somebody was trying to take my head off with a piece of chain. The whole lot of them were caught up in a web of corruption. I'd roused their wrath by lifting up a tiny corner of the carpet which hid the dirt they'd swept out of sight.

The police were playing an ambiguous role. Oh yes – they'd have a clean-up of the little men, the pushers, from time to time. But did they dare to take on the big boys, the property speculators who were using the cash generated from drugs to turn Manchester into a collection of vacant lots, car parks and empty shopping precincts?

What could I do about it? I was like one of those people who ran across a cricket pitch with no clothes on – a streaker – an amusing diversion, but not a player. Not someone to be reckoned with.

I walked up Seymour Grove but instead of carrying on I turned left down the King's Road, through the Asian quarter, heading for Whalley Range. My legs were taking me this way without conscious direction from me. Part of me was saying 'go home', another part was forcing me down King's Road towards Manteh and his luxury pad.

Of all the players in this drama Manteh seemed to be the weakest yet he'd been the most deadly or at least his lieutenant, Leon, had.

Manteh's weakness lay in the fact that he wasn't playing on his own turf. He relied for support on his power to charm a volatile bunch of teenagers. Dyer had sent his crew of incompetent North Manchester ruffians to sort me out with local methods – boot, knuckleduster etc. They were as traditional as a bunch of Morris dancers. It was Manteh who employed Australian hitmen armed with shotguns.

I decided to go round to Manteh to tell him his friends had failed and to encourage him to get out of town quick. Maybe I could catch him off balance. He might tell me why Thwaite was killed and why Rachel Elsworth had become such an important pawn in the game he and his friends were playing . . . On a rational level it was a crazy decision but this was Manchester not Chicago: my home town not his.

As I walked along deciding this I passed a phone box so I rang Margaret McNeil but there was no reply, perhaps she was out walking the dogs. Waste disposal must be a problem with animals on that scale.

On impulse I phoned Sylvia at her home number. She answered at once. I apologised for standing her up, explaining where I'd been. Then I told her I was on my way to Manteh to find out what was so important about Rachel Elsworth.

'Don't be such a bloody fool Dave, that man's really dangerous. Say you won't go!' she said after a sharp intake of breath.

'That's rich coming from you. I'm fed up with behind hounded around my own town and Manteh is the guy with the answers.'

'What do you mean, "rich coming from me", everyone knows that Manteh has a lot to do with the Charlies. If you think I've had anything to do with your troubles you're quite wrong.' This was said in such convincingly indignant tones that for a moment I almost believed her. However, the late Leon

Grant, so well known to Sylvia, had worked for Manteh. So Sylvia was linked to Manteh, either directly or indirectly.

'I only phoned to apologise for standing you up. I hope I'll see you later.' I put the phone down and continued on my way. There was no point in accusing her of anything now. In possible future dealings with her, I might need the tenuous advantage my knowledge of her link with Leon could give me. Accounts might still need to be balanced with Sylvia, and as the Sicilians say, 'Revenge is a dish best eaten cold'.

Dressed in my best blue suit, I attracted no more than average interest as I walked along. The neighbourhood has more than its fair share of weirdos. Anyone who did try to place me probably put me down as a council official.

The street, with its houses painted in vivid colours, was a real death-trap for slow-footed pedestrians. Asian youths raced cars up and down at suicidal speeds, making a contrast with my steady pace as I strode towards the 'luxury pad'.

At the flats I presumed on my respectable appearance enough to walk boldly into the central enclosed area. There weren't many cars there but sitting outside Manteh's building was the white BMW with mirror windows that his punks had used at the airport. It stood out among the Fiestas and Golfs like a great white shark in a kiddies' swimming pool. There was no sign of activity from the glassed-in deck where Manteh lived. No one on guard, no one on the lookout for me; so Sylvia Mather hadn't tipped him off yet.

It was easy to spot the button for his flat with the black star next to it. I rang, and got an immediate response from the squawk box. I announced myself and in his deep, grating voice Manteh asked me what the hell I wanted.

I said I wanted to tell him about Leon.

'Fuck yourself, buddy,' was the pleasant reply.

I pressed the button again. 'I want to talk to you Manteh. I want to know why you sent Leon and that Australian pervert for me.'

'Chase yourself, you white motherfucker,' he snarled.

The rage which I'd been nursing all along the road from the police HQ burst into life. I banged on the speaker and kept my finger on the bell. I was getting the brush-off from a con-man who, it seemed, felt entitled to decide on my life or death.

There was nothing I could do, not even a stone that I could pick up and throw at his window. I took off my shoe and began pounding the speaker. My frustration went into every blow. The communicator smashed to pieces and I pulled the wreckage away from the wall. At least that would put the bastard to some inconvenience.

I slunk away from the porch into the central area. Manteh was at his window. He was wearing a white jacket, not his African robes. He threw back his head and roared with laughter at me; then stuck his finger up, American style. The anger I'd partly sated by smashing his intercom returned. I had to lash back at my tormentor, who was now giving me an obscene parody of a papal balcony performance.

I'd wipe that smirk from his face if it was the last thing I managed to do in this life. My eyes scanned the area for something to throw at him, but the whole place was immaculate with not even a stray stone lying in a gutter. Neatly weeded flowerbeds and lawns contained nothing with which I could hurt him.

Then my eyes fixed on the BMW.

I ran towards it, coming closer to Manteh as I did. His angle of vision narrowed and he must have climbed up on a stool or chair to keep me in view. I tried the doors. In his arrogance, or certain knowledge that no criminal dared to touch his vehicle, he'd left it unlocked. I wrenched it open and swung the door back as far as it could go. The hinge groaned but the German workmanship was good, it didn't break. I swung it back again and again, really putting all my strength into it. On the fifth swing something gave. There was an awful creak and the door fell off. I picked it up, raised it above my head and then hurled it into the half-empty car park. The noise echoed round the enclosed space.

I looked up at Manteh. He was now in a towering rage, pulling at his hair with both hands. I'd touched a sensitive nerve. He was going to get more of the same. I clambered into the car and pushed the driver's seat back as far as it would go, then put both feet against the windscreen and heaved. Nothing, it didn't even budge.

I smashed both feet into it again and again. Then, with a faint popping sound, the screen fell out on to the bonnet. I jumped out and hurled the screen after the door and as I did so glimpsed something coming at me out of the corner of my eye. I looked at the ground, Manteh had thrown a small hatchet at me. It must have only missed me by a fraction of an inch but I was delighted to see it.

The rage and anger I'd felt were transformed into pure pleasure which washed over me in waves. I looked up at Manteh and waved, then picking up the hatchet, set to work on his BMW.

The mirror-windows went first, then I got onto the body panels. There were people looking from the windows of some of the flats but nobody came out to stop me. Who was going to stop a well-dressed lunatic smashing a perfectly good car to pieces? They probably thought it was a stunt for TV, with Jeremy Beadle lurking round a corner.

I reckoned I'd at least five more minutes of fun before the police arrived. I slashed the tyres, smashed the lights and fittings and pulled the fancy CD player out and tossed it onto the growing pile of wreckage. I looked up at Manteh, he was still there. He hadn't seen anything yet.

I managed to get the bonnet up and then went to work on the engine, pulling out what I could and wrecking with hammer blows whatever I couldn't shift.

That must have been Manteh's limit. He cracked at the point that perfectly tuned German engine bit the dust.

Lacking anything else lethal to throw at me he launched himself. Two minutes later, he was out of the front door and on me in a flurry of fists and angry inarticulate curses. He landed several heavy blows and kicks before I was able to push him back but I didn't feel them. I was impervious to anything he could do, such was my eagerness to batter him back.

Taller than me, he'd a longer reach. When I pushed him back he began to circle round and round looking for an opening. He was no street fighter: he had lots of little thugs ready to do any dirty work for a few quid. Only his rage at the destruction I was wreaking on his beloved vehicle had driven him into making a physical challenge.

He must have watched too many Kung-fu movies, because he tried to use his long legs to get a kick in while feinting a blow at my head. Ignoring the blow, I grabbed his leg with both hands and jerked him back. He tried to hop away but I kept hold of him and we half danced and half lurched into the very centre of the enclosure.

Windows were open now and shouts of encouragement were coming my way. Manteh obviously wasn't popular with his neighbours. I twisted his foot and threw him over. He didn't give up; he stumbled back to his feet. I gestured him forward and he may have struck me but his blows didn't register. I hit him hard in the face. He came back again and I began to lose control.

I went for him; butting, kicking, elbowing, punching, using every ounce of my strength to hurt him or even kill him. I would have bitten him if I could, such was my fury. There was nothing scientific or clever about the way we fought, just sheer bloody madness from the frenzy gripping us both.

I was on the ground on top of him when I came back to myself. There was a screeching of brakes and the blaring of a car horn right behind me. The bottom dropped out of my stomach. It must be the police or the Charlies. I felt a sense of relief that at least I hadn't killed him. A pair of hands grabbed my collar and started pulling me off but the grip was feeble. I looked round. It was Sylvia Mather.

'Dave, get off him!' she yelled. I looked down at Manteh's battered face and let him go. As I stood up he rolled away with a snake-like movement. He retreated to a safe distance. 'You're dead Cunane! You won't see the morning,' he gasped but made no move towards me and when I stepped forward he turned and ran back to his flat.

'You're dead, you're fucking dead!' he wheezed as he went.

I stood there in a daze. I looked down at my suit. It was in tatters. Lying on the ground where I'd been battering Manteh there was a wallet made of brown and cream coloured leather, the skin of some scaly African reptile which I couldn't immediately identify.

As Sylvia tugged at my arm I stooped and picked it up.

Sylvia guided me into her car and, swerving to avoid the heap of BMW wreckage, drove us away at speed. I was shaking and trembling so much that I leaned back in the car seat and shut my eyes for a moment.

The pain from blows that I'd received while in my berserk

rage now began to register. My knuckles were painful, I opened my eyes and looked down at them. They were skinned and raw but otherwise my aches and bruises were no worse than any I'd received on a wet afternoon playing rugby. I didn't think Manteh was an expert at body contact sports.

An afterglow of the pleasure I'd experienced while smashing his car returned to me. Then I became aware that my rescuer was speaking to me.

'What kind of crazy performance was that? You aren't fit to be allowed out. You ought to be certified. Don't you realise he'll go to any lengths to get his own back now. Oh you fool Dave! You bloody fool! I was going to deal with him. He would've let you alone if he knew you were going to help me get rid of Dyer. Now you've blown it, well and truly.'

'Stop the car Sylvia, let me out. I won't put you to any more bother. Just stop and let me out.'

We were on the edge of Chorlton by now.

'So that's all the thanks I get for rescuing you, is it?' she said.

'What do you mean, rescuing me? I was doing all right.'

'Oh, don't be a fool! I got there just ahead of his friends. They'd have chopped you into thin strips with their machetes.'

I knew she was right. Manteh would stop at nothing to get me now. I had to get out fast. My clothes were in shreds, I needed to change and to get my car. I also needed a weapon, that first of all.

'You're right Sylvia, I'm sorry and . . . thanks for saving me. Do you think you could do me one more favour? Could you take me to a friend's house where I have to collect something. It's not far from here, in fact just round this corner.'

I indicated which house I wanted her to stop at.

'I hope this is important. For God's sake, hurry up,' Sylvia urged.

I rushed out and banged on the McNeil's door. There was no answer apart from the howling of the dogs locked in the kitchen. I rang again, maybe Margaret was having a sleep. I looked round the house. Her car was gone. She must be at the station picking Jim up. I went to the side and tried the garden gate. It was locked, but through the cracks I could see an aluminium ladder leaning against the garage.

I dodged out into the street and, to Sylvia's horror, scrambled over the garden fence. There was an explosion of noise from the dogs. I hoisted the ladder against the wall and began climbing to the bathroom window. The upper part of it was open. As I ascended past the kitchen the dogs saw me and I saw them; their hairy faces covered with foam, their red tongues hanging out.

An audience of school children gathered in the street. They were gazing at me with expressions of awe. I reached the window and inserted my arm but I couldn't reach the catch.

As I stretched, I listened to the juvenile voices debating.

'He lives there, he must have lost his key.'

'But why are the dogs howling if he lives there?'

'Look at his clothes, he looks as if he's been dragged through a hedge backwards.'

'I know who lives there and it's not him.'

Spurred on by desperation I climbed another rung on the shaking ladder, my head was almost touching the roof eaves. I forced my arm down and just managed to get my fingers on the window catch. Thank God the McNeils hadn't had security catches fitted. The windows opened.

I shimmied a couple of rungs down the ladder and put my foot on the window sill. The noise from the dogs changed. They started baying, the noise was almost unearthly.

I retrieved the guns from the loft and was out of the window again in no time. Slamming the window shut behind me I went down the ladder like a dose of salts. As I crested the garden fence the audience of children scattered. They were frightened by my battered face and fierce expression.

I jumped into the car. Sylvia's expression deserved to be photographed, her lips had shrunk as if she had been sucking a lemon.

'Now you've made me an assistant in a burglary! What have you got in that rug?'

'Just a couple of pump-action shotguns. Would you like to get a move on before the police arrive, or these children decide to whip up a lynch mob.'

We shot away down the leafy street and straight out into the traffic at the main road, just missing a bus. Sylvia took me home, driving fast through the early evening traffic. She dropped me off on the pavement opposite my home.

'You've got to get away or he'll kill you. Give me a ring when you get fixed up and I'll come and see you.'

There didn't seem to be much to say apart from thanks. I waved to her as she pulled away, thinking as she did that if you looked at it from one point of view it was Manteh that she'd rescued, not me. Her part in all that had happened still needed explanation.

I ran across the road and up to my flat. There were no lurking policemen and someone, probably Finbar Salway, had secured my door by nailing up the splintered lintel.

I was throwing clothes into a sports bag when he came in. 'You probably deserve the VC for what you did yesterday, Finbar, but I've nothing to give you except my thanks,' I said. I didn't interrupt my packing of a few essential survival rations.

He took a look at my face, 'My God Dave, you've been in the wars.' He made no reference to his part in yesterday evening's adventure. I pointed out that he had a black eye himself.

'That was yesterday, I haven't seen so much excitement since Suez. We never had so much fun at a reunion before. You don't half lead an exciting life.'

'You're right Finbar, but I won't be leading any sort of life at all if I don't get out of here quick.' Finbar was taking no notice of me. He was poking at the parcel which held the shotguns. He knew immediately that there were firearms in it. I dashed into the bathroom to get my battery razor and when I came back he had one of the guns out and was testing the action.

'You could make an awfully big hole in someone with one of these,' he said grimly.

'Well I confiscated them off someone who was trying to make a hole in me.' His eyes shone but if I was going to carry on breathing I had to get away. 'The people I took these off are likely to come round here looking for me. They probably won't bother you if they see that the car's gone but you'd better take one of these for your own protection.'

He took the gun eagerly. It was a greater reward to him than any medal yet minted.

'They'll expect me to have gone as far away as I can but I'm going to hide out locally. Could you leave a signal in your window when the coast is clear here?'

'Look Dave, why don't you let me come with you?' Finbar pleaded.

Great, just what I needed for protection from the Charlies: a sixty-year-old former paratrooper. If I got him, old Lumsden and my father together I could muster a real Dads Army to take on the drugs gangs. The police nightmare about vigilantes would become a reality.

'You can help me best by giving me a signal that it's safe to come back here. Leave the curtains undrawn and the light on in your bathroom. Take the gun but remember it's illegal. You're not in the Army now, you can't go round with it on your shoulder.'

I was desperate to get out and I ushered the grumbling Finbar through the door and hurried out to the car. It looked as if I'd made it. The Charlies had a slow reaction time, it took them a while to get organised. They probably had to keep on selling drugs until late and Manteh couldn't tear them away from profitable trade. How he must be screaming for Leon.

From the main road I turned on to the Meadows down a cobbled track lined with poplars. It led to an old farm site. The farm had been demolished and turned into a car park for use by twitchers wanting to get a glimpse of a moor hen or reed warbler.

The nature lovers use the site by day, but at night it's a favourite spot for motorised sex. Almost any evening in the week cars can be seen bouncing on their suspensions, while Peeping Toms lurk in the bushes. However, there was no activity on either the bird or the bonking fronts when I got there.

It was still early evening. I parked in the most heavily shaded area with a dense screen of bushes almost hiding the car from view.

I used my phone to bring myself up-to-date with the real world of crime and violence. A call to my answering service brought an interesting response. There had been five calls from different women claiming to be Rachel, wanting to get to know 'David' better. There was nothing else for me from the answering service.

I phoned Ted at his home number.

'So you've not been locked up yet Dave?' he answered cheerily.

'I thought they were going to. Benson and Sinclair saw me in person. Benson threatened to sue me if I allege police negligence again.'

'Nice one Davy boy! You'd better make sure that you don't park on a double yellow line for the next few months,' he joked derisively. 'Seriously though, you must be on to something or why would they bother warning you off? No smoke without fire is there?'

'Have you heard anything Ted?' I asked politely.

'Yeah, the senior police spokesman is suggesting that it might be suicide after all . . .' Ted paused before going on . . . 'Is there anything else I can do for you?'

It was all the opening I needed.

'Why don't you do an interview with the parents?' I urged. 'You know, run the police statement, and then have the parents on denying it?'

'Mmmm, you wouldn't be after my job would you, Dave? I'll run the idea past my editor, sounds like the sort of muck we like raking.'

Encouraged by his interest, I gave him the details and put the phone down.

I was only a few hundred yards from where I'd been mugged last week. Looking through the trees and reed beds towards the river bank I realised how Manteh operated. He planted a suggestion in his victim's mind and let fear do the rest.

When I saw him on Sunday he said I'd been riding down here on the meadows with the dog. I'd thought it was only the German Shepherd that had saved me from another thumping, but more likely than muggers behind every bush was that someone at the flat was reporting back to him.

His tactics worked. When I'd gone to see the Thwaites I'd been afraid of my own shadow for the rest of the day because I'd seen a black man on the same road. He was probably a perfectly innocent commercial traveller.

Manteh relied on his legend to spread fear. To survive my latest clash with him I had to find some way to hit back. Sinclair had made it clear that I was on my own.

Looking around at the trees, bushes and river I felt like an outlaw, a latter day Robin Hood, driven into the wilderness by the corrupt establishment. Benson must have some link with Dyer which he wanted kept quiet. No wonder I was unwelcome, poking my nose into their affairs. If I let everything simmer down I was likely to end up having an accident or an arranged 'suicide' like Thwaite.

Thinking of Robin Hood put me in mind of the Sheriff. I wondered if I could make an ally of Michael Rice now he had fallen from grace. I phoned the Royal Infirmary and got in touch with him far more quickly than if I'd tried to contact him at Police HQ.

'What do you want, you bastard? You've landed me right in it,' he growled as soon as he recognised my voice. He didn't sound too damaged.

'Look Sergeant,' I said in my most honeyed tones. 'What happened wasn't my fault. I phoned you to tell you to get out but you were too pissed to answer the phone. They must have thought you were me in the dark.'

'Rubbish, you fixed the whole thing up. Get off the phone . . .'

'No. Just listen before you get into more trouble. Your very high-up friend has some sort of link with Dyer. Your man knows about it. That photo you took him is part of the evidence. If we can work together to find out more then maybe we can get your career back on the rails.' I didn't want to say much on the car phone but I needed to convince him.

There was a silence for several minutes, then he said 'What do you mean, get my career back on the rails?'

'Haven't you heard?' Benson wants your balls. The best job you're going to get is traffic warden at a children's play scheme. Sinclair must be waiting till you're out of hospital to break the news to you. How are you anyway?'

'Oh, God! It's your fault Cunane, you're a disaster. I never should have gone within a thousand feet of you.'

'Come on, you're feeling depressed. With you on the inside and me stirring things up for Dyer we just might turn something up. You know your boss would jump at the chance to get something on either of them if we could find solid evidence. You've nothing to lose.'

There was another long pause. 'I'll think about it. You were lucky to find me here. I'm being discharged as soon as the consultant's had a look at me, and he'll be round soon. So don't try calling me again. If I decide to come in I'll give you a ring from home. What's your number?'

I gave him the number. I felt pleased with the call and could only hope no one else was listening in. Rice was well deflated, all the cockiness knocked out of him. It would be good to have him as at least a partial ally. It was more realistic than the idea of launching one-man raids on Moss Side from Chorlton Meadows. There weren't enough trees to hide me from the Charlies.

Manteh must be nursing his bruises. I remembered the wallet he'd dropped. In the excitement I'd forgotten about it. I rummaged about in my bag and almost panicked. Fortunately it wasn't lost. It was lying right at the bottom, next to the whisky and the crackers.

I opened it. Made from the scaly skin of some reptile, it had been well used, several of the scales were detached. It was of crude make, the leather was thick and it would cause a bulge in an ordinary suit even when empty. Inside there weren't any credit cards or cash, only slips of paper.

On the left-hand corner of each slip there were several capital letters. They might be initials or code. Then there was a four figure number beginning with zero, then a dash, then a twelve figure number. Under this there was a long series of numbers against a column of dates starting last December. The wallet contained nothing else.

Here was a puzzle. It looked like a series of messages in code. The letters might be someone's name. The first four numbers beginning with zero looked like telephone area codes. Yes, 0204 that could be Bolton, then maybe Liverpool. Area codes followed the initials . . . like an address and a name.

That left the twelve figure number. There aren't any twelve figure phone numbers.

Then it came to me . . . it was a series of bank statements. The initials and the numbers at the top were the name, address and bank account number, so the columns below must represent deposits. I added up one of the slips, which didn't have such high numbers on it as some of the others. Since last

December, if I was correct, the account had received more than £90,000.

One big problem in the dope peddling game is how to get rid of the money generated in such copious amounts. Many dealers like to stand in front of a fence taking the cocaine or heroin from an accomplice behind the fence and passing back the cash. That way there was never any evidence on them if they were stopped. One drawback was that they had to have a trustworthy confederate; another was that they still needed to stash large sums of cash.

So that was Manteh's game. The concerned leader was in fact operating a sort of piggy bank for the dealers of the area. He probably supplied them as well. This would account for his popularity and influence with the Charlies. He'd need to give them their balance at any time they asked, so he kept the figures in his wallet. He must be bitterly regretting his impulsive attempt to bash my head in. It had certainly cost him dearly.

I counted the slips. There were more than sixty and the one I'd added up had some of the lowest numbers on it. So if you counted £250,000 on an average slip and sixty odd slips that came to deposits of well over £15 million since December. Everything in this case seemed to lead back to bankers and property dealers. Here at last was the proof I needed of the very high stakes being played for. The life of a DJ must have seemed of very little account against profits like these. Whether it was the NMP, Dyer or Manteh who was the motivating force in this nasty struggle wasn't yet clear, but at least the motive was. I had irrefutable evidence of it. My crazy trip into the heart of Manteh's realm had achieved something tangible besides the personal satisfaction it had given me.

If only I knew the name of the bank I might be able to extract some of the money.

I looked at my watch, it was nearly five o'clock. I could probably get in touch with Fred Lumsden if he hadn't already gone home. I just caught him, he was putting his coat on to leave. I asked him to go into my office and take out the file on Rachel and hide it somewhere. He could also retrieve my Beretta from behind the cabinets and hide that as well. If he didn't hear from me in three days he was to pass them both on to

Mr Sinclair at Boyer Street HQ. Fred was mystified but, sweetened by the tip I'd given him earlier, he was willing to comply.

It struck me that Manteh might be willing to trade, something on the lines of my life for his money, the reverse of the highwayman formula.

There was nothing I could do while it was still light. Trust me to pick one of the longest days in the year to hide. I got out the crackers, munched a few and washed them down with whisky. I was careful not to drink too much, the alcohol would only give me a thirst later.

I pushed the seat back as far as it would go and arranged the shotgun in a handy position next to me under a rug. I shut my eyes and fell into a dreamless sleep straightaway. It had been a long day and it wasn't over yet.

20

The chirruping of the phone in my ear woke me. I was so stiff that I could hardly move my arm to pick up the receiver. Groaning, I hoisted it to my ear. It was Lovena Anderson. She was speaking so quietly that I couldn't hear her. I asked her to speak up but it was no better. I realised she was in shock.

'They took him, they took my Douglas,' she whispered.

'Lovena, who took him? Was it the police?'

'No, no! They took him. Them Charlies! They say they're going to cut him up bad unless you turn yourself in . . .' She didn't say anymore.

It was my turn to be shocked. My throat felt very dry. My grip on the phone was painfully tight.

'Do you know where they've taken him, Lovena?' I managed to croak.

'Oh, where do you think? They've got him round at Charlton Close some place. It's that Manteh. He says he won't do nothing until you phone.'

'God! Did he leave you a number?'

'No. He says it's in the book under Moss Side and Hulme Spiritual Guidance Group.'

'Bloody hell! Trust him to drag God into it. How long ago was this, Lovena?'

'Just watch your tongue David,' Lovena counselled.

'Sorry Lovena, but he's such a hypocrite.'

'It was about twenty minutes . . . David there's more . . . Jay was with them . . . he let them into the house.'

'You mean he handed over his own brother? I can't believe he knew what he was doing. I thought he was acting like Manteh's glove puppet on Sunday. How does Manteh get control over these lads?'

She didn't make any reply. I had to say something to comfort her.

'Look Lovena, the fact that Jay's involved should give us hope. I don't think he'd do anything to harm Douglas. He's weak, Manteh must have pressured him.'

'Well, the Lord alone knows,' she said firmly, 'but what about you David? Will you do what he wants? I've got to think about my boy – he's only fourteen and some of them that's got him, they'd love to stick a knife in him just to keep in practice. They're scum!'

Once again Manteh had shown talent for making the right move. He hadn't bothered sending out his crew to search for me. He only had to press the right button to make me coming running.

'I'll phone the swine and see what he wants. Can you look up the number for me and ring me back?' My reply sounded a lot braver than I felt. I could have phoned directory enquiries myself but letting Lovena find the number would give me a minute to think.

I opened the window. The night air drove out the faint lingering fumes of whisky I'd drunk at 5 p.m. I looked at the clock. It was 3. a.m.

I'd slept solidly for eight hours. No one had disturbed me, the car park was as empty as it had been when I arrived. The bonking brigade had been and gone, creeping back into their beds after a couple of hours of post-pub nooky.

What was I going to do? I ought to save Douglas. I owed Lovena that. It was my fault that Manteh had him. Phoning the police would do me no good. This was no domestic situation. The Charlies would top him at the first hint of police activity on the estate. He'd disappear.

So, if it was no use calling the police, what was I going to do? My last thought before going to sleep, that I could buy my life by giving Manteh back his wallet, had been sound. Manteh must be thinking on the same lines if he was raising the stakes by kidnapping Douglas. He must be really desperate to get the wallet back. Could it be that he was nervous about what might happen if his customers, the Charlies and their associated drug dealers, learned that he'd lost their banking records?

If Manteh had kept them in ignorance then I had a chance of surviving and rescuing Douglas. Whatever Manteh had told them about me, they could have nothing against Douglas. Although the press portrayed them as an utterly wanton and lawless band of desperadoes, the Charlies only maimed, tortured or killed two groups of people: rival dealers, and grasses.

They left the general public alone. By rescuing Rachel, I'd put myself in the category of a potential grass, or even rival – I'd have to find out which from Rachel if I survived. But Douglas was neither.

Odious hypocrite that he was, Manteh had shown concern about his 'image' in the community. I would have to face him, and bargain with him and hope that I could threaten to shame him in the eyes of the drug-dealing confraternity. Relying on the moral sensitivities of the Charlies gave a slim chance: the only chance Douglas and I were going to have.

Lovena rang with the number. I repeated it back to her without intonation. With not much hope that what I was doing would make a scrap of difference I dialled. Almost immediately the phony-sounding American accent of Manteh was booming in my ear.

'Is that you Coo-nane?' he said with a satisfied chuckle.

'You might have more to laugh at than my name before you've finished,' I replied.

'So it is you? Not lost your sparkling wit then? How dee-lightful! I was just thinking that now the boot is on the other foot, as your proverb says . . .' he laughed again. The sound was like a toilet flushing.

'What do you want?'

'You took something of mine. I want it back, simple as that, man. But then you got some paying back to do. You made me eat shit yesterday. You got some lumps coming or there's no way I can keep ministering to the boys.'

'That could be cool, man,' I interjected.

'It's true. They already think I'm too kind with trash like you,' he sounded as if he believed his own cant.

'You do surprise me, Manteh.'

'There's a consolation for you. If you spare me the trouble of finding your sad arse I might not hurt you too bad and I'll let the boy go,' his words were dripping with insincerity.

'What guarantee have I got that you'll let him go?' I asked.

'Guarantees come with washing machines, man. If you aren't here the boy won't be around at daybreak. The boys are all fired up against you and I won't be able to protect him,' he said sanctimoniously.

'You poor weak man. Why don't you let him go now? He's done nothing to get up your nose.'

'Can't do that. You've got something I want, and the boy's my guarantee you'll keep your fat mouth shut about it. You just hand it over. No fuss – no muss. You get your arse kicked and then I might be kind,' he wheedled.

'What do you mean, Albert Schweitzer? You might be kind? You've not got your paws on me yet.'

'If you don't want the boy to get cut, you'll come. Just walk into Charlton Close and the brother will show you where to go. If you don't make any trouble for me I might let you go. You got an arse-kicking coming. I got to maintain my street cred! No way I can let you walk. Either you come in and the boy goes free, or the posse comes and finds you anyway. Make up your mind. You've got an hour before we start sending the kid back to you a piece at a time!' he concluded with a snarl.

I looked at my watch – 3.10 a.m. Manteh had sounded more worried about his bank statements than anxious for revenge. He could revenge himself on me at any time but his 'customers' must be pressing him at this very moment.

I'd another hour of freedom. There was no point in phoning my parents or the McNeils. If there was going to be bad news they'd hear it whatever happened. The only person I knew who admitted to dealings with Manteh was Sylvia Mather. Any port in a storm, I thought. She might know something that would give me an edge.

I dialled her. Her phone rang but no answer. I waited impatiently, realising that I was clutching at straws. As I was just about to hang up she answered.

'It's you, what do you want? Don't you know what time it is?' There was something different about her voice, but I put that down to the early hour.

'Well you said to call when I got fixed up, and anyway I need your help,' I said.

'Where are you calling from? You ought to be out of the country by now.'

'I phoned you to let you know that I'm going to see Manteh in a few minutes. He's using a kid I know as a hostage. I just wanted to let you know . . .' There was no reply for a long time, so long that I began to wonder if she had been cut off, then she spoke.

'Are you trying to be noble? You must be crazy. First you beat him up and then you go visiting. Don't go,' she said. I'd always liked the way she hit the nail on the head first time.

'There's nothing else I can do. The kid hasn't got a chance otherwise.'

'It's not by any chance your own kid, is it?' she asked indignantly.

'Of course not. How many times have I to tell you, I'm single with no dependents.'

'Well then, leave it to the police! Why play the hero?'

I didn't answer.

'Are you still there Dave? Forget I said that, but it is three o'clock in the morning . . . Haven't you got anything you can trade with him instead. Bargain with him but don't go. I know about Manteh . . . I've an acquaintance called Leon – you saw him last week – he told me that Manteh's a psychopath, quite unpredictable. He's killed dealers who've welshed on him. He killed one with a pair of pliers!'

'That's just the confidence-building message I wanted to hear. Thanks Sylvia.'

'Dave don't go near him. He'll make you suffer after what you did to him.'

'Sorry, love, but I've no option. I involved the kid and I'm his only chance. He's only fourteen.'

'Dave, I'm begging you, go to the police. I haven't always been straight with you but if you go I'll come with you. I can tell them a lot they'd like to know. We can get together, make things right, go abroad . . . anything you like, but don't go there.'

'Sylvia, did Leon tell you anything that might give me some chance?' I was pleading with myself as much as with Sylvia. My impulse was to stay in the car and drive to Dover and the cross-Channel ferry as fast as I could.

'Don't go near him Dave. He has this like . . . chorus of followers. He whips them up into a frenzy and then makes them join in killing. Leon says it's like an insane rap session. He gets the victim to admit that he was in the wrong, then they all join in and kill him. That way none of them will ever grass on any of the others.

'I'm sorry Sylvia, but while there's life, there's hope. If I come through I'll let you know.' I hung up hurriedly. She hadn't told me anything I wanted to hear. Still, she'd confirmed my guess that she didn't know Leon was a killer. The only times I'd had luck in this case had been with Sylvia, two-faced as she was. Maybe she'd bring me luck again.

I drove out of the secluded car park, along the tree-lined road with tyres booming on the stone setts, and threaded my way through the narrow lanes of Chorlton to Wilbraham Road. There was no traffic at all until I turned onto Princess Road. I took a right at Great Western Street and came to the neat little close where Lovena lived, just four miles from where I'd hidden so far. Her home was one of a few newly built 'closes' which had been intruded into the traditional terraces which clustered round Manchester City football ground. It was apart from the main area of new housing in Moss Side, containing Charlton Close, which formed a compact block on the other side of Princess Road. I tucked my car in next to hers and, taking the wrapped-up shotgun with me, hurried in.

Lovena looked up at me, but I shook my head.

'I'm going round there now, the bargain is that he'll let Douglas go if I turn up.' I didn't look her in the eyes.

Lovena sat down and wept silently. Tears trickled down her face.

'I want you to have this,' I said, giving her the shotgun, 'and also this wallet. If I don't return and Douglas isn't back either, you take the wallet round to Alhambra Studios and give it to Ted Blake. Do you know who he is? He reads the local news on Alhambra TV. Give it to him and tell him it's from me. He'll know what to do with it. Keep the gun and if anyone . . .'

'I'll know what to do . . . Fear the Lord and keep your powder dry!' she cried fiercely, shaking the gun in her hand. I'd no doubt she'd put the gun to good use. I gave her my keys and then set off to walk the half mile to Charlton Close. My last sight of Lovena was of her getting down on her knees to pray again.

I cut through the litter-strewn terraced streets back to the bright lights of Princess Road and crossed into the new estate.

There were plenty of people still about, even an occasional police car in sight. Unlike the rational plan of the terraced streets, the new 'closes' were cul-de-sacs and crescents. They didn't lead anywhere. I had to retrace my steps back to Claremont Road and go along by the park. A poster on the gable end invited me to 'Fly to Jamaica'.

As I reached the park gates I could see plenty of activity in Charlton Close. The fence that so conveniently screened it from the road couldn't hide the vehicles coming and going. Commerce was taking place by the glare of the sodium lights. This was the one place in Manchester where trade was booming.

Although the housing in the area was new there was a stagnant air of rising damp about the place. The new brick hadn't weathered as well as the red brick of the old terraces.

My heart sank as I took in the scene. Anyone who got between these people and their profits hadn't a snowball's chance in hell of walking away in one piece. They'd strangle their own grannies if they had to. They had no fine feelings. So what chance did I have?

It was hard walking across the street. It was a far, far stupider thing than I had ever done before. A quick turn back would take me into the bushes of Alexandra Park and away, unseen. Then, as I walked forward I saw the face of Jay Anderson peering at me from the shadows. I noted sadly that he was wearing the standard disguise of the drug dealers – a bulky dark anorak with the hood pulled up. I was past the point of no return.

'Real sad man! What a mess you've got us in, man! If only my mother had never met you,' he bleated.

I grabbed his bony elbow.

'Shut up Jay, do what you've got to do!'

Without another word he led me into the Charlies' den – the tangled skein of streets of which one, Charlton Close, had given its name to the gang. There were lights on in some of the houses. Others were boarded up with heavy-duty plywood. The occupants didn't seem to be making the effort to make the place habitable that you found in other parts of Manchester – too much open space belonging to no one in particular. The broad white fence boards were covered in graffiti, the grass was overgrown and there was rubble lying in the streets. A perfect ambience for the Charlies.

Jay pointed to a house on the corner of the close.

'He's in there. Go in on your own.'

As I walked youths fell in step behind me, then my hands were grabbed and I felt a pistol muzzle being forced into the back of my neck. I gasped in pain and fear. The pressure forced my head down. I was frisked and then pushed into the corner house.

The house I was bundled into now was an abandoned home. I'd a good view of the floor from my bent position: used contraceptives, hypodermics and crap littered the floor. Someone had fractured a water pipe and water was seeping into the room.

I was in the midst of a group of about twelve men. Blacks were in the majority but there were whites and Asians there as well. Manteh walked up to me and, using both gloved hands, started smacking me about as hard as he could.

When he finished my head was ringing and my face felt two sizes larger. The place where I'd been hit with the gun butt was throbbing.

I tried to focus the pain out and keep my eyes on Manteh.

'So this is the hit man, the man who cut Andrew Thwaite's throat for him!' Manteh shrieked to his congregation.

'What the hell are you talking about?' I mumbled through bruised lips.

'Cut that out, liar! You were seen creeping out of Andy's flat in your socks. You killed him and I want to know who paid you!'

'I killed no one.'

'Don't fuck with me, man.' Another crack on the face nearly took the side of my head off. 'Leon saw you coming out and I told him to fix it up to look like suicide. I didn't want no police poking about and finding things that was none of their business.'

I didn't speak but I hardly felt the blows, I was so surprised at what he was saying.

'Don't think you're hiding Rachel Elsworth. I know exactly where it is that you've got that spoilt little bitch,' he screamed in triumph.

My battered face must have been capable of expression because Manteh clocked the look on my face.

'Ha, that shook you! A weasel called Kevin Spragg gave us the news today. Rachel told his girlfriend just where you were hiding her. I can put my hand on her any time I like, so your boss Dyer is going to be unlucky.'

He gave me another blow, my teeth felt loose. I swayed, the light glistened on the ring of faces. They spun round me. The young thugs holding me tightened their grip.

Manteh came back into vision, holding a Mini-Uzi machine pistol. It was in his right hand pointing down; then he swung it upwards, cocking it with his other hand at the highest point of his swing. The circling group scattered. Those holding me retreated out of the way.

He pushed the muzzle against the bridge of my nose. It only needed gentle pressure from his finger to blow my head off.

He leant forward and whispered. I couldn't catch his words but half-remembered lines passed through my dazed brain . . . 'This is the way the world ends, not with a bang but a whimper.'

I wasn't going to end with a whimper.

'What about Douglas?' I bellowed. 'You promised to let him go, you slimy bastard!' Manteh jumped back, startled by signs of fight in his intended victim.

'He's got your bloody money you fools! He's ripping you off!' I yelled.

Manteh leaned forward and muttered, 'You're supposed to keep your damned mouth shut about that, man,' between clenched teeth.

There was the sound of other guns being cocked. It began to look as if my execution might turn into a double execution.

'Hey, my man! Let's listen to what he have to say,' a tall muscular individual with a floppy cap said in a broad Jamaican accent.

Manteh's tongue flickered nervously over his gleaming teeth as he turned to face his little flock of dealers.

'He's lying to spin his time out. Use your brains! What would he know about our money?'

'I know you've all got numbered accounts,' I yelled desperately.

Pandemonium broke out. Cursing, shouting and stamping their feet the Charlies turned to each other. Every man in the room was armed.

'Don't you tell me to use my brains, you mother!' the big Yardie shouted. 'You tell me! How does he know about our accounts? That bitch knows everything, doesn't she? You said she couldn't know a thing, but she does. You told her. You and your friend Leon been cooking something up on the side with that Rachel.'

'He doesn't know! He's guessing, is all! You agreed to keep your mouth shut about them accounts,' Manteh said hurriedly. He looked almost as desperate as I felt. He was at least twenty years older than most of his followers. He looked older still now.

'It's a scam, he's blagging you all,' I said.

Manteh turned back with a vicious look on his face, put the gun to my head and pulled the trigger. Even as I flinched I realised that he'd left the safety on.

The man in the cap came up behind Manteh and pinned his arms. Manteh's blue-black skin showed marks from the pummelling I'd given him yesterday. The veins stood out on his neck. His eyes turned yellowish. He was blowing a fuse. Other Charlies came up and pulled the Mini-Uzi out of his twitching fingers. He looked as if he was having a stroke. I noticed that some of the Charlies were backing towards the door.

Manteh began screeching in a high-pitched female voice. The effect was eerie. Then he changed tone to a deep bass male voice, speaking in words I recognised as Asante.

There was only Manteh, the Jamaican and me still at our side of the room. The rest of the Charlies were cowering round the walls and some were already through the door.

'He's having one of his spirit talks,' the big Jamaican snarled. Grabbing me by the shoulders, he pitched me to the other side of the room.

'Fasten up this mashed-up piece of garbage with the kid,' he said contemptuously.

Hands grabbed me and three men, anxious to escape from the scene, hauled me off into the next room. I breathed a sigh of relief.

Regulation handcuffs were produced and my right hand was fastened to a radiator. Fastened in the same way at the other end was Douglas Anderson. Our guards pulled out cigarettes and immediately the sharp odour of ganja filled the room. Sounds of mingled moaning and shouting came from next door.

'Sounds like a long do,' sighed one of the Charlies to the other two. They all left the room.

Douglas gave me a nervous grin. His left eye was badly swollen so he must have put up a fight before being kidnapped. Impressive, especially for a fourteen-year-old.

'How are you Douglas? I came round as soon as your Mum told me you were here.'

'I'm all right. What about you? You don't look so good.'

Douglas's concern for me was touching considering that he looked battered himself. He'd obviously resisted the Charlies. I knew I had to get him out of here.

'I'm doing fine Douglas. We've got to think about getting out of here fast before they change their minds. Can you stand up?' Douglas struggled to his feet and watching what I did braced his feet and pulled at the radiator. Nothing happened except that the steel bracelets cut into our wrists.

I was conscious of the fact that the best chance for escape was in the first few minutes of captivity. I tried again, heaving with every ounce of strength. The radiator pulled loose at my end but not Douglas's. Water began glugging out. The noise was loud but there was plenty of racket coming from the other room.

I froze. I heard someone saying 'Yeah, I'll only give him a spliff,' then the door opened. Jay Anderson came in and shut the door behind him. He put his arms round his brother.

'I thought they'd let you go as soon as they got Cunane but they say Manteh's going to kill you both. The spirit voices are strong,' he sobbed. Keeping his face away from me he hugged his brother.

'Look, you've got to help us get out of here,' I pleaded.

Turning, he gave me a look of contempt. 'How man? I've no hacksaw and they got men on every corner even if you get out of this room.'

'Take a look out of the window Jay. What can you see?'

He crossed the room languidly. 'There's two of them in the alley outside,' he whispered.

I looked around the room, originally a kitchen/dining room. There was another interior door opposite the breakfast counter.

'Go and look where that leads,' I asked. He tiptoed over and opened it.

He shook his head. 'It only goes upstairs.'

'Jay, shape yourself. Have a look if there's anyone up there,' I ordered.

He went out, and returned in a moment.

'It's just the upstairs rooms. There's no way out.' He came back to his brother, hopelessness and despair written on every feature. He annoyed me. Was he prepared to sit here until Manteh came in and cut our throats? He was pathetic. Didn't he realise that they'd probably let him in here so he could be killed with us?

'Jay, you big wimp! Get hold of that bloody radiator and help Douglas pull it clear of the wall and for God's sake don't let it drop.'

Jay stirred himself into action. Fortunately, the row from the adjacent room masked the sound of the radiator tearing free. Douglas and I stood like Victorian convicts, free of the wall, but shackled by our hands to the radiator. There was no interruption in the wailing and shouting coming from the adjoining room. Either they were all as high as kites or they were used to prisoners rattling their chains.

I pulled the brothers after me as I headed towards the door. We moved as quietly as we could. Water was spraying over my ankles from the ruptured pipe. We were leaving a trail a mile wide. I led the brothers upstairs to the landing under the loft hatch.

I made a back. 'Get up,' I whispered to Jay. He clambered up on my shoulders and pushed the hatch upwards. There was no folding ladder to make it easy for us. Jay was making no move. He'd frozen.

'Climb up you fool, and help Douglas up after you,' I hissed at him. His instinct of self-preservation wasn't well developed.

Moving like a zombie, he climbed into the loft. Douglas swung up onto my shoulders as I supported the radiator. The two links of chain on the cuffs made it possible to move the radiator but I was balancing it with one hand. Douglas and I struggled like a pair of contortionists and we managed to get Douglas's arm and shoulder into the loft space.

Jay was acting woodenly. Why didn't he grab his brother's end of the radiator? Douglas twisted his body into the loft and pulled it with his left arm, taking some of the weight off me. Jay was still frozen.

'Jay, you clown, you'll be just as dead as Douglas and me if they catch you. Brace yourself across the hatch and help me up!' It would be too bad to be caught now just because Jay was too spaced out on ganja to help. He was the only one who could get me up into that loft. With the handicap he was carrying, Douglas didn't have the strength to support my weight as well.

Jay did as I asked. He lay across the opening with his knees bent, his feet jammed against one side, his shoulders against the other. He extended his right arm as far as he could. I grabbed his right in my left and with Douglas pulling the radiator levered my legs against the wall and got my left arm through the hatch.

I pulled myself into the loft, the radiator went the wrong way. It felt as if my wrist was being severed but I was in, lying across the open rafters, gasping. Once again there was no sound of alarm or break in the babble of noise coming from below. I didn't know what sort of show Manteh was putting on for his followers but he was holding their attention.

I gently closed the hatch cover. We were in total darkness. The volume of yelling and shrieking seemed to be rising to a crescendo as Manteh worked up his followers for a bout of killing. The sooner we made ourselves scarce the better.

'Jay, can you feel your way forward along the rafters and get us into next door's loft.'

A grunt was his only reply but I could hear him moving.

As our eyes adjusted it was possible to see chinks of starlight through gaps in the roof tiles. Douglas and I got to our feet and tried to shift the radiator until it was in a more comfortable position. Water was still gurgling out of the broken pipes and we ended up carrying our burden in our unshackled hands.

Jay returned and led Douglas forward. I hobbled behind.

There was a crawl space between the houses but it was tough getting through the narrow gap attached to a radiator.

The builders had left nails sticking out everywhere and it was hell staggering along. Several times I slipped and my foot went through the ceiling below but either the rooms were unoccupied or the inhabitants were used to having their lofts used as a passageway because there was no sound. By the time we reached the eighth house at the end of the terrace, our burden had become lighter as water drained out.

Jay felt and fumbled for the hatch. He opened it suddenly. A shaft of yellow light dazzled us. There was no sound of detection. Jay nimbly lowered himself and helped Douglas after him. The change in light altered my depth perception and made me clumsy but there was no time to hang about.

I lowered the radiator as far as my arm would go and dropped through after it. There was a resounding crash. We lay blinking at each other in fear. My arm felt as if it was going to come loose from its socket but there were no bones broken.

The only sound, apart from our own gasping, was heavy snoring. Jay opened the bedroom door, and the light revealed a pot-bellied man asleep on the bed. The smell of rum was overpowering.

We scarpered down the stairs and out of the back door. Jay knew his way round the footpaths better than I did. The designers of the closes had included many footpaths and ginnels to create a 'neighbourhood' feeling like a Cumbrian village. The design couldn't have been bettered as an aid for junkies and muggers. Those quaint Lakeland villages had been built for smugglers and highwaymen.

The design worked for us now as Jay guided us to Princess Road by winding paths. Douglas and I mastered a form of crabwise movement with the radiator. We looked like a couple of men encumbered by a long narrow white suitcase.

The police were certain to stop us if they saw us. Jay had overcome his narcotic torpor and entered into our escape, his enthusiasm increasing in direct proportion to the distance from Manteh. He scouted round corners and signalled us forward. We ran across the dual carriageway and were back at the Anderson home in minutes.

There were no sounds of pursuit but it couldn't be long delayed.

Lovena had a surprise in store. She'd packed all her suitcases and was sitting in her doorway with the shotgun across her knees. She embraced each of her sons and then me.

'I knew the Lord would preserve you, but now we've got to get out of here. Jay and Douglas, we're going for that holiday in St Kitts I've always been promising you. You're going to see your grandmother. It's something I should have done years ago.' Without any more fuss she organised Jay into loading the cases into her car.

She gave me back my keys and Manteh's wallet.

'You going to need this if you plan to stay around here,' she said, passing me the gun, 'but you seem to have become attached to my family!'

'Big joke Lovena, have you got a hacksaw? We've got to get this thing off.'

She shook her head.

'Well you'll all have to come round with me to a friend's flat. I promised to tell her if we got away and we need to put a few miles between ourselves and here before we stop to cut ourselves loose.'

Without a backward glance Lovena led Jay to her car. Douglas came with me. He had to clamber over the driver's seat of the Nissan, wedging the radiator awkwardly between us. I drove one handed.

We took the long route to Heaton Mersey, avoiding the parkway and main roads. We arrived at Sylvia's flat as dawn was breaking.

21

Somebody had given Sylvia a hell of a bashing. Her bruises matched my own. I was shocked by the sight of her face: livid purple bruises and puffy eyes made her face into a horrible mask. Her lip was swollen. Seeing her like this made me forget about my own troubles.

The damage seemed to be only to her face not to her body. I could see that because she was wearing a green silk dressing-gown which showed enough of her figure for Jay's eyes to be tracking her. She was delighted to see me in one piece but her own tangled problems had finally caught up with her.

Moving slowly she led us into her living room. This was the first time I'd been in her home. The flat was furnished with good-quality modern furniture. It was a lot larger than mine.

Before I could examine it I needed the smallest room. With co-operation from Douglas I was able to satisfy my need for a pee.

Back in the living room I stared at Sylvia. The sight of her battered face released the rage I felt about my own treatment. She looked small and fragile. Lovena and Jay were sitting stiffly on the low-backed settee looking very awkward. Sylvia was dazed, whether by sleep or the beating wasn't clear.

I asked her for a hacksaw – she looked at me as blankly as if I'd asked her for a gold bar. After explanations she was able to come up with a junior hacksaw which was part of a tool set. Jay insisted on freeing his brother first, which he did by sawing through the chain link. The hardened steel bracelet was too difficult to cut through. The clumsy way he sawed made me anxious that he'd snap the blade, leaving me stuck on the end of the radiator.

When Douglas was free I expected Jay to start on me but it took several minutes of shouting and arguing before he'd cut me free. We couldn't have escaped without Jay's help but he'd have to stop being such a pain in the arse before I began to like him.

'What you looking at me for, white man?' he said, curling his lip and sneering at me as he went on with his task unwillingly.

Despite having crawled through the lofts of eight houses, Jay still looked stylish and well turned out. His anorak had protected him from the dirt. He was wearing a new black leather jacket with a floppy off-the-shoulder fit, looking very cool. He had a new pair of trainers, different from the new ones he'd worn on Sunday. He also had a new, oversized denim shirt and two-tone Bloggs jeans. Altogether he must have been wearing £600-worth of gear.

'Shut up Jay and get on with it, don't you think we owe Dave something?' Douglas said.

'We don't owe him nothing! He ain't our father. Who the hell does he think he is? Who asked him to interfere?' Jay whinged.

'You've got a bad attitude problem, man. Chill out,' responded Douglas. He was set to go on but his mother interrupted.

'I don't want you two quarrelling, haven't we got enough aggravation without having you two at each other's throats. It was the Lord put it in David's heart to go and save you and we should all get down on our knees and thank Him!'

'Oh, it's always the same with you, Mother,' sneered Jay. 'You get down on your knees to thank your Jewish god for a few crumbs from Whitey's table. Where do you think they got the cotton that made this town rich? Black slaves picked every bit of it! Now we've got something that Whitey wants. They want drugs and we can get rich selling them!'

His ranting was punctuated by a resounding crack as Lovena hit him across the back of the head with all her strength.

She looked embarrassed. 'I'm sorry miss, I want to apologise for my son,' she said to Sylvia, who gave her a distant smile. Sylvia was getting a dose of family life served up raw on her own doorstep and she didn't know how to handle it. She said nothing.

Jay still hadn't finished cutting me free. His mother motioned him to continue.

'I'm sick of trying to bring up my kids in this country, the sooner I can get them into a different climate the happier I'll be. Maybe I should have belted Jay more when he was younger, but it's hard for a woman on her own. He was a lovable little scamp when he was a lad.

'If you hadn't dragged Jay round to see that man last Sunday maybe he would have left us alone, but now look, he's brainwashed Jay with his crazy ideas.'

Lovena started sobbing loudly after her outburst and Douglas put his arm round her. Jay carried on sawing at my manacle but gave me a venomous look. It wasn't a lovable scamp's look.

I was irritated. I'd put my head on the block to rescue Douglas but now I was accused of being the cause of the inner city problems of Manchester.

Jay had known all about Manteh long before I had. Before I said anything I would have regretted later Jay managed to finish cutting me free. He let the radiator fall with a crash and went to join Douglas in embracing his mum. She dried her eyes and gave her sons a hug. It was Andersons united against the world. I should have known I would be the one to get whatever blame was going.

I had to say something. Maybe Jay *had* been a lovable little scamp once but he'd grown into a lout and his greed had nearly cost his brother's life.

'Thanks Jay. Thank you for everything you've done tonight. You saved your brother and you saved me but you saved yourself as well. Do you really think your pal Manteh would have let you go wandering off round Moss Side?

'Either he'd have killed you to stop you blabbing or, even worse, made you kill your own brother as the price of admission to his band. Then you'd have been too scared for your own skin to say anything but your life would have been ruined.'

'No, he's not like that,' Jay replied, scowling fiercely again. 'He'd have let Douglas go. He was just saying that about killing him to frighten me. He might have killed you but then he says you're a murderer yourself. So you'd be no great loss. What have you ever done for me? You made me stay in that stupid college doing A-levels and for what? There's no jobs going for blacks in this town.'

'That's bloody rubbish Jay, and you know it. If you think the only job for a black boy is to become a crack dealer you must be mad, and it's very insulting to your mother. As for what you said before about selling drugs to wicked white people being the only way to get rich, well just ask yourself, do Manteh's dealers only sell to whites?

''Course they don't! Who do you think Manteh's working for anyway? He's probably got a Colombian boss. Who bankrolled him when he first turned up in Manchester? Somebody must have been backing him.'

Lovena joined in by saying, 'Just you listen Jay and listen well. Every penny I've ever earned has been honestly earned. All the food that's gone down your throat, and the clothes that's gone on your back, were bought and paid for with hard work until you started hanging round with those low-lifes.'

Jay was beginning to look chastened. He was an impressionable character who went along with the crowd. Lovena was right, if she stayed in Moss Side Jay was certain to go to the bad. He'd hang about on the fringes of easy money and let himself be drawn in. He wasn't tough enough to pull himself clear.

'What's all this about you being a murderer then, David? Where's Jay got hold of that idea?' Lovena asked.

'Well, you know I told you I was in trouble, and I went to see Sese Manteh,' I said, not disguising my irritation at her cross examination.

'Yes, but you didn't say nothing about any murder,' she butted in.

'That's because I wasn't involved in any murder. I found the body of a young man and one of Manteh's henchmen put two and two together and made five. I haven't been involved in any murder.'

'Well if you say so David, that's good enough for me.' She didn't sound too convinced. There was nothing to be gained by arguing with her, so I let it drop.

The Andersons sat down together to discuss plans. The little row and the blow across Jay's head seemed to have cleared the air between them. They decided to drive to Lovena's cousins in Telford before she booked their flights.

I advised them to drive there straightaway and to avoid the motorway but they didn't seem too interested in my ideas. They were trooping out of the flat almost before I got the words out of my mouth. Lovena wasn't warm in her farewells either.

She kissed me and gave me a hug but there was a certain coolness.

Jay didn't say a word but Douglas came up and made a fist and touched. He gave me a warm grin. 'See ya soon man!' were his parting words.

I didn't feel guilty about being the cause of them leaving Manchester. Jay had been going wrong for a long time and, as he was the one who let the Posse in to snatch Douglas, he'd got off lightly. If I hadn't been aching so much, I wouldn't have minded smacking him about the head myself. It might help to accelerate the learning process for him.

If Manteh had killed Douglas and me there's no way he'd have left Jay running around. Manteh didn't run his business on sentiment. It had come out during the illness of Carleton, her eldest son, that each of Lovena's sons had a different father. Not that it was any of my business, but she'd told me often enough that Jay's father was doing time. So Lovena couldn't lay all the blame at my door if Jay was taking after his father. There was something indecisive about the way Lovena had never been able to choose one of her men to be a permanent husband. The truth was, with her career as a midwife, she felt herself to be a cut above any man.

I'd sometimes felt that if I hadn't been so emotionally numbed after Elenki's death I could have been the 'fourth man' in Lovena's life, shared grief bringing us together, but the moment passed. I failed to meet her specifications.

She got religion and I found Delise.

While the Andersons had been making their curt farewells Sylvia had changed into jeans and a sweater. The sweater did a lot for her. I could feel the sap rising. For the first time since I'd met her she was smoking a cigarette. She took a deep drag and faced me.

'Dave I'd better be open with you . . . I've been using you . . .'

She started to weep and I was expected to comfort her but I didn't. What she had said wasn't news. Unlike Lovena, she hadn't got two husky sons to rush up and hug her so there was a hiatus until she finished sobbing.

I just sat and waited. I was determined not to speak. Eventually she went on. 'It's not that I didn't really like you or anything, but I've been trying to find someone who'd help me to get rid of Mike Dyer.'

I looked at her, raising my eyebrows interrogatively.

'No, I don't mean kill him; just take over his clubs. I'm the one who's been running the business side, he's just a drain on the organisation with his horrible boozing partners.'

'I thought you claimed to be a loyal employee?' I said.

'That's just it. I'm too loyal to the business to let him run it into the ground. Oh, it was great when I started working for him as his PA. He let me have more and more say in the day-to-day running. I'd just split up with my pig of a husband and I put my heart and soul into the job, but it wasn't enough.'

'What do you mean?' I asked sceptically.

'I was perfect for Mike, I could do all the hard parts of the job for him but I'd never be a rival. Hah! Everyone knows that mere females can't run nightclubs in Manchester!'

'Poor old Sylvia. So you're suffering from male chauvinism,' I said, glancing around her luxurious flat.

'Joke if you like, but it's true. My husband used to thump me around when things weren't going right for him in court. Then he wanted me to forgive and forget. He'd be as horny as a ram for a week after he'd battered me. That was supposed to make it all right,' she said bitterly. 'Do you think I'm one of these women that men like to use as a punch-bag? Is there something wrong with me?'

'Look Sylvia, I didn't mean to joke. I've seen quite enough wife beaters in my job to know it's not funny, but you were supposed to be telling me why you wanted to get rid of Dyer.'

'Yes, you're right. No one's interested in someone else's sob story.' She looked as if she was ready to start weeping again.

'Come on Sylvia. Big girls don't cry these days, they just get even. I thought you were a toughie,' I said coaxingly.

'No, they don't do they? . . . Well, at the end of my first year with Mike he was doing so little work in the business I thought he was going to retire and leave me in charge. Then I found out he doesn't even own the clubs. A property company called NMP is the real owner . . .'

I nodded encouragingly at her, as if this was news to me.

'NMP cheat the tax people by claiming dozens more employees at the clubs than we have, and Mike rips the NMP off by claiming we take in a lot less than we do. So I thought I'd try to get Mike in trouble with them. Andrew Thwaite came to me offering to arrange a big loan from the Northern Pioneers' Bank. We'd be able to expand the clubs into a large entertainment company.'

She gave a bitter laugh and again I looked questioningly at her.

'Well I don't see what's so wrong with that! You were only trying to help Dyer.'

'Was I? I could see Thwaite was a con-man straight away. I had him checked out. There was no way he could have got the loan although he did have the Elsworth girl in tow all the time. His father's a union official and the family's had a feud going with the Elsworths for years. There's no way Elsworth would touch a deal from Thwaite with a barge-pole.'

'So what!'

'I hoped Mike would make a fool of himself, fall flat on his face and that the NMP would hear about him trying to buy them out and that they'd sack him,' she said.

'And put you in his place, I suppose.'

She nodded, and stubbing out her cigarette, lit another.

'I didn't realise how desperate Mike was to get out from under the NMP. He swallowed the story. He boosted Thwaite into a top DJ slot. Thwaite was really convincing. He kept telling Mike that these things weren't arranged quickly but eventually he must have realised that Mike had rumbled him.'

'Why was that?' I asked, waving the smoke out of my face.

'Mike was getting shitty with him, threatening to see Elsworth himself. So Thwaite made another plan. He'd get the drug gangs to put up the money. It'd be perfect for them. They could launder their money through the clubs. He brought Leon Grant to see me.'

I must have squirmed in my seat when she mentioned Leon. She glanced up at me.

'Yes. He's the one you've seen me talking to, and jumped to the wrong conclusion about. Leon's very charming, very courteous . . .'

And now very dead, I thought to myself.

'Leon's deal was simple. He'd force Dyer out of the business in one way or another, either by steaming the clubs with his gangs or by making him take a golden handshake. Then he'd offer NMP a fifty-fifty deal. He'd put up hard cash to buy a half share and I'd stay on as Managing Director.'

'What did you have to do in return?'

'I was to turn the other way if a few mild drugs like Ecstasy were sold on the side, she looked away from me as she spoke.

We sat in silence for some time. Sylvia was quite a sweetheart. She must have known that Dyer wouldn't tamely roll over while his business was taken away from him. He was the last man anyone would expect to retire peacefully. Leon had more experience in handing out cement waistcoats than golden handshakes. She must have suspected.

'Say something Dave . . . you don't know how hard it is for a woman to get on in business in this town, some men are pigs! It's not my fault if people want drugs,' she pleaded.

'OK Sylvia. Where did I fit into your little scheme?'

'Well, when you barged into the club that night Mike nearly had heart failure. He thought you were doing some investigation for the Inland Revenue or the Serious Fraud Office or something. You see he's got the police sewn up,' she looked expectantly at me as she spoke.

'How's he managed that?' I barked.

'The Chief Constable's wife owns five per cent of NMP.'

'You're joking!' I almost laughed in her face.

'No it's true, she owns it through untraceable nominees registered in the Cayman Islands. Dyer and his property friends gave the shares to Benson and he put them in his wife's name. On the register the shares are listed as being owned by Chiefly Nominees, Cayman Islands Inc.'

'That's incredible. How did you find out?' the sceptical tone in my voice was intended to encourage further revelations.

'We'd just caught a little creep selling "E's". I was worried that the police would find out and close us down. Mike was well kettled that night. He just laughed and said that while the police were always threatening us they'd never close us down – they were all bark and no bite. I thought he was just bragging – and then he told me what I've told you.'

'It just seems fantastic, the Chief Constable on the take. I've never liked him but . . .'

'It's not for himself, not for personal gain. It's for politics. He needs money to finance his campaign for a national police force,' she interrupted.

So, unlike one of his predecessors who wanted to be God's Cop, Benson's ambition was to Britain's Supercop.

He'd come to Manchester from the rural hinterland trailing rumours of political influence. He must have felt he needed the Manchester experience to show he could handle inner-city crime. He'd spoken on the platforms of the Police and the National Decency League, demanding a national police force to restore national morality. Eyebrows had been raised, but this was the nineties: top cops were into policy making. What no one but Dyer and the NMP had known was that Benson was forking out hard cash so that the League would keep him in the public eye.

I wondered how this would go down with his political friends. They hadn't drawn the line at a girl from a grocer's shop or a boy from a garden-gnome works running the country. Would they permit a self-publicised supercop who financed himself with under-the-counter bungs from night-clubs to run the national police? Or even the Manchester police?

'Mike explained it,' Sylvia went on. 'It's like the Wild West; the Sheriff's always well in with the saloon keepers. In the old days clubs were seedy run-down places. The police were always shutting them down. There wasn't much money involved. That's all changed.

'Nowadays we have people fighting to get in. I've had men climbing drainpipes with £20 notes clenched in their teeth, desperate to be allowed in. We put the entrance fee up, we double-charge for drinks but still they come. Some nights I've turned hundreds away because of the fire regs. We give them a ticket to one of our other clubs.'

'So let me get this right. You're saying Dyer killed Thwaite because he couldn't get a loan and when I came along he was scared that some bigger fish than NMP or the Chief Constable was coming for a piece of his action?' I asked.

'No, I couldn't say that, I don't think Mike's capable—'

'All you're thinking about is getting your hands on his clubs.' I interrupted impatiently. 'Can't you see that what you've said is a perfect motive for murder? I know Dyer's on a short fuse.

He wants to bash my head in and all I've done is ask a few questions.

'Thwaite was promising him the means to get the NMP and Benson off his back,' I continued. 'If he'd been able to buy out the NMP all the Chief would have had was five per cent of a company completely unrelated to Dyer. If Benson tried to get stroppy Dyer could have told him to get stuffed or explain his wife's ownership of NMP shares to the Police Committee.

'Thwaite not only failed with the finance but then got into bed with Dyer's worst enemies. People have had their lights put out for a lot less than that.'

'That sounds very convincing Dave, but I know it wasn't like that,' she said maddeningly. 'Mike would never arrange a cold blooded murder.'

'Yes he would. Murder's murder – hot or cold, and what you said about Benson explains why the police are so unwilling to investigate. If he bumped off Thwaite for treachery you're probably next on his list, especially as you know all his trade secrets. Has he threatened you?'

'He hasn't threatened to murder me,' she managed to say before she turned on the waterworks again.

'Spare me the tears,' I said roughly. 'What were your plans for me Sylvia? First you tried to drop Dyer in it with NMP, then you tried to double-cross him with the Charlies. Was I supposed to be insurance in case Leon got rough or was I around for a third try at getting rid of Dyer?'

Sylvia looked frightened.

'No it wasn't like that, I fancied you as soon as I saw you being cheeky to Mike in his own club. I was frightened of Leon. I thought he'd toss me out like an old sock as soon as he had no use for me.'

'I see, so I was to be your toyboy and insurance policy combined.'

'No, Dave, no! It all got out of hand. Leon had something going with Rachel Elsworth. As soon as she disappeared he started pressuring me to find her. He said he'd tell Mike what had been going on. I was at my wits' end.'

'A likely tale. Anyway what's your problem now?'

'Mike found something out. When I went into the Paloma last night he smacked me around the room. He knows I've been seeing you and now he thinks you're working with the Charlies to frame him for drugs. He says I'm the only person who could have told them the code for his security system. He said he'll get his thugs to gang-rape me and cut my face if I don't get out of Manchester,' she wailed.

'Tough luck!' I said brutally. 'You should have thought of that before you started playing the field. You arranged with first Leon, then Dyer, for me to be beaten up when you thought I was going to find out too much about your double-crossing game. No, my only interest now is Rachel. I've got to make sure she's safe. At least you've no idea where she is. So this looks like goodbye.'

I got up to go, but she threw herself at me using every ounce of emotional and sexual appeal.

'Please Dave, I'm begging you, let me go with you. He'll kill me if I stay, but he's frightened of you. He can't make out who you are or who you're working for.'

I pushed her back – I've always been a mug where ladies in distress are concerned but even I'm not so stupid that I'd take up with Sylvia again because of an emotional appeal.

She thought I was a pushover. An easy mark for a pair of big tits and a come-on look. She did have the goods on Benson and Dyer though. I could just see Sinclair drooling when she told him her story.

No wonder Benson hadn't wanted me poking my nose into Dyer's affairs. He must know full well that top coppers are eager to believe the worse about each other. Sinclair must have some suspicion of links between Dyer and 'Wild Bill'. That was why he'd been so eager to get his hands on the photo. Still, Sinclair had made it very plain to me that he wasn't going to go against Benson.

Come to think of it, there had been a few odd things about that interview. I'd been too steamed up afterwards to work out what had been going on. I'd gone rushing round to Manteh's place to straighten him out.

Benson had mentioned the detective who'd interviewed Dyer. The detective said Dyer had been foaming at the mouth at the mention of my name, but before Benson said all that he told Sinclair to ask me how I'd been able to tell Dyer that

Thwaite was dead. He'd made a big point about the time – 23.30 on Thursday – when I'd told Dyer about the 'suicide'.

The inference he'd left with Sinclair and me was that he'd learned this from the police interview. But suppose he hadn't? Suppose he'd learned all this privately from Dyer? There might be a way I could establish how he'd got his information.

It would be interesting to see the transcript of the interview with Dyer. It would be even more interesting if there was no mention by Dyer of what I'd said. 23.30! Pretty specific for a man who was 'foaming at the mouth'.

Dyer wouldn't give the police the correct spelling of his name, let alone volunteer all kinds of fine detail.

The only chance I had of finding out about that interview now was through Michael Rice and it would be a pretty slim chance at that. Benson had probably moved Rice away from any contact with investigating officers by now. My guess that Rice would be demoted to turnkey might not be wide of the mark. The police holding centres were still bulging at the seams since the destruction of Strangeways.

On the other hand, Rice might be the only copper in Greater Manchester desperate enough to pursue inquiries which might implicate the force's chief constable in a web of corruption.

If he did help me it gave me a very slim chance of pulling through this quagmire.

That left me with the problem of what to do with Sylvia. I phoned Molly Delaney in the hope of getting Delise to come and babysit her. Delise should be back from Jersey by now and I knew that despite all her snide comments about Sylvia she'd help her in the circumstances. Even Molly would. All I got was the answerphone, so I left a message for Delise to get in touch urgently.

Meanwhile I'd have to cart Sylvia round with me.

22

Manteh's 'posse' should be assembling by now. I didn't expect them to get on my case right away. At least half an hour would have elapsed before they'd discovered our getaway. Then they'd go round to the Andersons' and draw a blank there. Next, round to my flat and leave a stake-out or renew the bribe of the neighbour who'd been informing them about my movements. Then they'd throw the net wider, they might come here. But it was most likely they'd try to grab Rachel. They knew I was committed to protecting her. It was unlikely that they'd trouble the Elsworths again while they had Rachel's address.

The moors around Bolton weren't a foreign territory to them. They had dealers in Bolton. So even at this moment they might be making a move towards my parents' cottage. I might have some time – the cottage was hard to find, even following directions. Still, I didn't want to hang about too long with Sylvia.

If she was coming with me, we'd better get a move on. I told her to throw a few things into the smallest case she'd got. I'd no idea where the day might end, but we weren't likely to be back in Heaton Mersey for a while. I went in the bedroom to watch her pack, I'd no intention of letting her out of my sight. She seemed very subdued and when she'd finished we went out to the car without speaking. I let her drive because I wanted to use the phone. She sat meekly waiting for instructions.

My uncomfortable eight hours' sleep at the lovers' hideaway in Chorlton and then the escape from the Charlies had given me the resilience to face the next round. With the pale morning sun shining, I felt as full of bounce as a dog food commercial. It was pleasant to think of Manteh worrying about his numbered accounts. The top of the greasy pole must be as slippery in the drugs trade as in politics; except that instead of the House of Lords, they had the knackers yard for the casualties.

I think having the uncertainty removed about Sylvia also contributed to my buoyant mood. I was probably punch-drunk from being hit on the head so often, but I felt things were going well for the first time since the whole mess started. My optimism contrasted with Sylvia's sullen mood.

She gave me a strange look when she saw the happy expression on my face but she didn't speak. She must be thinking that she'd said enough already. I'd used the opportunity to freshen up and change. Now I was no longer blundering about I ought to make sure that my next move was the right move. I ought to get hold of Rachel before the Charlies did, and then let her Daddy send her out of the country. I certainly ought to let Sinclair know the news about his boss. First things first. I must phone my parents and warn them to get ready to move right away. My father was already up when I phoned.

'Look Dad, your guest has let the opposition know where she is.' I usually call him Dad in normal speech. On the rare occasions when neither of us will be embarrassed by it I call him by his given name . . . Paddy.

'What are you talking about?' he barked irritably down the phone. 'Don't you know what time it is?'

'Rachel. She told a girlfriend where she is, and the friend told a creep called Kevin Spragg who sold the information to the Charlies.'

'My God, would you believe it? These females, nothing stops their tongues wagging. I told your mother that the visit was supposed to be hush-hush, she was supposed to keep an eye on her. Rachel must have used the phone when I was in the garden . . .'

'Hold on a minute Dad! It doesn't matter a damn how she did it. The bad news is that the Charlies might be on their way to you right at this moment. Get packed and ready for a move.'

There was a pause while he registered this information then he came back, 'I thought it was Dyer that you had the wind up about . . . Your mother and I can start our holiday a few days early, we were supposed to be touring Scotland next week, but you'll have to shift Rachel. I've got your mother to think of, I never expected that they'd find out where Rachel was after that conjuring trick in Southport.'

I was getting impatient with him, 'I know that Dad, I'm phoning from the car. I'm on my way to you as fast as I can and I've got somebody with me, a woman friend.'

'I wish I could work you out David, you never seem to get enough trouble and strife. Where are you picking them up from? You know these things come in threes, so if you find yourself with a third stray female, you'll know you're for the chop.'

'Well, thanks a bunch Dad. Proper ray of sunshine you are. I'll be with you in twenty minutes.'

All things considered Dad had let me down lightly, he usually told me I was a 'crate-egg' or a 'fool to myself' when he had knowledge of one of my schemes coming adrift. Of course, he never gave me any credit when something I'd arranged worked out well. That wasn't in the rules of his game.

Having phoned my old man, I thought of phoning Elsworth to tell him to get Rachel booked on an intercontinental flight but then decided against telling him anything. There were too many questions about Elsworth's activities to take risks. I was bothered about why he'd been out of the country so soon after his previous trip. He spent his time between Manchester and Brussels and maybe, as his own wife suspected, the explanation wasn't innocent.

That still left my aggressive friend Finbar. The least I could do for Finbar was to let him know that the posse might be playing on his home turf. He'd be delighted.

'Hello Finbar, I thought I'd better let you know that there's a better-than-even chance that the Charlies will be coming to pay you a call.'

He answered his early call without any fuss, 'Is that you David? Well it's all been quiet on the home front. I sat up waiting to see you for hours.'

'Sorry about that, but I changed my plans. Anyway if you see any of these lads hanging about just pick up the phone and get the police round.'

'Hmmmph, I don't know about that, I'm entitled to defend my hearth and home you know. I might just invite a few of my friends round.'

I knew it was useless to try to change his mind.

'Well that's up to you Finbar, but just bear this in mind. I've got a suspicion there's someone living not a million miles from Thornleigh Court who's been tipping the Charlies off. You might have a spy in your camp, some pot-head who owes them a favour, do you know anyone like that?'

'Spy, eh? Well I'll ask Fiona, she knows far more about the neighbours than I do.'

I knew he'd start mustering his friends straightaway. The Charlies could be sure of a warm welcome at Thornleigh Court. With any luck Finbar might wing a couple of them with the shotgun, or give them a good fright at least.

I wasn't worrying anymore about where Finbar's desire for a bit of a scrap led him. He seemed to like being in the thick of it – so good luck to him.

I couldn't think of anyone else to give an early morning call to. There were one or two more details to fix. I got the shotgun off the back seat and ejected a shell. The cartridge was carrying a full buckshot load, but the next had a solid lead slug. I ejected them all; half were buckshot, half lead slugs.

A 12-gauge slug would make a very large hole in an elephant. It also came in handy for smashing locked doors. There were more cartridges in the glove compartment. I didn't tell Sylvia that I'd come by the gun courtesy of her late buddy Leon. Anyway, I was armed with a deadly weapon, the Viking Arms 12-gauge pump-action shotgun was accurate up to about fifty yards.

Too bad I hadn't got the Beretta as well. Having had a glimpse of what the Charlies were armed with I could understand now why the police outside the Bank of England had carried so much iron. While I was making my preparations Sylvia wrinkled her nose in distaste.

'What comes next Rambo? The band round your head, or the survival knife?' she sneered. I gave her a cheery grin. She flicked her hair back and lapsed back into a sulky silence.

Apart from Sylvia, the only flies in the ointment were the steel bracelet on my right wrist and the fact that my face was swollen thanks to the combined efforts of Leon Grant and Manteh. I found an old pair of sunglasses in the front of the car and shoved them on. They helped to disguise the puffy eyelids. Looking at my beaten up face in the mirror I decided to shoot first and ask questions later if Manteh's mob got near me again.

We made good time along empty roads to Bolton. There was

hardly any traffic on the M62. We reached the turn-off for Bolton, which was named St Peter's Way. I hoped that wasn't an omen that I was shortly going to be visiting the Pearly Gates. At the end of the motorway we took the road for Belmont, the moorland village where my parents lived.

There were only a few milk floats on the move as we drove up Blackburn Road through Astley Bridge and took the turning for the West Pennine moors. Sylvia maintained her silence and I wondered what was going on in her head. What game was she playing; what profit did she hope to make by tagging along with me? I knew she was a gambler.

The answer wasn't flattering, having failed to play both ends against the middle, Sylvia was sticking with me because I was her safest option. Dyer had already threatened to maim her and God alone knew what Manteh might do. Still, why should I try to cheer her up? She'd got herself into this mess with both her pretty eyes open. We stopped the car for a moment and I changed placed with my grumpy passenger.

Leaving the built-up area behind, the road began climbing into the moorlands. It ran along the side of a steep slope. On the left there was a rough edge of moorland – all tussocks and heather pitted with holes where coal had long ago been extracted from shallow pits; a jagged crest loomed over the narrow road. On the right, sloping down steeply, there were green fields with encroaching settlements and estates in the far distance. The main kind of farming practised round these parts was extracting grants from the state.

As I rounded a bend a stone-built pub, the Hilton Arms, came into view on the left. My turn-off point, a plunge down the steep incline, was about half a mile further on the right. Everything looked fresh and clean in the clear, early morning light.

I recognised the semi-derelict farm buildings which marked the settlement where my parents, on a crazy impulse to return to nature, had located themselves. An odd choice for two people who had lived their entire lives in big cities.

The track leading down to the cottage was a one-in-three slope: the steepest section was made of ribbed concrete which then gave way to a pot-holed lane. Easy to miss because it disappeared down the edge, it was hardly visible from a driver's viewpoint. As usual, maddened dogs from the dilapidated farm buildings rushed the car. My father always tried to run them over, so far without success.

The farm was littered with broken-down machinery, much of it brand new, left lying about in all weathers. It was nominally a dairy farm but the hill-billies who ran it were interested in grants rather than milk. They were never short of money. They'd increased their income by selling off the leaky and damp old weavers' cottages surrounding the farm to such as my parents. Where weavers had toiled retired policemen, motor traders and butchers now resided.

The stone-built cottages had been renovated and extended by the immigrants. The squalid homes of the hill-billies made a stark contrast, with their broken front doors and cracked windows. Making life difficult for their new neighbours was the main pastime of the hill-billies. They loved blocking the narrow lane with a broken-down tractor or driving their cattle through carefully tended gardens. Paddy fought a perpetual battle with them.

He enjoyed his rural residence. It reminded him of his early days on the beat in the slums of Manchester but I don't think Eileen cared for it much.

They'd seen my car coming down the hill and were waiting round the door. Paddy, always good at getting up early, looked genial and well rested. My mother was making an effort to smile but I could see she'd have preferred a couple more hours in bed. It took me about six turns to back into the protected harbour by their front door. The dry stone walls were awkwardly sited for cars but I got in without scraping anything. I watched my mother looking Sylvia over and smiling at her. If I wasn't careful she'd get the wrong idea and start giving Sylvia her recipes for apple pie. Rachel was there flashing a shy grin.

My feelings on seeing her were mixed. Was she friend or foe? If some of the Charlies felt that she knew about their secrets she must be involved in some way. She was definitely a cuckoo in the nest in my parents' home as far as I was concerned. Her cool and aloof expression might have irritated me on another occasion. Stepfather or not, there was a lot of Harold Elsworth in Rachel. Standing alongside my parents there was something condescending about the impression she gave. I felt that she looked as if she had made herself too much 'at home'. Still, if I was going to get everything sorted, I needed her willing co-operation. So I smiled right back at her. Calming nervous females and encouraging them to confess is supposed to be one of my fortes.

I introduced Sylvia to Paddy, Eileen and Rachel and we went inside. The solidly built house was crammed with antiques and bric-a-brac but was warm and cosy. It reflected my parents personalities well: my mother's pride in her possessions and my father's never-ending work as a home improver.

Sylvia and I sat facing my parents and Rachel. Eileen made quite a contrast with Rachel. Unlike her, she is definitely not the physical type that the up-market clothes catalogues are aiming at. Short and dumpy in build, she conforms to the standard stereotype of a north-western mature female. However, no one could mistake her for the typical mother-in-law or seaside landlady type. She has a sensitive and intelligent face, which is what people notice first; then her hands. Wide, with short fingers, they're never still. She's always making, shaping or smoothing something into place. She paints and does 'wood collages' with oddly shaped branches she finds.

'I just want to say I'm very sorry about all this,' I said, 'normally I wouldn't have involved you but I had to find somewhere safe to leave Rachel while her parents made arrangements. I'm just sorry that this gang of Manchester villains have found out where she is. A chap called Kevin Spragg told them.'

We were all looking at Rachel, but she didn't lose her self-possession. Unlike Eileen and Sylvia who looked haggard and gaunt without their make-up, Rachel's fresh complexion needed no artificial aids.

'No, that stupid, stupid man! Oh my God! I'm so sorry. I just had to talk to someone and Lisa's my best friend in Manchester. I'd no idea her boyfriend knew the Charlies.' Rachel spoke coolly, with no trace of regret.

'Never mind love. No use crying over spilt milk, then. Come on. We'll all have a cup of tea,' said Mum, dispensing her healing balm. 'It's too early in the morning to get worked up about what happened yesterday.'

'No I don't think we've time for that,' butted in Dad. 'We'd all best get on our way. Least said, soonest mended.' Paddy has always had a neurosis about getting to his destination on time and Eileen smiled at him, humouring him. 'No, I'm serious. These hooligans are deadly. They're capable of bumping the lot of us off. We'd best get on our way.'

Sitting in that cosy room the menace of the Charlies seemed unreal. The sun went behind a cloud and the room darkened for a moment.

Turning to me Paddy said, 'Do they know what car you're driving?'

'Well I suppose they do,' I agreed reluctantly.

'Right then, I'll take that one and you take mine. I don't suppose you've bothered to fill her up have you?' he said briskly.

He was adopting his old style of speaking to me as if I was a half-witted recruit on the force.

'There's plenty of fuel in it. But you can't have it. I need the car phone to keep in touch.'

'No you don't,' he said in his domineering way, 'they'll mark you straight away if you drive round Manchester in that red Nissan. You'll be a hell of a lot safer in the Vauxhall.'

He stood up in front of me. I stood up too. Paddy Cunane, the rock hard cop – he was an inch taller than me and although his cheeks were slightly sunken in and the skin at his throat was loose he was still as strong and dominating as he'd always been. His hair was only just beginning to go grey and he hadn't lost much of it. Age hadn't softened him.

'Give over, you two!' Eileen interrupted sharply.

'They're always going on like this but they don't mean anything by it,' she explained to Sylvia and Rachel, resuming her lifetime role as mediator between quarrelling father and son.

'Look Dad, they might not be here for hours. If I know anything about that dozy lot . . .'

'Rubbish! You know nothing about them. You've got something they want very badly.' He indicated Rachel. 'They might be here any minute. You can help me get the luggage into the car after you've had a word with your mother. She's something to say to you in private,' he said sternly. He gave me the keys of his car and then strode off upstairs.

Sheepishly, I followed my mother into the kitchen, I knew

there was something unpleasant going to happen. Dad always left the really serious telling-off to Eileen.

She peered short-sightedly at me over the top of her granny glasses, with an anxious expression on her smooth and unlined face. 'David, what have you been doing to yourself? Just look at your poor face and that young woman too. I went through enough of this with your father for one lifetime, but at least he had the Force behind him, while you're just on your own.'

She shook her head and wiped the tears out of her eyes. I knew I was going to be put through the emotional wringer. I'd already had enough but there was more to follow.

'That girl of yours Delise Delaney's been in touch with us. She phoned last night to try to find out what's been going on,' Eileen said. 'She says she came to see you early on Saturday and you had another woman installed at your flat. It wouldn't have been Sylvia would it?' she continued, looking at me severely over her specs.

I nodded.

'Now David, we don't want to tell you how to lead your life. We just want you to be happy, but isn't it time you got yourself sorted out?' she admonished me, with total inaccuracy.

She and Dad never did anything else but tell me how to lead my life.

'Promise me you'll sort things out with Delise? Your father and I want to see you with children of your own before we're too old to enjoy them.'

I nodded again.

I was saved from the need for a more prolonged response by a yell from Dad ordering me to come up for the luggage. With a shrug and a look at Eileen I obeyed him. This was why I'd never felt the urge to join a 'disciplined force' myself.

Delise had played her cards well by enlisting my parents on her side in her campaign of emotional blackmail.

When I came down the spiral staircase from the recently built front bedroom, the three females had their heads together. It wasn't hard to work out what they were talking about as the name David recurred several times. Eileen was smiling at Sylvia and squeezing her hand. Typically, Paddy took charge of the luggage, loading while I supplied the labour. He was looking out of the back-bedroom window towards the main road.

'Do you really think they'll come?' I asked doubtfully. At this distance from Manchester the Charlies seemed like a bad dream.

'Of course they will, if only half of what Archie Sinclair tells me is true. You always were too optimistic, lad. You're too good-natured for your own good. Just get a move on and we'll get out of here. We're in a trap in this house, there's only that road up the hill and the winding lane by the bleach works to get out by. All they need do is park at either exit and they'll have us corked in.'

When I came back up for the next load, he was looking out of the window with the binoculars he used for bird watching. He passed the binoculars to me.

'What does that look like then?' he asked grimly.

Parked at the top of the hill was a four-wheel-drive Suzuki jeep. I glanced at my watch. It was still very early, just before 6 a.m.

Cursing myself for my complacency, I was about to run down and get the shotgun when he grabbed my arm.

'Steady on, we don't want to get your mother upset. There only seems to be that one FWD here. They'll be waiting for reinforcements. There'll be a chance to get out in a minute. Now this is what we'll do. That bloody idiot farmer drives his cows along here just after six every morning. As soon as he gets them past the front door I'll be off with your mother down the bleach works road. We'll not go up the hill, we'll go down the lane and turn out on to the main road at the far end.'

'But they'll follow you, and what happens if they catch you?'

'They don't want me and I know every back lane and side turning for miles round here, besides I'm armed.'

He unzipped his golfing jacket to show me the Webley and Scott mark VI 0.455 revolver in a holster under his left shoulder. He'd confiscated the old cannon from a drunken ex-RAF officer who'd been threatening to do in his errant wife with it. It had been lovingly maintained and would put a stop to anyone who interfered with him.

I agreed to his plan. Not that I could have disagreed. There was no alternative really.

I joined Paddy at his observation post. I was biting my

knuckles with anxiety, yet he seemed perfectly calm and relaxed. He continued observing the Suzuki with the patience which made him a good bird watcher.

'You did say it was the Charlton Close mob that was after you?' he said meditatively.

I agreed.

'Well, I can definitely make out three Afro-Caribbean males in that vehicle. So it's likely to be them and not your other playmate, Dyer,' he said. I admired the cool way in which he spoke, using the same tone of voice in which he might have noted the presence of some common species of bird.

As we stood there, I told him everything that had happened in the last few days – apart from the shooting of Leon and Trevor, which I kept to myself. Justifiable homicide or not, I wasn't bold enough to tell Paddy about that. I did include the fact that the chief constable of his old force seemed to be a crook. He didn't comment but seemed to age a little as I went on to tell him about the interrogation session with Sinclair and Benson.

'Archie Sinclair was robbed of that job,' was all he would say, shaking his head sadly.

After what seemed like hours, but was actually only ten minutes, the yipping of dogs and mooing of cows could be heard approaching. Paddy and Eileen got into my red Nissan. I remained on the look-out. Our hope was that the Charlies would see my car disappearing down the lane when Paddy and Eileen made off. They'd follow and Paddy would lead them a merry dance. Eventually they'd discover that Rachel and I weren't in the car.

However long this took would be the lead I had.

When the last cow had lurched past the door Paddy shot off down the lane without making any fuss about farewells. His own car was in the garage which he'd built on the side of the house. I took Sylvia and Rachel up the spiral staircase into the front bedroom. Sylvia was showing understandable signs of nervousness. She was pale and shaky on her feet. Rachel, by contrast, seemed almost too calm. She might endanger the three of us if she didn't become more aware of the situation.

The front bedroom into which I led them, part of Paddy's renovation job, looked out obliquely over the narrow lane which snaked down from the main road. It also gave the tactical advantage of allowing me to look down on anyone coming from the lane to the front door. The lane curved in front of the cottage and led off towards the old bleach works. I nipped into the back bedroom for another peek at the opposition. I raised my eyes above the window frame. Sure enough the Suzuki was coming down the hill at reckless speed.

Within seconds the Charlies found themselves stuck in the cluttered farm yard. Mooing cows, yapping dogs and grinning yokels blocked their exit to the bleach works lane. Retreating to the front bedroom I could hear their horn blaring. The window on this side of the house didn't give a view of the farmyard, but I heard a bout of cursing clearly enough over the farmyard babble.

The locals gave tongue in reply, 'Where the bloody hell do you think you're going? What buggering time do you think it is? What's your bloody rush? Get your hand off that fucking horn or you'll spoil the fucking milk.'

Inbreeding and stupidity hadn't robbed the three rustic labourers of the power of invective. When the occupants of the FWD continued with their horn blowing they counter-attacked with an even more blistering verbal assault. Their language could have curdled the milk over three counties but this time they weren't dealing with polite over-sixties looking for a rural retreat.

The cursing was concluded by gunfire. Startled cows staggered back down the lane past the cottage. Then the labourers followed and last of all their dogs.

Silence momentarily reigned in the farmyard only to be broken by the revving of the FWD.

I readied the shotgun. Sylvia and Rachel had taken refuge beside me, crouching beneath the window frame. The Suzuki halted right in front of us and its windows must have been open.

'I tell you I'm not getting out Leroy, you fucker, them's man-cows! I'm not going to get fucking gored to death to suit you.'

'Get out you mother, or you'll wish you was a fucking man-cow!'

'Who you calling a mother, Leroy? I don't have to take that

kind of crap from you. I paid £200 for these trainers and I'm not getting them all mashed up with that cow-shit.'

'OK Kingsley, man. Fool! You want to play it this way, fine by me then! I'm phoning the Reverend Manteh.'

We heard the dialling tone of a mobile phone.

Sylvia and Rachel looked at each other nervously, I gripped the gun. Then I heard the car door slamming. Presumably the animal-shy Kingsley was coming to give the place the once-over after all.

I heard him rattling the front door. A terrific sound of barking, and the car door slamming again signalled the returning farm dogs chasing Kingsley back into his vehicle. More heated argument followed. I smiled encouragingly at Sylvia and Rachel. The worst was over.

Then there was an almighty crash and bang. They had opened fire on the bedroom windows. Fine particles of glass were everywhere. There was a line of bullet holes stitched across the ceiling. I looked at Sylvia, her eyes were almost bursting out of her head. Rachel still seemed cool. Maybe she hadn't much imagination. The Charlies had reverted to their Moss Side practice of shooting up buildings. Should I return their fire, I wondered?

It must have been Kingsley who started giggling first, then they were all at it. There were four of them.

'What the fuck did you do that for, man? You was only supposed to check the place out, not give the place a licking,' one of them said.

'Well it's checked out now Leroy. We know there ain't anyone here. We saw the bastards clearing off. The Reverend ain't going to be pleased with you hanging 'bout round here when you should be using this fancy vehicle to chase them.'

That settled their argument, there was more giggling. Then the FWD drove off down the lane.

I risked taking a look and saw it churning round a bend in the dry stone walling of the lane.

Before I could let out a sigh of relief Sylvia started on me. 'That was nice and safe then, wasn't it? What would you have done if they hadn't been so easily fooled? Started a shooting match I suppose. Well count me out.'

'That's fine darling. I wasn't asking you to do anything.

There's a bus stop about half a mile away and the bus comes once every two hours. Or you could hitch a lift off the Charlies,' I replied.

'There's no need to be sarcastic Dave. I'm entitled to wonder what I'm letting myself in for,' Sylvia raised her voice in a hurt tone.

'Hush you two,' said Rachel, 'there's someone coming.'

Sure enough we heard the sound of the strayed cattle and dogs followed by the shouts and whistles of the cow hands as they rounded up their stampeded herd. Soon the foul-mouthed labourers were in earshot.

'Eeeah George, look what they done to that bloody copper's house.'

'Ar, serve him bloody well right. I reckon it was him they was calling on so early. Fly old bird though, in't he? Shot off down the lane like a startled rabbit just before 'em. Happen they was paying him back for sommat.'

'Bugger that, we've got to get these bloody cows milked. It'll be coming out of them like clotted cream. Do you reckon we can claim compensation?'

'Don't you be worrying about compensation, Zack, I'll look after that. Don't forget you've got that muck spreader to fix so we can get that slurry out of the tank.'

They went on their way, and peace returned.

It was time we were making our own departure. I checked the lane. There was no sign of the FWD coming back. I went into the back bedroom for a look up the hill.

Another white Suzuki FWD had replaced the one containing Leroy and Kingsley and their mates.

It couldn't be the same one. Manteh must have hired a fleet of FWDs. In the front bedroom Sylvia and Rachel were shaking the glass off their hair and clothing. They were congratulating each other on their escape. Sylvia still looked and sounded a lot more nervous than Rachel. She'd turned a delicate shade of green under all her bruises.

Rachel looked at my face, 'They've come back, haven't they?' she asked.

I nodded agreement. I felt so disappointed that I didn't trust myself to speak. There was silence for a moment, then it was Sylvia who spoke first. 'So Plan A was a failure. What's Plan

B? You must have a plan. A wonderful clever man like you who can take on Manteh and all his men! You must have some other amazing scheme!' At least her anger had put some colour back in her cheeks.

'He's done all right so far. Give him a chance!' said Rachel. I was surprised at her springing to my defence. I turned and went back to the spot from which I could see the new vehicle in its position at the head of the lane. Rachel followed me.

The route between the two bedrooms led through a bathroom, a fact which had often led to embarrassing situations when I stayed at the cottage. Now, cool as ever, Rachel stopped to freshen up and use the mirror to put some lipstick on.

I studied the unwelcome new vehicle using Paddy's binoculars, trying to observe as patiently as he had done. It was hard to see anything of the occupants through the tinted windscreen, but after a while a tall white man got out and took a leak behind the vehicle. Another white man let him back in.

'You'd better get settled for a long wait while I work out how we're going to get out of here,' I said over my shoulder to Rachel.

'Great! Just let us know when you're ready,' grumbled Sylvia, who'd joined Rachel in the bathroom. I glanced at her. She was combing powdered glass out of her blond hair.

I continued studying the FWD and its occupants as they came into view occasionally. All sorts of ideas passed through my head but none of them were practical. I was getting eyestrain gazing up the hill.

Milking finished. The cows returned to the fields and the hill-billies to their own aimless activities. One of them was tinkering with a large tractor attached to a tank in a field. Eventually he got it going and brought it down to the back of the milking parlour.

I remained on sentry duty. The rare glimpses I got of the men in the FWD convinced me that they were definitely not the ones who'd blasted the windows in. None of them were West Indian, unlike the two who'd quarrelled outside the house. These must be some of the Charlies' white hangers-on. The farm workers were closer to them than me and they didn't identify them as the ones who'd fired earlier because two of them got in a battered Land-Rover and drove off past the parked FWD without incident.

In the distance I heard a pump start. A nasty smell drifted into the room through the broken windows. I looked at Sylvia and Rachel. We all pulled faces. The stench got worse. It was gagging us, a mephitic odour. Just when I thought I couldn't take any more I heard the tractor roaring away. It got louder and I looked out through a tear in the curtain down on to the lane. The tractor and trailer were parked right in front of the cottage, there was no driver. A peek through the window revealed him strolling into the farmhouse.

'Listen you two, this is our chance. Get the car out of the garage. I'm going to use this filthy muck-spreader to block up the lane.'

I pressed the keys of my father's Vauxhall into Sylvia's hands and we all hurried down the spiral staircase. I went out first and gave a cautious look up and down the lane. There was nothing stirring, not even the farm dogs.

Dad's decoy plan hadn't reckoned on the Charlies turning up in such numbers so quickly. There must have been two Suzukis. One with Leroy and Kingsley blocking the hillside exit, and the other at the bleach works end. When Leroy had gone in belated pursuit of Paddy this one must have taken his place on the hillside road. They couldn't see us getting the car out unless they came down the hill.

I got on the tractor. I'd never driven one before but it was shit or bust. I forced the long gear lever into reverse and slowly let the clutch in. Backing up with the muck-spreader trailer attached was difficult but I shunted the trailer out of the farm-yard and on to the hillside with no interference from dog or man.

I revved the motor and released the clutch fully. The tractor and spreader shot backwards up the lane swinging from side to side under my erratic steering. The trailer scraped into the walls on either side several times, but I kept it moving in front of me. My crazy plan was to block the road at the narrowest point. I'd just reached the steep, final, ribbed-concrete stretch of the track when disaster struck.

There was a loud twang as the steel pin joining the heavy muck spreader drum to the tractor broke. I jammed my foot on the tractor brake. As I looked over my shoulder the spreader continued up the slope under its own momentum, pivoted on its wheels and went over backwards. The steel drum split and a cascade of filth poured out down the lane all around me. In a panic I tried to get the gearstick into a forward gear. Nothing happened. The motor had cut out when I slammed the brakes on.

The sound effects and smell accompanying all this were terrific. Even the strongest nerves would have been jarred. As the tractor juddered to a halt the drum began bouncing back down the steep slope towards me, slowly at first, but gathering speed. I frantically forced the gear lever into neutral and let the tractor gather momentum down hill. It began to race forward. I tried to start up again but too late I realised why the yokel had left it with the motor running: the starter didn't work.

I wrestled with the steering and tried to work the brakes at the same time. Nothing happened. The tractor continued silently speeding down the hill like a runaway juggernaut. My main danger had changed from the menace behind to that in front. The farmyard was coming up fast. I jumped for my life as the tractor smashed through the wall of the milking parlour. Fortunately the filthy habits of the hill-billies paid off now. They'd left enough heaps of muck and manure lying around to cushion my fall.

There was a clang as the muck-spreader tank came to rest at a bend in the road.

Emerging from the farmhouse, the remaining rustic scratched his head as he tried to make sense of the scene. What had been ruinous and dilapidated before now looked like a bomb-site. I don't think he connected me with the damage, or maybe he didn't notice me in my camouflage of farmyard waste. He may even have thought the tractor had taken off on its own and I would be after him for compensation.

While he stood gaping open-mouthed, with his dogs growling at his heels, the white Suzuki shot away from its position. Its occupants must have clocked me jumping off the tractor. The speed at which they hit the slope was a tribute to Japanese engineering and the bounty Manteh must have put on my head.

It was a four-wheel-drive and built for rough conditions but there was no vehicle in the world which could safely come down a one-in-three, grease-covered slope at that speed. The Suzuki rolled over once, then again, and then bounced at least twenty feet into the air before coming to rest upside down on top of the smashed muck-spreader drum in a pool of liquid filth.

No one got out.

23

Quickly taking my chance I dashed to the garage and got into the big Vauxhall. Rachel and Sylvia were already in it with the engine running. It took forever to back out on to the narrow lane but eventually I got it out and pointing in the same direction taken by Leroy and Kingsley. I restored my father's anti-cow and dog barriers and drove out slowly along the walled lane. There was nothing to impede our progress except piles of cow dung and the farm dogs.

Passing the bleach works I drove slowly up the hill in second gear. It was an adventure turning out on the main road at the best of times as there was little visibility in either direction until you crested the brow of the hill. I moved forward intending to turn left, back towards Bolton and Manchester.

I thought I was seeing things. There was a white Suzuki FWD tucked into the side of the road on my left.

I swung the wheel round and let the power assisted steering of the big Vauxhall take me to the right. I put my foot down to the floor. Reinforcements must have arrived just as Leroy and co. set off down the farm lane. Manteh had certainly got his act together.

The big car accelerated down the straight road. I looked in the mirror; they were following but I would outrun them on this clear road. But the road ahead was not clear. There was yet another Suzuki, the fourth I'd seen, and it was swinging out to block my path.

Sylvia was shouting something at me but I didn't hear. There was one hope remaining. On the left, just before the junction where the Charlies were attempting to intercept me, another lane zig-zagged up the steep slopes towards the moorland summit. It met the main road at an acute angle. Without taking my foot off the accelerator I slammed on the hand brake and did a sharp turn to the left. The car brushed against the verge but we held the road and shot up the steep, twisting lane.

I flung the car into left and right bends. At the top there was a perfect ambush spot where the road turned sharply right, leaving a two-hundred foot drop on to rocks for anyone who missed the hairpin, but there was no time for any tricks. I drove as fast as I could push the car, cresting the steep hillside.

The road was now straight and level across the moors. On the left was a vista of Bolton laid out below us and on the right more bleak moorland and tussock grass rising to the flat top of Winter Hill. There would be no danger now, the Vauxhall would outpace the Suzukis and I only needed to drive along the moorland road and join the motorway at Horwich to make good my escape.

The car didn't seem to be pulling very well. I looked down at the instrument panel. The pointer of the temperature gauge was on 'Danger'. There was a light flashing.

The fan belt must have snapped when I accelerated up the hill. Now the engine was over heating and if I didn't cool it down it would seize up. I switched the heater on to draw heat from the radiator and there was a drop in the engine temperature. The three-litre engine might seize up at any second, leaving us at the mercy of the posse.

'Sylvia, take your tights off!' I yelled, but she shook her head angrily.

'I'm not wearing any, you fool, but I wouldn't take them off for you if I was!' she said.

'You don't understand! The fan belt's gone and I need something for emergency repairs. Rachel how about you?' I pleaded.

Rachel was wearing a little denim skirt. She did have tights on and started pulling them off. We'd reached the highest point on the road, there was no other traffic. I didn't dare turn off the engine because I'd lose the steering, but I tried free-wheeling on downhill stretches. The heavy car kept up a fair speed and the temperature gauge stayed stable just below the danger mark.

We passed a golf course on the left, which offered no cover whatever, and then on the right a few isolated cottages.

I was frantic for somewhere to stop, but as we went on the country became more open, just space and dry stone walls. I reached the old road between Horwich and Bolton. Left, the obvious choice, went downhill all the way into Bolton: an open road without turnings or hope of cover.

Rachel gave a cry of alarm. She'd spotted a Suzuki a few

miles behind us. For the first time today she was beginning to lose her cool. I caught a glimpse of her dark hair in the mirror as she looked back down the road.

I turned right, climbing again towards Horwich and the higher moors. There must be somewhere to turn off. Bends in the road hid us from our pursuers as we rolled down the other side of the hill into the small town. I spotted a right turn down a leafy lane and took it. We rolled down a couple of hundred yards and parked in a shady bend.

I switched off the engine and gave Rachel the shotgun. She knew how to handle it.

'You stand guard while I try to get the fan belt fixed,' I told her.

Rachel gave me a funny look but took the gun and stood by the back of the car out of sight. As she turned away I couldn't help noticing what an attractive girl she was. The green blouson she was wearing did nothing for her figure, but the short denim skirt showed off her long legs to perfection.

'Sylvia you'd better help me,' I said gruffly, turning back to the job in hand. I was embarrassed to see that Sylvia had noticed my surreptitious examination of Rachel's trim figure. She didn't say anything but her expression said it all for her.

When I opened the bonnet a wave of heat gusted out. It would take at least fifteen minutes for it to cool. Sylvia stood beside me, with a grim expression on her face. She flicked the hair out of her eyes and looked at me directly. The mop of curly blond hair falling over her battered face couldn't hide her emotions. She seemed to be on the point of tears.

'Come on Sylvia, at least we're still alive and free,' I cajoled.

'But for how much longer?' she asked sourly.

It struck me as an odd thing for her to say. It was Dyer, not the Charlies, who'd threatened her. Maybe she thought the Charlies would punish her for the failed double-cross on Dyer. Manteh was certainly ruthless enough for that, but he had to catch us first.

'There goes one of them!' whispered Rachel urgently, 'and another and another!' She could see them passing the end of the lane.

That meant Manteh had sent four, possibly five Suzuki loads out to get Rachel and me. He was taking no chances. I could understand him wanting his revenge on me: he couldn't afford to have his prestige lowered in the eyes of the posse by letting me remain unscathed, and he wanted his bank account numbers. But why was Rachel so important to him?

As I struggled to fasten the tights without burning my hands on the red hot engine I asked Sylvia what she thought.

'She must have the same value to Manteh that she had to Dyer – as a means of reaching her father,' Sylvia replied scornfully. 'What other importance could she have? You don't think she's some sort of teenage Mata Hari do you? She doesn't know anything, she's as green as grass.'

'I should have known better than to ask you, I said.

'Can't you stop being horrible to me?' she pleaded. 'I know I've been stupid and greedy but you're making everything worse.'

'All right, we'll drop it for now, but there's a hell of a lot you haven't told me. When we get clear, I want to hear everything you know about Dyer's criminal buddies and your dealings with Leon.'

By way of response Sylvia gave her characteristic little nod of the head and flicked her hair back out of her eyes again. I felt a returning surge of the sexual chemistry which had first drawn me to her. She was an exceptionally attractive woman.

We stood in silence for a few minutes waiting for the engine to cool but then our reverie was broken by a cry from Rachel. They were back! We could see a white Suzuki parked in the lay-by at the end of the lane. It was hard to tell whether they'd spotted us and were waiting for reinforcements or were just on guard in the neighbourhood. The safest guess was that they *had* seen us.

Our means of escape were limited. The car might be temporarily repaired but where could we go? The rocky little lane we were on looked as though it might peter out beyond a few cottages two hundred yards further along.

I could creep back along the other side of the hedge and try to ambush the goons in the FWD but I would be pushing my luck. I'd no idea how many there were. There might be another three or four loads of them parked on the main road. The whole thing was turning into a Suzuki rally.

That gave me an idea.

Although I knew it was sensible to run, my feelings towards the men in the FWD, whoever they might be, were almost crazy. I was tired of being chased and wanted to hit back. Why should I keep taking whatever they wanted to hand out? It was time someone put the heat on them.

There was a phone box halfway between me and the Charlies. Taking the gun off Rachel, I asked Sylvia to go and phone the Countryside Rangers.

'Tell them there's some kind of rally of white FWDs on and that there are vandals out, shooting up the moor. Get them moving, tell them they're frightening the lapwings, tell them anything you can think of but get them here.'

'Don't be stupid. I'm not going down there,' she said.

'Why not? It's Rachel and me they're after. If you go and phone and Dyer and his mob don't arrive to reinforce the Charlies, then I'll know I can trust you,' I said. The logic was a bit tortuous but I needed to convince her.

'Yes, but what if they grab me?' she replied.

'I'll start shooting if they make a move,' I said, brandishing the weapon.

Shaking her head doubtfully, she set off.

Rachel and I watched her holding an animated conversation in the phone box, complete with gestures. Then she hurried back. The Charlies made no move. They were more used to shooting from ambush than facing people who might shoot back at them. Following a random path, as I was, gave them little opportunity to set up a trap along my route. They would play a waiting game, trying to surround me at some convenient killing ground as they'd nearly done at the cottage.

The Vauxhall's engine had cooled and it started easily. We set off down the yellow sandstone lane. We went about two hundred yards before the FWDs started to move in pursuit. Ahead the road trailed away downhill, which could only bring me back to the main road and more of the posse. On the right, between two of the stone cottages, I spotted a tarmac road leading straight uphill.

I slowed and pointed the gun out of the window. My passengers flinched and behind me the Suzuki paused. But the Charlies weren't my target. Hoping no one was hurt I fired four times into the cottages, taking out the bedroom windows.

It was vital that I rouse the entire neighbourhood: my plan was to draw the Country Park Rangers into the area as rapidly as possible.

I turned right and put my foot down. The road ascended the steep side of the moor by a series of long zig-zags. I soon had a good view over Horwich towards Rivington and the lake at Anglezarke. I realised I was on an engineers' access road to the massive television transmission mast on Winter Hill. A sign post confirmed my guess. I blasted it to splinters and reloaded. The more damage I could create along our route, the better our chances of survival. I wanted the Rangers to come straight for us.

Looking back I could see the two FWDs labouring after us a long way down the hill. There might even be a chance that I could make it across the moor and lose the posse. Sylvia was biting her lips but Rachel was taking in the scenery as if she didn't have a care in the world.

I fired at every sign post and man-made object on the way up, leaving a clearly marked trail of destruction behind me. The noise must have carried for miles. To a listener it must have sounded as if the 12th of August had come two months early.

We reached the summit and the slope became less severe. At the last bend the road was barred by a heavy iron gate secured with brand new padlock and chain. I slammed to a halt and grabbed the shotgun again. I put the muzzle near the lock and fired.

The lock held, so I fired again. This time the solid slug smashed it and I swung the gate open. Sylvia had the sense to get behind the wheel. She moved the car through the gate while I rewound the chain. Noticing a TV company sign post I blasted away again. No one could mistake what direction we'd taken.

I jumped back in the car and reloaded while Sylvia drove on.

The immense, thousand-foot mast dominated the landscape. At its base there was a windowless building for the engineers. Further along the road there were smaller masts belonging to the police and ambulance service, then the road came to dead stop. There was no way across the moor, at least not with the car.

I had ignored the first rule of tactics and left myself without a line of retreat. Unless the Countryside Rangers arrived soon things were bound to end in a gunfight.

We had a moment or two before the first Suzuki made it on to the flat top of the moor. We were the only things moving up there apart from the magpies. I told Sylvia to put the car into the engineers' car park next to the Land-Rovers already parked there. The mast stood on the edge of the steepest slope of the moor. While Sylvia and Rachel scrambled out of the car, I crammed every cartridge remaining into my pockets.

Winter Hill is a vast, wedge-shaped slab: one side sloping gently towards Bolton; two steeper sides in the direction I was travelling and the steep scarp facing north-west. The north-west face was nearest but there was no chance of us running down it. Outlined against the sky on the edge I could see shooting butts. I pointed them out, they were our only possible refuge.

We ran for the butts, jumping from tussock to tussock in ankle wrenching leaps. Rachel easily outpaced us. The going was soggy although it was nearly midsummer. Peaty water with the consistency of sump oil surrounded each clump of sedge. White bog cotton stood out against the black. Rain had made the summit into a giant sponge, the source of all the local streams.

We made good progress and were at the first butt before I heard the sound of an engine. Like magpies going to ground we jumped in. Thick turf walls on a base of rough stone sheltered us. There were cartridge cases lying about from last season.

Nothing was stirring apart from the birds.

A musical tone, like the humming of a giant harp, caused by the breeze whistling through the mast was counterpointed by the low rumble from the Suzukis and the hissing of air passing through the sedge and bog cotton.

Well concealed, we lay panting at the spot from which hunters had killed thousands of birds. Now I knew what it felt like to be hunted.

I risked a look over the parapet. One white FWD was parked

below the TV mast and four men had got out. The other was in the distance, well back. The group didn't seem to be carrying weapons and they were scanning their surroundings without much conviction. A life of drug-pushing hadn't prepared them for the great outdoors.

As I watched two formed a deputation and marched to the building. One of them was definitely black, with locks bouncing behind his head. Silhouetted against the skyline as they were, it was impossible to distinguish skin colour. One was extremely tall and thin, with a stork-like gait. I hadn't seen any of them before.

Two engineers emerged. Arms were waved and the faint sound of raised voices carried across the moor to us. The posse members were being told to clear off. They got back in their vehicles with the long-legged man driving. They turned out of the car park but not on to the road.

With wheels churning the soft black soil the FWD set off straight on to the moor.

At first it looked as if they were leaving but then I saw that they were looping along the edge of the scarp slope. At least, that may have been their intention, but they didn't make it. The Suzuki bogged up to the axles and three of them had to push. They would have done better to have left the FWD and scoured the moor on foot but perhaps my shooting had acted as a deterrent.

It took them about thirty minutes to do a quarter of their loop: stopping and starting all the time. Rachel and Sylvia began to look more relaxed. Our refuge was in a particularly sodden stretch, but there was the chance that they might abandon the motorised safari and start hunting on foot.

I looked anxiously at Sylvia. Had she phoned the Countryside Wardens or Dyer?

Suddenly a blue Land-Rover appeared. I'd been so intent on the Suzuki that I hadn't noticed its approach. It had a sign on top which I couldn't read but I could see that it occupants weren't reinforcements for the Charlies. Driven with much greater skill than the long-legged driver had shown, the long-wheel-base Land-Rover crossed the moor and cut them off. Two uniformed figures leapt out for a confrontation. One of the Rangers was shaking the chain with the smashed padlock.

Unlike the earlier quartet at the farmyard, these Charlies went peaceably. The Rangers escorted them off the moor, following in their Land-Rover. Quiet returned.

As the day wore on it grew warmer; it was a clear and brilliant day. From our vantage point, more than fourteen hundred feet up, we could see the coast, the Welsh mountains, the Lake District and even the Isle of Man.

We postponed the problem of what to do next. The tussocks of peat we were resting on were comfortable and we lay talking about our escape.

Unfortunately I wasn't too sure that we had escaped yet. There were only one or two roads off this moor and it would be easy enough for the Charlies to lie in wait for us. They must be using their portable phones to co-ordinate their search. On the other hand the attention from the Countryside Rangers might have frightened them off. If they were all drug dealers they wouldn't welcome attention from authority. So maybe we were in the clear.

Rachel began to tell us about her stay with my parents.

'Paddy is very forceful, but Eileen doesn't seem to mind a bit. She manages him so well and they both have their separate areas of operation. Paddy's outside laying drains or rebuilding the garage while Eileen's inside tending the house. I didn't know people lived like that any more. They're like something out of *Postman Pat,* such a wonderful old couple . . . so full of character,' she gushed.

I exchanged a glance with Sylvia. She raised her eyebrows.

'I've spent a lot of time with your parents too, Rachel,' I said.

Rachel gave me sharp look as if expecting an insult, but I changed the subject. She'd lost the fresh country-girl look she'd had earlier. She was pale and drawn, her cheekbones standing out prominently beneath her almost transparent skin. The raven black hair highlighted her pallor.

'There are a lot of questions I'd like to ask you,' I said, 'but only if you feel up to it. I was employed by your stepfather to locate you and restore you to your family but finding you turned out to be more complicated than I thought. You know about your boyfriend don't you?'

Rachel nodded her head and spoke in a low voice, 'Yes, Eileen told me what had happened.'

'Did Andy think he was in any danger when you saw him last?' I asked.

She looked across our little bunker directly at Sylvia before replying, 'Yes, he knew there was always a chance Dyer might do him harm but we never thought Dyer would kill him.'

'I know this is hard, but are you saying that you think Dyer had Andy killed?' I asked.

Rachel nodded affirmatively.

'So you know, for certain, that Andy didn't kill himself?' I continued.

Before Rachel could reply Sylvia broke in, 'You're crazy! Mike is every kind of rat you can imagine, but if you think he'd go to those lengths you're out of your mind. I should know . . . he's just not like that.'

'What do you know about it!' Rachel shouted angrily. 'Andy got Mike to do all sorts of favours because Mike thought I could get Daddy to help him, but then when Andy couldn't and Mike got nasty, Andy started threatening him with exposure . . .' she paused. 'That was Andy's mistake,' she added bitterly. This was the first time I'd seen Rachel showing genuine feeling. Even when her mother met her on Southport beach she'd stayed cool.

'What do you mean, exposure? What was that Rachel?' I said.

'Andy did a lot of research into Mike's background,' Rachel said, 'he even went to London and Cardiff to find out about the companies Mike was involved with. He found out that some of Mike's backers had criminal records. If he'd gone to the press that would have ruined Mike's chances of getting the licence renewed on his clubs.'

There was silence for a moment as Sylvia and I took this in, but it was Sylvia who spoke first.

'Even so, I could believe it if Andy had been killed in a beating-up that went wrong, but it's so unlike Mike to send an assassin round to cut the man's throat. Believe me, I've no reason to defend Mike Dyer but I just can't see him doing that.'

'Hah! Believe you! Why should I believe you? I suppose you think *I'm* a liar!' snorted Rachel.

'Well, accepting that it wasn't suicide, and assuming for a minute it wasn't Dyer, who do you think did it, Sylvia?' I asked.

'How the hell do I know? You're supposed to be the private detective,' Sylvia said angrily. 'It could have been anyone. I already told you Andy had met some of the Charlies. And Rachel knows Leon Grant, don't you Rachel?'

This reply sent Rachel in to a fury. Her normally fresh and healthy complexion was now bleached of all trace of colour.

'No, no I don't,' she said between clenched teeth, 'I've never met him. You're the one who was trying to do a double-cross. Andy knew all about it. He thought you were a pathetic joke.'

Sylvia looked angry, her bruised face coloured.

'It was your dear friend Dyer who was after Andy,' Rachel went on bitterly. 'Andy told me to lie low in Southport until it all blew over. Then he'd join me, he'd get gigs on Merseyside even if you and Dyer drove him out of Manchester.'

'Rubbish!' Sylvia said. 'The last time I spoke to Leon Grant he said he knew both you and Andy —' She got no further because Rachel launched herself from the other side of the shooting butt and waded into her, swinging both fists.

'You lying cow, you filthy bitch!' Rachel screamed. 'You helped Dyer to kill Andy!'

I grabbed Rachel from behind but she went right on biting, scratching and pummelling Sylvia. Sylvia was so surprised by the sudden attack that she didn't raise a hand to strike back. She just tried to cover her face. I was only able to drag Rachel off by knotting my hand in her thick hair. I pushed her down against the turf. So much for my capacity to radiate calm to troubled females!

'Stop it you bloody fool!' I shouted. 'Haven't we got enough trouble without you going mad? It's going to take us all our luck to get off this moor in one piece,' This sudden outburst was more shocking than anything that had happened today, it was so unexpected. For a moment I wondered if she really was insane. Was this what her mother had been delicately hinting at when she'd told me how the teddy bear came to lose its head?

While I spoke I saw Rachel's wild eyes turn to the shotgun which stood against the turf wall to my right. I hastily retrieved it and started dismantling it. I unloaded and then unclamped the barrel from the walnut stock.

Both women watched me in silence. A quick look round revealed that nothing was stirring.

The turn of events gave me plenty to think about. According to Sylvia, Rachel and Andy had both been involved with the Charlies.

Rachel claimed that this was lies and that Sylvia must have helped Dyer to kill Andy. My instinct was to trust Sylvia but what possible motive could Rachel have for lying? And Sylvia was a tough and determined character. She might have been ready to murder to save her career.

Sylvia was leaning up against the turf dabbing her lip with a handkerchief. Her lip was swollen up again and there was another bruise on her face under her left eye. It just wasn't her day. She looked up at me with a tearful expression.

I had to come up with a plan of action quickly before Rachel started knocking hell out of her again. I went over and helped Sylvia to her feet.

As I did Rachel stood up too. I tensed for another onslaught but she said 'Look, I'm sorry. I don't know what came over me. It won't happen again.'

'I'm sorry too Rachel,' I replied. 'I shouldn't have stirred things up by questioning you but it seemed like a good time to get some answers. You've been under a strain.'

Rachel's response was to start sobbing, at first gently and quietly. Then she started heaving, gasping for breath and wailing. I'd never seen anything like it.

Sylvia made her sit down again with her head between her knees. When I looked at Sylvia she snapped angrily at me, 'She's having an asthma attack, you big dope!' as if it was my fault. She put her arm round Rachel.

'Have you got an inhaler or anything you take?' Sylvia asked in a very tender and concerned tone of voice. No one witnessing the scene would have imagined that Rachel had been knocking nine bells out of Sylvia just moments before.

My idea that Sylvia was hard enough for murder evaporated.

'Her inhaler's in the car, you'll have to go and get it,' she said.

I set off across the quaking peat to the car. The distance

between the car and our hiding place seemed a lot further than it had when we'd run headlong for refuge. There was nothing happening at the transmitter, just the humming of the wind through the aerial, but on the road a small group of elderly people were walking along briskly. They were dressed in hiking kit and gave me a friendly wave.

A surprise awaited me when I got to the car. There was a big yellow piece of paper stuck under the wiper. I snatched it out: 'Penalty for illegal parking £80 . . . etc . . . etc.'

I stood back and laughed. Dad was going to be pleased. He'd insisted on me using his car. First the fan belt had broken; and now he was stuck with a hefty fine and possible legal action. At least the car was still intact. If the Charlies's had more time to themselves they'd probably have set fire to it.

I opened the boot and got out all our bags. Thank God we all had light bags. As made my way back to the shooting butt I tried to think what I was going to do. Apart from escaping from the moor, and getting back to Manchester, nothing suggested itself.

I'd no friends in the police force. The Charlies were out in force hunting me down, and Dyer and his mob wanted to hospitalize me. Emigration seemed to be my only remaining option. It would have to be to somewhere a lot further than Middlesbrough.

When I reached our bunker Rachel was still sobbing and being comforted by the victim of her assault. It didn't take Sylvia many seconds to extract the inhaler and soon Rachel was looking more like her normal self.

'There, there, Rachel love. You don't want to go getting yourself so upset,' Sylvia cooed. 'It's all Dave's fault. Men are so insensitive and callous.'

Then turning to me Sylvia said, 'Well, you great lump, have you thought of a way to get us out of here?'

'I have, but you're not going to like it,' I said. 'We're going to have to leg it. There's a footpath over there which leads down from the moor to a small village near Bolton. We're going to have to walk and then get a bus into Manchester.'

'What's wrong with the car?'

'The Charlies'll have it spotted. They're probably waiting for us at the bottom of the access road. No, our only hope of not being caught is to merge in with these hikers and picnickers.'

Sylvia took a look at the road. There were scattered groups of walkers hiking in both directions. She nodded her head, 'But what about Rachel? She's in no fit state . . .'

'No, I'll be all right,' Rachel said. 'Honestly, I get over these attacks quickly once I've used the inhaler. I'm sorry for all the bother I've caused. I'm really sorry for what I said to you, Sylvia. You were always nice and kind to Andy when he was doing gigs at the Paloma. I don't know what came over me.'

'Let's forget about it then,' I said hastily. 'Let's get moving. The sooner we get away from here the safer I'll feel.'

I took out the whisky and crackers and offered them round. Rachel shook her head but Sylvia and I both took a reviving dram before we set off. I took the opportunity to change my jacket and trousers, the ones I was wearing had been too close to the farmyard for comfort. I cast them off. Yet another set of clothes to bite the dust on this case. Without further fuss we picked up our bags. I was able to fit the parts of the shotgun into mine. There were only a few spare cartridges left.

The path off the moor was a long and winding one. We'd to cross the road which I'd earlier raced along from my parents' home but there was no sign of any Charlies. Manteh's arrogance in sending out a fleet of identical vehicles must have made it easy for the Rangers to round them up. Some of them were bound to be armed with shotguns, the weapons of choice in drug-dealing circles, so they'd have a hard time proving they hadn't done all the shooting.

Our descending path took us alongside a golf course and down a flight of sixty-odd steps on a hillside above a small brook. There were houses on the other side of the stream, each joined to the road by its own foot bridge. We walked through the village until we came to a phone box at the bus terminus.

While dialling my father I wasn't feeling as cocky as when I set out. Someone out there had raised the barriers on this obstacle course I was trying to complete.

Paddy answered the car phone straight away.

'I thought it was you,' he started, not giving me a chance to speak. 'Where are you? This damned car phone of yours is an infernal nuisance. It's not stopped ringing since we set off.

There's a copper called Rice wants you to get in touch with him at his home number . . . sounds as if he's up to no good.

'Then there's your friend McNeil, somebody called Salway, and an ignorant pig called Bob Lane. He's just given me a right load of ear-ache because I wasn't you. That secretary of yours has phoned as well, she was surprised when your mother answered. We'd better swap cars back, your mother can't cope with this constant telephoning. Any road, where are you?'

'Oh, can I speak?' I said. 'Thanks for letting me get a word in. According to what it says here I'm at somewhere called Barrow Bridge and I haven't got your car anymore.'

'Barrow Bridge, but that's only four miles from where you set out from,' he said in a dismayed tone. 'We're at the Services near Shap. What the hell have you been up to?'

'Don't give me that Dad. Your little diversion didn't work. Manteh had sent more than one lot. Luckily they had an accident on the hill. So we set out.

'As soon as we got on the main road more of them appeared and guess what? The fan belt of your wonderful car snapped and we were lucky to find somewhere to hide. If you want it back it's in the car park on the top of Winter Hill with an £80 fine on it.'

'Bloody hell fire!' he bellowed. 'I let you have my car and this is what happens. Is Rachel safe?'

'Yes,' I said, 'she's fighting fit and so is Sylvia. Look Dad, I'm in a jam . . .'

'I suppose,' he interrupted, 'I could report the car to the police as being stolen, then they might retrieve it without making me pay the fine . . .'

'Dad, can you forget about the car for a minute?' I pleaded. 'I said I'm in a jam. I don't know what to do. If I go to the police they're likely to throw me to the wolves and if I show my nose in Manchester there's two rival gangs waiting for the privilege of bashing my head in.'

'I should have thought the solution was obvious to a man with your ability for causing mayhem and grief wherever you go,' he said.

'That's unfair,' I said indignantly.

'No, I'm sorry. Just my little joke, don't take yourself so seriously,' he chuckled. 'You can't go to the police, so make them come to you. Make something happen that even Benson can't ignore. You're friendly with that television chap, Blake, aren't you? Well, plant some evidence about Dyer that they'll have to take notice of.

'Then you've got the Charlies on your back haven't you?' he said in a superior tone. 'Well, give them something else to worry about. Set this other mob on to them, play one lot off against the other and get the police to do something about it.'

'Yes, I've thought of all that myself,' I said, 'but how am I going to do it?'

'Look, David,' he said in a more fatherly way, 'when there's a really bad forest fire raging along in places like Australia or California how do they deal with it? They start other fires in its path to make a firebreak. That's what you'll have to do.

'Fight fire with fire.'

24

It was well past midday when we got back into Manchester. The bus drive into Bolton and then on to Manchester via Eccles and Urmston took hours. It was a journey through the region's industrial past. I'd plenty of time to think as the double decker jerked and crawled its way into Manchester. One comforting thought was that the top deck of a bus was the last place Manteh's underlings would think of looking for us.

Sylvia had managed to cover up her bruises with make-up but her lip was still swollen. She was chain smoking. Her leather jacket matched my own and we looked like a unisex couple. I kept fanning the smoke out of my eyes. Rachel was as cool and attractive as earlier in the day. Her complexion was a little better.

The reconciliation between the pair was holding up and from time to time they exchanged comments just to break the monotony of the journey.

Our bus went through Stretford, then along the road past my flat. I was able to get a quick look. There was nothing unusual. There were no policemen or squad cars near the area, no prowling gangs waiting to break in.

We stayed on the bus as far as Withington and got off at Wilmslow Road. Victorian villas lined the road, many converted into hotels. We chose one near the corner of Mauldeth Road called the 'Garden of Kashmir', because I fancied a curry in the restaurant. I booked a double room in the name and Mr and Mrs Mather and an adjoining single room for our cousin.

Lal, the Indian receptionist, was exceptionally polite and attentive. I could see he was suspicious of us – a false smile played on his lips.

Sylvia's fat lip, and my battered mug and sunglasses didn't do much for our credibility. God knows what he thought we were – a tag wrestling team? A real-life Punch and Judy show? I spun him a yarn which I could see him disbelieving as quickly as I told it, but he kept on smiling.

'We're here for a wedding. We've just flown in from Canada.

My brother's getting spliced for the second time and we thought he'd be putting us up but he can't. So we left our luggage round at his place. We might stay two nights, depending on how wild the celebration gets, meanwhile we're all exhausted and jet-lagged and we'd appreciate not being disturbed for at least eight hours.'

Lal smiled his acceptance. He nodded his understanding of every lying phrase, and then showed us up to our rooms with gracious courtesy when I paid for a night in advance. Rachel gave the place a very careful inspection on our way up – it was obviously a different class of hotel than she was used to. When Lal left us, I realised that he probably thought I was up to all kind of tricks with two glamorous females in my company.

As soon as the door closed behind us Sylvia turned on me.

'Just what kind of little game do you think you're playing, Cunane?' she said. 'You must be the most arrogant and conceited man in this country.'

'Hold it Sylvia!' I said. 'It was suspicion, not excessive lust, that made me book a double room. I told you when we set out this morning that I wasn't going to trust you near a phone and I'm sticking to that.'

'You trusted me to phone those Rangers!' Sylvia replied.

'That was then, this is now,' I answered.

'You make me sick!' she said. 'So you think I'd tell Dyer where you are? After what he threatened me with! Can't you get it into your fat head that I'm only tagging along with you because I'm terrified of him! He said he'd ruin my looks if he saw me again.'

Her anger and fear didn't seem false, but professionalism demanded some scepticism. I had to think about Rachel's safety, as well as my own. Rachel was listening to our exchange with an irritatingly superior smile on her face.

'Maybe he would, and maybe he wouldn't,' I said, favouring her with a look from the more battered side of my face. 'I noticed how ready you were to stick up for him this morning. You can't have given up on him completely and you're just going to have to put up with me being suspicious.

'The same goes for you Rachel,' I said, turning to her. 'There wouldn't have been any need for this morning's caper if you hadn't blabbed to your friend Lisa about where you were. I don't want to see either of you near a phone until we're home and dry.'

Rachel blushed and started up indignantly, 'How was I to know that Spragg would tell the Charlies where I was? I want to phone my mother and let her know I'm safe.'

'And I want to have a bath without you snooping on me,' chipped in Sylvia.

I could see that I was on a loser. There was no way I could hold them against their will. I tried persuasion.

'OK ladies, let's look at this another way? First you, Rachel. On Tuesday I found you a safe hideaway, complete with an armed bodyguard. I know the Charlies hadn't a clue where you were because that same night they broke into your parents' home trying to find you. Right?'

Rachel was stunned by this information.

'Yet by 4 a.m. this morning,' I continued, 'they knew exactly where you were, thanks to your friend Spragg.

'Now Sylvia. You must have guessed when I cleared off on Monday that I'd found Rachel. You gave a little whisper to a member of the Charlies that I had her. Isn't that right, sweetheart?'

'You don't need to be so sarcastic,' she said. 'It wasn't like that at all, I needed Leon's help, I was just keeping him up to date. I didn't realise what he was up to . . .'

'And I suppose you didn't know Dyer was on his way round to my place.' I countered.

'I went round to warn you, that's why he began to suspect me,' Sylvia interrupted. It was true that she'd come round just before Dyer and his thugs but then so had Popeye Lane.

'Fine,' I said, 'so I'll accept that you've fallen out with Dyer, but that still leaves Rachel and the Charlies. We don't know why Manteh's so desperate to get hold of Rachel.'

Sylvia and I both looked at Rachel.

She shook her head. 'What's it got to do with you? You've only been hired to look after me.'

Rachel's tone reminded me of her stepfather.

'Well Petal,' I said nastily, 'remembering you're speaking to a mere, rough, hired man perhaps you can tell me in simple words how I can look after you if I don't know who's trying to find you. You must have frightened of something to go and hide yourself away in Southport like that in the first place. Or were you starting a new career?'

'I can do without the sarcasm, too, Mr Cunane,' Rachel said. 'And the answer is . . . I don't know. I think they want to get hold of me so they can blackmail my father. That's the only reason I can think of.'

'I agree with you, I can't think of anything else either,' I said. 'But in that case, why did old Daddy-baby hire little-old Davy-boy to find you? He'd only to pick up the phone to get hundreds of coppers on the job willing and able to do it for nothing.'

Rachel's expression was one of genuine puzzlement.

'You've met Daddy,' she said. 'He'd go a million miles to avoid embarrassment.'

She sounded genuinely bewildered. 'Daddy would never let himself be "beholden" to the police, or people at the Bank, if he could sort things out himself. Surely you can see that?'

Her explanation of Daddy's motivation was plausible but thin. It still didn't explain why she'd kept out of touch with her parents for several days before Thwaite was topped. After all, Daddy had claimed he was hiring me to rescue his darling daughter from the clutches of plebeian Andy, not Dyer or Manteh.

Rachel must have seen the sceptical expression on my face.

'You don't have to believe me,' she said. 'You're not my judge. I've already told you Andy wanted me to keep away while he sorted things out with Dyer. I didn't want to go home, so that only left our place in Southport. I didn't want Mummy to know about that. She can be very old fashioned.'

'Right on baby! Rachel, you're one hundred per cent right,' I said. 'I don't have to believe you. I can see that you didn't know Manteh's posse, or Dyer, or anyone else was on the lookout for you. But why, oh why did you have to get in touch with Lisa Goody?'

'I was lonely,' she said. 'I wanted to speak to someone. You just whisked me off to a remote cottage in the hills. I would have phoned home straight after I spoke to Lisa but I could hear someone moving about.'

I didn't want to provoke Rachel into another asthma attack so I didn't push her any further. She'd been stupid in giving away her location but if everybody always did the sensible thing I'd be out of a job.

'It seems to me that we're all in the same boat,' I said in a more sympathetic tone. 'Dyer's after Sylvia. Manteh's after you and both of them are after me. Really great! I just hope that neither of you are so stupid that you can't see what will happen if either Dyer or Manteh finds out where we are. You can't touch the phone even to let your mother know what's happening.'

'Please, just one little call,' Rachel pleaded. 'If the house was attacked Mummy must be mad with worry.'

'Look, Miss,' I said in my bluntest tone, 'if you'd just gone home to your bloody parents in the first place none of this would've happened. I'd be at home with my feet up now. Get it in your head, you're not going to phone anyone! What more do I have to do to explain it to you? Draw you a diagram?'

'Dave,' Sylvia said, 'do you need to be so brutal? You might bring on another attack.'

Rachel was sitting on the bed with her head in her hands, Sylvia went to comfort her.

'I'm sorry Sylvia,' I answered, 'but you both seem to think we're playing a game. I want us all to survive this mess. Why don't you start thinking about ways we can get out of it? You'd enough tricks up your sleeve when you were in with Leon. We won't last an hour if half of Manchester know where we are. You know what Manteh did just to get his hands on me last night. I'm not going to give him another chance just because a spoilt girl needs to phone Mummy.'

Sylvia gave me a sour look and turned away. No more was said.

I opened my sports bag and spilled out the contents on to the bed.

My head was spinning. There were so many unanswered questions . . . When Rachel went to Southport was she hiding from Dyer or from her father? . . . Why were the Charlies after her? . . . Did they want to capture her or liberate her? . . . Maybe Leon had been at the beach on Monday to see that I didn't find her.

The permutations were endless.

I went in the bathroom and poured myself a stiff whisky. I

looked at my face in the mirror. I looked like a battered circus clown. Only a few days ago my vanity had been pricked because Delise had suggested that my nose was slightly out of alignment, and now look at me! Even my hair wasn't looking too good after the crawl through the upper stories of Charlton Close. I needed some personal maintenance time but I wasn't likely to get it.

Lal must have wanted trade badly. If I'd been a receptionist I'd have phoned the police straightaway if someone looking like me turned up. My face was only partly shaved, I must have been in too much of a hurry to get out of Sylvia's flat this morning, but worst of all were the bruises. One side of my face was purple and the other yellow-coloured. I looked more like someone in need of hospitalization than hotel accommodation.

While probing my bruises I noticed that I still had the handcuff shackle on my right wrist. I poured myself another slug of whisky and hoped Lal hadn't seen it. It made me feel even sorrier for myself than I had before. Maybe Lal would think I was into bondage and S & M rather than wearing a convict's identity bracelet. My gloomy speculation was interrupted by a light tap at the open door.

Sylvia came in.

'Can I join you?' she asked quietly.

I nodded and she poured herself a drink.

'Rachel and I have been talking,' she said, 'and we want to say we think you're right. But you've got to trust us. There's nothing to stop us walking out now if we wanted to. What could you do about it?'

'Nothing,' I agreed.

'We're worn out, we need food and rest,' she continued. 'Why don't I see if the hotel will serve us a meal in the room. We can say we're exhausted after our journey. I can pay with my American Express gold card.'

'Sylvia, that's the best thing anyone's said to me all day.'

She flicked her hair back and gave me that grin of hers.

I moved closer to her.

'Not now . . .' she said, 'later . . . Let me freshen up in here and then I'll order for us. Can't you nip out and get some clothes? You look as if you've been down a coal mine.'

So she'd also noticed that I'd wrecked yet another portion of my wardrobe.

I waved the wrist shackle at her, 'I can't go far with this on, I'll have to see about getting rid of it.'

I left her in the bathroom and went through the adjoining door into Rachel's room. When I saw Rachel, I tilted my head in the direction I'd come from and she vacated the room. I didn't feel any urge to be polite to her.

I lay on her bed and phoned Fred Lumsden at his lair in the Atwood Building.

He replied at once. I asked him to box up my Beretta and my keys and send them by courier service to the Garden of Kashmir Hotel for collection under the name of Mather. For once Fred was in a co-operative mood. Lacking Delise to service my needs I'd have to make use of what substitutes were available.

'Do you know a big Scottish bloke Boss?' he said. 'He's been round asking for you twice. I didn't like the look of him. I think he might get a bit er, heavy-like, if he comes again.'

'I know any number of Scots, Fred. You'll have to describe him.' It could only be Jock; Sinclair would never come looking for me himself.

'Well,' Fred said, 'this was a big, ugly-looking cove with a very bad complexion. He must have bad eczema or a really rough razor burn or something. He slipped me a tenner to give him a bell when you get back to your office.'

Trust Dyer's henchman to do things on the cheap.

'I hope you took it Fred,' I joked. 'Stick with me and you'll make your fortune. I'll give you another twenty if I get my pistol delivered safe and sound. OK, Fred?'

He grunted his agreement.

'Look,' I said, 'why don't you tell this haggis-basher that I phoned and told you I won't be back for a few days because I'm going to the Cayman Islands. You might also get some inquiries from Moss Side friends of mine. You could tell them I've gone to Zurich to do some banking.'

'How am I supposed to know if they're from Moss Side? Sounds a bit iffy to me Boss,' Fred replied cautiously. I could visualise him scratching his unshaven chin and baring his fangs.

Come back Delise, all is forgiven. At least I didn't have to bribe her to do the simplest thing!

'Look Fred, I'll give you £40 if you give the story to the Scot and £50 if you tell the dudes from Moss Side that I just called in the office in a rush and told you I was on my way to pick up some heavy money in Zurich. You'll know who they are, they'll be the only other people apart from the Scotsman who're interested in my movements.'

'Still sounds a bit funny to me, Boss,' the smell of money had whetted his appetite. I could only hope he didn't get too greedy.

'OK, then,' I said. 'Forget it. If you can't do me a little favour . . .'

'Now, no need to be hasty. I didn't say no. It just needs a bit of thinking about. I want to draw my pension. All right, I'll do it, but in my own way.'

'Great Fred, now have you got the destinations: Cayman Islands for the Scot and Zurich for the others?'

'Yes, but I want £50 for both,' he said. I was surprised that his demands were so modest. Perhaps I could trust him after all.

'Come on Fred! You've already had £10 from the Scot for the same information, and all you've to do is phone him.'

'No. I want £50 for both,' he said stubbornly.

'All right,' I agreed, 'but I expect that lift to be working next time I'm in the building.'

I put the phone down and stretched out on the bed. The destinations I'd suggested should cause maximum gloom and despondency in the enemy camps. My eyes closed.

Before I surrendered to sleep I remembered my earlier efforts to re-enlist Delise as a babysitter for Sylvia. I'd forgotten to ask Dad where she had phoned from and it didn't seem so urgent anymore. I fell asleep.

When I came to, Rachel was shaking me.

'There's a phone call for you,' she said. 'There's a parcel at reception and a courier to pay.'

I staggered to my feet and went down. It occurred to me that Sylvia and Rachel could have left while I slept and that the greedy old spider down at the office might have sold me out. There was nothing I could do about it now.

I'd find out soon enough.

At the desk I paid off the courier. Having the Beretta made me feel a lot more secure. When I got back upstairs Sylvia was standing by the door.

'We're in a private dining room just along here,' she said.

I followed Sylvia along the passage to a pleasant room overlooking the main road. Taking a glance out of the window, I saw nothing unusual. No white FWDs. A waiter served me chicken madras, pilau of saffron rice, poppadums, hot chutney sauce, and naan bread with a pint of lager to wash all it down. Sylvia and Rachel had already started eating.

Before I started I took my keys out of the parcel and soon had the steel cuff off my wrist. We took out time over the meal. I entertained Rachel and Sylvia by telling them about my training as a so-called SAS-style bodyguard.

We felt much more relaxed after the meal. Sylvia went to our room for her bath and I went with Rachel to her room. Sylvia was entitled to some privacy and I was getting paid to look after Rachel.

I decided to risk phoning Finbar and asking him to come round with a change of clothes. He was as eager as ever to join the fray. There'd been nothing happening, things were getting boring down at Thornleigh Court. I gave my warlike friend edited highlights about what had happened since I saw him last.

Just as I expected, this got his blood up and I had trouble calming him down. He agreed to bring a few clothes round by taxi and leave them at the reception desk when I promised to involve him in further developments. He'd seen no sign of Delise round at the flat.

It was the first time I'd been alone with Rachel and I was determined to find out more about her. I'd altered my first impression of her as a naive, easily impressed teenager. Judging by her performance this morning she was a strong character.

She'd taken the opportunity to change from the outfit she'd worn for the morning's adventures and was wearing black leggings, slip-on shoes and an attractive loose sweatshirt with 'Save the Whale' written on it. The clothes her mother had packed for her may not have been her own choice but they suited her well. She'd gathered up her heavy black hair into a ponytail.

'I see you're an animal lover Rachel,' I said.

'I think it's disgusting what they're doing to the whales. Did you know whales can send messages to each other across thousands of miles of ocean? They might be more intelligent than human beings.'

'Well as a matter of fact I did know that,' I replied. 'Have you read Heathcote William's "Whalesong"?'

'Yes,' she gushed enthusiastically. 'Oh, you've read it too! I thought it was great! I don't think there's a more important cause.'

'I agree Rachel,' I said. 'Seriously, what do you think about justice for human beings? It looks as if that rat Dyer's going to get away with what he did to Andy.'

Her expression immediately changed to one both sad and bitter.

'Isn't there anything you can do?' she asked wistfully.

'Well there is something *you* could do,' I answered. 'If you're really determined to nail him, you could swear out a statement naming him as the person who threatened Andy. Then we could release the statement to the press through Andy's parents' solicitors. They could bring a civil action for damages against him for the murder. That might force the boys in blue to get off their bottoms.'

'Wouldn't that be very dangerous?' she said. 'I thought you were terrified about us revealing where we are and everything?'

'No, we could do it all from this room without anyone finding out where we are,' I assured her.

'And you really think that would lead to Dyer being locked up where he belongs?' she said.

'Yes I do,' I replied.

'Well all right, what do you want me to do?' she agreed.

'Rachel, if you answer a few questions I could help you write out your statement. We could get someone to deliver it to the solicitor and go and make it all legal later.'

Rachel thought this over for a few minutes, then she said 'I trust you Dave, so I'm ready to answer your questions.'

'OK, now what was the hold Andy had over Dyer?' I asked. 'I know there was something because Dyer suddenly started giving Andy top billing at the Paloma.'

Rachel pouted and turned up her lip. 'That's not fair! Andy was good and he was improving all the time. He was terribly ambitious. He got a trial on Sunset Radio and they were going to offer him a contract. That was nothing to do with Dyer.'

'I'm sorry, but we both know there was something which persuaded Dyer to kick-start Andy's career, wasn't there?' I insisted.

'I suppose so. Andy told Dyer that Daddy might agree to re-finance his clubs. Dyer wanted a management buy-out of the clubs from the owners, some sort of property outfit called NMP. He was desperate, and when he found out that my father was the Managing Director of the Northern Pioneers' Bank, he couldn't do enough for us. It was embarrassing. He kept jumping to conclusions. We tried to tell him.

'I think that was what made Andy sick of working for him. Dyer's the sort of man who thinks you have to do a favour to get a favour. He told Andy all about his business affairs, a lot more than he let on to Sylvia. You see Andy understood about business,' she said.

'So was Andy interest in going ahead and being part of this management buy-out?' I queried.

'Was he interested?' she replied. 'Is a cat interested in cream? Andy was full of plans. It was the chance of a lifetime. He had a lot more plans than Mike. We'd start our own radio station, market our own music, promote Manchester groups, even start our own boutiques.'

'So what went wrong?' I asked.

'Daddy said the deal wasn't commercially viable. He was interested at first but when he found out we wanted to buy from NMP he went cold on the deal,' she said.

'I took Andy home to see if he could persuade Daddy to change his mind but then Daddy found out that Andy was from the same part of Yorkshire that he came from. I suppose Thwaite isn't such a common sort of name. If Andy had been called Smith he might still be alive . . .' Her voice trailed off into silence.

'Go on,' I urged.

'Well, I thought Daddy would be pleased but he was really horrible. He looked as if he was going to throw a fit. He really got on Andy's case. He said he knew that Andy was a drug-pusher as well as being the son of a union agitator. He practically ordered him out of the house, there and then. Andy was wild with rage,' she concluded.

'Andy took being turned down badly, did he?' I prompted. She seemed to have dried up again.

'Yes, he went to London to make enquiries about NMP. He didn't dare tell Dyer that the deal with Daddy had fallen through. He couldn't find out much about NMP because it's an offshore company, registered in the Cayman Islands.

'Andy had a terrific nerve really,' she said. 'He kept telling Dyer that things were going well, then when Dyer got pressing he'd threatened to drop the deal. I think he was trying to find someone else to put up the capital.'

This was getting interesting, 'Do you think he approached the Charlies to see if they'd come up with the cash?' I asked.

Rachel became vague and tentative. I could see she realised where her remarks were leading her.

'No. It wasn't like that,' she said. 'Dyer began to suspect that Daddy and Andy were plotting to do the buy-out on their own and dump him. That's when he started threatening Andy. Dyer went to see Daddy and Daddy said he knew nothing about any deal.

'That same week Dyer sent that naff, pimply Scotsman round to threaten Andy,' she said. 'I don't know what was said but Andy told me to go to our place in Southport and lie low. I wanted him to come too but he said Dyer had threatened to break both his legs if he didn't turn up for his gig that week.

'It was a dreadful week. I got thrown out of my hall of residence because of a stupid trick by Kevin Spragg and then I had to go to Southport and then Andy . . .'

She started sobbing bitterly.

'Of course it was Dyer who killed Andy,' she hiccuped. 'How could that woman think it was anyone else? She knows all about it, I'll bet.'

'Now Rachel, don't start that up again. Sylvia's got troubles of her own with Dyer. The best thing you can do is to write down all this and we can give it to the solicitor and then go and swear out an affidavit,' I said. 'Did you personally hear Dyer threaten Andy?' I added. 'I mean, were you ever present when he threatened him?'

'On the Monday when Dyer came back from seeing my father at the Northern Pioneers we were setting up the Paloma and testing for sound levels and so on. Dyer came in and in front of Sylvia, and that Bob fellow, and the Scotsman he said, "I could murder you Thwaite, all the trouble you've caused me". Those were his exact words and I'll swear to that on oath,' she said.

'Good enough. We'll get him on that. Now the Scot's called Jock, appropriately enough. I don't know his other name but I've got a photo of him. The smaller chap's called Bob Lane and his nickname's "Popeye". Have you heard him called that?' I asked.

Rachel nodded.

'You see Dyer's lawyer could argue that Dyer wasn't responsible for what his employees had done. He'd try to blame it all on them. Do you think its possible that they killed Andy on their own account?' I said.

'Come on, you've got to be joking!' she said. 'That Popeye doesn't tie his own shoe laces up without being told to. Jock's meaner, but he dishes out the rough stuff to order. I never saw him do anything on his own.'

'Yet you're prepared to swear that Jock threatened Andy at Dyer's request.'

'Yes I am,' she said. 'I want to see Dyer in prison where he belongs. I think he's done other things. Andy said there was a lot more involved than anyone ever knew.'

'That's right, this morning you said Andy threatened Dyer with exposure,' I said.

'Oh did I? Well I'm not sure about that. I was upset this morning.'

She sat back on the bed.

I felt that I had got as much from her as I could for the time being. There was certainly enough material to put a bomb under Dyer. I felt excited and happy at the thought of him getting his come-uppance. Nevertheless, there were inconsistencies in Rachel's story that a good lawyer might fasten on to.

Still, it wasn't my job to convict Dyer. I just had to give him enough worries to get him off my back. If there was more to be found out about Rachel's father and Wild Bill Benson it would all have to come out in the wash. There was only so much one man could do despite my own father's comments about my talent for spreading mayhem.

I sorted out some hotel stationery for Rachel and got her started on writing out her statement. We locked the door of her room to avoid any intrusions and she got on with it like a schoolgirl at her essay.

I sat with her for a few minutes but then remembered my handgun still wrapped up in the box Fred had sent.

I went through the connecting door to my own room. Sylvia was coming out of the bathroom. She was wearing a large bath towel wrapped round her middle and a smaller towel as a turban. As she stepped into the room the turban slipped and she put her hand up to hold it on, revealing her breasts as she did so.

She grinned at me as she restored her towel.

'Sorry, I didn't bring a bath robe with me but you've no false modesty have you?' she said. She laughed and smiled at me for the first time that day. As with Rachel earlier, there was a feeling of release of tension and return to normality after our weird morning and night. She continued to smile at me and then sat down on the side of the bed.

She patted the bed beside her, 'Would you like to come and dry my hair Dave? I haven't got my drier either.'

I would have had to be carved from stone to have refused her. I went over to her and once again her beautiful breasts popped out of their makeshift shelter. As I went towards her she signalled with her eyes for me to lock the adjoining door.

'Dave, I can't tell you how much I've missed you,' she whispered in my ear.

25

I could hear a tapping noise: tap tap, tap tap, as I swam back into consciousness. There was also a sound a steady breathing next to me. Sylvia was curled up beside me. The tapping continued, it was coming from Rachel's room.

I gave Sylvia a shake, she sat up with a jerk, and then grabbed my arm and pulled me back into bed. 'Dave don't be in such a hurry to jump out of bed. Come here for a cuddle.'

'We've no time for that. That's Rachel knocking. What time is it?' I said.

She reached across and looked at my watch on the bedside table. 'It's eight o'clock! We've been asleep for hours. It must be the country air or you tiring me out! Oooh Dave, you big hunk! I could eat you.'

She stretched her arms up and arched her back like a cat. Her full, firm breasts and pink nipples were as fine as any page-three model's. I swallowed hard, then pulled back the sheets.

'Come on love! We've got to get up. Rachel's knocking on the door. Go and tell her we'll only be a few minutes,' I said.

'Leave her where she is and come back to bed. I want you again. She'll keep,' she said eagerly.

'Come on, Sylvia, we've got to get going. I need a quick wash and shave.'

As I went towards the bathroom I realised that I didn't have a change of clothes unless Finbar Salway had delivered them.

When I came back into the bedroom, with the towel round me this time, Sylvia had let Rachel in and was chatting to her whilst she dressed. She'd no false modesty either. She sat in front of the mirror and started frizzing her hair up. Her bruises seemed less obtrusive.

Rachel wasn't offended by the sight of so much bare flesh, she gave me a smile. 'Have you had a good rest? I finished writing that statement and then when I realised what you two were up to I had a little rest myself. I haven't phoned anyone so don't get worried. Are we going to eat soon? I'm famished!'

I don't think I blushed but I must have looked slightly

uncomfortable because Rachel gave a little laugh. 'By the way, Dave, there's a suitcase of yours next door,' she said.

'Why don't you order some food to be sent up while I get ready? We won't be able to go out anywhere,' I said.

'Oh brilliant,' replied Sylvia, 'we wait here while the great detective cracks the case from his bedroom.'

'I didn't say I was going to stay here,' I said. 'I'll have to go and see some people. I hope to get a result soon. Meanwhile you stay here. Don't phone, don't go down to the dining room, don't go out on the street. Just stay here and lie low, the pair of you! Got it?'

'My, isn't he forceful Rachel? I suppose we'd better do what the great man tells us. But when can I expect you to return from your jaunt into the crime-ridden streets?' Sylvia said.

'You'll see me when you see me,' I answered. 'I can't tell when I'll be done. I may even be out all night. Now why don't you just go next door with Rachel for a bit while I get dressed and make some phone calls. It's better if you don't hear them.'

'What a real chauvinist pig you are! Send the women out of the way while you get on with the man's work,' said Sylvia, only half jokingly.

Rachel clearly agreed with Sylvia.

'Now Sylvia, I thought we settled all that earlier,' I said. 'It's nothing to do with sex discrimination. What you don't know about you can't tell anyone, whatever they threaten you with.'

'Fine,' she answered, 'just don't forget that works both ways Dave!'

Sylvia flicked her hair back, and flounced into Rachel's room. Rachel trotted along behind her. They passed me out the suit-case and I heard the sound of the door being locked from their side.

Finbar Salway had packed my biggest case and sent me a fine selection of clothes. I put on a rust-coloured shirt, plain taupe trousers and a loose-fitting, teal-coloured, double breasted jacket. The shoulder holster didn't make a bulge.

I called Michael Rice at his home number. While the phone rang I practised my draw with the Beretta a couple of times. I remembered that I still hadn't cleaned it.

Michael Rice came on the line. 'It's you, you slimy bastard!' was his greeting when I announced myself.

'Cut out the charm Rice,' I said. 'You were trying to ring me earlier today. What gives?'

'I'll tell you what gives,' he said, 'I've been suspended pending an inquiry into what went on at your flat. That's what gives, you monkey!'

He sounded really depressed.

'I'm sorry, that's rough, but I did tell you Benson was after your balls. Anyway, what did you want me for?' I asked.

'Yeah, I phoned your car all right and all I got was your father,' he said. 'Crusty old sod, isn't he? Like father, like son! Told me he out-ranked me. Someone ought to tell him he's not on the Force anymore.'

'OK, if all you wanted to do was let off some steam – fair enough,' I said simulating anger, 'but I've no time to listen to you insulting my family. I thought you might have some idea what to do next but I see you haven't.'

'Well, you're a right one to take offence, aren't you?' he asked. 'Considering the harm you cause other people with your blundering about? I don't have any proposition for you but what you said to me while I was in hospital about not having anything to lose: that was right. I'm not staying in the job if I can't work in the CID. If they want to put me back with the woodentops pounding the beat, that's it! I'll jack it in.'

Amazing that Rice thought I gave a damn what he did with his life. It wasn't my fault he'd tried to get clever and landed up arse over tip. If he wanted me to help him he'd have to ask. I'd already had enough of his domineering ways.

'Hey Rice,' I said, 'there is something you could do to get back into Sinclair's good book, but you've got to ask me. I'm not going to press you. It's up to you to ask me.'

I hoped that wasn't going to be taken as pleading with him. If he was going to come unstuck again it had to be his own fault. I wasn't having him coming round blaming me. He didn't answer.

'I'll tell you what Michael,' I repeated more soothingly, 'think about it and then meet me at the Manor House pub in Withington in about half an hour. I might be with someone so be on your best behaviour.'

'Right, well I'll think about it,' he said gruffly.

I guessed it was going to be hard for such a hidebound copper as him to take anything from a civilian, much less orders from the likes of me.

I knew I ought to phone my very own, personal, hidebound copper, Paddy Cunane, to see how he'd got on; having to alter his holiday plans again and return home was bound to have put him in a bad mood. I dialled him at home and got through right away.

'Hello David, I got the car back and it didn't cost me a penny,' the old bugger answered my greeting in his usual brusque tones.

'I told them it must have been stolen earlier this morning. The Lancashire CID said they were waiting to talk to the owner but once I explained that I'd been in the Force they couldn't have been more helpful. They sent a car round to take me up for it. Very smart young man drove me up there – detective inspector, just about your age, married with two little boys.'

'What! A detective inspector to act as your chauffeur!' I mocked. 'I hope you didn't let him pump you about what we've been up to . . . By the way, I notice that you've not got round to asking me how I am yet.'

'No,' he said thoughtfully, 'well he wanted to know what had happened round here but I couldn't tell him anything, could I? I'd like to know what the hell's been going on here myself. A river of shit down the lane and the bedroom windows blown in! I've never seen anything like it in all my born days! I'll put the cost of the repairs on your bill.'

Sarcasm was wasted on Paddy.

'I can tell you're all right,' he continued, 'you wouldn't be phoning if you weren't. How's young Rachel and that other lass? She's a fine figure of a girl. Your mother was only just saying that you'd think a well-made young woman like that would be settled down with a home of her own and a husband and kiddies by now instead of trailing around with a ne'er-do-well like you.'

He was insufferable.

'Well, maybe she doesn't want to settle down!' I snapped back at him. 'Have you both thought of that? There is life outside marriage you know! When I was married and settled down you didn't like it much, did you?'

'Keep your shirt on!' he replied. 'Getting a bit touchy aren't you? You're a bit long in the tooth now for thinking about settling down with a lass like that. Look at your brother, how settled he is.'

'Don't go on Dad, we've been all through that, time after time. I only phoned to see if you and mum were OK. The Charlies haven't been back, have they?' I asked.

'As a matter of fact they have.'

'What!' I shouted.

I felt the hairs rising on the back of my neck.

'When?'

'About lunch time,' he said. 'A very polite young man came to the door. He was white, looked more like a school-teacher than a drug pusher. Any road, he asked in a very nice way if we knew anything about the whereabouts of Rachel and you. He knew she'd been staying here like, but he didn't know we were your parents.'

'What do you mean? They must have known,' I said.

'No, you think about it, Rachel herself didn't know until this morning. When she phoned her friend she must have just said she was staying with a couple. All she knew about me is that I was an ex-policeman. I didn't tell her any more. "Loose lips sink ships – Be like Dad, keep Mum!" etcetera, etcetera,' he said smugly.

'Well, it's hard to believe that they didn't check up on you.'

'No,' he answered. 'If they knew they were looking for a retired policeman in an isolated farm cottage at Belmont that would have been enough to trace us. Unless you think there's been some slip-up at your end?'

This was just so characteristic of my father, if there was any blame attaching it had to be shifted on to someone else's shoulders.

'What do you mean, "slip up at my end"?' I asked angrily. 'There was only me who knew where Rachel was. If you hadn't let her go shooting her mouth off down the phone we'd all be sitting pretty now! Did you tell Rachel about how Thwaite met his end and all that?'

'I told you. She didn't find out anything from me. Hold on a minute, I'll ask your Mother?' I could hear him bawling 'Eileen!' and after a moment my mother came to the phone.

'Oooh! Doesn't he shout. You'd think he was on a parade

ground. David, there must be some mistake, I didn't tell Rachel anything about her young man's death. I was most particular, and I don't know how she managed to telephone either unless she crept down in the middle of the night,' she said.

'Anyway, I was thinking that if you don't get back together with Delise that Sylvia looks as if she needs someone to look after her, poor thing. She seems like a nice young woman. Do you know much about her?' she asked, reverting to her favourite theme. 'She was like a breath of fresh air with you, made you look years younger. Are you going to bring her to see us again? You need somebody to keep you out of mischief.'

'Mother, will you leave off? I can't talk to a female in your presence without you putting up the marriage banns.'

'Well you're not getting any younger. We know how sad you were about Elenki, but she'd have wanted you to be happy, wouldn't she?'

There was no answer to that. Obviously Delise would have to get her face bruised if she wished to retain my mother's sympathy. How my mother could compare someone like Sylvia, who looked as if she'd just done ten rounds with Frank Bruno, to a breath of fresh air was a mystery. She must be getting more short-sighted than I'd realised.

'What's this about the Charlies coming back then?' I said, to change the subject.

'Yes. Ever such a smartly dressed young man, and he offered us money to phone him if you came back. Of course your father refused, but he was very insistent. We shut the door but he pushed £500 in £20 notes through the letter box with his phone number attached. Your father opened the door but he was running for his car with the farm dogs after him and now the money's just sitting there by the front door,' she said.

'Why don't you use it to get the windows repaired?' I asked gracelessly.

This must be how the Charlies had tracked my movements at Thornleigh Court. With the sort of money they had available for bribery no one could be trusted. Even a man's nearest and dearest might be corrupted. I thanked Mum and asked her to give Dad my best wishes. They'd given me plenty to think about.

No sooner had I put the phone down than I realized that I

still hadn't found out any more about Delise's whereabouts. She hadn't been at the office this morning or at my flat, nor was she available at her own or her mother's phone number.

I glanced at my watch. Time was flying.

I quickly phoned Jim McNeil and asked him if he could meet me at the Manor House. I told him to bring the dogs with him if he wanted. He didn't sound pleased with me but agreed to come for a drink.

Lastly I phoned Popeye Lane's mum and asked her when I could come to see her son.

'You what?' she drawled. 'You want our Bob?' she continued in a wondering tone of voice, really rolling her broad vowels. 'You're not from the police are you?'

She was quick enough on the uptake when I explained that I wanted to give Bob some money. She gave me directions on how to reach her at Langley. Bob would be in during the morning tomorrow. His mother lived on the Manchester overspill estate which sprawled over hundreds of acres near Middleton.

I could have sat around phoning people all evening but now I had to take the plunge. There were bound to be people on the streets who might recognise me. I would have to take my chances. I shouted through the locked door to Sylvia and Rachel that I was going out.

The indefatigable Lal was still at his post in the lobby. It was hard to tell if the place was doing much business. There were people in the restaurant but I hadn't seen any more hotel guests.

'What time do you knock off Lal?' I asked.

He raised his eyes heavenwards as if to imply that it was in the lap of the gods.

'What time do you shut the doors? I might be late back,' I said.

'Just be ringing the bell if the door is locked, I will let you in sir,' he replied. The poor chap must practically sleep beside his reception desk.

'Fine,' I said. 'Mrs Mather and my cousin won't be going out. I don't want to be disturbed so if anyone comes asking for them don't let on they're here. We want to get well rested for tomorrow. You know how long these weddings can go on. I'm off to my brother's stag do.'

I decided that I would move to another hotel first thing in the morning. My story to Lal would start unravelling by then. There didn't seem to be much danger of him gossiping to anyone about the battered guest with two girlfriends. He seemed to be part of the fixtures around here.

It was a fine evening when I got out on to the streets of Withington. There was plenty of traffic going into town and the pavements were crowded with young people travelling up and down in groups. Few were on their own, most were with a companion, and groups of three or four were more common than couples.

The Edwardian houses had been converted into lodgings for the students crammed into the colleges. Shadows were lengthening on the dirty old red-brick buildings as I hurried along through Withington in the direction of the Manor House. Despite the tawdry surroundings there was a jolly and friendly feeling in the streets as people hurried off for their evening's pleasure. It was hard to sustain the feeling of menace.

A man approached me. Quite well dressed, he was smiling and seemed harmless but I instinctively looked over my shoulder. All clear, no sign of the posse creeping up on me. I was as jumpy as a cat on its ninth life.

'Could you help me?' he asked politely. I thought he was going to ask for directions but he went on, 'I'm trying to get to the Salvation Army in Wythenshawe, I stayed at a centre in Withington last night and I haven't got any bus fare. I wonder if you could help me?'

Without conscious volition my right hand found its way from the shoulder holster and the Beretta to my back pocket. I gave him two £1 coins which he pocketed sharply. He thanked me politely.

As he went on his way I wondered how much he'd have had on him if I'd pulled out the gun instead and made him turn out his pockets. He only needed to score with ten or twenty mugs like me every day to rake in a good living.

Distracted by this, I walked quickly through Withington Village, unworried about hit men creeping up behind me. I followed Wilmslow Road where it curved away from Withington and a horrid stink of sweat and stale clothing met me. I looked up to see the grey concrete walls of the Christie Cancer Hospital across the road. There was a ventilator fan working and I must have been getting the smell from the laundry.

I reached the Manor House and slipped inside. Looking across the lounge I spotted the stubbly face of Michael Rice. He saw me at the same time and signalled that he'd got the drinks in. A good sign. He owed me from our last drinking bout. His bruises were no worse than mine, but he was sporting a white plaster across his nose.

Seeing me sit next to him, several men got up and moved away from us. We looked like a pair of hard cases.

He'd already knocked back a couple of pints with whisky chasers judging by the glasses lined up in front of him. I drained my own whisky and started on the pint of bitter without saying anything. He was looking grim but it was up to him to speak. I'd already made that clear enough.

'Well, what's this scheme of yours then?' he grizzled. He sounded about as happy and cheerful as a Death Row convict ordering his last meal.

'I've got enough on Dyer to put him in the frame for the Thwaite killing,' I said. 'Just like you told me on Tuesday evening, I've got enough to flush the swine out into the open. I've got a statement which I'm going to give to Thwaites' lawyer, Nigel Gemelli. You know how persistent he is. Then Benson'll have to do something.'

I leaned over to him conspiratorially, 'What you could do is dig up some dirt on Wild Bill himself,' I said in a low tone.

'Huh, you don't want much do you? How am I going to find this dirt?' he asked.

Locate the detective who interviewed Dyer, and see if Dyer mentioned the exact time on Thursday evening when I told him that Thwaite had done himself in.'

'Well, what will that prove?' Rice asked.

'If the time wasn't mentioned at the interview,' I explained, 'if he said nothing at all about it, then it will show that Benson himself has been in touch with Dyer. He told me in the presence of Sinclair that it was 23.30 when I told Dyer about the death. You can bet Sinclair clocked that. He's still got all his chairs at home, whatever he's done to you.'

There was a gleam in Rice's piggy little eyes which looked suspiciously like hope. He knew if he could get Sinclair on his side with something like this then his career might be back on the rails. At the very least they should be able to twist Benson's arm enough to make him drop the suspension.

'Sounds like you're clutching at straws to me, but I'll see what I can do,' he muttered grudgingly.

At that precise moment someone tapped my shoulder and I turned to see Jim McNeil. He recognised Rise immediately. Rice stared back at him.

'Hello Jim, brought the bow-wow with you? My friend's just going,' I laughed.

Rice stood up and moved towards the door, rasping 'Phone me tomorrow and I'll let you know how I get on,' as he went.

Jim's expression was no more pleasant than Rice's had been. He'd bought himself a pint before he came over. I used the opportunity of Rice's departure to position myself on his stool, facing the door, where I could see who was coming in.

'What did you think you were playing at yesterday, man?' Jim demanded angrily. 'You bloody idiot! Leaving a parcel with Margaret and then breaking into the house to get it back. We worked out it was you from the description the neighbours' kids gave. You must be mad!'

'Then we couldn't get hold of you,' Jim continued. 'Margaret was really worried. I don't know whether to deck you for breaking in or pat you on the back for surviving so long.'

'Come on Jim,' I coaxed. 'That's no way for a professional man to talk. I suppose you've worked out what was in the parcel as well?'

'No, was it drugs?' he asked.

'It was the guns which two assassins were going to murder me with. I got this bash on the face from one of them on Tuesday evening. I'm ashamed about what I did and I know I owe you an explanation so here goes . . . If you don't accept it, just get up and go. Much as I love you and Margaret I'm in such a mess that I don't have time to make elaborate apologies.'

Jim looked me in the eye and said 'You don't need to explain yourself Dave. We were worried when we thought it might be drugs. If it wasn't, well . . .'

'No, you're both owed an explanation and this is it. I couldn't keep the guns with me because the police wanted me and I thought it would be better for Margaret if I didn't tell her what they were. We both know how honest she is – she'd have owned up straight away if anyone had asked her. I apologise for breaking in to retrieve them. I was in a hurry.'

Jim took a long drink of beer. 'You're serious aren't you? You've really got hit men after you?' He shook his head wonderingly.

'You know, I've read about these things, but I've never thought I'd get involved. How in God's name did you get away?'

I didn't reply, just looked Jim in the eye. I didn't want to tell him any lies.

'Hmmm, I suppose that means you don't think I ought to know,' he said. 'That man you were with was the policeman who Esau knocked over at my house, wasn't it? Scruffy-looking individual isn't he?'

'Forget about him Jim. He's in big trouble himself. He can't do you any harm. Can you do me a favour? Can you drive over to Hebden Bridge and give this letter to Andy Thwaite's parents? I wouldn't ask but they must get it tonight.'

Jim had always been a good friend and had done a lot for me but I'd never tried to involve him directly in my work. I knew he enjoyed listening to me telling him about the odd characters I met and that he and Margaret were concerned about me. He didn't look too happy at my suggestion. If only Delise had been around I wouldn't have had to ask him. I'd already imposed on him enough.

'I'm not going to get arrested am I? There's nothing illegal about this?' he asked doubtfully.

I explained to him exactly what was in the letter and how to get to Hebden Brige by the shortest route. Eventually he agreed. I hoped I wasn't putting a strain on our friendship.

I went to phone George Thwaite. He was eager to receive the statement; as a veteran of a thousand union battles he knew all about the need to keep the pressure up on the enemy. He would meet Jim outside the Shoulder of Mutton, so all that remained was to get Jim moving.

As we went to the car I could see that he was still worried. He had the dog in the back of the car. It was my friend, Esau.

When I sat in the front seat next to Jim its great wet tongue began licking the back of my neck.

'It looks as if Esau remembers you Dave. How long do you think it'll take me?' Jim asked.

'Only a couple of hours, the motorway should be quiet now. Can you drop me off in Fallowfield? I've got to see someone.'

A few minutes later we were passing the drive-in MacDonalds and coming to the junction at the centre of Fallowfield. Jim stopped at the lights and I hopped out. Jim seemed to have cheered up. He gave me a grin and said 'I'll get a front-door key cut for you Dave. Then next time you call you won't have to get in through the bathroom.' He seemed to have forgiven me.

Using my friends in this way was tough but it really was a matter of life and death. Mine.

I headed up Moseley Road and turned into the terraced streets by the Adult Education Centre. I soon found the street I was looking for. There were traders' vans parked on the pavements and turbaned boys playing cricket in the lengthening shadows. I stopped at the house with a battered Morris Minor in front of it. The brickwork had been painted a dull shade of cherry red with some kind of varnish.

I knocked on the 'Georgian' front door, which didn't match the house and clashed with the coloured brickwork. Out of the corner of my eye I saw a curtain twitch. There was no reply so I knocked again. I knew he was in there, my years of experience as a process server had given me a sixth sense about whether a house was empty.

I started banging on the door with my fist. The door frame began rattling. I heard footsteps approaching and the door-chain being taken off.

Fred Lumsden opened his front door.

'Oh it's you squire,' he said nervously. 'What do you want? Have you come to pay me? They've been round you know, down at the office.'

Fred isn't a Mancunian, he hales from Bristol and when he's nervous the West Country accent becomes stronger. He was really drawling this time.

'Aren't you going to invite me in Fred? I thought you weren't going to open the door at all.'

'Yes, sure. Come in Boss. Well, no one round here's in a hurry to open their doors after seven o'clock. You wouldn't believe what goes on in this neighbourhood,' he said by way of excuse.

'It's what went on down at the office that I'm interested in,' I replied.

'I phoned the Jock,' he said. 'Then those other people came round. There were two of them. I told them what you told me to say . . . OK Boss? I was just going down to the Sherwood for the last hour, you can come if you want to.'

I ignored his invitation, and gave him a hard look.

'Right Fred, now tell me how much they bribed you to spill the beans.'

'Don't be like that Squire, they didn't give me anything. I just passed on your message like you said – gone to Zurich to the bank. They weren't pleased. One of them was a great big Jamaican . . .'

'Yes Fred, but how much did you take to report about me?'

'No, no,' he shook his head. 'When they knew you'd gone abroad they weren't interested any more.'

So far our conversation had taken place in the narrow hall of Fred's home. I pushed past him into the lounge. His coat was hanging over the back of a chair. I grabbed it and felt the pockets. Sure enough there was a thick wad of notes in the right-hand pocket.

'Where did you get this?' I asked.

'It's me holiday money. Honest Boss!' he wailed.

There was £300 in used fivers in the roll. I counted out £120 and handed it back to him.

'That's the £120 I promised you. I'm keeping the rest till you tell me where it came from.'

Fred's story crumbled. 'I'm sorry, they did give it me. But if you'd seen the size of them you wouldn't have quarrelled with them either.'

'All right Fred, there's no need to whine. Now tell me exactly what you told them and I might think of letting you have some of this back.'

Fred explained that the Charlies had come round not ten minutes after he'd sent off the motorcycle courier. He'd given them the message about Zurich. He'd let them look in the office. Then they'd forced money on him and threatened him to tell them as soon as he saw me again. I had to believe him because if he'd passed on anything else they'd have been round at the Garden of Kashmir long before now.

I gave him back all the Charlies' money plus the extra £120 I had promised.

'Right Fred, now I want you to phone them again. I want you to tell them I came round here. You can say you were hiding my gun for me. I want you to tell them that you've got some interesting news. Tell them that I've done a deal with Dyer and I'm going to be round at the Paloma with him. Tell them I was bragging about it, and make it convincing.'

Fred's ugly face was a sight worth seeing. He hadn't shaved and his bristly jaws were churning up and down as he tried to think out what would be the best move for him. Emotions of fear and greed flickered alternately across his poorly aligned features.

'What are you offering me this time Chief?' he said with the light of greed in his rheumy old eyes.

'I'm not as well off as those dopers. I'll give you £20 now and another £40 when you've made the call,' I replied.

'Make it the round £100 and you're on,' he bargained.

After haggling I got him down to £75; one third now, two thirds on completion. He'd phone the Charlies around 11 p.m from his sister's house a few streets away.

The avaricious old stoat had an interest in keeping me alive if only so he could carry on playing me off against the Charlies for more bribes. I left his house as quickly as I could and walked back to Withington through Ladybarn, keeping to the side streets. The few youths and roaming hooligans I encountered kept their distance when they saw my face. I stopped at a chip-shop on Mauldeth Road and bought a bag which I ate as I made my way back.

Lal was still wearily propping himself up against the reception desk when I went in. He'd nothing to report. No one had been round asking for us. He looked weary yet was still as polite as ever so I gave him a fiver for his trouble.

The room was a trap for the passive smoker; both of them were at it. Rachel was lying on the bed filing her fingernails. There was the remains of a meal and two large bottles of

Lambrusco, one consumed, the other half gone. I crossed the room and opened the window. Sylvia gave me a feeble smile.

'Hello Big Boy, got everything sorted out then? We were getting worried you might not be coming back to look after us.'

They both giggled.

'Yeah, well I have. I didn't realise you were a heavy smoker. If you can put your fags down I'll tell you about phase two of our plans,' I said.

'Your plans!' Sylvia laughed. 'Why don't you get real Dave? You're never going to bring down Dyer, Manteh and half the police force. Rachel and I have been talking it over, and we think it's best if she goes back to her parents and you and I make a fresh start somewhere a long way away. I've got friends who'll send my things on when we get fixed up and you have to.'

'Do you think this as well Rachel?' I asked.

She nodded and gave me a sad smile.

'It's over Dave, accept it,' Sylvia said. 'We're already packed to move.'

I shook my head. 'You're right, we're certainly going to move, but not out of Manchester. We're going to sort these bastards out. You're going to phone Dyer and tell him exactly where Rachel and I will be tomorrow afternoon. The sweaty little git will be dying to get his hands on us and you'll screw every last penny you can out of him.'

Rachel started gasping, she fumbled in her bag for the inhaler. Sylvia turned on me like an angry mother hen. 'You absolute bastard! I thought you were straight!'

'Yeah, I am, just like you love. I'm not handing her over. Rachel's got to phone her flabby friend Lisa Goody and pass on the same message to the Charlies. Then, when they meet for their confrontation the police can grab the lot of them and we'll be in the clear.'

26

Surprisingly, Rachel and Sylvia accepted my plan. It wasn't much, but then everybody's always telling me I'm not very bright. If I could lure Manteh and Dyer and their henchmen to the same spot at the same time there was bound to be an explosion and the police could lock up the survivors.

It took over an hour to install ourselves in the Toll House: a concrete-box hotel in Northenden, handy for a getaway to the airport. There was still some light in the midsummer sky, clear for once. The late hour of our arrival – after ten-thirty – attracted no attention in this ultra-modern environment. Unlike the long suffering Lal, the staff here had been stamped out of identical moulds in plastic and took no interest in us whatever. I was able to hire a car at the reception desk without any bother.

When we got to our room I turned the radio on and tuned to a local FM station, Sunset. After a few minutes of the usual rap and soul a newsflash came on.

'Hey there House fans, reports are coming in of a riot at the Paloma Club. Fighting is taking place between security staff at the club and gangs of gatecrashers. Mike Dyer, the ever genial mine-host is unavailable for comment about this second serious incident of rioting at Manchester's most popular teenage night spot. We'll update you on this one just as fast as the news comes in.'

I'd done it, I'd pulled the Charlies' chain for them. I started dancing round the room with my hands joined above my head. Rachel laughed out loud and joined in but Sylvia went pale.

'Dave, this is your doing isn't it?' she said. 'I know all the people who work there. It just isn't a joke.'

She was on the point of tears.

'Sylvia, don't go soft on us now. You were ready to do exactly the same thing. I just passed on some false information to the Charlies, that's all. They think I'm hiding in the Paloma. They bribed a mate of mine to tell them.'

I was grinning so much that my face was hurting. She had to smile.

'If you phone him now to tell him that I've joined up with the Charlies he's bound to believe you. Offer him a deal,' I said.

I told her what to say and though her heart wasn't in it, she was carried along by the general enthusiasm. She picked up the phone and dialled Dyer's private number at the club.

'Hello Mike . . . yet its me . . .

'I know what you said but I've got something you might be interested in . . .

'Can't you just listen . . . Cunane came round, I'm with him . . .

'No, I'm not telling you where we are . . . will you listen? He's not here now . . . he's got Rachel Elsworth with him . . . he definitely wants to take over your clubs . . .

'He's doing a deal with Manteh . . . I know Manteh's after his blood, that's why he's doing a deal with him . . . Manteh's going to keep sending his mobs steaming into your clubs until the police shut you down, then old man Elsworth will come up with the money for Cunane to reopen them . . .

'Will you just listen a minute? He's going to get rid of you . . . Rachel will fit you up for the killing of Andy Thwaite . . . You'll be inside . . . She's swearing out oaths and depositions all over the place that you did it . . . No, she's not been to the police . . . Cunane's been warned off by Benson. The thing is Mike, I can let you know exactly where Rachel will be tomorrow . . . No, not for old times, sake. It's going to cost you plenty . . .'

There was a long pause, presumably while Dyer chewed all this over. I could imagine him, at bay in his lair, prowling up and down while his t-shirted stormtroopers guarded the entrance to the bunker. Sylvia gave me a nervous smile, her hand was trembling. Her performance was all the more convincing because she did it so unwillingly. The phone began to squawk again and she listened with an ever deepening frown.

My heart sank. It sounded as if Dyer was telling her just what she could do with herself. My plan looked as if it was going to flop at stage one.

'He says the club's under attack again. The Paloma's under attack. It's never been as bad as this before.' She put the phone down, looking shaken.

'You really have done a deal with Manteh, haven't you? What you made me tell him is all true,' she said accusingly.

'There's been no deal,' I retorted. 'Are you mad? You know what Manteh wants to do to me. The Charlies'd bribed an old caretaker and I got him to give them a little misdirection. That's all. Do you think Manteh would've let me walk away in one piece if I'd met up with him?'

She shook her head.

'What did Dyer say?' I asked.

'He said he'd think about it. I have to phone him back later. Dave, I'm really scared now. He'll kill both of us, and you too Rachel, if he ever finds out what's going on.'

'Well,' he's never going to find out, is he?' I said. 'I've got to get both him and Manteh off our backs.'

I turned to Rachel. 'You seem to be enjoying things so far, now you've got to perform your own little act. You've got to get in touch with Lisa and tell her we're meeting Dyer tomorrow afternoon.'

'That won't be so easy Dave,' she said, all serious now.

'Why, she should be back from the pub by now and tucked up with that lout Spragg,' I argued.

'I know that,' she said, 'but there's only one phone in her block and it can ring for hours before anyone answers, and fetches the person you want to speak to.'

'Well, Rachel, you'd no trouble getting through to her before, so I suggest you start right now,' I said.

I passed her the phone and she dialled. As she'd said it was a long time before there was a reply and even longer before she started speaking to her friend. She gave Lisa the news of the coming meeting with Dyer. The reason she gave for the meeting was that Dyer had agreed to pay her off. I was going to be present as her protector.

Lisa had no trouble accepting that Rachel would be prepared to meet her boyfriend's murderer to receive some 'compensation'. She'd do the same herself if some public benefactor disposed of Spraggie.

It would only be a matter of time before the news was circulated to Manteh by Spragg. It would be with him quicker than it takes a dose of clap to get round a Bangkok brothel.

Thinking of news turned my thoughts to Ted Blake. He

would've finished for the night at Alhambra and just might have given his usual boozing club a miss. He did have the occasional sober evening. I might catch him at home.

My luck was in. He answered the phone right away.

'Have you heard the news Ted? Manteh's mob has declared open season on Dyer's clubs,' I said.

'You're still in the land of the living are you Dave? What did you say?' Ted answered groggily. He sounded as if he'd been woken up. It was unusual for Ted to go to sleep before one or two in the morning. He must be feeling the strain of life in the fast lane at Alhambra.

'Tune into Sunset will you Ted? There's a mob trying to smash up the Paloma,' I said.

'The hell there is! I'd better get down there with a crew. This isn't just your obsession with Dyer is it, Dave?' he asked.

'Of course not. Listen, there's more. The girlfriend of Andy Thwaite has testified that Dyer threatened to murder Andy just before he was killed. Thwaite's parents are going to bring a private prosecution against Dyer if the police won't act.' I was only anticipating the news slightly.

'Just hold on a minute Dave, let me take a few details down. You might have the makings of a story here. What's the girl's name and age? Is she a looker, you know . . . er . . . big boobs?'

'Her name's Rachel Rankine, she's eighteen and she's attractive. She's quite well-developed but I don't see what that's got to do with it,' I said in a mildly indignant way.

'No you wouldn't, Dave old son,' Ted replied. 'I was just thinking of packaging the story for the *Planet*, we might just get something into the late edition.'

'Can't you get something on to the morning television news?'

'I can and I will,' he said, 'but there's a limit to what you can say on the television news, whereas the story's got everything the *Planet* likes to go to town on: sexy young bird crying for justice against the establishment, randy older man . . . Yeah, the story's got a bit of pizazz now, it's not just you bellyaching about how naughty Dyer is. A spicy love interest is just what is needed. I suppose she did cohabit with this Thwaite, didn't she?'

'Oh yes, they even had a secret "love-nest" in Southport.'

I winked at Rachel as she blushed crimson. Sylvia put her arm round her.

'Great! You don't happen to know if Dyer gave her a bonk as well do you? He's known to be partial to a spot of nooky with fresh young birds,' he said.

'Look, why don't you interview her? I can give you exclusive access but it'll have to be in the morning, you can't see us now. Why don't you get on to Thwaite senior? I'll give you his number. He'll be only too delighted to release Rachel's statement to you and you can probably get on to Nigel Gemelli the solicitor as well.'

Ted wasn't too pleased that I wasn't going to hand Rachel over to him right away, but in exchange for an exclusive he was prepared to wait. I could tell he thought this story might be his ticket to the big time. I'm sure he could see himself as 'Sir Edward Blake', the media mogul, knighted for his services to news. I promised to phone him in the morning and arrange a meeting.

When I put the phone down neither of my damsels in distress was looking pleased with me. I didn't care.

'So this is what all the secrecy is about,' Rachel said. 'Just an opportunity for you to make a bit on the side at my expense. What do you mean by telling him that my name is Rachel Rankine?'

'It'll save trouble all round Rachel,' I said. 'After all, it is your real name and your parents have paid me a fortune to keep their name out of this mess.'

This didn't suit poor Rachel at all, she started howling. Sylvia gave her a handkerchief, but Rachel stood up and went to the door. I stood in front of it.

'Can't I even go to my own room then?' she demanded.

'No, I think it's better if you stay in here with Sylvia. I'm going out now for two or three hours.'

Rachel pulled a face and turned her back on me. 'I'm going to phone my mother then, and you won't stop me,' she said over her shoulder.

'All right,' I compromised, 'but let me speak to her first.'

Dee answered the phone after the third ring. She must have been sitting next to it. I told her that she'd have Rachel back with her soon.

'Why can't she come home now? I want her here now. Where are you?' she asked.

'You're going to have to trust me Dee. I can't tell you anything and I don't want you to tell anyone, even Harold, that Rachel's been in touch. Just tell her to be co-operative. It's all for her own good!'

'Please, Dave. Harold's here now, he's upstairs. Can't I tell him?' she said plaintively.

'No. He might be compromised. You know what you told me on the road to Southport. If you can just trust me for a bit longer we're all in with a chance to come out of this smelling of roses. Even Harold.'

There was a pause and then she said, 'I suppose I've no alternative but to trust you Dave, especially after all . . . well, you know, but he'll want to know who phoned.'

'Tell him it was one of Rachel's friends phoning to say she's safe,' I said and handed the phone to Rachel.

'Keep it brief, and don't tell her where we are,' I told her.

Giving me a curious look, Rachel complied. She did more listening than talking and then slammed the phone down angrily.

'How did you get her to jump through hoops for you?' she asked bitterly. 'She never does it for me.' I didn't reply.

There was an awkward silence for a moment then Sylvia said 'When am I going to phone Mike again?'

'I think we should let him stew for a bit and phone when I get back. If there's trouble at the club he'll be there all night won't he?' I replied. She agreed.

'Why don't you and Rachel get a few zeds Sylvia?' I suggested. 'You're both going to need to be fresh in the morning. Keep the door locked and don't open it for anyone but me, I should be back about 4 a.m.'

Neither of them looked sorry to see the back of me, and I felt relieved to be leaving them on their own. They should be safe enough if they kept their noses indoors.

I located the hire car – a Ford Fiesta – and drove out first to the M56 and then on to the M62, eastbound. There was a fair amount of traffic but not so much that I didn't have time to think.

It was wearing me down having to get Sylvia and Rachel to

agree to every step I took. I felt a sense of relief to be doing something on my own. I was sick of telephoning people too.

I'd gone back to believing in Sylvia, not just because we'd slept together. She'd let her ambition nudge her out of her depth. Believing in wasn't the same as completely trusting her. Who could say how she might jump if Dyer put out the welcome mat and she convinced herself that I'd caused all her troubles?

With Rachel things were even less straightforward. For an innocent runaway that was a wild attack she'd made on Sylvia – and then there was the fact that she'd either known Thwaite was dead before she went to ground in Southport, or Lisa had told her – but why had she said it was my mother?

Could she be shielding Harold Elsworth? She knew more about the Charlies than she'd let on. Maybe she'd put Thwaite up to blackmailing dyer and she felt guilty about the result.

I still didn't have as much going for me as I wanted. All the phoning and stirring I'd done in the last few hours could be a waste of time. I had to make sure. I had to take Dyer and Manteh out of the equation, but arranging for both of them to be at the same spot wasn't enough. I had to take more active measures.

The weeds in the Lane's garden were growing up to the level of the upstairs windows, the gate was off its hinges and the short path to the front door was blocked by what looked like the remains of a turret lathe.

I'd had no trouble finding my way to the crescent where Popeye lived. When I'd started work as a debt collector and process server some of my fattest fees had been earned on the Langley – an estate where debt collectors soon learned to abandon hope as they entered. I'd been young and desperate in those days.

I pressed the doorbell but it didn't work and so I gave the door a bang. I was anxious to get inside as mangy dogs were gathering at the end of the path and looking me over, their eyes glinting in the yellow light from the street lamps.

Popeye himself, wearing a blue tracksuit, opened the door and invited me in with a surprised but friendly expression on his face. I was reassured by this because what I wanted to ask him to do might get up his nose.

'Come in Mr Cunane. This is my mother.' Popeye introduced me to a pleasant-looking lady in her fifties. Neither of them seemed surprised at the unconventional time I'd chosen for my visit.

His mother had a smiling face which made an impact on me after the doom and gloom from Sylvia and Rachel. She was of medium height with her hair done up in an old-fashioned bun. The old-fashioned look was enhanced by the dressing-gown and long nightie she was wearing.

'So you got here then, a bit earlier than I thought you would,' she said. 'I'm going to apologise for the state of the garden. Bob's father's a handyman, which means he'll fix anyone else's house up before he'll do up his own. The garden's been so bad that the neighbours got up a petition against us, which considering the state of some round here, gives you an idea of how bad it was. It's quite tidy now compared with what it has been, innit Bob?' She spoke with a broad local accent.

'That's all right, Mam. Mr Cunane hasn't come to see the garden,' Bob said.

'His car's in the street Bob, I'd best send Clint out to look after it before those Maltese from down the street have the wheels off. Talk about what makes a Maltese cross, we've all got to bear a Maltese cross round here, but our Clint'll see 'em off.' From the way she was speaking I imagined Clint was a dog.

'Good idea, Mam,' Bob agreed. 'Why don't you go and make us a drink? Tea OK for you, Mr Cunane?'

I nodded, and as soon as his mother went out handed him an envelope containing £300 in £10 notes. He opened the envelope and looked through the money quickly, before putting it in his back pocket.

'I didn't tip you off about Dyer coming round for the money you know, but I'm grateful anyway,' he said. 'It'll tide me over till I can get a job. I'm not with NMP now. I had enough of that little swine Dyer and that Scots bugger.'

He looked quite bitter. Thanks to me his wrist was in plaster and I was glad he was mad at Dyer and not me.

'How've you been Mr Cunane?' he asked. 'It looks as if someone else has been trying to put your light out since we had a go at you.'

'I'm afraid you're right there mate,' I said. 'I'm in trouble with the Charlies as well as with your ex-boss. In fact, you wouldn't be far wrong if you said I was on the run.'

'You can stay here if you like,' he offered. 'Folk round here know how to keep their mouths shut.'

'That's very good of you all things considered,' I said, indicating his broken wrist – heavily plastered and supported by a sling round his neck.

He grinned and said, 'Well there were three of us, and we were supposed to be professionals. So I suppose it was what you might call an occupational hazard. Did you see the big soft Scots git back off when you went for him with the bat? I'll bet he crapped himself. Likes giving folk a beating does Jock, but doesn't like it when they hit back.

'I've been sick of working with him for a while,' he continued. 'He always had me holding some poor bugger up while he kicked shit out of them. I'm grateful to you for giving me the chance to get out. Jock's killed people, you know – loan sharking – a sideline the Boss ran for the NMP. They never involved me in that but they would've done if I'd stayed around.'

'Were the NMP just a bunch of club doormen then?' I prompted.

'No, that's just a small part of it. So called respectable businessmen most of them. Members of the Rotary Club, JPs and suchlike. They just need Dyer and his doormen as their enforcers, most of the time they treat him like shit. You'd be surprised at the names of some of the people connected with NMP.'

Not as much as you might be at one of them, I thought.

All the feuding and fighting between Dyer and the Charlies; what did it come down to? Manteh and the Charlies had got most of the inner-city drugs market sewn up. They wanted to expand their outlets into the clubs. The NMP, under pressure from the collapse of property prices, were equally determined to develop that market for themselves. They wanted to see homemade Ecstasy tablets as opposed to imported heroin and cocaine. A turf battle like the struggle for supermarket shelf-space between rival brands of washing powder. Dyer and Jock were just front men.

'Do you think Jock did for this DJ, Andy Thwaite?' I asked.

'He could have, he went out with Dyer after the club shut. We took the takings down to Dyer's house, that's down Handforth way. Then they both cleared off. They were both as pissed as newts when they came back.'

Popeye must have seen the gleam in my eye.

'No, Mr Cunane, I'm not grassing them up to the police,' he said. 'I want to go on living round here, I'd need a lot more than you gave me to risk grassing on Dyer and the NMP.'

His mother came in and put the tea on the table. She was frowning. 'I'd better not stop round here if you're talking about grassing on someone,' she said, as she went out.

'Well I don't want you to grass, Bob, but there is something you could do for me. Do you think you could go round some of the NMP crowd and tell them that Dyer's cooking the books? Tell them that he makes a hell of a lot more profit than he ever lets on to them?'

Popeye's change of expression was comical. He gave me a look of surprise, then fear, then he began to grin from ear to ear.

'You're joking, you must be joking! Some of those guys in the NMP make the Mafia look like a bunch of social workers. If Dyer's ripping them off then he can kiss his arse goodbye.'

'He's ripping them off and I can give you the evidence you'll need to convince anyone.'

Popeye began giggling and rubbing his hands together. 'Bloody hell! They'll rip his arm and legs off. You've got to credit his nerve if it's true.'

'Well, would you be interested in exposing him to his friends – not to the police mind you! I've nothing to do with the police, in fact I think they're looking for me as much as everyone else,' I said.

'You're a right head-case Mr Cunane! Have you got any friends at all? A man who's daft enough to get Dyer, the Charlies and the Fuzz after him, all at the same time, deserves help,' he said. Then, looking more businesslike, he asked 'Have you got the evidence with you?' I could see the pound signs gleaming in his greedy eyes.

I showed him the heavily creased photocopies of Dyer's books and bank statements that I'd been carrying round with me. He studied them with me. I pointed out where there were contradictions.

'It looks as if he's been on the fiddle right enough, but what's in it for me? Like I said, it's bad news for Dyer.'

I took out the photo of Dyer and his henchmen that I'd nicked. 'I should think everyone in that photo would pay you well for a copy of those papers. You could go round them all. Most of them are respectable businessmen with offices in Manchester. You'd make a bomb.'

Popeye started grinning happily.

'You jammy bastard! It was you that hit me on the head that night wasn't it? You've got a bloody cheek coming round here!' he said.

I didn't speak. We stared at each other, then he laughed again.

'Would you object if our Clint came with me?' he asked.

I shook my head and he gave a whistle.

I was expecting to see a pit-bull terrier and got a surprise when Clint ambled into the small room. He was a huge man – at least six foot six in height and built like an over-stuffed sofa.

'He's my kid brother,' Popeye explained.

A beatific and empty smile played over Clint's gentle features. I felt a faint chill. It was just as well I hadn't come to do anything unpleasant to Popeye.

'He suffers from learning difficulties like,' said Popeye, 'and he's very friendly with my pals but if he sees anyone ill-treating me he goes berserk. Shake hands with him Mr C.'

An enormous paw, with digits the size of Cumberland sausages, enveloped my own hand. I expected to have my fingers crushed but Clint knew his own strength and didn't squeeze at all.

'Mr Cunane's a friend of mine, Clint. Be nice to him!' Popeye said.

Again I felt a tingle of fear. Being around Clint was like playing Russian roulette with five chambers loaded. He gave me a friendly hug round the shoulders, he must have been at least twenty-five stone and most of it felt like muscle.

I asked Popeye if he knew who all the men in the photo were. He did. He'd often driven Dyer to meetings with them and it would be no problem to visit them. 'They're all in the Yellow Pages, Mr C.' he joked.

It was still only 2.30 a.m. on a fine quiet night when Popeye and his brother walked me to the car. Sure enough, there were signs of furtive movement as we looked down the street but the car still had four wheels. Otherwise it was a peaceful scene, only the distant wails of police sirens on the main road helped me to recall my purpose.

I had to drive several miles before I found an unvandalised phone box. Despite not wanting to use the phone again it was essential to check if Rice was in before calling on him.

He answered straightaway.

'I need to see you, Rice. Have you been able to follow up what I told you about the interview?'

'Look Cunane, get off my back! You'll have to wait, it's only been a few hours since I saw you. I can't tell you anything on the phone anyway and it's too late to do anything. Ring tomorrow and arrange a meet.'

If everything went according to plan some very nasty events were going to happen: in private to Dyer, and in public between Dyer's men and the Charlies. So public that even Benson wouldn't be able to look the other way. Manteh wouldn't be with 'the youth' when they went up against the NMP. He'd be lying low, but I needed to make sure that the police dealt with him. That was where Rice came in.

I was desperate enough to plead with him.

'No, no wait, Rice . . . er, Sergeant. Don't hang up, please. Something's come up, something I haven't told you about, something to do with those inner-city friends you were so worried about on Sunday.'

My change in tone must have had an effect on Rice, the whining made him feel powerful again.

'It's better be good, I'm not going on any more wild-goose chases for you. Are you sure it won't wait until tomorrow?' he said.

'No, you'll want to do something when you find out what I've got to tell you,' I said ingratiatingly.

Rice gave me directions to his flat in Palatine Road, Didsbury. That was very handy. Rice's flat was only a couple of miles from the Toll House and if I got there quickly and set Rice moving in the right direction I should get back to Sylvia and Rachel by 4.00.

From what he'd said it didn't sound as if he'd had much luck in proving Benson had a link with Dyer.

Rice's flat was one of eight in a converted Victorian house. At 3 a.m. there was still a smell of boiled potatoes lingering in the air when Rice let me in the hallway and led me upstairs to his flat on the top floor.

It was a downmarket place in which to find a police sergeant, a crash pad for bachelors by the look of it – nothing like as respectable as Thornleigh Court. The impression of being in a student's flop was heightened when he let me into his room. Strong smells of cat pee and whisky pervaded the air. Rice moved a heap of dirty clothes and underwear off the sofa to make a place for me. There were the remains of take-away meals lying about on the floor.

He must have seen me turning my nose up, because he said, 'I don't think you're going to get your clothes mucky. We don't all earn enough to have cleaning ladies and five changes of clothes a day like you, you know.'

'What are you on about!' I said angrily. 'I bet you pull in twice as much as I do. I don't have any cleaning lady either.'

'We all know you get all kinds of non-taxable expenses, you're rolling in it,' he said stubbornly.

'OK, have it your own way,' I replied.

There was no point in antagonising him. I thought he was going to be too ignorant to offer me a drink, but as if reading my thoughts, he went over to a cupboard and got out a bottle of whisky – Happyways' 'own brand'. It took him several minutes searching round on the floor to find two glasses. No wonder he hadn't been anxious to let me see how he lived.

'I didn't get far with your bloody clue, Cunane. Sinclair remembers Benson giving the time but neither of us can get hold of the transcript of the interview.'

'Well, why can't you?' I asked.

'The inspector who took the interview is a lodge-brother of Benson. He won't do anything to drop Benson in it. Says he can't remember if Dyer told him about the time with the tape recorder off. His sergeant says the same . . .'

'Haven't you got the actual transcript of the interview? That's all we need,' I said.

'You're not listening are you, thick-head?' he snarled. 'They won't turn over any evidence that might put Benson in the shit, nor get me out of trouble, just to oblige Sinclair. They're mates of Benson. You know – rolled up trousers and fancy aprons. Anyway they must reckon Sinclair's on his way out, too. Why should they offend Benson? The only way we could get that transcript is by an official inquiry that would have to be initiated by Benson himself and if you think Sinclair's going to try starting that just to please you or me you must be barking mad.'

I looked at him glumly.

'If that was your only clue, you're up shit-creek mate,' he said cheerfully.

There didn't seem to be much to say. I raised Rice's chipped glass to my lips and sipped his supermarket whisky. I still had one shot in my locker. I took out Manteh's wallet and passed it over to Rice.

'Have a look at this and tell me what you make of it,' I asked.

'What's this?' he snapped. 'More clues that lead nowhere? You're a loose cannon you are. You've wrecked this bloody investigation.'

'Just look in the wallet. I got it off Manteh. And for God's sake stop feeling sorry for yourself!' I told him.

Rice removed the thin cards and began studying them with interest. He went over to the table and cleared away some of the chip papers and dirty mugs. He began spreading the cards out and humming to himself. The miserable expression on his face began to slowly change. He started crooning a word – 'Sledgehammer . . . Sledgehammer . . . Sledgehammer . . .' and rocking backwards and forwards as he re-arranged the cards and then re-arranged them again.

'What do you think they are then?' he said, turning to me after a while.

'Oh no you don't,' I said. 'I'm a loose cannon, a rank amateur. You tell me what they are.'

With that sudden change from surliness to charm which marked him, Rice grinned broadly.

'They're only my route back into the CID. You've only handed me a list of drug dealers and their bank accounts. Sinclair's going to wet his pants when he hears about this.'

He phoned Sinclair right away and told him what he'd got. He read out the list of initials, slowly so they could be checked off a list.

Then he said, 'So Sledgehammer's on then, sir . . . When can we mount it? Too late for today isn't it? 4 a.m. tomorrow, all arrangements as planned.' Then he listened in silence for a long while and after 'Yes sir, . . . thank you sir . . . yes sir,' for about five minutes, put the phone down.

He went over to the table, picked the whisky bottle up and put it back in the cupboard. It wasn't hard to guess part of what Sinclair had been telling him.

I laughed at him and for once he laughed back.

'I'm reinstated, Sinclair wants me to take these round to him right away. He's going to get the Bank of England to try to block the accounts. The shit's really going to hit the fan for our religious friend Manteh when his pals find out. Then we're going to put "Sledgehammer" into action.'

'What's that?' I asked.

'Well, I shouldn't tell you, but we've been planning a massive clean-out of the Charlies for months. Hundred of officers are going to assemble at the Police Training Centre then we're going to motor into Moss Side like an armoured column. The only thing that's been holding us up has been precise information as to who the main dealers are. That's the info I was looking for last Sunday when I saw you coming out of Manteh's house.

'Anyway, Sinclair said I wasn't to ask you where you got the lists. Probably illegal, eh?' he said, smiling broadly.

'Not at all, I found the wallet in the street and now I've turned it over to the first police officer I've met, like any honest citizen would.' As we spoke Rice had been putting on various grubby articles of clothing and now he steered me to the door.

The first streaks of dawn were appearing in the sky as I drove quickly back to the hotel. I felt carefree for the first time since Delise had left me. I could understand Rice bursting into song. The strain of the last few days was beginning to lift. I'd put the skids under Dyer and Manteh, this would probably be the dawn of the last day they'd still have the power to terrorise others.

When I got back to the hotel room it took some time before I could rouse Sylvia. I told her as much as I thought she needed to know: that I'd made plans to dispose of Dyer whether she helped me or not. I could see that she was still torn. In the end my pose of indifference convinced her. She phoned Dyer, very reluctantly.

He was desperate to trade, he wanted to get his hands on both me and Rachel. He was ready to take Sylvia back as an equal partner, split the profits right down the middle.

Sylvia told him I would be on the forecourt of the G-Mex building with Rachel at 4 p.m.

Before we all settled down for a few more hours' sleep Sylvia went over to her case and took out a wig of straight black hair. 'I thought I could wear this. It'll make us less obvious tomorrow.'

'That's a great idea Sylvia,' I mumbled as I fell asleep in the armchair.

27

'No, no TV cameras and no photographs,' I was shouting as I stood outside the door of our room barring the path of Ted Blake and his Alhambra news crew.

'You shit, Cunane, you absolute shit! You promised me an interview,' Ted raved at me. 'Let me see her, let me speak to her in person!'

'Yes Ted, an interview. A verbal interview, no cameras, no pictures. I'm in the body-guarding business, do you expect me to paint a target all over Rachel so Dyer's mates can take pot shots at her!'

Ted is bigger than I am but he's not in very good condition. However, with his crew behind him, and with his bloodshot boozer's eyes rolling, the crazy fool was getting ready to rush me. You don't keep your job in the Alhambra news room for very long if you can't force awkward customers to give interviews. My jacket was unbuttoned, and my hand happened to brush it open – revealing the automatic in my shoulder holster.

The news-hound drew back. 'Look Dave, can't we be reasonable about this? I've given you loads of help.' He looked me straight in the eye. 'Well, I have, haven't I? Just give me this interview. I'm pleading with you. The rest of the press'll be here before long. I'm begging you, for old times sake, just let me file this story before everyone else? Please, my editor will break my neck if I don't get the follow up I promised. Please, Dave, my job's on the line.'

I wasn't taken in by his journo's cant. He'd have told me he needed the interview to feed his sick wife and ten starving kids if I hadn't known all about him.

'Look Dave, if people seeing her is what's worrying you how about doing the interview with her face blanked out and her voice altered? Come to think of it, that might have more impact anyway. Come on, Davy baby, we can take you all down to the studios and tape in secret. We can settle your hotel bill and get moving right away.' He put his hand in his wallet and pulled out a thick wad of notes. 'If it's money that's the problem Dave . . .'

'Put your money away Ted. You've convinced me. We'll do it like you say.'

'You'll not regret it Dave, you'll not regret it, old son. We'll get it on the national lunchtime news if you can get a rattle on.'

Ted despatched one of his crew to charge our hotel bill to Alhambra and bribe the desk to deny that we'd ever been here. The rest of them raced us down to the car park, forming a solid phalanx round Rachel and Sylvia. Ted insisted on getting into my car with the three of us. He wasn't taking any chances that I might slip away. We went in convoy behind the news crew to the Alhambra studios.

This wasn't working out as I'd intended, things were slipping out of my control. When we got to the studios Ted would have lots of his own minders to take care of me.

'I hope you haven't got any plans to ditch me when we arrive Ted. We've got to be out of the studios by 11 a.m. at the latest. I've got an even bigger story for you if you're a good boy, one that you can film live,' I said.

Sylvia, sitting next to me in the front seat, shot me a puzzled glance.

'I can give you the time of the next big raid in Moss Side if you play ball,' I murmured.

Ted, who had been chatting up Rachel, immediately gave me some attention. 'What raid? You mean the Charlies attacking these clubs? That's old stuff. We've already got that in the can.' Ted spoke in that cocksure, nasal Manchester tone of voice that so many trade union leaders had used to inflame their opponents in negotiating sessions.

'No, Ted, I mean the police rounding up the Charlton Close mob,' I said as patiently as I could manage.

'Get away. They'll never try that,' he replied in his know-all voice again.

'OK, you can read about it in the newspapers. But if you let us out of here with no trouble, no funny business with Rachel, I'll give you the biggest scoop of your life.'

'Right Sunshine, you're on,' was his laconic reply.

When we got to the studio Ted was as good as his word. He

arranged the interview with maximum speed and discretion. Rachel put as much melodrama into it as if she was auditioning for the Royal Shakespeare Company. What the viewers would see would be the silhouette of a poor victimised girl pleading for justice against the cold-hearted killer of her lover. It was perfect for the camera. Even her voice, speaking slowly in a low register, was calculated to appeal. If this was trial by television, Dyer was as good as convicted.

When she openly accused Dyer of ordering her boyfriend's killing, I could see Ted's editor whispering nervously to a producer. If they were frightened of the libel laws, too bad. It didn't really matter now whether they broadcast the interview or not. Popeye and Clint would be doing their rounds of Dyer's backers at this very moment.

As far as Dyer was concerned, the interview was overkill.

During the interview Sylvia stood by me. She hadn't spoken once throughout the journey from Northenden, or in the studio. She had the dark wig on and my sunglasses. Not surprisingly, I noticed several of the Alhambra people studying her.

When he'd finished with Rachel, Ted swanned across. 'Do I know you lovie? I'm sure I've seen you somewhere before,' he said, flashing his teeth.

Sylvia rewarded his attention with an enigmatic smile. It was time we made our move. I told Ted I'd phone him one hour or so before the raid to give him time to get set up. As I drove out of the Alhambra studios and up on to Deansgate I was racking my brains for somewhere for us to lie low until after the showdown between Dyer and the Charlies.

Rachel seemed particularly nervous but I put that down to excitement after her TV interview.

'Why don't we go to my flat in Heaton Mersey Dave?' said Sylvia. 'Mike must have enough on his plate now. He won't be calling at my place.'

'Sorry Sylvia, but we don't just have to worry about Dyer. We'll have the press after us as well. It won't take Ted Blake long to work out who you are. I don't think your disguise was too convincing.'

'Well, we can't just drive round all day and I'm not spending another minute in a hotel room,' Sylvia insisted, 'besides I want a change of clothes.'

In the end we drove to Heaton Mersey.

I was too drained to resist and Rachel had gone very pale and quiet. I didn't want her to start hyperventilating. We went by a roundabout route and observed the flat for ten minutes before going in, but my precautions were perfunctory. I felt Dyer and Manteh would have plenty of other things to occupy themselves with at the moment.

Once in the flat, Sylvia headed for her wardrobe.

Rachel said she didn't feel well and went to lie down in the guest bedroom and I settled myself in front of the television. I didn't have long to wait for the news.

An edited clip of Rachel's interview was included, along with a statement about the Thwaites by Nigel Gemelli, as an item at the end of the midday news. It was just part of a brief background piece about crime, drugs and the clubland scene in Manchester. It was all cleverly done . . . 'Allegations have been made against a prominent club owner.' No accusations made directly, but the clear impression left was that there was a case to answer.

The issue the news editor had picked out was the novelty of a private prosecution for murder. Denials of inactivity by a police spokesman left the police looking very bad.

Maybe it was because I was feeling tired but for once I felt a flicker of sympathy for Dyer. He must be desperate now. I could imagine the sweat pouring off his fat red face as he tried to work out his next move.

He shouldn't have killed Thwaite. Arrogance and fear of betrayal had led him into that crime and now he was going to pay for it. His friendship with Benson wouldn't be worth a brass farthing to him now. Benson would have to arrest him, maybe this time Spotty Jock would rat on him to save his own skin.

My musings were interrupted by the sound of the intercom buzzing. Sylvia rushed out of her bedroom to answer.

'It's that friend of yours from the TV, shall I let him in?' she said with an expression of contempt on her face. 'He did a right demolition job on Mike, didn't he? And you still haven't got one scrap of proof that Mike did kill Andy, not one scrap, apart from what Rachel says.'

Sylvia's expression showed what she thought of Rachel's denunciation.

I felt a rush of anger, 'I know more than you think. Dyer and the Scotty went out at 4 a.m. the morning Andy was killed, they didn't come back till much later – both of them drunk. That's when they went to kill Thwaite.'

'Hah, you call that evidence! Mike often went playing poker. How many times do I have to tell you he couldn't kill anyone! He can be all kinds of a swine but he wouldn't need to cut Andy's throat. He'd never do that!'

The door buzzed again.

'Shall I let this creep in? He's not likely to go away.'

'Yeah, let him in. It looks like I need a friend in here.'

'Oh, Dave don't be so childish!' she said. 'I'm not saying Dyer's an angel. I know he tried to put you in the hospital, and he's ready to do the same for me, but he's not a cold-blooded killer. You've got this idea fixed in your head, anybody could have killed Andy, anybody at all.' Sylvia was exasperated and angry but I knew her affection for her former boss was clouding her judgement.

There was a rap on the door and Sylvia let Ted in. His blocky frame filled the doorway. He was on his own. Sylvia gave him a look of concentrated loathing that would have blistered an asbestos fire door. 'Come in, why don't you? Come in and join your dumb friend,' she said, angrily flicking her hair back. 'I've better things to do than sit around solving non-existent crimes with you two.' She went back into her bedroom.

Ted's presence seemed to fill the room. He did take up a lot of space but it was more than that. After the long claustrophobic session I'd had with Rachel and Sylvia I wasn't ready for his domineering ways. His big fleshy red face seemed to loom at me. Ted's head is square and sits on his neck surrounded by a big fold of fat which flops over his shirt collar. He knows how to exploit his appearance when he wants to. He can be genial and caring one minute, then his eyes narrow and he goes for the jugular. That's why he keeps his job at Alhambra despite his many faults.

Now, in his excitement to get a 'big' story his red face was gleaming with sweat. He looked as he had when I'd first met him, like a prop forward going down on a loose ball at the end of a hard game.

'So that's Sylvia Mather. She doesn't seem to be terribly impressed with you, old son. I hope it's nothing to do with me. Look Dave, old fruit, my editor has put me on this story full time, I recognised your friend Mather despite her disguise . . . Well to be honest, a research assistant remembered seeing her at the Paloma. So I guessed you'd be here. Where's the Rankine bird?'

Ted's eyes were peering round the room as he spoke.

I knew what he was looking for, and it wasn't Rachel. 'There's no drink here Ted. Even if there was you're not getting any. I thought we had a deal that you'd leave us alone.'

Not at all put out, Ted took a hip flask from his inside pocket and raised it to his lips. 'That's right, that's why I've come, old buddy boy,' he said between gulps. 'If I could work out who the bimbo in the black wig was, others can. Half the staff in the newsroom are stringers for the nationals. So you can expect a whole gang of them to be door-stepping you any minute now.'

I gave a groan of sheer weariness. Would I ever be home free? Yet again I was on my travels. I went to get Rachel. She looked young and vulnerable, lying there on the bed. When I woke her she was confused and scared. I told her we were moving, she just looked at me wide-eyed. It crossed my mind that she wasn't going to come but she took my hand and hauled herself up.

'Can't we go home? I'm sure they won't be looking for us in Tarn,' she said, in a low, dispirited tone of voice.

'I'm sorry, love. I know it's hard. It'll just be a few more hours now and then you can go wherever you like. Just stick with me for a little while longer, if we go to Tarn we might put your mother in danger.'

I'd no intention of going within five miles of Tarn for a long while, still less of leading a squadron of press and police in that direction to stumble about over the graves of Leon and Trevor.

'Besides, Rachel, you know your father doesn't want his name involved,' I said piously.

'You're right, I was only thinking about myself.' She leant against me, put her head on my shoulder and gave me a hug.

When we got back to the living room, Sylvia was glaring at

Ted Blake. Her expression softened slightly when she looked at me but not by much. 'If you think I'm going on another mystery tour with you Dave, you must be out of your skull. I'm not setting foot outside this flat, and don't try telling me Mike Dyer's after me – he's hardly likely to come here with half of Fleet Street sitting on my doorstep, if what your tame so-called media expert here tells me is true.'

'It's not Fleet Street anymore, lovie. It's Wapping and the Isle —' Ted tried to interject.

'Oh, shut up you lush!' Sylvia yelled, cutting him off. She didn't seem to be very open to persuasion by me and what she'd said was true.

'Sylvia, I've got to go. Rachel and I have had all the publicity we need for today. I'll phone you later and see how you are. Don't forget what we agreed yesterday . . . don't get in touch with him again.'

My worry was that Sylvia might be tempted to arrange a grand reconciliation with Dyer now that she thought he was being victimised.

She kissed me, 'Go on, you big lump, get going. What d'you take me for? I've only room for one man in my life at a time and that's you, you dope.'

My stomach lurched and I felt ill. I could have no doubt now that Sylvia meant what she said despite all her treachery. I knew I wanted Delise back in my life more strongly than ever. I had cooled towards Sylvia, but her feelings had grown more ardent towards me. We were pulling in opposite directions, doomed to misunderstanding.

The attraction I'd felt towards Sylvia had been purely physical. It was a relief to be getting away from her. I'd have to tell her when the time was right. She deserved more than a curt brush-off, but Delise was the only woman for me. If I hadn't been so jaded after a night's stake-out on Rochdale I'd have gone after her when she left me that letter. It wasn't just that I was missing Delise's services as a partner in detection or as a lover. Delise was the only person who really understood me and took me at my own valuation. I needed her.

Sylvia was a seething mass of contradictions. I knew instinctively that if I tied myself to her in any way she would bring me down. I could never fit into the pattern she would want to make. I cursed myself for making love to her at the Garden of Kashmir. If I hadn't done that I could have continued with the high moral line towards her that I'd had yesterday morning after her revelations of deceit.

On my way to the car, Ted grabbed my arm and tried to get me to go with him. I knew he wanted to get Rachel on her own. What he'd said about warning me about the press pack was a load of bull. He could have phoned if that was all he wanted. Quite likely too, he was the only person who'd worked out that Sylvia Mather was my companion. I pushed him into his car with unnecessary roughness and made him drive off before taking the opposite direction. I took a winding route through Stockport and then back on the M53 towards Chorlton.

Once in Manchester, I drove to the McNeil's house by the most direct route, the risk was surely slight at this time of day. Margaret was in and, despite my previous escapade of breaking into her home, she was glad to see me.

'So this is Rachel. Come in love. You look as if you need a rest. What have you been doing to the girl, David? She doesn't look at all well,' Margaret said with professional concern. I explained that Rachel was asthmatic. 'So, of course, you'll have been getting her highly excited and worked up like you have with Jim,' she said, pursing her lips in disapproval. 'Come and lie down on the couch love, and I'll make you some soup.'

Even while Margaret spoke, I heard the dogs start howling in the back room. The hairs on the back of my neck rose and I looked at her nervously. She laughed, 'Yes, they're here! So you'd better make sure you behave yourself this time!'

Margaret settled Rachel down in her living room and in no time at all she bustled back with two bowls of chicken soup. Rachel hadn't lost her appetite despite her wan appearance and she made short work of the soup and of a second helping as well.

'That was all to do with you on the news, wasn't it?' Margaret asked me.

I nodded but didn't reply and Margaret took the hint that I didn't want to discuss events in Rachel's presence. We made polite conversation, mostly about the dogs. Margaret didn't take the risk of bringing them into the room, but we could hear their claws scratching about in the kitchen.

The day was beginning to drag. Once Dyer had been arrested and 'Operation Sledgehammer' had taken care of Manteh and the Charlies I could send Rachel home and my life could return to its usual predictable routine.

Suppose it wouldn't return to the old pattern, suppose Delise really had had enough of me? Well there could be no question of any kind of partnership with Sylvia. If she wanted to build an empire in Club City she'd have to get on with it without my help. Whatever sort of relationship Sylvia wanted with me – hot, cold or lukewarm – I'd have to end it now. I must find some way to let her down gently. Maybe Margaret could think of something.

Thinking of Delise and the old routine reminded me of my expenses. As a distraction I got out a piece of paper and began working out how much Elsworth owed me, the expenses on clothes alone should come to a small fortune.

Sylvia's attitude still bugged me.

She was so sure Dyer was innocent, so certain. It struck me for the first time that the only reason she could be absolutely sure of his innocence was if she'd topped Andy herself. No, that was ridiculous. I'd crossed Sylvia off my list of suspects a long time ago; still, on her own admission she'd been involved with Leon and he hadn't been too worried by the prospect of bumping me off.

Yes, perhaps Leon had been to Clydesdale Road that morning. If I could get in easily then so could he. Did he even need to, if, as Sylvia said, Andy knew him? Andy might have let his own killer in. Then after doing the job Leon reported to Manteh, who told him to go back and make it look like suicide. That was when Leon had seen me slinking out of the back door in my socks.

But this was all speculation, I'd been through it all a dozen times before. The murder could have been committed by Elsworth or even by Dee. Benson had a motive if Andy had been poking around into the affairs of the NMP, and he'd certainly done all he could to suppress a murder inquiry. Then again, it might have been a completely random killing by some crazy junkie.

I shook my head, if I went on like this I'd be suspecting everybody, including the McNeil's dogs.

I'd been hired to find a missing girl and I'd done that. The odds were still very long on Dyer being the murderer. He had had the time, opportunity and a good motive. If Popeye and Dad's friends were to be believed, he'd killed before. I had a witness who'd heard him threaten Andy. He'd certainly threatened me and gone out of his way to carry out his threat when he thought I was a business rival.

It must have been him, you just can't prove these things in real life as straightforwardly as in an Agatha Christie novel . . . Look at all the miscarriages of justice the police and legal profession had been responsible for lately.

'Dave, just give me a hand with these chairs in the hall will you?' Margaret asked me. When I got out in the hall she closed the living-room door and started rattling chairs loudly.

'Sorry, Dave I just had to speak to you. What is the matter with that girl? She's not at all well,' she said anxiously.

'What do you mean? I told you she had asthma. She's got her inhaler with her,' I answered woodenly.

'No, it's more than that. Is she on something? Has she been acting strangely?' Margaret persisted.

'She might have snorted coke, but not for a few days,' I replied.

'That's it then, you want to be careful with her. They can get very paranoid when they're coming off coke. Just don't do anything to upset her. She should be with her family, you know.'

Having given her professional advice Margaret led me back to the living room.

No sooner had I sat down than the doorbell rang. The dogs barked, Rachel looked at me in alarm and I pulled out the Beretta.

'Just stay where you are, it could be the postman, it could be anyone,' Margaret said calmly. I let her go to the door but stood behind her with the gun ready.

Through the frosted safety glass I could see the rugged features of Michael Rice. 'You'd better let him in Margaret,' I said.

'I thought I'd find you here,' he said cheekily. 'I've been looking everywhere for you. You're responsible for that pantomime on the TV news aren't you? Mr Sinclair's really pissed off with you. He thinks you might have compromised "Sledgehammer".' He sat down without invitation and picked up the half-finished bowl of soup I'd left.

'Have you got any more of this, Missus? I love chicken soup, Jewish penicillin! Just what I need to keep me going.'

He turned to Rachel, who'd now got some colour in her cheeks again. 'You must be the lass all the fuss has been about. Is he looking after you all right?'

Compared with the glum specimen I'd met last night Rice was now as full of crap as a Nigerian con-man. Even his bruises weren't as livid as they'd been.

Rachel nodded and smiled at him as Margaret hurried off to provide yet another uninvited guest with soup.

Soon he was quaffing his soup, which he mixed with torn-up pieces of bread. There was something unstoppable about the guy. I could see why Sinclair liked him. Speaking with his mouth full, he said, 'Sinclair wants me to bring you in, but there's no great hurry. He says we can't afford to risk you shooting your mouth off to someone about "Sledgehammer".'

I took the opportunity of him filling his mouth again to respond. 'What makes him think I would blab? I'm not going anywhere until Manteh, Dyer and the whole crew are banged up.'

'Interesting you should mention Dyer, Benson himself is out looking for him with an armed response team,' a spray of soup particles accompanied Rice's reply.

The armed response team was the recent innovation of having a van-load of heavily armed coppers cruising round the inner city on the off-chance that they could respond to armed robbers.

'Yeah, the word is that Dyer's armed, so Benson's in the van with the response team waiting to zoom after him when he's spotted. It's been one hell of a while since Benson took an interest in an actual operation.'

I looked at my watch, it was twenty to four.

'I might be able to help you there, Rice, if you can forget about finding me until tomorrow,' I said.

I exchanged a glance with Rachel, she nodded. She knew what I was going to say.

'Spit it out Cunane, what do you know?'

'Dyer will be waiting to meet me in front of the G-Mex Centre at four o'clock. He thinks I'm going to be doing a deal with the Charlies.'

I thought he was going to hit me, 'Christ! Cunane, nothing's ever simple with you is it? What the hell would the Charlies want with you unless you've sold us out.' He pulled out his radio, then angrily put it back.

'Bloody thing's useless, they listen in the whole time. I knew I should never have trusted a civilian.' He turned aggressively to Margaret. 'Can I use your phone, love?'

She showed him into the hall and he quickly relayed the news to Sinclair. Then he bounced back into the living room.

'On your feet Cunane, you're coming with me. If Dyer's expecting to see you, then he bloody well will see you.'

'No you don't understand. I never intended to be there. I just hoped . . .'

'You just hoped there'd be a second Peterloo Massacre in which all your enemies would be wiped out for you,' he said. 'God! I've got to hand it to you Cunane, you're ambitious. You're not as small-time as you look. I bet it was you who arranged all these attacks on Dyer's clubs wasn't it?'

'I'm not arguing with you, I'm staying here. I'm being paid to look after this girl, and that's what I'm going to do,' I answered, raising my voice.

Rice lost control completely.

He grabbed the lapels of my jacket with both hands to haul me out of the door. I smashed my arms up between his, broke his grip, and shoved him back. He tripped over the low table he'd been eating soup off, but as he hit the floor I could see him going for the ankle holster where he kept his pistol. I could have kicked him in the balls and stopped him but I didn't want to smash up the McNeil's living room.

'Don't do anything foolish Rice,' I yelled. 'I'll come with you.'

The dogs had started their usual frenzied baying. They'd be through the kitchen door in seconds by the sound of it. Margaret rushed out of the room, grabbing Rachel's hand and pulling her along as she went.

'Go on, we'll be all right,' Margaret shouted.

I stretched my hand to Rice, still on the floor fumbling with his trouser leg. By the time he could have got his pathetic pea-shooter out a real villain would have had him dead and buried. My reward for kindness was that he grabbed my arm and twisted it up my back. I could have countered by raking the inside of his ankle with the back of my heel but instead I relaxed completely.

'Look, I've said I'll come with you. Calm down. You tripped yourself up, you fool.'

Not releasing his grip, but slackening the pressure slightly, Rice bundled me out of the house and into the front passenger seat of his clapped-out Cortina.

I was glad Margaret and Rachel weren't there to watch.

Rice did one of his racing starts away from the kerb and we charged off towards Wilbraham Road and then down the Parkway in the direction of the G-Mex.

'What're you going to do you idiot? Drive right up on to the forecourt and stake me out for Dyer? At least drive into the underground car park.'

Rice bared his teeth at me. 'You'd deserve it if I did stake you out, you tricky swine. No, Sinclair says you just need to show your face long enough for Dyer to see you and then Benson can have his big moment of glory and arrest him. You'll jut be there long enough to let the dog see the rabbit.'

It looked as if his comments about the Peterloo Massacre were about to come true. My little plan had come unstuck. I was going to be the meat in a sandwich between two savage groups.

We drove into the car park. It had once been an underground warehouse for the Midland Railway Company's station, which still stood above us, transformed into an exhibition hall.

God! What an exhibition there was going to be in a few minutes. At the original Peterloo, on this very same spot in 1819, the soldiers had guns and the mob only had stones.

This time there'd be three sides, all armed to the teeth.

We had to go to the lower level as the upper level was full. When we got out, I looked round warily. There was no sign of the Posse. Rice took out his radio.

'Damn, I'm not getting any signal at all,' he muttered.

I could have told him that would happen.

'You'll just have to go on up to the forecourt and dodge back down here if you see him,' he ordered.

We started off. The massive brick arches deadened all sound. There was a lifeless and musty feel to the air, like in a deep cave. My throat felt constricted, I undid my collar.

'Getting windy, are you Cunane? You're not going to bottle out of this one,' said my companion.

We passed the vaults, each separate one holding about eight cars, my eyes straining to detect any movement. There was a long line of vaults before the stairs leading up to the daylight. I was expecting to be jumped at any moment. I undid my jacket and pulled it back for a quick draw.

Rice suddenly grabbed hold of my arm, 'You crazy bastard, you really are expecting a bloody massacre, aren't you?'

I didn't speak but he knelt down and retrieved his pop gun from his ankle holster. He pulled the radio from his inside pocket and began calling for assistance but all he got out of it was static.

'Who's bottling out now then, Rice? We'll have to go on or Dyer'll clear off. It's five past four already.'

'Well move it then, get up to the forecourt and I'll try to cover you myself,' he said.

We ran, our feet making no sound on the black asphalt roadway. We came to the exit, there was a motionless escalator and a steel stairway beside it. I ran up the steel staircase, my feet making muffled ringing sounds. Rice made no noise at all going up the escalator.

I emerged cautiously from the gloomy cavern and, hugging the side of the exhibition building, peered round the corner on to the downward sloping forecourt of the exhibition area.

I looked behind me. Rice was signalling frantically. His radio was working, he pointed down the road which ran between a new office building and the Midland Hotel.

'Benson and his team are down there in that contractor's van. They'll see everything,' he whispered from concealment.

I nodded and crept out towards the closed doors of the G-Mex building, scanning left and right desperately. There was nobody moving, no Posse, no Dyer. It looked as if the rendezvous I'd arranged was going to be a flop.

I dared to release my breath.

A woman with black hair and sunglasses dashed out from the back of the Midland Hotel. She ran across the road and on to the cobbled paving of the forecourt, looking straight at me.

It was Sylvia wearing her stupid disguise. I ran towards her to get her out of the way. We met in the centre of the forecourt.

'Oh Dave, I had to be certain that you weren't doing a deal to hand Rachel over. I'm so glad—'

Just as she spoke a grey Ford Scorpion pulled to the halt sign at the one-way street which ran between the G-Mex site and the Free Trade Hall. It had tinted windows. With great deliberation the passenger window slowly opened, a shotgun poked out and a shot was fired.

Sylvia caught the full blast in her back, she was blown right into my arms. I went down. I rolled over her, trying to shield her.

The door of the car opened and Dyer stepped out, aiming his gun for a second shot. As he did so the back doors of the contractor's van parked down the adjoining street were flung open. Two blue overalled policemen jumped out, levelling handguns at Dyer. There must have been a challenge, or maybe Jock, who was driving the Scorpion, spoke; but Dyer turned, took in the armed police with Benson right behind them, and throwing away his gun, hoisted his arms in surrender.

Benson tapped the officer on the shoulder with his chief constable's swagger stick. Both policemen fired simultaneously. They hit Dyer in the head maybe four times, the position of the car masking the easier body shots.

Jock tried to rev. the car and they shot him too, four times through the closed car window.

Behind me I could hear Rice swearing.

I looked at Sylvia, her head and face were uninjured but she'd taken the full blast meant for Rachel right in the centre of her back. I didn't have to look twice to see that she was dead. The black wig that had made Dyer think he had Rachel in his sights had come loose.

I released her and stood up. The irony of the circumstances struck me painfully. Her last words had been to express relief that I hadn't betrayed Rachel. She hadn't trusted me any more than I had trusted her. It was too painful to look at her. I looked up at the sky – a typical silver-grey Manchester sky. There was no meaning or purpose to it.

Rice rushed to me, 'Sweet Jesus, who is it? I thought it was the girl you were with earlier. She took the shot meant for you.'

He looked down at Sylvia, then at me. 'It's Dyer's assistant, isn't it? She meant something to you, I can see that. God I'm sorry, Cunane. I can't understand it. They had all the time in the world to cut him off,' he said, gesturing in the direction of the swarming policemen who were now coming out of concealment towards Dyer's car from all directions. 'It's Benson, he gave the word too late,' Rice said bitterly.

He held my arm for a moment and then slipped his tattered jacket off and placed it over Sylvia's face. None of his colleagues had yet come towards us, they seemed to be waiting for the word from Benson.

Eventually Benson and a couple of uniformed officers strode towards us.

Benson was smacking his swagger stick into his gloved hand, his little moustache twitching nervously on his upper lip. He bent over the corpse and, lifting the jacket, flicked the wig away revealing Sylvia's blond hair.

To my amazement, he folded the wig up and put it in his pocket. 'It's his mistress, isn't it?' Benson said. 'What was her name Cunane? You would know it. Dyer was obviously hunting her down, she must have betrayed him.'

I swung at him with all the strength in my body, but his sergeant had been reading my body language because he kneed me in the groin before I could connect. I went down, and he followed up with a boot in my ribs.

'Get him out of here, Rice, he's just a bystander. Get him away before I'm forced to take more drastic action.'

Picking up his jacket with one hand and pulling me with the other Rice obeyed his Chief Constable. Somehow we stumbled back down the steep stairs. From a long way away I could hear my own voice gasping. 'It was an execution Rice. He meant to kill Dyer whatever happened. You saw it.'

Although I was deeply shocked, part of me was still expecting more trouble from the Posse. I was tense. Rice didn't speak to me at all, he just kept up a steady stream of curses under his breath.

Then I realised. The Posse weren't going to turn up. They must have discovered that their funds were frozen and they'd probably already killed Manteh. None of his hocus pocus would save him if they thought he'd ripped them off.

So Manteh was gone, and Dyer was gone.

Dyer had probably died thinking he'd rubbed out Rachel, the only person who could testify against him.

Why did Sylvia have to turn up? Was she really there to stop me turning Rachel over to the Charlies? Or was she still hoping to get back into Dyer's good books by fingering me?

I'd never know now.

28

Rice dropped me back at McNeil's.

He wasn't a man to give sympathy or show much feeling, but he said 'Bloody rough luck, mate,' as I got out of the car.

I didn't feel numb, I didn't feel shocked, I didn't feel grief . . . I didn't feel anything. I was a man in a void, a man walking in the calm eye of a storm.

Margaret stopped me at the door. 'Dave! What's the matter? You look dreadful. What's this on your jacket? It's flecked with blood! Are you hurt?'

I didn't trust myself to speak. She led me into the living room I'd left such a short time before. I sat down. The weird feeling of being at the centre of everything and of looking at the world through the wrong end of a telescope persisted. Margaret pushed a glass of brandy into my hands. I looked down at it and then drained it in one swallow.

Both Margaret and Rachel were looking at me with the most intent expressions.

'It's all over. Dyer's dead, he killed Sylvia,' I said.

Rachel covered her face with her hands, like a small child, and began to sob. She wasn't hysterical, just weeping quietly; no great dramatics.

Margaret hadn't known Sylvia, her face assumed a professional attitude of concern. 'How did it happen?' she asked quietly. 'It's better for you if you can talk about it, David.'

'It was a set-up. I went to lure Dyer out of hiding and Sylvia appeared instead. She said she'd come to see that I wasn't really going to hand Rachel over to the Charlies. Dyer was there, the police must have seen him going down those narrow streets, but they just let him shoot Sylvia. Then they gunned Dyer down too, but after he'd surrendered. Benson knew just what he was doing, he'd have let Dyer shoot me as well but Dyer was just a little too slow about it to make it look credible.'

'How dreadful for you, but why did Dyer shoot Sylvia? I thought she worked for him.' Margaret asked gently.

I looked down at Rachel, with her head in her hands and

her dark hair spilling down in front of her face. 'I'll never know now, the shot might have been meant for me, or he might just have been mad,' I said.

Rachel continued with her weeping. Margaret looked at her anxiously. 'Hadn't you better take her home if everything's all over?' she asked.

'I suppose I better had. Come on Rachel, we'll go to my flat and get your father to come and pick you up.' While Margaret tended to the still tearful Rachel I put our bags in the car. Margaret kissed me warmly and hugged Rachel, then we got in the car.

I drove sedately to Thornleigh Court and parked the hired Fiesta in my garage. We were intercepted by Fiona Salway on the stairs. She must've had radar. I wasn't ready for another sob session with her, so I said I'd see her later. She gave Rachel a curious look and retreated to her flat.

My own flat was in good condition. The door looked battered but everything inside was in order. Although it was great to be back inside my own four walls the rooms had an air of unreality about them, as if I was seeing them for the first time. I left Rachel to phone in private and went to freshen myself up.

When I came back into my living room Rachel was sobbing again. I made her a cup of tea.

The sudden death of Sylvia had crystallised all sorts of feelings and ideas in me. My intuition for recognising a villain had always been strong. I am convinced that it exists; perhaps it's an inborn instinct from two generations of coppers in the family, or it could be my upbringing surrounded by the heavy boots of police but more likely it's the product of a childhood misspent in watching countless crime films and TV series.

When I'd been on that beach at Southport abducting Rachel with her mother's assistance my instinct had been that there was something wrong. I'd thought I was being spied on, but it wasn't that. I now felt that whoever had killed Thwaite, it must be somebody close to Rachel.

Sylvia had died trying to convince me that it wasn't Dyer. She had been right. Dyer had deserved to die a thousand times over for his actions, but that didn't include killing Thwaite. I was the one who had provoked Dyer into action, I was the one who'd provoked the NMP and their hitman Benson into executing him as surely as if I'd pulled the trigger myself.

My instinct was telling me now that whoever was coming to collect Rachel was in fact the killer. She knew who it was, it was someone close to her. That was why she'd been so anxious to support me in blaming Dyer. Rachel must have contacted whoever it was to tell them the coast was clear. It could be Manteh in search of whatever it was he wanted from Rachel, or one or both of her parents, or even Lisa and Spragg.

'Come on girl, snap out of it now. It's no use going on like this. These things happen. Dyer was a violent man, Sylvia should have kept clear of him, but she wouldn't believe he was a murderer.'

'She was right. He didn't kill Andy. I did,' she said and carried right on with her snivelling.

I sat down heavily in the chair opposite her, I couldn't believe what I was hearing.

'It was me, I couldn't stand any more of his bullying and blackmailing,' she wailed. Her face was streaming with tears and there was mucous running from her nose. Her eyes were red and puffy. She covered her face with her hands.

I leaned across and took her hands in mine and gently pulled them away from her face so that she had to look at me when she spoke.

'You're going to have to explain yourself Rachel.' I didn't speak harshly but I thought she was raving, the shock of Sylvia's death had unhinged her.

She looked me in the face and began to explain.

'When I started at the Metropolitan University my parents wanted me to stay at home and travel in with Daddy every day but I wanted my independence. So I managed to get a place at Abbotsford Hall. I wanted to be just like any other student. Mummy and Daddy were so protective, I felt I couldn't breathe.' She'd stopped weeping, but she paused to rub her eyes.

'Well, I met Andy Thwaite, Lisa Goody and Kevin Spragg. They were into the nightclub scene and they took me with them. It wasn't long before I was sleeping with Andy. He was so mature and he seemed to have contacts all over Manchester, I suppose I was impressed. He did drugs, just a little pot or a line of coke when we were making love and E's when we went on a gig.'

I could feel my stomach turning over: so Thwaite had never broken his youthful connection with drugs. His old man must have been lying or self-deceived. I got out the scotch and poured myself a glass.

Rachel went on with her revelations. She looked up at me shyly, 'When I first went with Andy I wasn't a virgin, I hadn't been quite as sheltered as Mummy and Daddy thought, but it seemed to worry Andy. He kept coming back to it, "How had I lost my virginity?", it really mattered to him and he kept going on about what a wicked family the Elsworths were. His family knew Daddy's from Yorkshire, he was obsessed with Daddy and with my virginity. In the end he made a tape of me saying that Daddy had raped me when I was thirteen.'

There must have been something in my expression which made her pause. She started wailing again.

'Look Rachel, you'd better tell me the whole rotten story. I'll never rest unless I know it and you need to tell someone. No one will ever know. How could I show myself up by telling the story?'

She stood up and went over to the window. For once the weather was sympathetic to my mood. Masses of grey clouds were forming up over the Meadows. It would rain later. Rachel was looking down into the road. She didn't look much like a murderess.

'Daddy never touched me really,' she went on. 'I used to tease Mummy sometimes that I would run away with him and leave her on her own but of course he never would have. I was such a little fool. I was drunk when I made the tape. Andy said it would inspire him to write a rap or a lyric.'

She gave me a sad grin, 'Once he'd got the tape Andy was like a dog with two tails. He and Kevin got in touch with their dealer and that man Leon came round. Andy promised to find a safe way to launder their money by blackmailing my father. They were very impressed . . .'

'I'll be they were, how much did they pay him?' I prompted.

'Oh plenty, but money was never the main thing. It would have been better if money *was* all he wanted.

'Not that he didn't find ways to spend it. He moved out of

hall into a flat and bought masses of equipment. Then he bought a new van and we got another flat in Southport for the weekends because he didn't want to draw too much attention to himself in Manchester. He gave Kevin Spragg and Lisa plenty of money too, but they just spent it on booze and drugs and clubbing every night.'

'And your stepfather? Surely he could have gone to the police,' I interjected.

'No, he thought the police would be bound to believe the tape, no matter how much I denied it. Even if he wasn't prosecuted the publicity when they put Andy on trial would mean he would have to resign. He loves his job. It would all be a terrible shock for Mummy.'

She was right. Elsworth would never risk his reputation in the courts. The smell of this story was just too fragrant to stay out of the sensitive nostrils of some rat after a headline, whatever effort was made to protect Elsworth's identity.

'When did all this start?' I asked.

'About the middle of November. They just wanted Daddy to take small sums at first and only every few weeks. But then when they found they could trust him, he was given more and more. He was having to take suitcases just full of twenty- and fifty-pound notes. It wasn't worth their while to send small stuff. The money they had was incredible. They were frightened they'd lose it all if there was a raid, and of course if any of them were convicted money they had in bank accounts here would be lost as well. The idea of secret accounts being opened for them by a highly respected banker must have seemed like a dream come true.' Rachel explained all this in a perfectly rational voice.

'What about Andy?'

'Andy was crazy, he was getting plenty from Leon but he wanted something else. He wanted to take over Dyer's clubs. There was no way Daddy could have done it, even if he'd wanted to. NMP, the company that had backed Dyer, would never give up control. They were in trouble because the property market had caved in. Andy wouldn't listen. We told him he could start his own club but he had to have the Paloma.

'The more Andy was told he couldn't have the Paloma, the more it seemed to madden him. When we wouldn't do anything he went back to Manteh and threatened that he would pull the plug on their operation if they didn't do something. They made a few moves to keep him quiet but they weren't serious about getting rid of Dyer. They started cultivating someone on the inside of Dyer's operation. That was Sylvia. She'd lost a lot of money gambling and was desperate. Leon Grant was her contact with the Charlies.'

I went to refill my glass. 'Do you think I might have one?' Rachel asked timidly. I poured some whisky and went in the kitchen for water, but when I got back she was sipping the neat whisky.

'I think Andy was mad at the end. He knew he was never going to get the clubs. He started playing spiteful tricks. He got me expelled from the hall of residence. He sent me off to Southport to upset Daddy. He phoned me to say he'd either be in control of the clubs or he'd have ruined Daddy by the time I came back.

'I'd had enough. I couldn't stand it any more. I came back from Southport, very early in the morning, went round to his flat and cut his throat with his own razor. He kept one to trim his designer beard. Then I went back to Southport.'

'What, just like that? Are you sure you're not imagining things? You wouldn't be covering up for your father, would you?' I said numbly.

It was just too hard to believe that this girl could have done for Thwaite just like that. Why, this morning she'd given a wonderful performance on television to accuse Dyer of the crime she was now confessing to. She looked so innocent and weak.

'No. I didn't tell Daddy anything. It was easy, I just got in the van and drove over before it got light, went into the flat and did it. He never even woke up, just gurgled and flopped about a bit, and that was it. It was easier than dissecting rabbits at school. I got in the van and drove back to Southport. I burned the tape and threw the razor into the Mersey.'

'Well, what about Leon? Where did he come into it?' I asked.

'Oh, what do you think? He just wanted Daddy to go on laundering his filthy money! They were perfectly happy to go on blackmailing Daddy, this time because I'd done a murder. You see they knew it was me straightaway. Leon always called round at Andy's early in the morning to give him his stuff for the day. He found Andy. It could only have been me. They knew they hadn't done it, Daddy was in Brussels and no one else would have wanted to kill Andy,' she said calmly, almost with an air of satisfaction.

'Just a minute, I don't follow this. Did Daddy know what you'd done?' I asked. I noticed that as Rachel progressed with her confession she was looking better all the time. Her tears had dried up and her eyes had lost the puffy look. She was returning to her role as an innocent young country girl. We might have been discussing the latest episode of *The Archers*.

'They phoned Daddy at his hotel in Brussels and told him. I phoned him as well. I have no secrets from Daddy. He told the Charlies that they'd have to get everything cleared up, but nobody reckoned that you'd come blundering on to the scene so quickly.'

'Oh thanks. So your father knew that you were in Southport even before the murder?' I said.

'Of course he did.'

'Why the hell did your father hire me to find you the day before the murder took place? What did he want me for if not to take the blame for what he knew was going to happen? And why didn't you just go home and resume your normal life when you'd done it?' I asked angrily.

'I would've done in a few days when everything had blown over. Daddy only hired you to put Mummy's mind at rest. We didn't tell Mummy anything. Daddy wanted Mummy to think something was being done but he wasn't worried about me himself. He didn't think you'd find me and, of course, he didn't know what was going to happen to Andy.'

I'd only her word for that. It was just as likely that the decision to dispose of Thwaite had been a mutual one between father and daughter.

'So you were in touch with your father all the time? Never missing at all?' I repeated incredulously.

'Yes, and the Charlies knew where I was. They didn't want you or Mummy to find me though. They thought either of you would have gone to the police if you'd got the truth out of me. Of course that would have ruined their game.'

'Did Sylvia know?' I asked. The colour had come back into Rachel's cheeks now. She was breathing normally.

'I don't think so, but she may have had some idea from Leon. I think she knew it wasn't safe for you to go looking for me. She didn't want you to find me.'

'Why did you keep accusing Dyer?'

'No, that was you Dave. You were so determined to find someone to blame for the murder. I couldn't let you think it was Daddy or Leon because if anything came out in the open then all I'd done would have been for nothing. I thought Dyer would be able to look after himself.

'You see, he could never have said anything to you or the police about what Andy had done. He knew nothing about it. And now Leon seems to have gone to ground somewhere, so if he stays away there's no one to tell anybody anything is there? Except me, you and Daddy.'

I must have looked uncomfortable as I squirmed in my seat. Rachel mistook my embarrassment for something else: she thought I was going to turn her in.

Andy Thwaite had probably been messing around with the drugs he'd been feeding to Rachel. Speed and cocaine was a lethal mixture to give to anyone. It could turn destructive feelings into suicidal ones and Dee had hinted that Rachel had been destructive as a child. Thwaite ought to have known that feeding her cocaine and speed was like sending a kiddy to play with a box of matches in a gunpowder factory.

Perhaps he did know . . . The frequent result of these drug cocktails was that the user topped him or herself in despair. Perhaps Thwaite was hoping that Rachel would kill herself.

He'd paid the price for his mistake. Rachel, contradicting all that I'd thought earlier about her spinelessness, had been individualistic enough to reverse the usual course of events and do for her supplier instead. The police had been right all along. Thwaite had died as a result of amphetamines; but not any he'd taken himself.

Dyer had paid the price for being ignorant and arrogant. If he'd given a display of conventional grief when I told him about Thwaite's death I never would have suspected him. But he had to show how callous and hard he was in a way that would have aroused anyone's suspicions.

Sylvia had simply paid the price for trusting him too much.

Leon and Manteh may have thought that I was trying to move in on their money-laundering racket. Harold had been so anxious that I didn't meet Dee. Had he been told to see that I didn't? They must have feared that I was gathering the pieces of the jigsaw. Harold had probably warned them that his wife was getting suspicious about the frequent trips. Manteh must have credited me with a lot greater skill than I possessed. In his dog-eat-dog world anyone getting too close to the meal ticket earned himself a one-way trip to a building site.

I must have been sitting in silence for a long time. Rachel's voice penetrated the fog of self-pity I was surrounding myself with.

'You wouldn't tell anyone would you Dave?' she said. 'I never meant any harm to come to anyone except Andy, and what's happened is as much your fault as mine. It's all worked out for the best really.'

Rachel thought I was about to turn her in to the police. What a joke! How could I tell anyone?

'No, Rachel, I'll never tell anyone that I've been a perfect bloody fool. As you say, everything's worked out for the best. Yes, you must be really buzzing,' I said bitterly.

She didn't take the remark as sarcasm. She appeared to think it was perfectly normal to bump off your boyfriend and expect to escape any consequences. Rachel now seemed completely composed, no more tears or upset. She was flashing that enigmatic half-smile at me, the same one she'd had in the wedding photo. She and her father had planned everything. I was just there to help keep Mummy in the dark and help provide an alibi if necessary.

I remembered what Dee had said about Rachel's hunger for perfection, her contempt for failure in others. She must have been the one who'd transformed Thwaite into a top-line DJ. Then she must have realised that he was just a grubby little no-hoper, a blackmailer from a clapped-out Yorkshire mill town. The memory of her stepfather's earlier contempt for Thwaite must have been like a blow in the face to her. How accurate Harold's contempt must have seemed when she woke up to what Thwaite was. Thwaite the scumbag who was trying to wreck the career of the one man she really admired: the only man who was as perfect as herself.

Her underlying paranoid tendencies, heightened by rage and drugs, had been enough to push her over the edge into murder. Yet she'd been so cool about it, so intelligent. She'd arranged to be out of the way while Daddy managed the clean-up operation.

She must have been startled when Dee and I turned up on Southport beach and hauled her off to the moors. The phone call to Lisa had probably been to ask her to lay in a stock of cocaine as well as to alert the Charlies and Daddy.

Margaret had warned me to be careful not to upset Rachel – how true! I'd better be careful to keep her away from any sharp cutlery. If I gave her cause to fear that I'd turn her and her Daddy in she was capable of dealing with me as decisively as she'd dealt with Thwaite. She made the strutting Dyer and menacing Manteh look like a pair of posturing amateurs.

'I know you're upset about Sylvia, but you'll find someone else won't you Dave?' she said with a kindly smile.

I stood up so quickly Rachel jumped back in fright. I went into the kitchen and started cleaning the oven. I pulled out all the sides of the oven and got them into the sink and began scouring every last trace of grease off them. How clever I'd been! Elsworth had only hired me because I was expected to be incompetent! I banged away furiously. The noise coming from the kitchen must have been sufficient to deter Rachel from entering. She really thought everything had worked out well, like the plot of an Australian soap opera.

I was vaguely aware of the doorbell ringing but I was too furious to answer. Then the kitchen door opened and there was Elsworth himself.

The sight of him standing in my sanctuary made my stomach heave. Yet I knew I had to be very careful. He smiled his best banker's smile at me.

'Rachel tells me you're upset at the turn of events. You're not going to do anything foolish are you? It's all worked out so well. Look at the paper.'

He held out a copy of the evening paper. '**WANTED BOSS KILLED IN SHOOTOUT**' read the headline. 'Look what it says here,' Elsworth said eagerly, pointing to the paragraph at the end of the page:

> Police have announced that they are not seeking anyone else in connection with the mysterious death of Paloma DJ Andy Thwaite following the death of Mike Dyer, previously sought in connection with the slaying.

'You don't need to worry Mr. Elsworth, I'm not going to go round bragging about my part in this. Who would believe me anyway? Rachel thinks it's all worked out very well.'

'Naturally you're tired and upset, it's a normal reaction Cunane. I'm sure when you get back on to an even keel you'll see everything has worked out well, all the loose ends seem to be tied up. I'm more than satisfied with your services. I'm prepared to be generous in the circumstances.'

He took out his cheque book and, resting on the kitchen counter, wrote out a cheque and handed it to me.

I picked it up, 'You do surprise me. I thought you liked to do these things with a cash payment.'

I wanted to throw his filthy cheque away, even though it was the largest fee I'd ever received, £20,000. No doubt as a true banker Elsworth had found some way to divert part of the Charlies' profits into his own pocket.

I looked from Elsworth's smiling face to that of his daughter standing behind him. Her face was calm but her expression was oddly unfocused. I knew that to rip the cheque up and throw it in the bin would be to sign my own death warrant.

'I don't expect we'll be meeting again Mr Elsworth,' I said. 'I can't say it's been the sort of job I'd want to do every day of the week but here's your daughter, safe and sound, and as you say, things'll look better in the morning. Remember me to Mrs Elsworth won't you.'

I held out my hand and Elsworth shook it warmly, no doubt feeling as relieved as I was that he didn't need to unleash his lethal stepchild again. They departed rapidly.

I wasn't left to sulk about my problems for long. Shortly after the departure of the Elsworths Finbar Salway rang to say he was coming up. I felt obligated to him so I didn't put him off.

He came into the lounge and saw the whisky bottle on the table.

'I don't mind if I do, old man,' he said. 'Make it a stiff one. I've got something awkward to confess.'

'No, I've had enough confessions today. Go to church and tell your priest,' I begged.

'No, no really. Don't joke. You know what you said about a spy reporting your movements. I found out who it is . . . It's Fiona.'

I must have looked startled. Finbar swallowed his whisky and poured us both another.

'A smartly dressed young man convinced her he was from the police and that she'd be helping to protect you if she phoned him and told him when you were coming in and out. He showed her a warrant card and everything. He didn't offer any money. She found he wasn't from the police when she phoned them yesterday. I'm very, very sorry Dave. I'll make it up to you any way I can,' he said.

He looked at me nervously.

'That's all right Finbar, think nothing of it. People deceive me all the time, they can take anyone in . . . Fiona mustn't blame herself. Honest people are the easiest to trick. If you don't mind going now, I've had a very heavy day and I just want to be on my own for a while.'

He got up smartly, downed his drink and went.

I turned the volume switch on the telephone down to zero and ran myself a bath. I needed to feel clean. I took the bottle into the bathroom with me and fell asleep in the water. There were no nightmarish dreams to plague me this time. When I woke in the cold bath I put on a robe and fixed myself a meal. Then I sat in my living room and watched the daylight fade.

When it had just turned fully dark, about eleven-thirty, the phone rang. It was Delise.

'Dave, I've just been reading in the paper about Sylvia Mather. You've been with her all that time since I saw you last, haven't you?' she asked.

I felt a powerful response to her words. It was as if the feelings which had been dammed up since the death of my wife two and a half years ago had been released by the death of Sylvia Mather. Thwaite had paid a price, Dyer had paid a price, even Elsworth had had to cough up some of his ill-gotten cash. Now I would have to pay a price. I would have to forfeit the affection of the one woman I really wanted to be with.

'Yes, Delise I was with her at least part of the time,' I said sadly.

'Was she very special to you Dave?'

'She wouldn't have been anything at all if you hadn't left me. I've been missing you. I need you. I know that sounds easy to say now, but it's the honest truth.

'I'm on my way round. I'll be with you in half an hour. I'm at my Auntie's in Blackley. You haven't changed the locks or anything have you?' Delise said. Her voice sounded warmer than it had done for months.

'No Delise, that wouldn't be right. We'll get together tomorrow. I just need some time on my own tonight.'

'Please, Dave, I've been missing you too. I've been a fool.'

'Delise, I really want you. I want us back together, I need you in my life, I can't manage without you, but it'll be better for us if we start again on a fresh day.'

In the end Delise agreed to be waiting at the office for me in the morning. This time I hoped we could get our relationship off to a better start. I realised now that I'd started my love affair with Delise when I was still sandbagged by the death of Elenki. I'd never really shared the emotional side of my life with Delise, it had been business and pleasure with her, in that order. She'd been right to leave me. I'd been a swine.

I was ready to go anywhere with her. If she wanted me to go to Jersey I'd go.

No wonder Rachel and Harold Elsworth had been able to run rings round me. Oh, I was good. I could sort out some of the hard men but it was Delise who had built up Pimpernel Investigations. She'd propped me up for two years and what had I given her in return? Nothing.

It was Delise who had gone round drumming up trade. Delise who had sent out the well-written promotional material. Delise who had worked out the finances and sent in the expense claims, and I'd been ready to forget her, ready to jump into bed with an ambitious opportunist.

Although I felt some guilt for my part in the destruction of Sylvia Mather and grief at her death, it wasn't a heavy burden.

I knew Sylvia was only out for what she could get; when somebody with more to offer her came along she would have traded me in without a second thought. That was what had attracted me to her that Friday night only a week ago: she'd been so refreshingly direct about going for what she wanted, with none of the hang-ups that Delise and I tormented each other with.

Had she been skimming a percentage from the profits at the Paloma, I wondered? All that jewellery, her interest in gambling and her luxury flat suggested it.

I remained in my chair. It was pleasant to be able to sit on my own for a while.

I stirred myself at about 2 a.m. to phone Ted Blake about Sledgehammer. However I felt about the way things had worked out, a bargain was a bargain. He was delighted. Another satisfied client.

I sat watching the dawn come up. Another new day, and it was going to be a fine one. The clouds had cleared away. Sylvia would be lying in the mortuary now, probably next to Dyer and Jock, and no one gave a damn about it, except me. Benson hadn't paid any price yet, but he would.

At six I put a tracksuit on and went down for a bike ride. I got down on to the Meadows, over the river at Jackson's Boat bridge and slogged my way down past Sale Water Park, right down the side of the motorway. There were a few early windsurfers on the lake, taking advantage of the moderate breeze.

The exercise worked the whisky fumes out of my brain, but it did nothing to relieve my mood. I went back by Jackson's Boat and turned towards the path through the reed beds where I'd been mugged on that morning. It seemed so long ago. I might as well try to exorcise that particular demon.

Keeping my eyes down on the narrow track through the marsh I cycled round bends and twists in the path.

Suddenly there was someone in front of me.

It was Sese Manteh, his face gaunt and twisted, his expression mad. Until he grabbed hold of my handle bars I thought I was seeing things. He gave a mighty twist and jerked me to the ground. My feet were caught in the toe clips and he pushed the bike down on top of me.

The man was roaring like an animal, he shoved his foot on

my chest and held me to the ground and then whipped out a machete from inside his jacket. I felt curiously detached and distant from what was happening. In a way I partly thought it was right. This was how I ought to pay for Sylvia's destruction.

As the machete whistled down towards my head I managed to avoid it by jerking to one side. I thrashed about desperately but there was no way I could disentangle myself from the bike and claw my way up in the slippery mud.

Manteh shifted his position, moving like a snake, and raised the machete high above his head with both hands in that same theatrical gesture he'd used with the Uzi machine pistol. I saw the sun gleaming on the blade as it came down for a killing slash at my head.

Then there was a blur of red at the side of his face and instead of the machete descending it reversed its trajectory, Manteh himself jack-knifing over backwards, buckling at the knees. I lay there panting for breath.

Seconds later another figure came pounding towards me. I braced myself, but it was Finbar clutching the pump-action shotgun I'd given him. I couldn't take it in immediately.

The lightning attack from a quarter I'd considered already neutralised, followed by equally swift deliverance by my friend Finbar, had the effect of lifting the deep and numbing depression I'd been feeling. I pushed the bike to one side and scrambled to my feet.

Finbar was looking down at the remains.

'Don't half make a mess these things, don't they?' he said wonderingly, looking at the gun.

'What are you doing here?' I asked.

'I saw him skulking in here when you crossed the bridge on your way to the water park. When he didn't come out I knew what he was up to and . . .'

'No. I don't mean that. Why are you out on the Meadows with a gun at 6 a.m.? Oh, never mind. Tell me later.'

I could hear the shouts of other people approaching the reed beds. 'Say nothing at all,' I said. 'We found him here.'

I grabbed the gun from Finbar, cleaned it carefully with my vest and entwined the nerveless fingers of Manteh's right hand in the trigger. They were almost on us as I grabbed the machete and shoved it into my saddlebag. A crowd of early-morning joggers and dog walkers quickly gathered and immediately jumped to the wrong conclusion. A number of them claimed to have actually seen Manteh shoot himself.

Later, Detective Chief Superintendent Sinclair himself arrived to take my statement about Manteh's deliberate suicide.

'Bit of a coincidence that,' he commented, 'lucky for you that there are so many people able to corroborate your story. In view of all the circumstances I'd like to interview you at Chester House at 11 a.m. You might like to bring your brief with you laddie, Benson'll be there and I've no idea what he's going to say.'

He gave me one of his most corpse-like smiles as I wheeled the bike away . . .

It was certainly lucky for me that Finbar Salway, guilt-stricken by his twin's unwitting spying for the Charlies, had decided to make reparation by standing sentry duty over me all night. Lucky that the old paratrooper had been nimble enough to scramble down to the Meadows and kill Manteh with a single shot at fifty yards.

29

The atmosphere in the interview room at Boyer Street was very different from that at my last session there.

Benson, Sinclair and Rice were present when I was shown into Sinclair's office on the tenth floor. There was some shuffling of chairs as I was ushered in and this time no haze of blue tobacco fouled the rarefied air. Benson, as usual, was smothered in his uniform. He hadn't discarded the uniform jacket even on a warm day. Sinclair was looking cool and businesslike in a light-coloured suit, and Rice's appearance was transformed by a Marks and Spencers sports jacket and slacks. He'd washed his hair and even got the dirt out from under his nails.

To my surprise Benson extended his hand to me.

'Hello, Mr Cunane, I understand that you have some hard feelings about the events of yesterday. I just want to make it clear that what happened outside the G-Mex building, though deeply regrettable, was also inevitable. I'd like to extend our official sympathy to you if you feel we should have acted sooner. Unfortunately, we believed the situation was under control and had no way of knowing that Dyer was armed as he was.'

Lying through his teeth and confident as the Devil, he stood with his hand extended making a prepared speech. I could see that Rice was tensed, probably expecting me to go for Benson as I'd done yesterday.

Always ready to disappoint Rice I accepted the proffered handshake. It felt like pressing the flesh of a month-old corpse.

If Benson was prepared to kill the fatted calf for me, I was prepared to go along with him just until I could see how the land lay. I had my own guilty secrets to conceal and couldn't afford to let the bitterness and hatred I felt for this lamentable excuse for a policeman show.

'I believe Mr Sinclair has already taken a statement from you about the death of Sese Manteh,' he continued, his East Anglian accent revealing itself in a slight twang as he spoke.

'The operation in Moss Side has been a complete success and I shall be making a very favourable report about it to the Home Office. Thanks to your efforts in supplying us with those bank account numbers we have been able to apply for sequestration orders against the accounts of all the drug dealers arrested. Of course, they will have to be convicted but there's little doubt of that. Your name will be forwarded to the Home Office and consideration given to a suitable reward.'

I must have looked surprised. Benson's transparent attempt to buy my silence startled me, but I was even more astonished by Sinclair's apparent willingness to take part in the charade. I looked searchingly at him, but apart from a thin smile playing on his almost bloodless lips his face was giving nothing away.

They expected me to respond, so I made a noise somewhere between a grunt and a groan which could be taken any way they liked.

'Manteh must have been in great despair to take his own life in such a dramatic way this morning,' Benson continued. 'The Detective Chief Superintendent would like to brief you about that, and then perhaps you can tell us something about what you have found via your more, shall we say, unorthodox route? We're particularly interested in knowing anything about the methods by which the gang transported their funds abroad. Then we can close the file. Anyway, I'll leave that till later, Mr Sinclair can I hand over to you?'

Benson delivered this little address in the crisp manner he must have refined at a thousand such briefing sessions.

I still hadn't said a word since I entered the room. If they were making secret tape recordings they were going to be disappointed by my discretion.

Sinclair cleared his throat and started fiddling with his unlit pipe. 'Well I'd like to say David that it's not my idea to give you this briefing, but if Mr Benson thinks it will do some good who am I to disagree,' he said cautiously in his purest Midlothian vowels.

I thought, he's either hinting heavily or the room really is bugged.

'We've been aware for some time that Sese Manteh was the principal agent in this part of the country for the Colombian drug cartels. In particular, we think he was an agent for the

Cali cartel, which is making great efforts to overhaul its rival concern, the Medellin cartel, as the leading supplier of cocaine and derivatives to Europe and this country.

'Although there is a thriving criminal underworld in this country there's nothing to compare with the Mafia in the USA. The Mafia is able to play the part of middleman in the drugs business in America, wholesaling the drugs, setting up retail chains and disciplining the dealers, and above all placing nice steady orders for large volumes of the drugs. Which is what the cartels need to expand their business. They want to develop a big market for base cocaine in this country and to supply in bulk by the container load. That way they can fight off their competitors from Africa, the Middle East and the Indian subcontinent.'

I'd listened to enough of this malarky, Sinclair was trying to bore me to death. I decided to put a spoke in his wheel.

'That's very interesting Mr Sinclair, but if you knew all this about him why wasn't he deported months ago?' I asked.

'Well, that's another issue, rather outside my scope David,' he said with a pointed look at Benson.

'Deportation is a sensitive political issue, Mr Cunane,' Benson said seriously. 'Manteh was granted a residence permit here as a religious minister. The Home Office was satisfied that his claim to be a minister of the Ethnic African Church was quite genuine. The church has registered offices in New York and Ghana and there were people here in Manchester ready to sponsor him.'

'I hope you're investigating these so-called sponsors,' I said bitterly, thinking of the 'ethnic minister' with his machete poised above my head.

'Yes, indeed! Some of them are enjoying our hospitality at this very moment,' said Sinclair with a chuckle. I took him to be referring to the drug dealers he'd rounded up in the early hours.

'It's easy to be wise after the event David, but we only got on to Manteh following a report from Trinidad about his activities there. You must understand that there are lots of people of real goodwill working among the youth of Moss Side and South Manchester to try to alleviate the drug problem. If we are seen to be vetting them or deporting them there'll be an outcry that will set policing in this area back for years. In fact we might be back to 1981 with a vengeance.'

'OK, so you're frightened of riots and only deal with such as Manteh wearing kid gloves, but what did Manteh do in Trinidad to arouse suspicion?' I said.

'Look David, if you're going to keep interrupting me and putting the most unfavourable interpretation you can on our actions, I'll never get to the end of this story,' Sinclair said irritably, flapping his arm like a cow using its tail to flick a fly off its backside. He was missing his pipe.

'I'm sorry,' I said grudgingly, but I felt that after what I'd been through in the past few days I'd every reason to take a jaundiced view of the police. I also had another reason for wanting to speed him up. I looked nervously at my watch.

Sinclair raised his eyebrows, 'Well David I'm sorry too if we're taking up your precious time . . .'

'No, I'm sorry, really. I'm aware that I'm being given privileged treatment,' I responded acidly, 'please go on.'

I was aware of Rice frowning at me: how dare a mere counter-jumping private investigator like myself interrupt his revered chief in full flow? I didn't care, let him radiate all the disapproval he liked. He wasn't the one who'd been on the receiving end from Manteh.

'All right, well to cut a long story short since I'm obviously boring you, young man, Manteh allegedly went to Trinidad as part of a fact-finding mission to promote goodwill among the Afro-Caribbean community here in Manchester, although there are comparatively few Trinidadians here in the North-west. While there he went in a small boat for a sailing trip in the waters of the Gulf of Paria, a notoriously dangerous stretch of water, with fierce tidal flows.

'When he didn't return a search was launched. He wasn't found until several days later when reports came in that he'd landed at Guiria, a small town in Venezuela which is regarded as a staging post for the Cali cartel. Cocaine is moved from there to several parts of the Caribbean for despatch to the States. Presumably, Manteh was passed back on up the chain to report to his superiors in Cali. Anyway, any British resident having links with Guiria is automatically flagged when their documents go through the Home Office computer, but nothing would have been known about Manteh apart from the fuss about him being missing.

'Since then he's been under surveillance, which is what Michael Rice was doing when he spotted you paying a visit last Sunday.'

Sinclair gave me the benefit of one his zombie-like grins.

'That brings us up to today, when Manteh killed himself in front of you with a firearm that was part of a batch listed as stolen from a warehouse in Harrogate six months ago and which have been turning up in Manchester recently. He must have been well aware of what his fate would be once his masters in Colombia learned of his failure. We'd like you to fill us in on what you know of his movements over the last few days.'

The three of them looked at me expectantly.

'No,' I said and folded my arms.

'It's just as a formality. Nothing will be held against you. We appreciate that you may take certain short-cuts. I can assure you that no charges are being considered,' said Benson, unctuously. 'Nothing's being recorded, if that's what's worrying you.'

He was rubbing his hands together like a pork butcher in a pig farm.

'I'm saving my evidence for the judicial enquiry,' I said in my mildest tones.

'What? What enquiry? What are you talking about?' Benson asked. Two little spots of red had suddenly appeared on either side of is face just where his cheeks met his sideboards. The moustache was quivering slightly.

'I'm talking about the judicial enquiry there's going to be when the Manchester MPs, the national press, the Inspector of Constabulary, the Home Office, the Director of Public Prosecutions, the Crown Prosecution Service and whoever else you care to name; yes even Her Majesty the Queen herself, receive the folder of evidence about your links with Dyer, the NMP and the deaths at the G-Mex yesterday. She's very efficient is my secretary, she's copied a full account of everything that's happened, including the photo of you drinking Dyer's health taken not long before you had him executed. Unless she hears to the contrary from me in fifteen minutes she's going to post them.'

I spoke in a monotone throughout and surprised myself at the calm, flat way in which I delivered my message. I suppose the events of the last few days had squeezed all emotion and capacity for feeling out of me.

The three of them were on their feet. The cosy atmosphere shattered. Benson looked as if he was having an apoplexy; it looked as if his gold-braided, metal-sheathed uniform had become a vice which was squeezing him to death. Almost everything I'd gone through was worth it to see this.

Benson seemed to be jerking towards me, his mouth opening and closing as he tried to get words out. God, he really is going to pop his clogs, I thought.

'Surely we can arrive at an acceptable solution to all this, in house. We can settle it in house . . . in house. Where is she?' he spluttered, gasping to get his mouth round the words.

Sinclair came round the desk to him and took his arm. He whispered something which I couldn't catch.

'We'd like to adjourn this meeting to another reception room where there's some coffee prepared,' Sinclair had the cheek to say. So the meeting was bugged. They'd been hoping I'd make some damning admission which they could then trade off against me keeping quiet about what I knew.

I laughed in their faces and opened the jacket of my mohair suit to reveal the voice-operated tape recorder nestling in its holster under my arm.

'Smile, you're on Candid Camera,' I laughed, tapping the hidden mike in my top pocket. I noticed that Rice, solemn as a judge up to this point, was having trouble keeping his face straight. 'Well what am I supposed to say? Snap?' I asked. Then, remembering that I had to live in this town, long after Benson had gone to that bourne from which chief constables never return – retirement – decided to stop cheeking the still-formidable Sinclair and comply with his wishes.

When we reached the reception room he sent Rice off to round up the coffee and as Benson still looked as if he was battling an invisible strangler it was Sinclair who went in to bat for the GMP.

'You can turn that off and put it down on the table,' he said grimly, 'whatever's going to be said is off the record. I never did think recording was a good idea,' he said, more for Benson's benefit than mine.

I obeyed his order.

'I'm surprised at you David Cunane. Your father and grandfathers all achieved high rank in this force and here you are about to drag us through the mud. You know the gutter press will have a field day, don't you?' Sinclair said.

Fortunately a lifetime of dealing with my father had immunized me against such blackmailing emotional appeals.

'Don't you think the press ought to know about a chief constable who owns shares in a company which has such deep-rooted connections with the underworld?' I asked Sinclair. 'And don't try to pretend that you don't know all about the NMP. Someone who's had his nose as close to the ground for as many years as you must know exactly what they're up to.'

Rice came back with the coffee. Benson signalled him to go away again. Sinclair motioned him to stay.

Rice stayed where he was.

'What's this about shares then,' Sinclair said to Benson, and taking out his pipe, lit it. He puffed the blue smoke in Benson's direction. He glanced at me and I obliged him by looking at my watch.

Benson had stopped gasping for air and was now merely perspiring heavily. 'Look, can't we keep this in house. Can't you do something to persuade him not to send the letters, you're supposed to know his family. I'm perfectly innocent but the publicity will wreck my marriage. Its just that the circumstances are bound to look bad for me.'

'You should have thought of that before you registered the shares to Chiefly Nominees, Cayman Islands, Inc. in your wife's name. A bit cocky that. Still a British possession you know, the Cayman Islands. Shouldn't take the judicial enquiry long to find out who the beneficial owner of those shares is,' I said.

Benson didn't think he was a bad man any more than Hitler or Stalin had done. He must have felt that his career was the supreme good and that if he needed a little extra cash to push it along why shouldn't he get it. Give me an honest crook like Dyer any time. All Dyer wanted was money, whereas Benson was after power. If Benson had achieved his aims he'd have had the whole country trembling when he tweaked his moustache.

Sinclair wrote down the name 'Chiefly Nominees' in his notebook and then rolled his watery eyes as if to say, 'I've heard this tale a thousand times before from bent businessmen caught with their fingers in the till'. He put his head back and studied the ceiling. There was no help for Benson in that quarter. Rice was examining his fingernails.

The silence lengthened. I looked at my watch again.

Eventually it was Sinclair who spoke, 'David, you'll phone your young lady and tell her not to send those letters. Your name will still go forward for a reward from the Home Office, although knowing them I can't promise it'll be much. The searching enquiry into your activities that we were going to start if you hadn't said the right things this morning will never start. In fact, all cases involving you and your clients are now regarded as closed and Rice and I will see to it that there's such an odour of sanctity round your name with this department that you're never short of work . . .'

He spoke with such a heavy weariness and slowness of speech that both Rice and I were sitting on the edge of our seats waiting for him to conclude. He hadn't finished yet.

'And . . .' I prompted, as he seemed to be straining for words.

'And Mr Benson's not well. He'll be applying for premature retirement in a few months' time and making quite a substantial donation to the charity of your choice immediately.'

We all looked at Benson. He nodded his agreement curtly, stood up and left the room. It was hard to believe that he was getting off so lightly. Could it be that in his self-absorption he believed that even now there was some way that he could salvage the wreck of his career. I felt that I could trust Sinclair to see to it that there wasn't. Manchester was about to lose its third chief constable in as many years.

'Say nothing gentlemen, say nothing,' continued Sinclair in his lugubrious tones. 'What's happened is an absolute disaster, a day of such shame as I never thought to see in my life. The less that is said, the less the damage.' For the first time since I'd known him Sinclair looked shattered. He seemed to have shrunk from the malevolent vulture-like figure of my imaginings to be merely a wrinkled and ageing man.

Still, I couldn't feel sorry for him. He was part of a system of which I wanted no part, including his offers of patronage. It was a day of shame for Sinclair but yesterday had nearly been the last day of my life thanks to his wretched boss. So why should I join him in his lament for the lost purity of the GMP?

'Michael, see he phones and then go with him to collect the material, or better still don't bring it back here. Destroy it. Don't speak to him unless you have to,' he said bitterly.

He was treating me as if I was a bearer of some contagion, and I resented it.

We stood up to go but before I went said, 'That cheque, get him to make it out to the Children's Hospice in Didsbury, and I'll want to see it before it goes off.'

Sinclair just grunted and waved me away with a flick of his hand as he was leaving the room. The audience was over.

Rice bustled me to a phone and I reached Delise two minutes before the deadline was up. Part of me, the anarchic part which enjoyed creating chaos, was sorry. If I told Delise to go ahead and post the envelopes it might cause the biggest scandal to hit the police force since . . . well since the last big scandal. I think Rice could sense that I was having second thoughts because he said 'You heard the boss, get on with it Cunane!'

That wasn't a very wise thing for him to say in the circumstances. He saw the gleam in my eye. 'Go on, phone her! You know as well as I do that you've no alternative.' I phoned Delise but not because I had no alternatives. She was sitting in the car outside the main post office in Ashton under Lyne and when she got my call she headed back into central Manchester. As usual Rice had got it wrong. I could indeed have told her to post them. I was capable. I didn't because I didn't want to spoil my father's retirement by besmirching the police force he had given his working life to. Benson was only one bad apple so why should his corrupt ambition and power-mania be allowed to tarnish the reputations of thousands?

Rice drove me into town in his battered Cortina and we parked on a double yellow line near the Atwood building, waiting for Delise to appear with her parcel. Rice had only spoken in monosyllables since we left Police HQ but now he said, 'Do you really think there would have been a judicial enquiry into Benson? You're naive. They'd have smothered it, Benson's got friends all over the place.'

'If I'm naive, you're too cynical. Why do you think Benson agreed to go? The press would have crucified him,' I replied.

He lapsed into silence again.

Delise finally showed up. We went into the building and once again used the facilities of Glo-Worm Enterprises. They had a shredder as well as a photocopier. Rice pushed all the envelopes through the shredder and collected the resulting paper into a binliner which he carted away with him. He didn't bid me any fond farewells. I took Delise out for lunch at a little French restaurant in a cellar on Portland Street. They did a good steak.

Over our second bottle of Beaujolais I explained all that had gone on since a week on Wednesday, all that is apart from what had happened that night at Tarn. I didn't ask her where she'd been or if she'd had someone with her. I didn't care, I was glad to get her back on her own terms. She didn't judge me.

We arranged to go to Jersey together. We would work more closely together and build up our relationship from there.

Later that day it was Delise, more practical than me, who arranged for a business answering service to forward our mail and re-route phone calls to Jersey. It was she who saw to our packing, booked us into a hotel until we could get somewhere else and managed all the arrangements.

She even phoned Sims at Happyways. To my surprise he was quite amenable to me working for the firm in the Channel Islands. Happyways didn't have any hypermarkets there but they did have a giant liquor store which had been leaking profits through the back door. So Pimpernel Investigations Limited was still in business.

As we were in the car preparing to leave for the airport it was Delise who opened her briefcase and took out the master copies of the documents incriminating Benson. When I raised my eyebrows she said, 'You didn't think I was going to destroy these did you? And I've got another copy squirelled away. You don't think I trust that old man Sinclair, do you? You're too generous Dave, that's your trouble. And don't think you're going to rip up Elsworth's cheque either. We can bank it in Jersey. You need me to look after you.

'You think life's like a John Ford western,' she sighed,

'you want to ride off into the sunset and forget all your problems.'

We set off to shake the dust of Manchester off our feet for four months.

Epilogue

Four months later . . .

Shortly after we returned to Manchester at the end of October I received a visitor at my office. Delise showed Dee Elsworth in and closed the door behind her, but not before she'd given me a very searching look.

Dee was dressed in loose-fitting but stylish clothes quite unlike those I'd seen her in before. She looked out of place in my office, re-decorated and re-equipped though it now was.

There was something different about her but I couldn't decide what it was. I was very nervous. My relationship with Delise was well settled, with no more tempestuous clashes. The last thing I needed was to renew an affair with Dee if that was what she'd come for – maybe it wasn't, she seemed very happy and pleased with herself.

We spent five minutes talking about nothing in particular: the weather; the new chief constable's policy towards clubs; how upsetting Mr Benson's sudden retirement had been; whether Benson's massive donation to a charity associated with royalty gave him a chance of a knighthood; the antiquities of the Atwood building; horse riding. We talked on and on until the strain must have begun to show in my face. All this could only be leading up to something deeply unpleasant.

Then she stopped fencing, smiled sweetly at me and said, 'I thought you might have been in touch. Harold would like to see you again. He's not stopped singing your praises to all his friends. He hopes you don't feel too badly about the stand-offish way he treated you when he first met you, but that's how he is I'm afraid.'

I thought, this is it, she's going to get me to call one evening when she knows Harold's out.

I couldn't believe she'd come here just to make a belated apology for Harold, but I explained that I'd been out of town for some time. Still, she didn't seem satisfied, 'Look, Dee I don't have any feelings about Harold one way or the other,' I said.

'He was just a client in a case that very nearly went badly wrong. I find it's best to let sleeping dogs lie in those sort of cases, don't you agree that's a good idea?' I smiled at her and then said, 'You do think that don't you?'

'No Dave, there's more to be said. Harold told me he'd paid you well but I doubt if he could pay you in full for all that you did. Rachel's improved tremendously, she's more her normal self again. We feel that we've got our daughter back. She never went back to the University you know. Harold's arranged for the Bank to finance a Hollywood film and she's going to have a minor but quite important part.'

As Dee spoke so optimistically about Rachel I had to remind myself that she didn't know what part Rachel had really played in the events of June.

'Things between Harold and myself are much better, all that travelling backwards and forwards stopped the night he brought Rachel back from your flat. That was something to do with you wasn't it? Harold won't say, and I don't like to ask.'

'Now Dee,' I interrupted, 'this isn't getting us anywhere . . .'

'No Dave, hear me out. You did something for me as well . . .'

'Look Dee,' I said, getting heated, 'I thought we agreed never to talk about that. What's done is done, and they both got what was coming to them.'

I got up to check that Delise wasn't listening at the door. She wasn't. She was typing up our latest expenses claims, so there was no danger of her eavesdropping.

'Dave it isn't that. I've already forgotten all about that. It was what happened afterwards,' she said, smiling demurely.

I was beginning to feel seriously embarrassed. It crossed my mind to get Delise to come in, or to make some excuse for leaving.

'Dee you know that was a one-off, something exceptional and out of the ordinary. I thought we'd agreed never to discuss that either.'

'David Cunane, you're being deliberately obtuse. Exceptional events can have exceptional results. You're supposed to be a detective. Can't you see I'm pregnant! Harold's in raptures, he's having palpitations. Of course he thinks it's his. He's just as self-centred as you are! I just want to be sure that you won't ever interfere to spoil our happiness.'

I was stunned. The case of Rachel Elsworth was turning out to be a never-ending story with consequences rippling on into the future. What was going to happen next? Was someone going to dig up those mouldering corpses at Tarn? As I tried to grapple with the unwelcome idea of unexpected paternity my naturally suspicious nature asserted itself. After a long interval I spoke. 'How can you be sure it isn't his?'

'Be serious Dave, a woman knows these things. Besides we've been trying for years and nothing's happened, and now bingo! The hospital think it's twins!' she said, smiling at my comical expression of bemusement.

'Dee you know I'd never interfere unless you asked me to. You know that don't you? Now we've got two mutual secrets.'

'I knew you'd say that Dave. I just had to be sure.'

She gave me a warm smile, a peck on the cheek, and left.

Delise came in as Dee closed the outer office door.

'What did she want Dave? She seems pleased with herself,' she said.

'She just came to tell me that her daughter is getting a part in a Hollywood film,' I lied.

'Well that's the best place for Rachel, Tinseltown! She'll probably go right to the top there!' Delise said firmly. Then she came and stood beside my chair and ran her fingers through my hair. 'At least her mother is pleased. You seem to have pleased a lot of ladies lately, Dave. Even my mum is talking a bit more favourably about you becoming her son-in-law.' Delise twined her fingers in my curly locks and gave a slight tug. I had the feeling that she knew or guessed a lot more about what had passed between Dee and me than she was saying.

Two days later a parcel arrived containing the better of the two Lowry paintings I'd admired at Tarn.